IN PRAISE OF RYANN WATTERS

Eric Reinhold has delivered a fantastic adventure that clearly distinguishes right from wrong. It's a great moral compass of a read!

—KARL HOLZ, PRESIDENT, DISNEY CRUISE LINE

Eric Reinhold takes ordinary children into an extraordinary world. When they return, they know more about Jesus, and so do the readers who enjoyed this fantastic adventure. *Ryann Watters and the Shield of Faith* is an interesting tale with a backbone of faith.

—DONITA K. PAUL, BEST-SELLING AUTHOR
OF *THE DRAGONKEEPER CHRONICLES*

Set in the real-life town of Mount Dora, Florida, this enchanting tale of fantasy combines a compelling storyline, riveting action, and excellent characterization, culminating in a breathtaking novel with the potential to be for Christian youth what *Harry Potter* was to a more worldly crowd.

—DELIA LATHAM, AUTHOR OF *GOLDENEYES*

As a father who has raised five children and now has eleven grandchildren, I realize the importance of quality, faith-based literature. Eric has done a remarkable job of putting this story together in an interesting and compelling way.

—RON BLUE, BEST-SELLING AUTHOR
MASTER YOUR MONEY

Eric is passionate to encourage kids to develop their character by becoming equipped with biblical principles.

I believe this book will help them to seek out answers for their lives from God, their parents, and Christian leaders. This intriguing, suspenseful plot will keep readers engaged.

—ARTO WOODLEY, CEO, FRONTLINE OUTREACH

...the perfect blend of fantasy and the spiritual world... Eric Reinhold releases his brilliance...in a fantastical tale that will leave his readers encouraged and yearning for more!

—SIMON BAILEY, AUTHOR OF *RELEASE YOUR BRILLIANCE*

What a delightful read—a children's book that adults can enjoy, one that immediately starts you on a fantastic journey that takes you from small-town USA to another world and back, all the time introducing new characters and following a plot that reveals itself with creativity and excitement. Rare are books for children that will create a desire for additional reading, and this one is clearly biblically based. How much better can you get?

—NAN MCCORMICK, SENIOR VP
CB RICHARD ELLIS

As adults we have the awesome task of capturing both the minds and imagination of the next generation, founding them in biblical truth and creative expression. Eric has done that. In twenty years the fruit [of his work] will be born and we will all be grateful.

—LARRY KREIDER, AUTHOR OF *BOTTOM LINE FAITH*

What a wonderful work of art this is.

—SHANNON BROUILLETTE, CEO, CFO STRATEGIC PARTNERS

When we got your book, we actually loaned it to sisters that are very good friends of my daughter. They both loved it, and one said that it made her want to be sure to read her Bible every day—that is wonderful! My daughter, Abigail, is nearly finished with it, and this is the most excited she has ever been about reading.

—FRED BEERWART, COLUMBUS, IN

I was captivated! I traveled with your characters through their journey, experiencing everything that happened to them. I finished your book, changed for the better.

—JON MAIOCCO

I was captivated by the book due to the descriptive language and the way Eric Reinhold created the characters. I stayed up late reading it, as I couldn't put it down—and that's a fact! I highly recommend this book to readers ten to fourteen years of age, but this exciting adventure novel would appeal to anyone. I am looking forward to reading about Ryann's further adventures.

—ERIN RELZ, AGE 11

Thank you so much for the wonderful book. It is the best book I have ever read in my life.

—JOSH ROY, AGE 9

Eric Reinhold's imagination is contagious. By the end of chapter one I found myself engrossed in a world of fantasy, entertainment, and engaging lessons in spiritual warfare. Eric weaves into the story the inspiration and motivation for the young reader to develop character traits of integrity, accountability, discipline, perseverance, leadership, commitment, and respect. Illustrations and the cover design by Corey Wolf add to the excitement of the world of Aeliana and the quaint town of Mount Dora.

—RICHARD R. BLAKE, SAN LEANDRO, CA

What a wonderful, wonderful story! My eight-year-old son...loves to read it at night lying in bed. He's been so excited that he's even been going to bed early...I love the fact that the entire story is built around His Word. I have to say this book is the best book I've ever come across for children (and adults, too, I might add).

—MARCI WILLIAMS

I really enjoyed your book because it shows the life of an ordinary child could be chosen to do important things. I like how it combines gospel teaching with adventure, excitement, suspense, and overcoming evil.

—JOEY, AGE 11

This fast-paced story is a great way to introduce fantasy to young readers. The author firmly grounds his tale in the real-life town of Mount Dora before his characters enter the fantasy realm of Aeliana. Talking animals, brilliant colors, and supernatural visitors will delight even the most reluctant readers.

—JULIE DICK, WI

Eric Reinhold is a wonderful storyteller who has a wonderful story to tell. This book is a page-turner that is hard to put down.

—WAYNE S. WALKER, AFFTON, MO

Thanks for creating an awesome book full of great characters. I loved it.

—VICTORIA JOHNSON, AGE 12

Ryann Watters
and the
Shield  of Faith

Eric Reinhold

BOOK 2
Annals of Aeliana Series

CREATION
HOUSE
A STRANG COMPANY

RYANN WATTERS AND THE SHIELD OF FAITH by Eric Reinhold
Published by Creation House
A Strang Company
600 Rinehart Road
Lake Mary, Florida 32746
www.strangbookgroup.com

Unless otherwise noted, all Scripture quotations are from the Holy Bible, New International Version of the Bible. Copyright © 1973, 1978, 1984, International Bible Society. Used by permission.

Design Director: Bill Johnson

Cover Designer: Amanda Potter

Cover art, maps, and illustrations in chapters 8, 23, 25, 28, and 31, and page vii by Corey Wolfe, coreywolfe.com.

Illustrations in chapters 1–6, 9, 11–22, 24, 26, 27, 29, 30, 32–34, and 36–38 by Jared Sloger, jaredsloger.com.

Library of Congress Control Number: 2009922334
International Standard Book Number: 978-1-59979-626-0

First Edition

09 10 11 12 13 — 987654321
Printed in the United States of America

Solo Christo

Sola Scriptura

Sola Gratia

Soli Deo Gloria

Sola Fide

The light shines in the darkness,
but the darkness has not
understood it.

Acknowledgments

I WOULD LIKE TO thank a variety of special people who made a positive deposit into my life over the past year as I wrote this book. To the band of merry authors who traveled the West Coast on the 2008 Fantasy Fiction Tour—Bryan Davis, Donita K. Paul, Wayne Thomas Batson, L. B. Graham, Jonathan Rogers, Christopher Hopper, and Sharon Hinck—the experience and memories will last a lifetime. Thanks to Real Armor of God for providing swords for the tour. The unicorn shield on the front cover is from their Web site: www.realarmorofgod.com.

A summer vacation to the Northwest last year provided an opportunity to meet with cover artist Corey Wolfe to sketch out the cover. Awesome work, Corey!

Thanks to the new interior artist, Jared Sloger. He's a tremendous up-and-coming artist, and I'm excited to have my book be his first major effort.

Thank you to Cathy Hoechst, President of the Mount Dora Chamber of Commerce, and Stephanie Haimes, Director of the W. T. Bland Public Library in Mount Dora for all of their support.

A very special thanks to my three children: Kara, for spending hours reading my early manuscripts and providing insightful comments into the minds of kids who will be reading my series; Kyler, for taking trips out to Mount Dora with me and taking the picture of me for the cover; and Kaylyn, for her encouraging smile and spirit.

Much gratitude goes to Donita K. Paul, who volunteered for the arduous task of helping me polish this work, chapter by chapter. Donita is a saintly "grandma" with a quirky sense of humor (like mine) who had me laughing out loud with her comments.

Lastly, I'd like to thank the many parents, teachers, librarians, church youth leaders, and kids who send e-mails of encouragement. It makes the many hours poured into this work worth the effort. For those who posted reviews on book Web sites, bought copies for friends, and spread the news about Ryann Watters, thanks and keep it up. Word of mouth, e-mail, and blogs are the best way to get the biblical message contained in this series out to the world! Eric

Contents

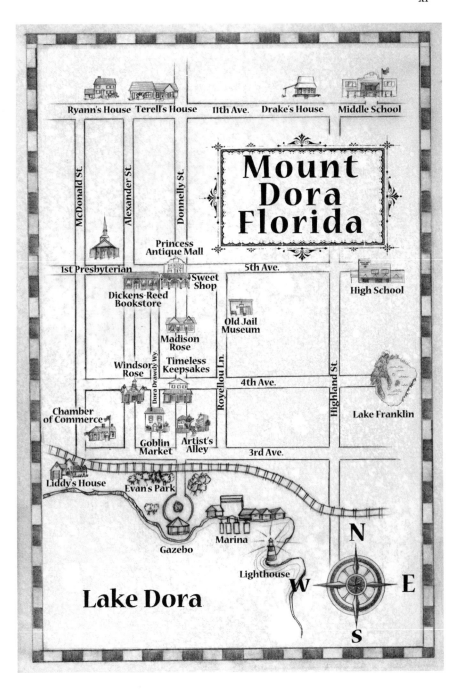

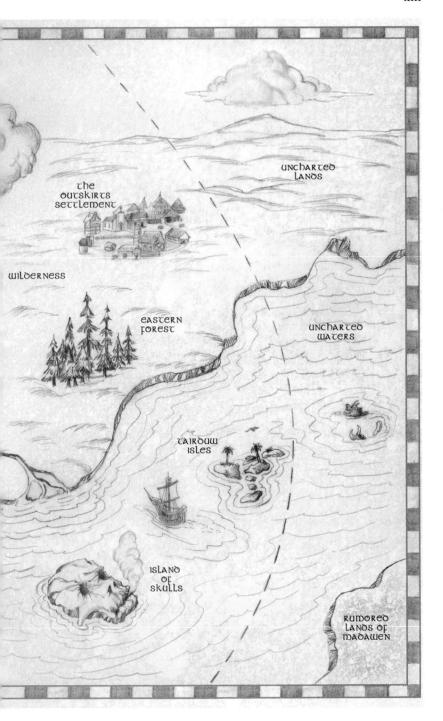

Characters

Ryann—age 13; tasked by Gabriel to find the shield of faith

Terell—age 13; Ryann's best friend

Liddy—age 13; friend of Ryann and Terell

Drake—age 14; Ryann's archrival

The Word—God

Gabriel—archangel of the Word

Lord Ekron—dark angel who fell from heaven

Don Korrel—drifter; lives in Mount Dora

Ireth—elf; member of the Chosen

Sorcha—white dragon; member of the Chosen

Eljon—red dwarf; prophet

Narcissus—black unicorn; self-appointed king of Aeliana

Carwyn—white unicorn; leader of the Chosen

Rowan—halfling (half-dwarf/half-elf); member of the Chosen

Garnock—river dwarf; member of the Chosen

Taran—bull; name means "thunder;" member of the Chosen; Mellt's twin

Mellt—bull; name means "lightning;" member of the Chosen; Taran's twin

Adain—Pegasus; name means "winged;" member of the Chosen

Bishop Dridak—religious leader of Myraddin

Hugons—the half-human/half-dragon race of peacekeepers who guard Aeliana

Raz—raccoon; Ryann's close friend from their previous visit to Aeliana

Essy—leopard; Liddy's close friend from their previous visit to Aeliana

Texting Interpreter

wuu2	**What (are) you up to?**
cya	**"See ya" or "see you later"**
cw2cu	**Can't wait to see you**
sumr	**Summer**
cul8r	**See you later**
zup	**What's up?**
l8r	**Later**
bfn	**Bye for now**

Discover the Powers and Record Them Here

RING

Blue	_____
Orange	_____

STAFF

Button 1	_____
Button 2	_____
Button 3	_____
Button 4	_____
Button 5	_____
Button 6	_____
Button 7	_____

CHAPTER 1

Into the Crypt

CHOES FROM UNSEEN singers filled the cavernous space inside the United States Naval Academy Chapel. Row after row of precisely aligned dark wood benches were broken up by a single swath of navy blue carpet running the length of the church. The perfectly blended voices seemed to come from everywhere and nowhere in particular. Ryann, who had just celebrated his thirteenth birthday, was drawn into the melodic *a cappella* song.

> Eternal Father, strong to save,
> Whose arm hath bound the restless wave.
> Who bidd'st the mighty ocean deep
> Its own appointed limits keep.
> O hear us when we cry to Thee
> For those in peril on the sea.

Goose bumps popped up along his arm in the silence that followed. He felt alone, yet he was one of the hundreds sitting stiffly upright in the ornately fashioned pews. Squirming in the hard seat, he tried to displace the chill running down his back. He peered forward over the unmoving heads packed into the hundreds of rows in front of them. The white shirts with black and gold shoulder boards, identifying the rank of each midshipman, dotted the otherwise drab congregation.

Focusing further ahead into the base of the circular, domed room, his eyes widened to capture the openness rising heavenward from the brown pulpit. Ryann jerked as blasts sounded from massive golden

1

pipes shooting up from both sides of the altar, cracking the eerie silence. Windy bellows cascaded around the dome, two hundred feet up. The novelty of such an instrument held his attention until the rays of the early morning sun began illuminating the stained glass mural outlined by the pipes. The face of Jesus radiated with the morning glow as He walked calmly across the tossing blue-green waves. Above the stained glass were the words "Eternal Father, Strong to Save."

Without moving his head, Ryann glanced left down the pew. He had positioned himself perfectly, or so he thought, with his sister, Alison, next to him, followed by his brother, Henry Jr., and then his parents. To his right was an open aisle. As the white-robed pastor strode purposefully from his highback chair to the podium, Ryann's hand crept along his pant leg with the stealth of a spider. Reaching into his pocket, he pulled out his cell phone, suppressing a smile as he silently congratulated himself on picking out one so small. He was grateful his parents had bought the phone but struggled with the rules that had come with it, like their prohibition against texting in church.

The sound of the pastor's voice launching into the sermon provided the perfect diversion for him to slide the phone down the side of his leg. A quick glance provided the needed confidence to continue, and Ryann's thumb moved with robotic precision to select his two best friends and then type out a quick message.

here in academy chapel. wuu2?

Ryann had received the phone as a gift for moving up to seventh grade. Liddy's and Terell's parents had quickly followed his parents' lead, and now the three of them could get in touch with each other at any moment. Being scattered around the country for summer vacations didn't seem quite so bad when they could quickly share moments with their best friends.

Ryann put his father in the category of "techie" and patiently sat through his instructions on all the features of the cell phone, but the real education came from his friends. He was going to be taking his first year of Spanish when classes began, and Ryann figured it would actually be his third language after English and texting. He smiled. Who would have known a month ago that *wuu2* meant, "What are you up to?" Sliding the cell phone under his leg to keep it hidden, he shifted in the hard bench and sighed, waiting to see if there would be a response.

Bzzzzz...

Liddy's back pocket buzzed as she followed her parents down the white marble stairs of the grand foyer. She slowly reached around to pull out the hot pink phone as her parents and other tourists listened to the tour director.

"The Breakers is the grandest of Newport's summer cottages and a symbol of the Vanderbilt family's social and financial preeminence in turn-of-the-century America. Commodore Cornelius Vanderbilt established the family fortune in steamships and later in the New York Central Railroad, which was a pivotal development in the industrial growth of the nation during the late nineteenth century—"

Liddy rolled her eyes. *Cottages? Who are they trying to kid? This is the biggest mansion I've ever seen.* Flipping open her phone, she read Ryann's message and quickly responded.

at huge mansion in rhode island. doin 3.5 mile hike along ocean cliff trail later today. cya

Liddy enjoyed the change of scenery as her family took their annual summer vacation to Rhode Island to stay with her grandparents. With the trip winding down, her parents had suggested a day trip to the famous Newport mansions. It sounded boring to Liddy until they mentioned the ocean cliff walk. Two-thirds of the trek was supposed to be fairly easy and scenic, but the last third was described as "treacherous" in the colorful brochure her parents had given her. Seventy-foot drops off the rocky shoreline into the turbulent ocean waves sounded exciting to her.

The abrupt silence of the tour guide erased her vision of the future, and Liddy's thoughts turned to Terell. Her thumbs glided across the black keys, typing out a quick message.

wuu2? last few days cw2cu

Bzzzzz…

Terell jerked in his seat, his elbow jabbing his mother in the ribs. Glancing about, he ran his hands up and down the top of his pants, smoothing them out. His mother's upturned palm came down on his leg.

Busted, Terell thought, pulling his cell phone out of his pocket and handing it to her.

Terell watched his mother flip it open so only she could view it. As he looked up into her face she mouthed the word *later.* He leaned back and tried to focus on the sermon. His mom was pretty consistent about quizzing him about the content later in the day.

"Terell, you know you're not supposed to have your cell phone on during church," his mother began as they headed out to their car. "It's a distraction."

"I know, Mom, but it's probably important."

"Well, when you become a doctor and you're on call, then you can have it on during church. Otherwise keep it off or don't bring it."

Later as they reached the car, he asked, "Can I have it back now?"

His mother fumbled around in her purse, then handed it to him. "By the way, what does 'cw2cu' mean?"

"Mom! That's 'can't wait to see you,'" Terell breathed exasperatedly while shaking his head.

"Watch it, Terell. A cell phone is a privilege, not a right."

"Yes, ma'am," he acknowledged while flipping open his cell to get the message.

He quickly scanned the text and typed back.

> **have fun. church is havin end of sumr dinner picnic at evans park. cul8r**

Ryann strode hastily down the granite steps outside the chapel doors with Alison trying to keep up. Red brick walkways running parallel to orange and yellow flowerbeds greeted him. The famous Herndon Monument his father always spoke of towered off to the left.

The twenty-one-foot, gray-speckled obelisk sprouted out of the ground in stark contrast to the rich green grass and brown oak trees surrounding it. He tried to picture hundreds of sweaty midshipmen scaling the greased monument to replace the plebe "dixie-cup hat" on top with a midshipmen cover. This marked the official end of the difficult first year and an elevation from plebe to midshipman third class. As his father had recounted numerous times, legend held that whoever replaced the dixie cup hat was destined to be the first in his or her class to become an admiral, although in reality it had not yet occurred.

"Hey, Ryann!"

He turned in time to watch his older brother, Henry, race down the steps two at a time. "Dad's talking to some old classmates of his and will be down in a few minutes. He's got our schedule laid out for the whole day."

"Really?" Ryann replied in mock sarcasm. "Who would have thought?"

"He wants us to check out John Paul Jones' crypt before we go to lunch," Henry said, ignoring Ryann's comment.

"What's a crypt?" Alison asked.

"It's where his bones are buried," Ryann said, widening his eyes and curling his fingers like monster claws.

"Oh, gross!" Alison replied, scrunching up her face and turning away.

"Where is it?" Ryann asked.

Henry turned to lead the way. "It's underneath the chapel. Come on, let's go! He said the entrance is around the side."

The two boys raced along the narrow sidewalk outlining the left side of the chapel.

"Hey, guys! Wait for me," Alison cried out from behind them.

Rushing down the steps, Henry and Ryann slapped the thick wooden doors with open palms, jolting the heavy entrance open. Pushing their way in, they stopped just inside at a sign with old type-face, pointing the way to the crypt.

"Hey!"

Both boys jumped as the high-pitched yelp echoed around the small foyer entrance.

"Shhh," they whispered in unison, glaring at their sister.

"Sorry." Alison shrugged her shoulders, the light dimming quickly as the bulky doors swung shut with a loud bang.

"Do you think it's open to the public?" Henry whispered.

"The door wasn't locked, so it must be, right?" Ryann hesitated momentarily. No one besides the three of them was in sight, but that made the exploration more intriguing. "Come on, this way."

The small room's walls hung with ornate religious symbols. A large black wooden door beside an altar caught Ryann's attention, and he rushed to examine it.

"Well, Mr. Know-it-all, what next?" Alison asked in her snootiest voice.

"We go through the door, of course." Pushing the door open, Ryann expected to be at their final destination, but instead the door's echoing groans resounded through a hollow chamber. The catacombs of the chapel basement seemed unending, and the more up-to-date style of this room appeared nothing like a crypt.

"Are you both sure John Paul Jones is down here?" Alison continued with indignant pessimism.

Ryann's and Henry's eyes locked briefly, and Henry winked. "Sure, he's just down the hallway here. C'mon."

Another rustic black door with an ancient doorknob awaited them. Henry reached it first. He turned the ornate metal doorknob and pulled back firmly.

Creeeeaaaaaaak!

Ryann glanced over his shoulder and gave Alison a sinister grin, hoping to increase her anxiety. A dimly lit room of swirling black and white marble awaited them. He followed his brother into the room and nearly collided with him when Henry stopped. Pushing him aside, Ryann grinned at the sight. A massive, almost totally black coffin dominated the center of the room. The base, rising out of the white marble floor, was adorned with four dolphins leaping out from each corner. Eight thick swirled-marble columns surrounding the coffin held up an ornately carved, octagon-shaped ceiling. Glowing blue light formed a halo in the recession above the tomb, cascading down eerily over the marble casket of the immortalized John Paul Jones.

"Ahh!" Alison cried out. Her voice echoed across the marble floors.

Both boys jerked around in Alison's direction. Standing at attention next to her like a suit of armor was a Marine guard Ryann hadn't noticed upon entering. His immaculate dress uniform molded to him as if he never took it off, like a painted statue. Ryann scanned up from the dim light reflecting off the soldier's polished black shoes, past the crisply pressed blue pants with red stripes down each side to his coat-like black top with gleaming gold buttons from neck to waist. His thick white belt with a highly polished Marine Corps emblazoned buckle, white gloved hands and white cover broke up the dark colors that had kept him hidden. He stared into the expressionless face of the guard to see if he could catch him blinking.

"Hey, kids, I see you made it down here!" their father said from the other side of the room as he walked over to join them. He didn't try to conceal his smile. "Looks like you took the long way."

"Kinda creepy, Dad," Alison said, then whispered, "and there's a guard over there."

"Yeah, honey, the military posts uniformed guards at significant memorials to honor those who died in service to our country."

"Dad, I've heard of Davey Jones from that pirate movie, but who's John Paul Jones?" Henry asked.

Mr. Watters glanced at his watch. "We've got to meet some friends for lunch, but in short, he's the father of the American Navy. All of the dimly lit, recessed alcoves down here have artifacts and details of his life. See there?" He pointed at the floor in front of the marbled coffin. "Etched into the floor, circling the sarcophagus—which by the way is made of twenty-one tons of Grand Pyrenees marble—are the names of the seven ships he commanded during his life."

"*Sarco* who?" Henry asked, wrinkling up his brow.

"Sarcophagus. You know, a receptacle for a corpse carved from stone. As a plebe you have to memorize that type of important information." Ryann's father smiled.

"Yeah, right." Henry rolled his eyes.

"Okay, gotta go, guys. And this time, let's go out the right way," Mr. Watters said as he led them around the room to the exit.

Ryann read off the names of the ships etched into the marble as they walked—*Providence, Ariel, Ranger, Serapis, Alliance, Alfred*—and some other name he couldn't read as they went out the door. As they walked toward their car, he sent a text to Liddy.

just left wicked cool tomb of dead guy under the chapel...zup?

CHAPTER 2

Shades of Blue

STANDING AT THE western end of Easton's Beach on Memorial Boulevard, Liddy waited, arms crossed, dividing her stares between her mother, who was going back to the car for one more thing they "might" need, and the eastern shore of Rhode Island, which awaited them.

"Come on, Mom! It'll be dark before we finish if we don't hurry up."

She stared in the direction of her father, who stood halfway between the car and her. His nodding head of mutual frustration gave him away before it changed to a "that's no way to talk to your mother" look.

Liddy tapped her foot in sync with the secondhand on her watch. Cooped up inside listening to the history of the famous Newport mansions, she was ready for the hike. Liddy closed her eyes and drew in a deep breath. She held her breath for just a moment as the afternoon sun warmed her face.

"Whhhooooo..." she exhaled through pursed lips, her arms now dangling at her sides.

"All better now?" Mr. Thomas interrupted.

"Yep. All good," she smiled.

Reaching into her pocket, she pulled out her cell phone and saw the red light blinking. Scanning Ryann's message, she tapped out her own as her mother walked their way.

scary...ha! going on cliff walk now. l8r

Heading down the short side road to the trail entrance, Mrs. Thomas pulled out the guidebook she had retrieved from the car.

"In 1975 the Newport Cliff Walk was designated as a National Recreation Trail, the sixty-fifth in the nation and first in New England. The walk runs three and one-half miles and about two-thirds of the walk is in easy walking condition, while the southern half is a rough trail over rocky shore line—"

"Mom," Liddy interrupted, "let's get going! I don't want to miss the hard part at the end."

Henry, Ryann, and Alison ran along the Santee Basin, a small inlet off the Severn River, in an impromptu game of tag. Dozens of navy blue and gold-striped sailboats bobbed up and down, their white sails billowing in the salty breeze like white sheets hanging on a clothesline.

"Tag, you're it," Ryann laughed, running away from Alison.

"No fair. You have to tag Henry sometimes," she shrieked.

"Hey, kids!" Mr. Watters yelled from behind. "Head left at the end of the street toward the sailing center."

They came to an abrupt stop just outside the pointy-shaped building designed to resemble a flotilla of sailboats. Ryann pulled on the door to the center. It didn't budge. Cupping his hands, he peered through the reflective glass. It was dark inside.

"We're a tad early," Mr. Watters announced as he and Mrs. Watters strolled up.

"And how much is a tad?" Ryann's voice rose sarcastically.

Mr. Watters glanced at his watch. "Well, let's just say we have time to take a little walk. Come on. I'll show you something cool." He turned with Mrs. Watters, hand-in-hand, and began walking away.

The kids scrambled to catch up until they were all walking in a parallel line along the cement pier. Mrs. Watters shook her head to get the hair out of her eyes as the gusty winds off the Severn River swirled around them. The soft glow of the retiring sun, now at their backs, reflected orange-brown light atop the murky water. Off to their right, motorboats idled toward the city docks and the pier-side restaurants bustled with early diners paying homage to the nightly sunset. On their left, the lapping waters of the river provided a barrier between them and the hillside mansions that dotted the opposite shoreline. Closing in on the far corner of the academy grounds, they were greeted by the open waters of the Chesapeake Bay. Sailboats too numerous to count took their best angles in to rest for the night. The Watters family stopped in unison, admiring the panoramic view of the river, bay, sailing vessels, and downtown Annapolis.

"What's with the green light thing?" Ryann asked, pointing at the globe balanced on top of a four-foot, grated-metal stand just up ahead of them.

Mr. Watters didn't hesitate. "That's Triton light, named after the submarine *USS Triton*. The globe beneath the light contains water from the twenty-two seas the *Triton* sailed through as it circumnavigated the earth."

Ryann read the bronze plaque, which had weathered to a light green.

This light is dedicated
to the safe return
of all those who go down
to the sea in ships

"Cool!" Henry said, interjecting a question of his own. "What about that giant mast over there sticking out of the ground?"

Swiveling around to their right, the white metal mast sprouted out of the small grassy area, dwarfing several trees surrounding it.

"Ah," Mr. Watters smiled, "the foremast of the *USS Maine*. It blew up in Havana Harbor in the late 1900s, killing half the crew and sparking the beginning of the Spanish-American War."

"Dad, you're a walking Wikipedia!"

"Well, here's a little trivia to go with it. Did you know that the *Maine* is considered the longest ship in the navy? Her foremast is located here, and her mainmast is located in Arlington National Cemetery in Arlington, Virginia."

Ryann laughed. "Great, I think I know something that even Liddy doesn't know now."

Mr. Watters looked at his watch. "Okay everyone, let's head back to the sailing center. Our guests should be arriving for dinner any minute now."

Evans Park was a flurry of activity as Terell and his mother walked down the gently sloping street. Summery picnic smells of burgers smoldering on the grill, baked beans simmering in metal pots, and the regionally famous Zellwood corn boiling in large vats tickled Terell's nose. His arms strained to hold on to the cool watermelon beading with wetness in the humid Florida afternoon. Mrs. Peterson held her homemade peach cobbler out in front of her. Still warm from the oven, the mouth-watering smell extended far beyond her reach.

"Terell, come on. We're getting ready to start a game!" a voice yelled out off to one side of the park.

He turned to see a football flying through the air. "Mom! Where can I set this down?"

"Over there will do." His mother pointed to one of the picnic tables.

The late afternoon sun glistened off the tiny droplets of sweat on his ebony skin as he gently set the watermelon down and ran off.

"Don't get all dirty. We're gonna eat in thirty minutes!"

Wild bushes and stringy weeds lined the winding path the Thomases hiked along. Liddy ran on ahead. "Keep to the right!" Mr. Thomas shouted. "That's a seventy-foot drop down to the ocean from here."

"Here it is!" Liddy yelled back.

She bounced on her toes as her parents caught up. "Here are the forty steps the brochure talked about. It goes down to a rock platform right at the edge of the incoming waves!"

Mr. Thomas gave a firm response. "We don't have a lot of time before sunset, Liddy, so we have to make it quick. We still have to get through the toughest part of the trail."

Thirty minutes later, Mr. Thomas caught up, gulping deep breaths of air as he bent over to put both hands on his knees. Liddy looked to her mother, just behind him, who didn't appear to be out of breath. Her mother smiled and winked. Glancing back down the steps, shadows brought on by the setting sun erased their travels.

"We're...going...to have to...exit...just after The Breakers," Mr. Thomas said, his chest rising and falling between words. "It won't be safe to keep going after that in the dark."

"Aww, Dad!"

Mr. Thomas's hand went up.

"All right," Liddy said softly, rolling her eyes as she turned.

The pathway changed to varying size rocks, causing them to carefully choose their own steps, testing each rock for stability. Crashing waves reminded them how close the cold waters were, despite being hidden in the new twilight.

"I think we're almost there," Liddy called back to her parents. "I can see the lights of The Breakers Mansion." She could barely make out the darker shapes of the boulders she crossed. Dropping down to all fours she felt ahead before bringing her feet along. Light-colored pavement marked the end of the rugged section of path as Liddy hopped off the last rock, landing with both feet while yelling out, "Made it!"

"Stay there, hon. We'll be with you in just a sec."

Liddy faced the sounds of the waves calling out from complete blackness. She slowly raised her head, her mouth opened in amazement at the clarity and brightness of the multitude of stars draped across the sky. In the opposite direction, a few streetlights provided enough lighting for the Thomases to see their way back to the road.

She gazed up toward The Breakers expecting to see the familiar white lights coming from rows of windows across each level of the mansion. Instead, her eyes honed in on a blue glow coming from an attic room. She blinked several times. The blue illumination distinctly contrasted with the white light coming from the other windows. Liddy stared transfixed as the light glowed brightly, then dimmed, then glowed brightly again. The gentle squeeze on her shoulder startled her.

"Ahh!" she cried, jerking around.

"Whoa, it's okay, sweetie. It's just us."

"Mom, Dad, check it out!" Liddy turned to point out the blue illumination. The light had vanished.

Ryann put down his fork, quickly scanning the faces at the dinner table. When his pocket vibrated for the third time, he reached under the table and slipped his cell phone out. Pulling it out from beneath the tablecloth, he glanced down and read the message:

strange blue light coming from mansion then mysteriously disappeared

That's odd. I wonder what was so strange about the light that made Liddy text me? Reversing his movements, he slid the phone back into his pocket.

"Ahem. Dad, can I be excused for a moment?"

"Sure, son," Mr. Watters replied automatically, then reengaged his guests in conversation.

I wonder what else happened. I can give a quick reply from the bathroom. Ryann made his way toward the bathrooms along the second-floor glass wall of the sailing center. Even at night, the panoramic view of the harbor was inspiring. Twinkling stars provided a backdrop to the tiny green and red running lights of boats still crossing the channel. A full moon reflected off the choppy waves in the bay, and the rhythmic blinking of Triton Light kept some semblance of order.

Ryann entered the bathroom, pulled his phone out, and typed.

anything else happen? what was so odd about it?

Heading back toward the table, he looked outside again and froze. Triton light was no longer blinking. It was one continuous glowing blue light.

"Hey, Terell, can you get my football? I left it in the gazebo," the older boy asked as he helped the youth pastor load tables into the church van.

"Sure," Terell answered. "Mom, I'll be back in just a sec."

Mrs. Peterson waved a hand in his direction as she continued chatting with a small circle of women.

Terell walked cautiously across the dimly lit grass toward the gazebo. The sun had long since set and the nightly background chorus of buzzing bugs had begun, highlighted by the occasional firefly popping on and off. He entered the darkened gazebo, just barely recognizable from the street lamps back by the picnic. Reaching under the wooden seats, he patted the pavement, moving around the floor until his hands hit the familiar shape of the smooth, leather ball. Rising up, Terell stared across the dark inlet of Lake Dora and his body stiffened.

Instead of the normal white glow coming from the lighthouse, it was blue! Stumbling back off the wooden gazebo flooring and onto the grass, Terell turned and ran back across the grass field to the remnant of church picnickers.

Grabbing his mom's arm, he pulled her away from the lone woman she was now talking to.

"Terell? What are you doing, son?"

"Mom, you gotta check this out!" He continued pulling her another few feet across the grass and pointed in the direction of the lighthouse.

"Look!"

The familiar glow of white light greeted them both.

Ryann, Liddy, and Terell all lay awake staring at different ceilings in three towns along the East Coast: Newport, Annapolis, and Mount Dora. Each of them tried to make sense of the strange blue lights they had seen. With more questions than answers, they grabbed for their cell phones as if on cue. They had all programmed their phones to send messages simultaneously to the other two with a simple click. Soft glows lit up their faces in the darkened rooms as they began to type.

we all saw a blue light tonight. any idea what it means? (Liddy)

none here. my mom thought I was freakin out (Terell)

I checked my watch just after seeing the light. it was 8:05. how bout u? (Ryann)

my text message to both of u went out at 8:04 (Liddy)

no watch. lighthouse comes on at 8. must have been just after that (Terell)

do u think it has to do with aeliana? (Ryann)

don't know. b back tues. cya then (Liddy)

nite (Terell)

nite (Ryann)

CHAPTER 3

Attic Antics

OUNT DORA'S TYPICAL summer day called for cloudless skies, temperatures in the nineties, and scattered afternoon showers lasting twenty to thirty minutes. Ryann was thankful for the breeze, which almost always blew easterly across Lake Dora. Without it, the muggy air would have felt like a heavy weight pressing down on him as he hiked toward the ice cream parlor. The Sweet Shop was their agreed-upon meeting place, not only to get out of the blazing sun but also for the homemade Thomas Sweet fudge and ice cream. The Dickens-Reed Bookstore right next door lay empty and closed indefinitely for business. Carved books, vines, sculptures, and pillars covering the length of the exterior still attracted attention. Ryann hoped a new owner would come along and restore the establishment to its original glory.

Bells jingled overhead as he entered. He stopped abruptly, shocked at the sight before him. Terell and Liddy were already seated at one of the small, round high-tops, returning his jaw-dropping expression with broad smiles. Ryann glanced down at his watch, which read 9:50.

Terell laughed. "You're on time. We just decided to beat you for a change."

"Actually, we're anxious to talk about what happened the other day," Liddy said.

Ryann plopped down in the remaining chair. His favorite, Cherry Coke, was on the table waiting for him.

"Thanks, guys," he said, sucking down a big gulp. As he exhaled with a breathy "ah" Liddy began the conversation.

"So, we've already established that each of us saw a blue flash of some kind at approximately eight o'clock on Friday night, right?"

The boys nodded their heads.

"What exactly did your light look like, Terell?"

"We all know what the lighthouse light looks like at night," Terell answered. "But this was different. The light was blue, and it didn't shine the same way. It was almost like the glow was bigger than the light itself."

"Yeah, mine was the same way," Ryann cut in, "and I couldn't see through the light. It reminded me of a mist or fog."

"How long did the blue light last?" Liddy asked.

"Not long. By the time I shouted for my mom to look, it had changed back to its normal color," Terell said.

Ryann nodded. "Same here. Just a few seconds."

Liddy pondered aloud while glancing up to the ceiling. "It's as if it was meant for just the three of us to see." She addressed Ryann, "Your ring hasn't been doing anything funny, has it?"

"No, I thought the same thing, but remember, Gabriel only said the ring 'might' lead the way. What do you think we should do now?"

"I don't know that there's anything we can do," Liddy answered. "We're all back in town, and school starts tomorrow. We'll just have to wait and see what happens next."

"Ugh, I'm not big on waiting," Ryann groaned.

"Hey! I just remembered," Terell jumped in. "I heard there's supposed to be an eclipse of the moon this Saturday night at ten. Why don't we get together and check it out? It's not supposed to happen again for three more years!"

Liddy raised her eyebrows. "That was random."

"All this talk about lights at night reminded me of it."

"Hey, it sounds cool to me," Liddy said. "My dad has a huge telescope. I bet he'd let us set it up in my backyard. I'll ask my mom if it's okay."

"Great!" Terell said, changing the subject. "You guys ready for school tomorrow? Kinda lame goin' back on a Thursday."

"I think the idea is to use Thursday and Friday to get everyone acclimated to the new school year before a full week," Liddy said.

Terell rolled his eyes, "Yeah, more like brainwashing us to forget about the summer."

Ryann stared out the storefront window.

Liddy was the first to notice. "What are you thinking about, Ryann?"

"Huh? Oh, I'm just wondering what Drake is gonna say tomorrow. We haven't seen him since we got back from Aeliana just before school ended for the summer."

Terell shook his head. "I'm sure he'll be the same old Drake. But I wouldn't worry about him after the whoopin' Gabriel and you put on him!" he laughed.

Ryann grinned. "Yeah, you're probably right." He glanced at his watch. "I'd better get going, guys. I promised my mom I'd mow the grass before dinner."

Terell raised his glass of soda up in the air, "Here's to straight As this year!"

Ryann grinned at his best friend, lifting his Cherry Coke up to clink Terell's glass.

Liddy rolled her eyes. "I know you're just mocking me, Terell, but it's a worthy toast just the same!"

Liddy yelled down the stairs, "Mom! Have you seen my backpack?"

"Did you check your closet?" her mom called back over the rattling of dishes as she prepared for dinner.

"Yes, Mom. Not there—" then mumbling, "—first and most obvious place to look."

"How about the attic? Your father put a bunch of stuff up there at the beginning of the summer."

"We have an attic?" Liddy yelled back down. *We've lived in this house for two years, and I never knew we had an attic.*

Mrs. Thomas walked into the family room to respond. "Yes, hon, at the end of the hall there's a rope that hangs down from the ceiling. If you pull it, the ceiling board comes down and the ladder staircase will unfold."

Draped over the railing on the landing, Liddy looked down at her mom incredulously. "I can't believe I've never known about it."

"You've worn a path from your room to the bathroom. I suppose you haven't had a reason to go to the end of the hall by the guest room."

"Weird," Liddy muttered, heading back down the hall.

"Be careful up there. It's dark and dirty," Mrs. Thomas yelled.

The white rope dangled from the ceiling precisely where her mom said it did. Liddy stared in disbelief. A black line outlined the white rectangular board, which closed flush with the same color ceiling. Stretching up on the tips of her toes, she grabbed the thick knot at the bottom of the rope. Liddy tugged with the full force of her weight, pulling the ceiling board down with a resounding *creak*. A ladder, folded in half with hinges, clung to the ceiling board. Liddy unfolded the ladder.

Looking up, she was greeted by a dark hole. *This is so cool!* she thought. Scrambling up the ladder, she hesitated at the top, letting her eyes adjust to the darkness. Stepping into the attic, she was met by the smothering, steamy air from the late afternoon sun beating down on the roof. Spotting a string dangling from the rafters, she gripped the thin cord and gave it a snappy tug. A lone bulb clicked on, casting a dull glow around the space. *Wow! This place is huge!* Liddy breathed in the stale air. *Now where's that backpack?*

Brown moving van boxes lined the walls. Liddy recognized her dad's messy handwriting in black marker identifying the contents of each box. She shuffled across the plywood boards, testing the creaky old flooring with each step. A green-and-red Christmas tree stand and several broken glass ornaments lay next to a box marked "XMAS." A white oscillating fan sat upright covered in a fine layer of dust. She bent over and opened the top of a ratty box, revealing a wooden tub inside. The side of the box said "Homemade Ice Cream." A half-empty, taped up bag of rock salt lay crumpled in the center of the container. *Just a bunch of junk*, she thought, taking one last glance around her dim surroundings.

Against the far wall, a large wooden chest outlined in tarnished gold bands sat in the shadows. *What's that?* Liddy stepped over for a closer inspection. A latch on the front slipped over a brass hasp. It was intended for a lock, but there was none. Her imagination jumped quickly from gold coins to rare, sparkling jewels as she lifted the latch and pulled the heavy lid open. *Clothes?*

Liddy fumbled through the multi-colored fabrics and odd-shaped hats. One brightly striped hat was bent over with a tassel, like something a court jester might wear. Another was a black satin top hat, which seemed fit for a magician or circus ringleader. She set them aside and began pulling out the dresses, shirts, capes, belts, and scarves. *These don't seem like costumes Mom and Dad would collect.*

Peering into the depleted chest, the last item was a thick brown leather belt adorned with metal studs and an oversized oval buckle. She grasped the weighty belt, which lay coiled like a snake, and lifted it from its cozy corner. Her nose tickled. Liddy reached with her other hand to rub it. She sneezed, losing her grip on the heavy belt. She winced as it landed with a hollow thud on the bottom of the chest.

Instead of removing the belt, she balled up her fist and knocked on the bottom of the chest. *It's hollow,* she thought, stretching out her fingers and running them along the smooth bottom of the chest. Her middle finger grazed across a small dip. Pulling her hand back, like she'd been bitten, Liddy peered into the dark recesses of the chest, trying to see what she had touched. Unable to see anything, she reached a trembling hand back inside. Sliding her finger along the chest floor, she felt for the same spot with her index finger and stopped when she located the small hole. Looking over her shoulder, she didn't see anything out of the ordinary but had the eerie feeling someone was watching her. Liddy pushed her finger through the hole, curling it just enough to get a grip and pulled up. The false bottom that had been wedged into the ornate box folded back on itself, flush against the front of the chest. She squinted, trying to see into the darkness of the false bottom. *Note to self, bring a flashlight the next time I come up here!*

Liddy delved into the chest one more time. The edge of the large chest pressed into her armpit as she extended her arm as far as possible. What's this? Her fingers ran across and around the edges of a smooth, rectangular object. Grasping at one of the sides, she closed her hand around it and lifted the familiar-feeling item out. A book?

Liddy gripped the book in both hands and stared at her findings. A dark brown leather cover wrapped itself around frayed pages sticking out on three sides. There was no title on the front, so she flipped it over and checked the binding. No writing.

Her mom's distant voice brought her out of her trance. "Liddy, time for dinner!"

She scurried about, first replacing the false bottom to its original position, then haphazardly tossing all the items back into the trunk. With the latch back in place, Liddy tucked the book under her arm and gingerly backed down the flimsy ladder until her feet reached the familiar hallway floor.

"Liddy!"

"Just a sec, Mom!"

She folded the ladder back into place, pushing up on the ceiling board, which retracted back up into the ceiling. Liddy hurried into her room, opened the bottom drawer of her nightstand, and hid the book. Closing the drawer, she hesitated, then opened it again and pulled the book back out. Liddy's mouth dropped open as she read the fanciful script on the first page:

All About Dragons

CHAPTER 4

All About Dragons

RYANN GLANCED DOWN at the card with his class schedule as he sauntered along the open-air walkway leading to the seventh-grade classrooms. "First period language arts, Mrs. Biggebottom, room 111," he read with a monotone drawl. "Surely this name is a joke."

Brrrrrrrrrring.

The five-minute warning bell clanged above the din of hundreds of sixth-, seventh-, and eighth-graders frantically looking for their rooms. Ryann spotted a blue door across the courtyard with "111" printed in white. Picking up his pace, he marched in a direct line across the open ground. His goal in view, he blocked out the large shadow moving into his path from left to right.

Bam!

"Uhh." Ryann landed on the ground, three feet to the right.

A familiar yet deeper voice chastised him. "Watters! You aren't the only one walking here! Why don't you watch where you're going?"

Ryann looked up into the sneering face of Drake Dunfellow.

"Sorry, Drake. I didn't see you coming."

"No joke, genius!"

"Hey, I said I'm sorry," Ryann countered softly, getting to his feet.

"You'd better steer clear of me this year, Watters!" Drake bellowed, causing numerous kids to turn and stare. "You get on my nerves."

Ryann stood motionless, staring into the older boy's stern face. Drake's narrow, dark eyes glared back at him. Ryann kept his voice calm. "Right, uhh, have a nice day, Drake."

Drake hesitated, scrunching up his brow. "Whatever!" he barked, then continued plodding along the invisible line he had been following.

Ryann recalled the advice his dad had given him to combat a bully: "Be calm and pleasant; they won't know how to respond." He shrugged. *That's odd. It's like he didn't even remember our confrontation in Aeliana last year.* Ryann found himself standing in the open doorway of room 111. Other kids rushed around him and through the door to be seated before the final bell. Crossing the threshold, he thought, *This is it, the beginning of seventh grade.*

Hundreds of kids jabbered excitedly about the events of the first morning. Ryann winced at the raucous roar of the cafeteria as he dropped his tray on the table next to Terell's. Out of habit, they had arrived at the same spot where they spent forty-five minutes a day the previous year.

Terell stabbed at a dark piece of meat covered in thick, brown gravy. "I can't believe we didn't get any of the same teachers for morning classes."

"I know," Ryann said. "Who do you have for afternoon classes?"

"I've got a Mr. Molten for history and then Ms. Rollio for Spanish 101."

Ryann looked at his schedule. "Cool, dude. I've got the same classes!"

"Hey, guys!" Liddy said, hopping into an empty chair next to Terell. Ryann knew exactly what would happen next. Liddy reached into her brown paper bag and pulled out a napkin, then lined up an apple and celery and carrot sticks neatly on top of it. Next came a mini water bottle and half an egg salad sandwich with green olives cut up and mixed in.

Liddy bounced up and down in her seat, rearranging the food on her napkin until Terell couldn't take it anymore.

"Liddy? What up, girl? You look like you're gonna bust any minute."

She stopped bouncing and looked both ways to see if anyone was paying attention. "Okay, you're not going to believe this, but I found an old book up in the attic of our house yesterday."

"You have an attic?" Ryann asked.

"Yeah, I didn't find out until yesterday. Anyway, the title of the book is—"she lowered her voice—"*All About Dragons.*"

Ryann and Terell looked at each other then back at Liddy.

"And?" Ryann asked, his eyebrow cocked to the side.

"What do you mean, 'and'?" she asked.

Terell butted in. "Hate to be the bearer of bad news, but you can buy a book on dragons at any bookstore."

Liddy huffed, "Oh, this one's not like that. What I mean is it's old. It has a worn leather cover and brittle, yellowed pages with old Celtic-looking words. And it's handwritten. I bet it's a hundred, maybe a thousand years old."

"Really?" Ryann asked. "What did it say inside?"

"Well, I haven't had much time to look at it. I just found it last night."

Brrrrrrrrrring.

The five-minute warning bell rang for afternoon classes. Liddy choked down her last celery stick. "Gotta get to class, guys. I'll check it out in detail tonight and text you if I find out anything interesting."

"Cool. Maybe it ties in with the blue flashes we saw," Ryann said as he and Terell gathered their books and headed off to class together.

By eight o'clock, Liddy had finished her homework, said good night to her parents, and was finally alone in her room. Opening the bottom drawer on her nightstand, she carefully pulled out the leather-bound book and laid it on her bed. A few of the pages were pulling loose of the binding. Using two hands to keep from tearing the pages, she carefully opened the book and turned to the second page. She read what looked to be the table of contents.

Anatomy of a Dragon
Dragon Warfare
Stages of a Dragon's Life
Types of Dragons
A Dragon's Lair

Liddy's hands shook as she turned the yellowed page. The paper felt thicker than normal, and she noticed it was imbedded with small slivers of bark. The texture reminded her of the birch tree bark she had peeled off one of her grandmother's trees up north. She looked over the artfully handwritten lettering and began reading the first few paragraphs.

Anatomy of a Dragon

By Ireth Silimaurë

A dragon's body is covered with hundreds of hard scales. They are fitted together like a suit of armor, overlapping one another to form a protective coating to the body beneath. The scales continually grow and multiply as the dragon matures. They do not fall off, and the dragon never sheds its skin.

The dragon's wings closely resemble those of a bat. The frame of its wing is like long fingers whose tips are visible. Dragons prefer to take flight by leaping off cliffs. Otherwise, they can run, gaining speed, and then leap into the air, snapping their tail downward and pushing off with their hind legs.

She continued reading the next several pages, eagerly devouring detailed descriptions of the skeletal and muscular structure of a dragon. Biology was one of Liddy's favorite subjects. Sometimes she even considered becoming a doctor. Several crude drawings labeled various body parts and internal organs. Liddy was most fascinated by the "Draconis Fundamentum," which described how the dragon's breath worked.

All of the dragon's blood passes through an organ called the Draconis Fundamentum before continuing through the rest of the body. Chemicals made in this organ travel into the lungs, where the dragon's breath weapon is produced. A dragon's breath weapon varies by the type or color of the dragon.

Liddy reviewed the comments on dragon senses and was not surprised to find that dragons' sight is exceptional, since they are geared for hunting. She was, however, amazed that dragons have a blind sense, which allows them to see things that are invisible and even see with their eyes closed. *Hmm, again, kind of like a bat,* she mused.

Glancing across the room at her wall clock, she noticed it was 9:30 already. She thought of Sorcha from their previous visit to Aeliana. She was the only dragon Liddy had ever seen, and even at that, she hadn't seen her up close. Liddy gently lifted the pages to skip ahead to the section on types of dragons. A chart caught her eye. It was titled "The Stages of a Dragon's Life." She placed her finger at the beginning, "0–5 years old," and ran it across to the stage of development, "wyrmling." Running her finger down the chart, she was surprised. *Wow! A dragon is an adult when it is between one hundred and two hundred years old.* She was only halfway down the page. Her finger passed by "ancient" at ages eight hundred to one thousand years old and finally came to rest at "great wyrm," the name for dragons twelve hundred and greater years old.

Liddy carefully turned page after page, past black, green, gold, and blue dragons, all of which looked like they were hand painted with watercolors, until she found the one she was looking for—white.

No way!

She flipped her phone open and tapped out a message to Ryann and Terell.

reading dragon book. turned to chapter on types...white... sketch looks just like sorcha!

Liddy set her phone on the bed and returned to the charcoal sketch. Seeing a dragon in Aeliana had burned an image in her mind that could never be erased. This was Sorcha, unless all white dragons looked exactly the same. On the next page she read the description.

The scales of the white dragon are a brilliant white, glittering in the sun. Their wings are tinged a pinkish blue and look a bit frayed along the edges. White dragons have chins with a distinguishing flap of skin and a row of spines. They have a small, sharp beak at the end of their snout, which curves sharply downward. Whites' heads are noticeably streamlined from the tip of their snout to the staggered crests blending into their neck.

Mature white dragons can climb ice cliffs with their talons. They enjoy swimming in icy cold waters, which proves to be their favorite hunting ground. Their breath weapon is frost, and they will use it to freeze their prey before eating it. They grow to a maximum height of 16 feet, and their mortal enemy is the red dragon.

White dragons live in ice caves, most often dug into the side of a mountain; however, they have been known to carve their lair into a floating iceberg. A

white dragon has one of the best memories of all
dragons and rarely forgets anything.

Bzzzzz…

Liddy jumped as her phone buzzed on the bed next to her. Flipping
it open, she read the message Ryan had just sent.

wow! when can I see it?

Her mom's muffled voice called from beyond the closed door,
"Liddy? Are you still awake?"

"Yeah, Mom," she yelled back, typing frantically.

"Bedtime!"

"Okay, just a sec!"

**busy with the fam tomorrow. how bout sat. when you come
for the eclipse? bfn**

Liddy shut her phone, turned off the overhead light, and continued
reading by a small, portable book light. After a few more chapters,
she glanced at her clock. *Eleven? Wow! It's been two hours!* Hopping
out of bed, she returned the book to the bottom drawer in her nightstand. *Tomorrow is going to come way too early.*

Ryann looked at his watch for the second time. "Where do you think
she is?" he asked Terell as they wolfed down their food.

Terell laughed, "She probably stayed after class to talk to a
teacher."

"It's only the second day of classes," Ryann said. "We don't even have homework yet." He surveyed the noisy cafeteria full of kids racing in all directions. "Here she comes!"

Liddy dropped her backpack with a loud thud behind her seat and plopped down. "Whew. I don't know if taking all honors classes was a good idea."

Terell responded in his most serious tone. "Really? Do they have honors P.E.?"

Liddy tilted her head and raised her eyebrow.

Terell's bright white smile beamed back at her. "Just kidding!"

"So tell us about the book!" Ryann said as Liddy pulled out her napkin and began spreading it out.

"Hi to you too," she snapped without looking his way.

"Oh, sorry. Hi."

She set her apple down and began laying out the carrots and celery. "That's okay. I didn't get much sleep, so I've been a little short with people today."

Terell couldn't pass up the opportunity to tease her. "Ah, that would explain the dark circles under your eyes." He made a circular motion with his hand around his face.

Liddy ignored his remarks, her face brightening with her next comments. "Guys, this book is so cool. You wouldn't believe how much there is to know about dragons. And that picture I told you about? I'm confident it's Sorcha."

"Who wrote it?" Ryann asked.

"I wondered that at first too. It's written by someone named Ireth Silimaurë. I think that's how you pronounce it. But there's not the typical date, publishing company, and all that other stuff you find at the beginning of a book—anywhere."

"Oh, man, I can't wait to see it," Ryann said, rubbing his hands together. "What time are we getting together on Saturday?"

"My mom said to come over for dinner. The eclipse begins at nine and should be over around ten, so your parents can pick you up then."

"We'll be there," Ryann answered for both himself and Terell.

CHAPTER 5

Mystery Man

RYANN PEDALED HIS bike down Highland Street. His normal route home took him along Eleventh Avenue, but today he had to make a detour. Mrs. Watters had received a call from their church informing her that her Bible had been found and turned in to the office. "No problem, I'll pick it up after school," Ryann recalled volunteering as he turned right onto Fifth Avenue. Looking up at the cloudless sky, he was thankful it appeared to be an atypical August afternoon. The daily thirty-minute downpours in the summer were often accompanied by a powerful display of thunder and lightning, making Central Florida one of the lightning capitals of the United States. Mount Dora's massive trees blocked Ryan from the blazing rays of the early afternoon sun. The combination of shade and wind blowing through his dirty-blond hair as he pedaled made for a bearable ride.

First Presbyterian Church sat on a small hill overlooking the town and Lake Dora. Ryann coasted to a stop in front of the old Dickens-Reed Bookstore. The neon red For Sale sign in the darkened window was a constant reminder of how fun times could end in instant.

Ryann checked his watch. *Two forty-five; the church office doesn't close until four on Fridays.* Looking up toward the church, he noticed someone lying on the park bench out back. *No way. It couldn't be, could it?*

Ryann's eyes widened. "Noah!" he cried out.

The figure didn't move.

He looked both ways for cars, then pedaled across the street, calling out again as he approached the bench.

"Noah, I didn't think I'd see y—"He didn't finish his last word.

The old, rumpled suit was similar, but the dark, long hair was different. Straddling the stationary bike, Ryann stared at the middle-aged man, wondering if he should wake him and ask the whereabouts of Noah. One eye opened, followed by a promising smile.

"Do you make it a habit of staring at people? " the man asked, turning from his side onto his back.

"Oh, uhh, no. I'm sorry, I thought you were someone else," Ryann stammered.

"And who would that be?"

"Never mind, just someone who used to sleep on this bench."

"Sorry to disappoint," the man said, putting his hands behind his head. "Anyway, the name's Don, Don Korrel, to be formal about it. And you?"

Ryann hesitated, evaluating the brown eyes and smiling face of the relaxed vagrant. He smiled back. "Ryann, Ryann Watters. I go to church here," he informed him, pointing to the red brick building behind them.

The hobo nodded, "That's cool."

"Well, sorry to have bothered you," Ryann said as he turned to go.

"Wait! I'm curious."

Ryann hesitated as the man swung his legs around and sat up. His long brown hair outlined both sides of his quizzical expression. Ryann thought he looked like an aging rock star.

"Most people give me nasty looks when they see me lying here. I'm just curious to know why you stopped to talk with the other guy who used to sleep here."

Ryann relaxed his shoulders. Laughter from children playing in the church playground and the cars passing behind him on Fifth Avenue made him feel he wasn't alone with a stranger. "He was interesting, and," Ryann paused, "he gave great advice."

"Aha! Well, old Don has been known to give pretty good advice himself," the scraggly man said.

Ryann looked him up and down again. His leathery skin made him appear old and young at the same time. The deep bronze tan gave him a youthful appearance, but the wrinkled skin from years in the sun had ripened him like a dried piece of fruit. Ryann guessed Don was in his late fifties.

He scratched his head. "Now that you mention it, I do have a question that's been bothering me. Do you think you could be of help?"

"Shoot."

Ryann wanted to make sure he was wording his question in a way that wouldn't reveal too much information. "Okay, hypothetically, what would you say to three people who were in three different parts of the country when each of them saw an unusual blue flash at the exact same time?"

Don reached up and rubbed the black and white stubble on his chin and cheeks. "Hypothetically?"

"Yeah."

The drifter looked Ryann in the eyes and answered in a hushed, gravelly tone, "I'd say they were being contacted to come back to a place they'd been before."

Ryann's eyes widened, "Really?"

Don looked both ways. He scooted forward on the bench and continued in a hushed tone. "Yep, when three blue flashes occur at the same time, it definitely means a portal to another world is going to open up soon."

"Wow," Ryann mouthed.

The drifter leaned back on the bench. "So, hypothetically speaking," he began, a slow grin forming on his face, "who might these three people be?"

Ryann looked down and kicked at the dirt. He answered softly, "You know, people."

Don waited patiently until Ryann looked up again. "If I were able to, I'd tell those three *hypothetical* people that they should get ready for the adventure of a lifetime," he winked, "because it's coming soon."

Ryann froze, captivated by the hobo's words. *How can he be so sure?*

"Uhh, thanks Mr. Korrel."

He grinned. "Call me D. K., and don't mention it."

Walking quickly around the side of the church, Ryann stopped and typed a quick text message to Terell before heading to the office.

i think i just spoke with gabriel

CHAPTER 6

Moons and Mist

RYANN PLOPPED DOWN in the oversized brown leather chair in his father's study with a loud huff. "Whew! I'm glad that's over."

The rhythmic clacking from Mr. Watters typing on his keyboard masked his son's entry. He finished the sentence he was working on and then looked up.

"So, son, what seems to be the problem?"

"Well, not so much a problem as a conclusion…I think."

"Does this have to do with Drake?"

"Good guess, Dad," Ryann grinned. "It was kinda weird today. We 'bumped' into each other, literally, and he acted like we never battled each other in Aeliana."

"Maybe he learned something from it and put it behind him."

Ryann laughed. "Ha! I doubt it. He still acted like a jerk. I'm just glad to be done with him."

Ryann sank deeper into the chair, waiting for his father's response.

"You know, Ryann, a shut door is closed on both sides."

"Huh?" Ryann looked quizzically at his dad. "What does that mean?"

"If you shut the door on someone's ability to interact with you, it may seem like a good idea, especially if it's someone like Drake. But," he held up his hands, "then you've also blocked your ability to show forgiveness. That not only affects them, but you as well."

Ryann mulled over his dad's words, trying to make sense of them. "So what you're saying is, if there isn't any contact between us, then—" he hesitated to make sure he was saying it right, "—then it's like a closed door, so he can't interact with me?"

"That's right, and what else?"

"I can't have a positive impact on him or really forgive him."

Mr. Watters smiled. "How would he know?"

"He wouldn't."

"Exactly. Ryann, do you remember what Jesus said after He told His disciples how to pray the Lord's Prayer?"

"No, sir."

"He said that if you forgive people when they sin against you, your heavenly Father will also forgive you. But if you don't forgive people when they sin against you, then God won't forgive your sins."

"Wow! That seems a little harsh."

"He said that, Ryann, because people who are unwilling to humble themselves and forgive other people are not willing to truly receive forgiveness from God. So now, what do you think about you and Drake?"

"I think I'll leave the door open," Ryann answered, struggling to get up out of the enveloping, soft leather chair. "At least a crack, anyways," he added, laughing as he hustled toward the door.

Terell's mom swung her car into Liddy's driveway. Ryann and Terell jumped out quickly, slamming their doors behind them.

Ryann smiled. "Thanks for the ride, Mrs. Peterson."

"You're welcome, dear." She looked over at her son. "Terell, Ryann's folks are takin' you home tonight."

"Got it, Mom," he replied as she backed out of the driveway.

Terell immediately turned to Ryann. "Are you sure he was Gabriel?"

"Pretty sure. I mean he didn't look like him, but—"

"But what?"

Ryann kicked at a rock as they sauntered up the walkway to Liddy's front door. Her house was Old-world European in style, with varying sizes of brown and gray stones outlining the windows and doors. Two dormers highlighted the roofline, and the moss hanging from the sprawling oak limbs added to the picturesque Southern charm.

"He sounded like him," Ryann continued. "I asked him about the blue flashes we saw, and he said that they indicated a portal to another place is about to open."

Terell knocked on Liddy's door.

"Really? How would he know about that?"

"That's the point. Who else would bring up a portal to another world? The kicker is, he winked at me when he said it, as if to say, 'It's me.'"

The door swung open, and they were greeted by Liddy's beaming smile. "Hey, guys, let's head around back to the deck. My dad's cooking burgers on the grill."

Strolling across the thick St. Augustine grass, Terell kept the issue alive. "Ryann, tell Liddy about meeting up with Gabriel."

Liddy stopped, her hands moving to her hips. "You spoke with Gabriel and you didn't text me?"

Ryann sighed. "Thanks, Terell." He returned his attention to Liddy, "No, it's not exactly like that." He quickly relayed the conversation he had with the drifter behind the church. "And I was just telling Terell why I think he's Gabriel in disguise."

Liddy crossed her arms, "Why would Gabriel change the way he looks?"

"I don't know. Why would he look like Noah the last time around? I think it might be part of the quest to find the shield of faith."

"What did you say his name was again?"

"Don Korrel."

She let her arms relax back down to her side. "And you say he winked at you?"

"Yeah, after he told me about the blue flashes opening a portal into another place."

Liddy pondered the unusual circumstances.

"I smell burgers!" Terell interrupted. "Come on, let's go."

Ryann stared into the orange sun as it calmly sank behind the still, dark waters of Lake Dora. Full from the cheeseburger, potato salad, and chips settling in his stomach, his mind drifted back a few months to this same picturesque scene.

Liddy and he were standing out on the dock. Ryann's ring glowed as he tried to prove to her that Aeliana really existed. That was the moment Drake's voice had interrupted them.

"Hey! Whatcha guys doin'?"

Both Liddy and Ryann inhaled sharply as they whirled around to see Drake, arms crossed, his head cocked back and a sneer across his face.

Ryann stole a glance at his ring—black—then back to Drake.

Liddy spoke up first. "Drake, you weren't invited, so you can just leave now."

"Hey, Miss Smarty-pants, maybe I'm inviting myself. Something

*odd is going on out here, and I intend to find out what it is." Drake
dropped his arms and stomped off across the yard toward them.*

"Liddy," Ryann whispered without moving his lips.

"Yeah."

"Will you trust me?"

*In a split second, Liddy's eyes darted from Ryann, to Drake,
and down to the ring. It was flickering between black and gold.
Without enough time to work through her usual analysis of a
situation, Liddy went with her intuition, "Yes, I trust you."*

*As Drake approached the dock, Ryann grabbed Liddy's hand.
"Jump!" he yelled, yanking hard on her arm and pulling her off
the dock. Liddy's high-pitched scream filled the air as the two of
them plunged into the bubbling gold water.*

They were headed to Aeliana.

"Hey, dreamer boy!" Terell sang in a silly voice, lightly punching
Ryann in the arm. "Snap out of it. You want any dessert?"

"It's my mom's famous homemade Key lime pie. If you don't want
yours, I'll give it to Terell," she laughed. "I'm sure he'll eat it!"

Ryann smiled at Terell. "Sorry, dude, that piece has my name on
it." Dessert pushed the vivid memories of the confrontation with
Drake to the back of his mind.

The three friends and Mr. Thomas scooped up the sweet-tangy
dessert as Mrs. Thomas cleared the table. Terell pressed his fork into
the remnants of the graham-cracker crust to get one final taste. Dusk
transformed itself into early evening as a soft orange glow from far
across the lake blended into the darkening black sky.

Mr. Thomas's chair screeched as he backed away from the table,
announcing his departure. "I'm going to get my telescope and begin
setting up in the backyard," he said.

Some daylight remained because of daylight saving time. Ryann checked his watch. *It's 8:25. We still have thirty-five minutes until the eclipse.* Peering in the direction the sun had set, blackness marked the ground where Lake Dora rested. Above the black lake, tiny white dots identified houses and streetlights on the opposite shoreline. A lone carriage light hanging off Liddy's house lit up the deck. Moths of varying sizes banged senselessly against the light's glass panes, keeping them from getting burned or prematurely ending their lives.

Ryann thought, *Sometimes I feel like those moths, trying so hard to get to their goal, frustrated they can't reach it. Yet, unbeknownst to me, I'm being protected by a loving God.*

"Hey, zombie!"

Ryann jerked his head around in the direction of Terell.

"That's the second time you've zoned out tonight, man. What's up with that?"

"Uhh, yeah. Sorry."

"What are you thinking about, Ryann?" Liddy asked.

"Just some of the memories of the last time we were here. Ya know, when we jumped into the water to Aeliana. I wish we could find our way back in."

His last statement punctuated the moment as the constant buzz of uncountable bugs played their nightly one-tone song. Liddy reached over to the outside wall and turned off the light. Like a camera coming into focus, their eyes adjusted to the darkness. The nighttime sky, blanketed by precisely placed stars, shone back at them.

"Sometimes I come out here by myself," Liddy confessed, "turn the light off, and just stare up at the stars. It's amazing, isn't it?"

Terell put his finger and thumb close together. "Makes ya feel kinda small."

Ryann shifted in his seat to rest his head on the back of his chair as he stared skyward. "Have you ever thought someone's up there looking back at our little planet? And then at each of us individually on this little planet? God created all of this," he waved his arms to emphasize his point, "but He cares for each of us individually."

"That's my man," Terell said with a touch of sarcasm, "thinkin' deep thoughts!"

"Well, it's true," Ryann said, ignoring him. "I was talking with my dad about it the other day. If you believe all these stars and planets, including our own, are just some sort of cosmic accident that occurred without a God, then life eventually gets pretty meaningless."

"You know, Ryann," Liddy chimed in, "that one issue of believing God created everything versus everything somehow coming into being on its own determines so many other important issues."

Ryann sat up. "Like what?"

"Well, take for instance your comment about each individual person. If you accept the notion that it all just happened and slap on a few billion years to make it seem possible, then what is each individual person's value? People have no souls; they're born, they live, they die, and that's it."

"Thanks for the depressing thought," Terell said.

"Well, it's true," Liddy continued. "Take it a step further. The shortness of life then becomes a selfish issue of people making decisions based upon what makes them happy or helps them avoid unhappiness."

"Yeah, how so?" Terell sounded interested for the first time.

"Think about it. Those that believe we are a cosmic accident have maybe seventy-five to eighty-five years to get whatever they can out of life. They basically do whatever feels good to them. If you believe you live forever, like the Bible says, then you'll wanna follow God's rules for living."

"I think I get what you're saying," Ryann chimed in, "but what do you mean about avoiding unhappiness?"

"I listened to my parents discuss ethics with our pastor," Liddy said. "You know, how you decide what's right and what's wrong. He said that how people view different situations and decide what to do is determined by their worldview. Those with a non-Christian world-view, I think he called it *humanistic*, don't believe in God. Instead, each person can decide what's right for them and do it."

"Wait a second," Terell sat up, clearly interested. "What about laws?"

"Yeah, that was my question, too," Liddy continued. "Laws change all the time, just like the people that make them. He said there were laws when he was growing up that didn't allow you to do certain things, and now they've been changed so you can do them."

"Isn't that a good thing?" Terell asked. "I always want to do more than my mom lets me."

"He said it depends. Some new laws are made that help people, and others are made that allow people to avoid taking responsibility for their actions."

"Something doesn't sound right about that," Ryann joined in. "I mean, how do the people that make the laws know what is right or wrong, and how can they just up and change their minds over time and decide that something that was right is now wrong and what was wrong is now right?"

"Scary!" Liddy laughed. "You're thinking the same way I was. It kind of goes back to whatever everyone as a group thinks, you know, majority rule. Over time, as people change, the rules can change."

"That ain't right." Terell shook his head. "You can't go changin' the rules of the game in the middle of the game."

"Ha!" Liddy laughed. "I think you summarized it better than our pastor did. Then he said the people that believe in God have a biblical worldview. They believe God has determined what's right and what's wrong, and it's written down for us in the Bible. So, we don't have to worry about the rules of the game changing." She nodded at Terell. "We're just supposed to follow the ones He gave us."

"That makes a lot more sense to—"

Just then, Mr. Thomas yelled to them from the backyard. "Kids! If you don't get down here now, you're gonna miss it!"

Chairs screeched. Terell's chair fell over with a loud bang. Liddy yelped as they scrambled off the deck in a hectic dash to see who could get to the telescope first. Ryann came to a frenzied stop in front of Mr. Thomas, followed by Terell and then Liddy.

Mr. Thomas smiled at Ryann, "Ladies first." Liddy calmly walked to the front of the line, shaking her ponytail.

"Wow! I can't believe the detail of the moon you can see through this, dad. It's almost like I can reach out and touch it."

"It'll look really cool when the eclipse begins," Mr. Thomas said proudly.

"Neeext," Ryann's voice rose steadily behind him.

"Okay, Ryann and Terell, we'll keep rotating you through so everyone gets a chance."

Ryann stepped up for his turn. "Whoa! You weren't kidding, Liddy. This is amazing. I've read about the darker areas on the moon being valleys, but through here you can actually see them! Hey, what's the darker shadow off to the right?"

Mr. Thomas answered, "That's the eclipse of the moon starting. It occurs when the sun, earth, and moon are exactly aligned, with the earth in the middle. A full eclipse, like the one we're going to see tonight, only happens once every few years. Terell, your turn."

Terell squinted as he took his place behind the telescope. Mr. Thomas continued, "The shadow will slowly cover the moon, and it will actually begin to appear red."

"Why's that?" Terell asked.

"The red coloring happens because sunlight reaching the moon has to pass through the earth's atmosphere, where it's scattered. Shorter wavelengths are more likely to be scattered by the small particles, and so by the time the light has passed through the atmosphere, the longer wavelengths dominate. We perceive the resulting light as red."

"Uhh, that's cool. Now could you say that in English, Mr. Thomas?"

"Well for now, Terell, just think of it as the same effect that causes sunsets and sunrises to turn the sky a reddish color."

Terell laughed. "I'll take your word for it, but only because I don't have something better."

"Liddy, you're up," her dad announced.

The rotation continued for the next ten minutes until they were interrupted by the pleasant arrival of Mrs. Thomas carrying a tray with four glasses of lemonade. "Time for a quick break," she smiled, holding the tray out so everyone could grab the cold, wet glasses.

"Dad, how long will the eclipse last?"

"Usually around fifty minutes or so. You have enough time for one more look before it begins."

Terell smacked his lips. "Mrs. Thomas, I have to say that this is probably the best lemonade I have ever tasted!"

"Why, thank you, Terell," she beamed.

Ryann looked at Liddy and rolled his eyes. Parents loved Terell. It wasn't that what he said wasn't true, but he was famous for grandiose thanks that walked right up to the edge of believability.

"Well kids, we'd better get back to it," Mr. Thomas said. "Liddy, we ended with Terell, so I believe you're up again."

Liddy took one last swig of lemonade. "Okay, Dad," she said, setting the empty glass down in the grass.

"Dad!" Liddy shouted. "I thought you said the moon was supposed to turn a reddish color?"

"That's right, I did."

"Well you'd better take a look, because it's turning blue, not red!"

"What? Here, let me see," Mr. Thomas said, quickly taking Liddy's place. "Whoa, this is strange. I've never seen anything like it. And I've seen dozens of these."

"What do you think is causing it, Dad?"

"I don't know, Liddy, but does anyone mind if I connect my camera to the telescope and take a few pictures?"

"Sure, no problem," Liddy answered. She felt a tap on her shoulder. Whirling around, she looked into Ryann's anxious face. "What do you want?" she whispered.

Ryann didn't answer. He pointed instead. Liddy followed the direction of his finger, aiming up to the top of her house. A blue glow flashed from the highest window.

CHAPTER 7

Portal to the Past

IDDY GASPED, THEN quickly put a hand over her mouth.

Ryann motioned for Terell to look. "What do you think it is?" he whispered so Mr. Thomas wouldn't hear.

Liddy regained her composure. "I don't know, but we need to check it out. Fast. Come on!"

Ryann scrambled after her. She called over her shoulder, "Dad, we'll be back in a few!"

Mr. Thomas mumbled an incoherent response as he feverishly attempted to attach his camera to the telescope.

Terell followed closely behind Ryann, slamming the back door shut behind him. Liddy put her finger to her lips as Ryann and Terell followed her toward the stairs.

"Liddy, is that you?" her mom called from the family room, the chatter of a television show blaring in the background.

Liddy motioned for them to follow and took the stairs two at a time to the second story. Ryann knew Liddy starred on the soccer team, but he hadn't realized how fast she was until he had to hustle to keep up.

She stopped abruptly at the top of the landing, signaling with a finger to her lips again. She reached for the hall light, then hesitated, leaving the switch in the off position. Ryann followed with Terell close behind as Liddy crept down the dark hallway. Blue light glowed from around the corner.

"That's not right," she whispered. She inched her head around the corner and gasped. Ryann jumped around her, not knowing what to expect.

All three stood motionless, gazing at the ceiling. A bright blue light outlined the attic entryway board, showering them in an ominous glow. The pull cord dangled above them.

Terell's stutter returned. "Sh–sho–should w–we pull it down?"

Ryann looked down at his ring. "Guys, look at this," he said.

Ryann held his ring hand up for them to see. The ring flickered back and forth between blue and its normal clear state.

"That's a sign we've gotta check this out," Liddy said.

Ryann leapt in front of her. "I'll pull it down." Reaching for the rope, his ring lit up with the same bright blue glow the moment his finger made contact.

"I knew it," Liddy cried out. "And that confirms it."

Ryann counted down, "Three...two...one!" Then he tugged hard on the cord. The ceiling board opened like the door to a spaceship, flooding the hallway with an eerie blue glimmer. He stared into the attic entryway and was confronted with a sparkling, frosty-blue glaze.

Ryann finished unfolding the ladder, then smiled. "Who's gonna be first?" he asked.

"A–ar–are ya–you kidding me?" Terell stammered.

"Don't you want to go back to Aeliana?" Ryann teased, knowing Terell had confided his greatest wish was to have another adventure.

"H–ho–how ca–can you be sure it goes to Aeliana?"

"What?" Ryann's face scrunched up. "It has to go to Aeliana. How many worlds do you think there are?"

"Ryann's right," Liddy beamed. "It all makes sense now. The three blue moons we saw in Aeliana on our last visit, the three blue lights we saw on vacation, now a blue moon tonight, and Ryann's ring turning blue. I don't think there can be any doubts that this is a way into Aeliana."

"And don't forget Don Korrel, aka Gabriel, confirming that a portal would open up in the near future," Ryann said, putting the final piece of the puzzle in place.

Liddy swept her arm toward the ladder. "Ryann, why don't you go first? After all, Gabriel gave you the second quest to find the shield of faith."

He acknowledged her statement by stepping onto the ladder. Ryann gripped each side of the ladder firmly as he stepped up, peering into the sparkling swirl. The dense light kept him from seeing what was on the other side. *Liddy seemed so sure this was a portal into Aeliana. Normally she'd want to gather facts by conducting an experiment.* Two more steps, and he was face-to-face with the mesmerizing swirl of blues and whites. He broke his hypnotic stare to look down. Liddy stepped up on the first rung of the ladder. Terell remained firmly planted on the hallway floor, hands on his hips.

"Come on, Terell, it's an adventure," Ryann said. "You've got to trust that all of this isn't just a coincidence, that God has brought us all together as part of His perfect plan."

Ryann watched Terell's demeanor change as his arms slowly lowered and a weak grin spread across his face. "That thing had better not close up after the two of you get through," Terell replied as he reached out to grab the ladder. "Now hurry up before I change my mind!"

Ryann grinned at his friends, then turned back to face the icy-blue mist. He squinted and thrust one hand in and out of the mysterious aura, hoping it wasn't burning hot or freezing cold. His hand registered neither, so he pushed it forward again and left it in place. *Nothing.* Emboldened by the immediate lack of danger, Ryann put one hand out in front of him and stepped up into the swirling blue mist.

CHAPTER 8

Annals of Aeliana

RYANN WASN'T SURE what to expect as his head entered the mist. It felt like entering a dark room in the middle of the night from a brightly lit one as his eyes tried adjusting to the change. One hand gripped the attic entryway for balance, while his ring hand was extended out in front of him. *Who knows what I might run into?* Starbursts flashed all around him as he lifted his knee to take another step. *It feels like I'm in the attic.* He looked down into the same dense fog that was above him.

Ryann cried out, "Hey, guys! Can you hear me?" His voice seemed confined to the area just around him, like he was in a small, enclosed room.

"Guys?" he muttered.

This is so weird. I can't tell what's up and what's down, but I feel like I'm still moving up.

He hesitated, trying to focus on his hand gripping the attic entryway. *To move ahead, I'm going to have to let go.* Everything in him wanted to maintain his grip, his last bit of security, yet he knew they were being called. Ryann lifted his leg for one more step and let go with his hand at the same time. A white flash exploded, blinding him. He thought he heard himself scream as the light enveloped him.

Liddy and Terell watched Ryann disappear into the misty blue swirl. One step, a hesitation, and then another. Liddy moved up the ladder as close as she could to Ryann's last foothold without running into him.

"It's going to be all right," she reassured Terell and herself. "He wouldn't keep stepping up if something were wrong."

Both of Ryann's feet were fixed as if waiting for something. Liddy could still see his white-knuckled hand clenching the side of the entryway.

"Ryann? Are you okay?" she asked.

Her question was met with his feet stepping up into the mist and out of sight.

For a moment, Ryann's world was bright white. It was as if a giant camera flash had gone off. Nothing existed but the whiteness. Ryann opened his eyes as wide as possible, hoping that something would come into focus. *Still white!* He closed his eyes tight, waited a moment, then he opened them. Everything was black, except for a circle of light out in front of him. *Do I run to the light? That's what people say to do when you die.*

Ryann steadied himself, waiting to see if his surroundings would come into focus. Unsettled as to what was up or down, he lowered his head in what he thought was the direction of his feet and made out his shirt and legs. The sparkling, icy-blue mist he had stepped up into was now swirling around the ground below him. He couldn't see his feet. He held up his hands. They appeared normal. As his eyes adjusted to the darkness, the circle of light in front of him became clearer. *It's not a circle. It has jagged edges,* he realized.

"Whoa!" a loud voice yelled behind him, echoing several times.

Ryann turned to his left to see Liddy, holding out her hands to steady herself and blinking repeatedly. Her feet were covered in the same swirling mist.

"Uhh," a reverberating groan called out to his right.

Ryann twisted around to see Terell standing in the same mist. His fogged-over glasses hid his eyes.

"Guys, we're here!" Ryann's bellowing voice echoed around them.

"Wherever *here* is," he said in a normal tone that reduced the effect of the echo. Looking down again, he could see his shoes. The mist was gone. Turning away from the light, Ryann faced his friends. Having the light source at his back helped him focus more clearly on his surroundings. Endless blackness backed Liddy and Terell, but off to the sides the light cast a gray hue on the dark walls. Ryann squatted down and felt around his feet. Hard and smooth. Running his hands along the surface, there were bumps and dips. His eyes continued to adjust to the mild darkness around them. The rough wall to his left became clear.

"Where are we, Ryann?" Liddy questioned softly.

"I think we're in a cave."

"A cave?" Terell asked. "Are you sure?"

"I got here a little before you, and my eyes are finally adjusting to the differences in darkness and light. You should be able to see for yourself in just a minute." As he spoke, still looking around, Ryann was more convinced. *The echoes, rough stone walls, rocky ground.* His nose tingled in the stale, musty, enclosed space. He turned around toward the light and could clearly see the outline of the cave entrance and blue sky outside.

"Can you see it now? The walls? The ground? The entrance?"

Liddy answered first. "Yeah, it's getting clearer to me now."

Terell replied next. "Whoa, okay now. Yeah, I think it's all clearing up. Boy, what a trip!"

Ryann walked toward the opening. Each step allowed him to see more and more on either side of him. He stopped abruptly after a few more feet. "No way!"

"What?" Terell and Liddy said in unison.

Ryann reached out to the cave wall on his right. Leaning up against the wall was his metal staff. Four buttons were lit up.

"Hey guys! My staff is here, and now there are four buttons lit up on it instead of three!" Ryann grinned, shaking his head. "And my horn's here too."

Liddy and Terell rushed to his side. Gabriel's gifts had somehow transported themselves from Ryann's closet to Aeliana each time he arrived. It appeared this time would be no different.

Gabriel had first given him the smooth metal walking stick when he had tasked him with finding the King's sword. To Ryann, it felt like a pool cue, long, shiny, and smooth, except for the seven bony-white buttons along one of the ends. He vividly recalled the transformation of each button to a soft glow. Each one had a different power. He had pushed buttons one and two on Liddy's first trip into Aeliana. Button 1 sprayed a fine mist, which grew in dimension as he waved it around, creating an area that was difficult to see through. It had come in handy when they were travelling down the Elan River and were confronted by Drake and his army.

Button 2 spewed a wall of fire, which Ryann could move by simply pointing the staff. He shivered thinking of the last time he had pushed that button. The wall of flames had repelled the black-shrouded horde chasing them into the canyon, then the outstretched wings of Lord Ekron swooping in from above extinguished it into a tiny, candle-like flame. Ryann shook his head to rid his mind of the piercing black eyes of the demon.

Button 3 was glowing the last time all three of them had arrived in Aeliana together. The sheet of ice it produced was extremely versatile. Surrounded by the horde on the top of a sand dune, Ryann had sprayed the ice in front of them, creating a slide for them to escape. It was better than any theme park ride he had experienced, yet under the circumstances he hadn't enjoyed the ride. Then, after finding the sword and heading back through the canyon, they were ambushed by Drake's army, who rained fiery arrows down at them from above. Button 3 produced a shield of ice over their heads until they figured out how to respond.

"Here you go." Ryann handed the curved, ivory horn to Liddy.

She ran her hands across the smooth yet pitted surface. The worn brown-leather strap, attached at both ends, allowed her to put it over her head and have it rest on her hip. It had served its purpose on their last visits in many ways. Depending upon how the horn was blown, short or long blasts, and how many times, there had been different results. Once it had sent fear through the ranks of their enemies, causing them to scatter. Another time it had caused an avalanche in the canyon, defeating their enemy and revealing the cave of the King's sword. The last time they used the horn, it had called Gabriel to their defense. It was a potent gift, which Ryann had entrusted to Liddy on her first visit to Aeliana.

"Hey! What's this?" Terell shouted from the shadows behind them.

"What's what?" Ryann asked.

Terell smiled, coming out from the shadows. "Yo, check it out." His arms grasped a pottery jar, blanketed in thick dust.

"Let's move over to the entrance so we can see better," Liddy said.

"Good idea," Ryann nodded, "but let's creep over and sit down in case there's someone outside we don't want to see us."

Terell grimaced as he hauled the jar the extra few feet necessary to carry out their plan. Setting it down gently on the hard cave floor, they looked over their newfound treasure. Standing two feet high, its base was the size of a small wastebasket, narrowing up to the opening at the top.

"It looks really old," Liddy noted as she reached over to brush some of the surface dirt away.

"Ya think?" Terell questioned sarcastically, a grin broadening across his face.

Liddy shot him a threatening glare.

"I'm just saying, Lid," Terell held his hands up in front of himself in mock surrender, "you're probably right." His grin transformed to serious contemplation as he held up one finger. "Seriously, how old do you think it is?"

"Who knows?" Liddy shook her head and returned to her task of scraping away the dirt. "But based upon the amount of dirt covering it, I'd bet it's been here hundreds of years."

The jar's exterior changed from a grayish-brown where she had brushed away the cave dust to a burnt-orange color. A design was etched near the top. Liddy studied the markings while the boys looked on. "You know," she concluded after a brief moment, "I don't think these markings are just a design. They look more like words of some sort, or maybe symbols that represent something."

Ryann leaned over, running his hands along the etchings, then moved his hand up to the opening.

"No!" Liddy cried out as Ryann's hand shot into the dark hole at the top.

Ryann jumped. "Huh?"

"You don't know what's in there," Liddy said. "What if it held a sharp object or, worse, some sort of poisonous snake or spider?"

Ryann laughed, "Liddy, your imagination has the better of you. Is that what happens in those adventure novels you read?"

The glare she had directed at Terell earlier came back.

"Oh, I think you're gonna like this, Liddy." Ryann smiled as his arm moved around in the container.

"What is it?" Terell asked, inching closer.

"This!" Ryann announced, pulling out a brown leather-bound book with ruffled, feather-like pages escaping from three sides.

"Ahh!" Liddy's shriek echoed around the cave.

Gripping the book in one hand, Ryann brought it down to rest in between them and began lightly wiping off the dust.

"What do you think it is?" Terell asked.

"There's one way to find out," Ryann answered, looking over at the puzzled expression on Liddy's face. "What, Lid?"

"That book. It's got the same leather cover as the dragon book from my attic, only this book is smaller."

"Are you sure?"

"Positive. I bet the same person wrote both."

Terell nudged him in the side. "Whatcha waitin' for, Ryann? Open it up."

"Careful, Ryann. I'm sure it's brittle, and you don't want to tear any of the pages," Liddy warned.

Ever so gently he pinched the leather cover and pulled it open. Emblazoned on the first page in a bright red script were the words:

The Annals of Aeliana

CHAPTER 9

Broken Beyond Repair

"WHAT ARE ANNALS?" Terell asked.

"They're like journals or archives, reporting on things that have happened over a period of time," Liddy answered matter of factly.

Terell shook his head. "Thanks, Miss Dictionary."

Ryann grinned at their banter. "You know, guys, this book could tell us something about the history of Aeliana."

"Let's take a look and see," Liddy said, moving in closer to Ryann's right side, while Terell moved in on the left. Daylight poured in from the entrance, providing more than enough light for them to see the decorative script as Ryann carefully turned the next page.

By authority of Aurelia, princess of the elven clan, as ordered by Aodan of Myraddin, these are the recordings of Inwë Silimaurë, scribe and keeper of the annals of Aeliana. No words may be taken away from this book, and new chapters may only be added through the testing by the fire of the Word most high.

Book Two–The Aodan Years

Chancellor Aodan was inaugurated in front of the Tree of Life upon the departure of Madawen, the first overseer of Aeliana. Madawen was called by the Word to set sail across the Morganwyn Sea with fifty others, and to be fruitful and multiply in a new land. It was upon the watch of Aodan that darkness and death entered Aeliana, which is recorded in this book.

Liddy stopped reading. "Chancellor Aodan was the head of the high counsel when we were here, but I don't recall Inwë."

Ryann's eyes grew wide. "Do you remember what Aodan told us the last time we were before the counsel? He was going to have Princess Aurelia's elven clan record everything that had happened—in a book!"

"This must be the book!" Liddy squealed. "I can't believe we're actually holding it!"

"Ahem!"

Ryann and Liddy turned to face Terell. "Aren't the two of you forgetting something?"

"What?" Ryann asked.

"I may not be the brains here," Terell smiled, "but if she recorded what happened during Aodan's life, then that means that the three of us should be in this book."

"Genius!" Liddy squealed a second time. "Scan ahead and see, Ryann."

Returning to the open book, Ryann moved his finger down the page. Seeing nothing, he flipped to the next pages and continued the effort. "It looks like the beginning is an account of Aodan's rulings and decrees as the new leader."

Liddy reached over. "Here, let me look."

"Okay," Ryann conceded as he moved it over to her lap, "I see someone's a little impatient."

Liddy flipped to the next page. "Here it is!"

"Hey, I was almost there," Ryann said.

"No need to get upset," Liddy grinned. "Okay, here I go." She cleared her throat.

> Raz the Raccoon and Esselyt the Leopard were the first to encounter the human boy from another land. His name was Ryann Watters and he hailed from Mount Dora, Florida. He was sent by the Archangel Gabriel and tasked with finding the King's sword. As proof of his calling, he had in his possession three gifts from the angel for assistance in his travels: a metal staff, a glowing ring, and an ancient horn.

As Liddy read further, her animated expressions made for an exciting recounting of Ryann's first visit to Aeliana. "Ooh, here comes the good part—when I come in!"

"Oh, brother," Terell sighed. "I saw that coming."

"Ahem!" Liddy cleared her throat again while lifting up her nose in a display of superiority. "And now, may I continue before I was so rudely interrupted?"

Terell shook his head. "Sure, whatever."

Liddy tried to suppress her grin as she read about her first visit to Myraddin.

> Upon his second visit, Ryann Watters returned with Lydia Thomas, also of Mount Dora. The two of them, along with Raz and Esselyt, attended the one hundred and forty-fourth feast of the Word at Myraddin. The truths from the Word are recorded in the Proclamations of the Feast by another scribe from our clan, Amroth Silimaurë.

Screeeech!

They jumped at the unexpected noise. Ryann swiveled like a gunfighter, pointing his staff toward the cave entrance. Liddy and Terell hunched over, low to the cave floor, behind him. Surprised by how quickly he moved, Ryann figured his reflexes from previous visits had returned. Creeping forward on his hands and knees, Ryann peered just outside the cave and scanned the skies for the creature that had emitted such a powerfully shriek.

"There!" Ryann whispered forcefully, pointing off to their left.

Large brown wings flapped in a heavy sweeping motion, propelling the creature away from them. The size of the wings seemed no match for the golden-brown body of a lion, to which they were attached.

Screeeech!

The winged lion turned its head to give them their first glimpse of its lion-sized eagle head. "If I have my mythological creatures correct," Liddy whispered, "I believe it's a griffin—half-bird, half-lion."

"Whoa, I–I wouldn't want to get in its way," Terell said as the griffin flew away.

"Guys, check this out!" Ryann said, motioning them forward.

Liddy and Terell edged forward outside the shadows of the cave, stopping at Ryann's outstretched arm. Together they glanced down in the direction he was looking.

"Ahh!" Terell gasped, backpedaling until he fell awkwardly on the ground. "I hate heights!"

Ryann and Liddy peered down to the sandy beach a hundred or so feet below them. Waves crashed onto the shoreline then flattened as the seawater ran up to the beach and immediately retreated backwards to start all over again. Looking up the cliff, the craggy rock face continued at least the same distance in the opposite direction.

"Now what?" Liddy asked, clutching the book to her side.

"Well, it appears as if we're in a cave about halfway between a beach and the top of a cliff," Ryann said.

"Okay, thanks for stating the obvious." Liddy rolled her eyes. "Any recommendations for some course of action?"

Ryann ignored her sarcasm. "I don't recall seeing something like this in Aeliana. If I had to guess, I'd have to say it was the Morganwyn Sea, mentioned in the book. As far as what to do, unless there's another way out of the cave, which I doubt, then we'll need to climb down to the beach."

"Wh–why down?" Terell asked, still huddled behind them just inside the cave entrance.

Ryann scratched his head. "Hmm, if we head up, that's farther to fall," he smiled.

"Not helping," Terell answered.

"Actually, Terell, I think there are enough places to hold on to that we shouldn't have too much trouble scaling down the side. It certainly looks easier to go down than up, and we can't wait here to be rescued by someone who may never come."

"What about the book?" Liddy asked, tucking it under her arm.

"I don't see how we can leave it in the jar. We haven't even finished reading it. There might be important information in there about what happened after we left," Ryann noted. "I've got the staff. Do you think you can carry it on the way down?"

"I'll give it a try." She moved it over to her hip, where the horn rested and then had an idea. "If I position it through the horn strap, it kinda holds it in place. That should work."

"Great!" Ryann said, turning toward Terell.

"What?"

"Are you going to be able to make it?"

"It doesn't look like I have much of a choice, do I?"

"No, not really."

"Then I guess I'm in."

Ryann scanned the cliff wall for the best place to start down. Tucking his staff firmly under his left arm, he found a narrow crevice to take hold and begin the descent. "I'll go down first, then Terell. Liddy, you follow Terell."

Ryann caught Liddy's attention before she could question the order and mouthed, "He might need help." She nodded and moved into position behind Terell.

A quarter of the way down, Ryann felt good about his decision. The descent wasn't as hard as he had thought, even carrying his staff under his arm. He wondered if something in the atmosphere in Aeliana made physical activity easier, or perhaps the skills he had learned on his previous quest were gradually returning.

Alone in his thoughts, Ryann almost lost his grip when Liddy screamed from above. "Look out!"

Something whizzed by his head. Ryann's first thought was that Liddy or Terell had dislodged a rock. Several high-pitched clatters and a loud crack from below was followed a groan from Liddy.

"Oh, noooo!"

"Liddy? You okay?" Ryann called up, straining to see around Terell. *Could the clay jar that held the book have fallen somehow?*

The only answer was, "I'm sorry," between heavy sobs. "Liddy?"

"Dude, she dropped the horn," Terell answered for her.

Horn? It took a moment for Ryann to fully process the word. *My gift from Gabriel?* Anger boiled up from deep within. He clenched his jaw tightly to suppress the scream seeking a violent escape out of his mouth. What would they do now? The horn was their only way to call for help. Ryann pressed himself securely against the cliff. Ryann closed his eyes and sucked in a deep breath. Holding it for a few seconds, he exhaled slowly and repeated the process again.

Terell called out over Liddy's sobs, "Uhh, guys? Sh–shouldn't w–we keep moving? I–I don't want to be here if that griffin comes back."

Ryann yelled up, "Liddy, it's okay. Don't worry about it now. Let's get to the bottom, and we'll figure out what to do next."

A soft "okay" escaped her lips.

Half an hour later, Ryann released his grip from the wall of the cliff and hopped down to the soft white sand. Large boulders of varying shapes and sizes spotted the hundred or so feet between the cliffs and the crashing surf. The roar from the pounding seas had grown as they neared the bottom, and now he could actually taste the salt in the air. He looked beyond the surf and his mouth opened wide in awe.

Rising out of the clear blue-green waters was a stream of vibrant, sparkling colors. He felt a presence on either side of him and knew that it was Liddy and Terell coming alongside to gaze at the amazing sight before them. Bright, clearly defined bands of red, orange, yellow, green, purple, and violet hues rose out of the water. The rainbow sprouted out of violently churning waters like a pot boiling over on the stove. Unlike the misty rainbows they were accustomed to seeing back home, this rainbow's colors were full and bold, almost like you could reach out and grab hold of them. Following the colorful swath painted across the canvas of a light blue sky, they traced its ending to a crown of green protruding from the cliffs a few miles down the beach.

"Ryann, I'm sorry," Liddy spoke softly from behind him. He turned to see her downcast head. In each hand she held a piece of the horn, sheared almost exactly in half.

"It's okay, Liddy. I know you didn't mean to do it."

"The strap, it just broke. There was no way I could catch it."

"Liddy, really, it's okay. I'm not gonna hold it against you," Ryann said reassuringly.

"Well, this is great!" Terell cut in. "Now that you two have made up and we're one happy family, whatcha say we decide where to go before the evil bird thing comes back?"

Ryann glanced over at his friend with a sly smile. "Okay, Terell, which way should we go?"

"Well, if you buy into all that stuff about Leprechauns and a pot of gold at the end of the rainbow, I say we follow the rainbow. This is the most amazing one I've ever seen. Who knows what treasure might lie waitin' for us at the end?"

"Sounds like a plan, Terell. Liddy? How 'bout you?"

"What? Sure, whatever." Her shoulders slumped around her slim frame with the book tucked tightly under her arm. "Oh," she looked up, "what should I do with the horn?"

Ryann stared at the two pieces, recalling how the horn had produced fear in the hearts of Drake's army and then how they had called Gabriel to help defeat the enemy forces when they were surrounded. It was a shame to no longer have its powers.

"We don't have a way to carry it with us. Let's take a second to bury the horn pieces by that large boulder over there. Gabriel may be able to fix it. If so, we'll know where to find it."

Within minutes they had completed the unfortunate but necessary task. At first they walked along the cliff walls to stay out of sight, but the deeper sand proved to be a struggle to make any serious headway. Ryann suggested moving to the tightly packed sand by the water as they continued in a northerly direction. Along the ocean's edge it was impossible to get the sparkling rainbow out of their sight, but Ryann wondered how many other potential friends or foes it might attract.

"Okay, remember the plan," Ryann said above the continuous

sound of crashing waves. "If we see something in the sky, we run for the cliffs. If we see someone coming toward us, we run for the largest boulder, and I'll protect us with my staff." He held it up for emphasis, then returned to using it as a walking stick.

"Speaking of your staff," Terell said. "Why is the fourth button blinking?"

"What?" Ryann spun the staff around and reviewed the buttons. One, two, and three were lit; five, six, and seven were the normal bony white; and the middle one, number four, was blinking on and off. Ryann glanced at his ring. It was blue, which he would expect from being close to water.

"That's odd. I've had my ring flicker between colors before, but the buttons on the staff have always either been on or off."

"Push it, man!" Terell urged. "What are you waiting for?"

Ryann's thumb moved forward along the staff.

"Ahem!"

The boys turned to face Liddy, her downcast continence now replaced with a pleasant grin. "Don't you think you should point it out toward the water so no one gets hurt? Remember the first time you pushed a lit button."

Ryann recalled both the embarrassment of pushing an unlit button and watching it sputter, and the shock of seeing mist shoot out the tip when he pushed button 1 after it first lit up. *Would a blinking button do something or not?* he wondered.

He did a quick scan of the sky and then up and down the beach to make sure no one was coming. "Stand behind me," Ryann announced, pointing the staff toward the sea and incoming waves. His thumb inched along the smooth metal surface until it blocked out blinking button 4. Squinting in preparation for what might happen next, he gently pressed down.

Nothing came shooting out of the end. Ryann pressed more firmly, wondering if he hadn't pushed down hard enough. Nothing.

"Look!" Terell pointed just beyond the crashing surf. An area the size of a small boat churned like the waters surrounding the rainbow. Bubbles popped on the surface with rising torrents of steam.

Ryann viewed the stirring waters in fascination, wondering what would happen next. They had yet to see anything come out of a lake, river, or, now, a sea in Aeliana. He imagined a large sea serpent rising out of the water.

"Ahh!" Liddy screamed.

"R–Ry–Ryann, look out!" Terell spat out.

He snapped back from his imaginary creature to the water in front of him. The same creature he envisioned was rising up out of the sea. The head was dragon-like, with large, flaring gills at the neck and a thick serpent body covered in scales, snaking down into the churning water. Ryann's eyes grew wider. In his vision the creature had been dark green, but the one in front of him was shiny and more translucent, similar to the color of the water. *This can't be!* he almost said aloud.

His mind shifted back to the rainbow and its churning waters. The sea serpent collapsed back into the ocean. An eruption of seawater shot up like a fountain, spilling out in every direction. Ryann released the button. *What in the world?*

"Whoa, that was wicked, dude," Terell said, lying on his back in the sand.

"What are ya' doing on your back?" Ryann asked.

Terell grinned sheepishly, "Uhh, backpedaling away from the sea monster?"

"How'd you do that, Ryann?" Liddy asked.

"Do what?"

"The sea monster. Button 4 must have done it somehow."

"I don't know. I was looking out at the bubbling water and started thinking about what would happen if a sea monster emerged, and boom! There it was."

"Try it again," Liddy urged. "Except think about something else this time."

Liddy and Terell bunched in behind Ryann as he held out the staff and pushed the blinking button again. The waters churned like before. Ryann shut his eyes briefly and grinned as an image came to mind. He felt both of them jump as a small fountain of water rose out of the bubbles and stopped five to six feet in the air. He concentrated harder on all the details of his image.

"Huh?" Terell uttered.

Liddy giggled.

An exact replica of Terell stood thirty feet off shore looking back at them. With the exception of the greenish-blue seawater coloring, every other detail, from the closely cropped haircut to his circular glasses, looked like Terell. It stared back eerily, then blinked, eliciting a gasp from Terell and Liddy. They looked on in amazement as the artificial image turned and began walking on the water parallel to them in the direction they had been heading.

"Sweet!" Terell acknowledged in a high-pitched voice, slapping Ryann on the back.

Ryann's grin widened into a full smile, breaking his concentration and causing the faux Terell to collapse in a watery heap.

"That power could come in handy," Liddy acknowledged. "I wonder how the staff can project whatever you think about into a watery replica."

"Okay, enough small talk," Terell said. "We'd better get going. I'm thirsty, and I'm sure this salt water isn't going to quench it."

"Terell's right," Ryann said. "We need to find a source for food, water, and shelter before it gets dark. Let's keep moving."

Turning toward the end of the rainbow, the trio continued their trek along the coastline. Liddy looked up at the dark forest covering the top of the cliff. "I don't know about you guys, but my skin's creeping with goose bumps with the feeling that someone is watching us."

CHAPTER 10

End of the Rainbow

ARE THE CLIFFS getting smaller, or is it just my imagination?" Terell asked, motioning ahead.

Liddy and Ryann turned away from the brightly blended hues of the colorful rainbow. At first glance it was hard to determine if the beach was rising or the cliffs were shrinking. Ryann stopped and looked back in the direction they had come. Besides their footprints disappearing in the incoming tide several hundred feet behind them, the distance between the beach and the top of the cliffs was narrowing.

"I believe you're right, Terell," Ryann acknowledged. "The cliffs and the shoreline are slowly merging."

"And we're getting closer to the end of the rainbow." Liddy pointed. "Look up ahead!"

They sprinted across the last stretch of sand, with Liddy easily outrunning everyone. The cliffs gradually sloped down until they merged with the beach. Liddy slowed to a jog and then stopped altogether. Ryann and Terell came to a halt just behind her, breathing heavily.

"We still have no idea where we are," Liddy said.

"Yeah, whatever." Ryann sucked in a big gulp of the salty air. "I'd do anything for a bottle of water right now."

Terell bent over at the waist, hands on his knees, could only acknowledge with a grunt. Sand covered all of them in splotches from the knees down. Ryann's and Liddy's blond hair scattered messily about their faces from the ocean breeze and sprinting. Terell's African-American heritage left him with the advantage of neatly cropped hair, but gleaming beads of sweat shone on his dark skin. The short break gave Ryann a chance to recoup and survey their surroundings. Looking back from where they had come, it was now apparent that the rocky cliffs had gradually shrunk until they were almost level with the beach. The treetops they had seen from below had become a forest off to their left. Ryann turned and peered further down the beach, holding his hand over his eyes to block the afternoon sun. Off in the distance, he saw water pouring into the sea. *Maybe it's the Pedr River*, he mused. Ryann recalled taking the Elan River out into the desert to find the sword, and he had heard the southernmost split in the tri-rivers flowed down to the sea.

Liddy recovered first. "Hey, look! The rainbow ends on the other side of those trees over there."

Both boys followed her and the glowing rainbow into the heavily wooded trees. Moving from the open area of the beach had its advantages and disadvantages. On one hand, it would take them away from where they could be easily spotted. On the other, they would no longer be able to see others coming their way. Ryann considered both options before coming to a conclusion.

"Let's stay close and head into the woods toward the end of the rainbow. I know where we come from if you try to find the end of the rainbow it keeps moving away from you; but in Aeliana, who knows?"

"It has to do with antisolar point theory," Liddy interrupted.

"Huh?"

"You know the reason why we see rainbows? Our eyes actually pick up light waves from raindrops at about a forty-two degree angle so that—"

"Um, hate to burst your bubble, Liddy," Terell stopped her, "but have you noticed any rain since we've been here?"

Liddy scowled at his interruption.

"Not that I'm not impressed with all the facts you pack in your brain!" he quickly added.

"Sometimes rainbows can form from other sources of water, like the ocean sea breeze, for example." Liddy pointed at the water. "But actually, beyond the intensity of this rainbow, I've been more intrigued by the fact that it only has six colors."

"Oh yeah, I knew that," Terell smacked his head.

"What do you mean, Liddy?" Ryann ignored Terell's drama.

"As I was saying before," she glared at Terell, "the top band is red because that portion between you and the rainbow is at about a forty-two degree angle from your eye. That's the angle that your eye picks up red light waves. The other six color bands below red—orange, yellow, green, blue, indigo, and violet—occur at angles slightly less than forty-two degrees."

Ryann took a quick glance at the rainbow. "Hey, where's the blue?"

"Exactly. I've been wondering the same thing."

Off to the side, observing the banter, Terell could no longer contain himself. "If you scientists are almost through, let me remind you that we're no longer in Florida!"

"Your point?" Liddy asked.

"Talking animals, the King's sword, griffins—I don't think things happen here the same way they do at home."

Liddy stared at him for a moment, processing his simplistic statement. "Good point, Terell." She turned back to Ryann. "Let's see if we can find the end of this rainbow!"

This proved more easily said than done. They looked up and down the thick forest tree line for the most promising entry point. Heavy underbrush, standing taller than any of them, blanketed the forest floor. In the end they decided it made the most sense to walk along the hard-packed earth, covered in sparse grass and sea oats, until they found a way in. Their newfound enthusiasm quickly faded with the strength of the brilliant midday sun as their steady pace slowed to a laborsome walk.

It was Terell's dry, scratchy voice that jogged them out of their funk with two words directed at Ryann. "Your ring!"

Ryann lifted his hand. The ring was blue; not the deeper, dark blue that shone when it was near water, but a brighter, light blue. It was the same blue they had seen in Annapolis, Newport, and Mount Dora, the same blue they had traveled through to Aeliana.

"When did it start?" Liddy asked.

"Just now, I think," Terell responded.

"Are you sure?"

"Well, it just caught my eye," Terell confessed. He hesitated, then added, "Yes, I'm positive."

Ryann recalled their first experience with the ring lighting up as they approached Lake Franklin to fish. Terell had run a little experiment and made Ryann step closer and then away from the lake, watching the ring change back and forth from clear to dark blue.

"Ryann, keep walking ahead of us for a few feet," Terell instructed.

He took a few steps and stopped. The ring sparkled back at him, unchanged.

"A few more steps," Terell said.

On the second stride, the blue light disappeared.

"Cool! Come on back."

The glow popped back on with Ryann's first step. He continued back to them and stopped.

"Keep going a few more steps," Terell said, stepping out of the way.

A few more strides by Ryann, and once again the ring's blue light turned off.

"Lady and gentleman!" Terell announced like a circus ringmaster. "I believe that we head into the forest, right here."

Terell pointed to the area where the ring had lit up while Ryann walked. They both turned to Liddy, who had been silently watching everything unfold.

"Seems the most logical conclusion to me," she said.

While the underbrush didn't appear more inviting than any other place they had seen along the forest line, they each had a confidence based upon the history of the ring.

Ryann pondered where the light blue color would lead them. He put together a mental list of what the other colors meant. White had confirmed someone was telling the truth, black had notified him of evil, red had indicated danger, blue was water, gold alerted them to the portal to and from Aeliana, and orange lit up when they were near the hidden sword.

They crunched through the dense wood as a team. One of them would hold the branches apart while the other two squeezed through, and then the new leader would reciprocate. Without realizing it, their process was a form of cooperative leapfrog, slowed down by Liddy clutching the ancient book and Ryann having to navigate the long staff through the scraggly branches.

"I can't believe how thick this forest is," Terell bemoaned as snake-like vines entangled his feet.

Ryann pulled a thorny branch away from his shirt. "A lot thicker than back home." The canopy of trees high over their heads brought welcomed shade from the blistering sun while at the same time shielding them from a view of the rainbow. When they stopped to rest, Terell asked, "Do you think we made the right decision coming in here? We can't even see the rainbow."

Ryann snapped a branch jabbing into his face. "Do you remember what the Book of Proverbs taught us? 'In his heart a man plans his course, but the Lord determines his steps.' I believe we've done our part in deciding the best course of action, but now it's up to God to determine what happens next."

"I suppose," Terell agreed. "But I sure hope that includes water. I'm dying of thirst."

"Guys, look here!" Liddy called out. While listening to the boys, she had continued to dig a hole through the thick underbrush off to the side. Stumbling over roots and vines, they joined Liddy in peering through the small opening.

A soft and drawn out "whoa" escaped from deep within Ryann.

On the other side of the forest window, an oasis of inspiring beauty awaited them. Rays of liquid sun pored through the light-blue hole in an opening in the majestic oak trees. Accompanying the sparkling sunlight was the dazzling array of colors making up the rainbow's grand entrance. Leaning further into the opening, they followed the vibrantly painted illumination to its end. Gentle, flowing water murmured from a small brook winding through the open meadow of bright green grass. The convergence of the clear pool at the end of the small stream and the rainbow crashing to earth in the middle of it resulted in an explosion of colors dancing on top of the inviting pond.

Overwhelmed, they could only stare at the magnificent vision before them until their eyes grew accustomed to the beauty. Ryann scoured the edge of the meadows for potential friends or foes.

"Man, look at that delicious-looking water," Terell said. "Who's up for a drink?"

Liddy pointed to a tiny island at the end of the rainbow. "Guys," she whispered excitedly, "don't you see it?"

"What?" Ryann and Terell asked together.

"There, in the middle of the water," she pointed, "there's a wooden box or something."

"You're right Liddy," Terell said. "Come on, let's go." He tore at the branches outlining the small opening.

"Hold on, Terell," Ryann cautioned, putting his arm on Terell's. "We've made enough noise here that I'm sure if there's anyone or anything around here, they've heard us by now, but we can still be cautious."

"Ryann's right," Liddy acknowledged. "If anyone else has been following the rainbow, it's going to lead them here as well."

"Okay, okay," Terell whispered. "But that's all the more reason to get to the treasure first!"

Tearing at the small hedge-window they had been peering through with a renewed sense of urgency, they created an opening big enough for them to push through one after the other. Rushing through the

wavy green grass, it was difficult to maintain a focus on the rainbow's end with every aspect of the meadow beaming with life. All of
their senses seemed to activate at once, reminding Ryann of when he
had first come to Aeliana. Earthy aromas of moist soil and fragrant,
blooming flowers rising out of the grass tingled their nostrils, while
the array of sparkling sunlight pierced by the brightly hued rainbow
captivated the field of vision ahead of them. The gentle breeze rustling
through the tall grass and the rapid waters flowing noisily over the
river rocks provided their background music. Coming to a halt at the
pond's edge, Ryann was the first to speak as he fixed his eyes on the
wooden box sitting on the small island out in the middle.

"I guess it was too much to ask to have the shield be at the end of
the rainbow!"

"Oh, yeah, that would have been way too easy," Terell smiled. "We
haven't been chased, fired upon, or challenged by something from
the dark side yet."

The need to quench their thirst drove them to their knees to scoop
up handfuls of water. After a few minutes of slurping, Liddy exam-
ined the pond. "It doesn't appear to be too deep. Who wants to try
walking out to the box?"

"Who, indeed?" came a strong, crisp, feminine voice from across
the waters.

CHAPTER 11

The Prophecy

THE THREE TEENS jumped, startled by the unexpected voice, and turned to see who had spoken. Staring back at them was a slim woman of similar height. Her silky cocoa hair was parted in the middle and flowed straight down around both sides of her face. Noticeably high and prominent cheekbones sat just below two large green, almond-shaped eyes. Her brown clothes and dark green cloak blended in with the thick forest growth behind her.

Terell noticed the tips of her ears poking through her hair first. "Look at her ears. I think she's an elf," he muttered without moving his lips.

"You are correct, dark one, and those same ears are capable of hearing quite well."

Terell grimaced. "Sorry about that. Uhh, my name's Terell, and these are my friends, Ryann and Liddy."

Her eyes widened even larger, but otherwise her expression remained unchanged.

"We're not from around here," Ryann said, looking back and forth from Liddy to Terell. "What part of Aeliana are we in?"

She bowed her head. "It is an honor to meet the three written about in the ancient books." Her eyes glanced at the book in Liddy's hand before continuing. "I am Ireth Silimaurë, and you are in the South Woods."

"Ireth? No way! You wrote *All About Dragons,* didn't you?" Liddy asked excitedly.

"She did?" Ryann asked.

"Yes, I'm sure I read your name in the book." Liddy answered his question while directing her attention back to the nodding elf. "How did it get into my attic?"

"I'm not so sure what an attic is, but how you came to possess it must be part of the mystery of its disappearance. While writing in the woods one morning, as is my daily practice, a swirling blue illumination appeared before me. I was curious, yet cautious, and did not want to touch it with my hand. I chose the only thing at my disposal and stabbed at it with my book. A powerful force pulled it from my grip, and before I could shout for help, the blue glow was gone."

"I've read through it and kept it safe, but I'm sorry to say that I don't have it with me now," Liddy noted apologetically.

The elf glanced down at the book in Liddy's hand.

"Oh, um, this is a book we just found in a cave along the coast." Liddy shifted back and forth guiltily. "Wait a second. It was written by Inwë Silimaurë. Is she your sister?"

Again the elf's eyes grew large, but this time she shuffled a few steps towards them, blinking eagerly. "No, no, Inwë is an ancestor of mine who lived almost five hundred years ago."

Ryann made the connection and joined in the conversation. "Five hundred years ago? How can that be? We've just finished reading some of the book, and it refers to us in the past, which would mean hundreds of years have gone by here. But we've only been gone from Aeliana over the summer."

"Legend has it that Inwë wrote a book and hid it before she mysteriously disappeared. Your names have been passed down in stories by other members of our clan, but no written record has existed. Until now."

Ryann's eyes squinted, perplexed, then he cautiously drew his conclusion. "So, that means that no one we knew…is still living?"

"That would be correct," Ireth noted unemotionally. "Except for possibly a dragon. They can live for several thousand years."

"Sorcha!" Liddy said giddily.

Ireth raised an eyebrow. "You know the ice dragon?"

"We met briefly at the annual Feast of the Word," Liddy answered.

"I have never met Sorcha, but others in my clan have spoken of her, a rare, friendly white dragon. It would be good for you to meet. Many things have changed since you've been gone." Her gaze returned to the book. "May I see it?"

They still faced one another across the small pond. The illustrious rainbow and shimmering white light faded from their view amidst the conversation.

"Sure," Liddy answered. "It seems as if this book rightly belongs to your elven clan. But, what about this rainbow? What does it mean?"

Ireth's eyes sparkled at the question. "The rainbow is spoken of in our book of prophecy. I have never seen such a beautiful sight. My mother and her mother spoke of a rainbow that would come someday and so wanted to live to see it."

"In our world," Liddy explained, "God sent a flood to destroy almost everyone on Earth for their rebellion against Him. Only Noah and his family were spared. The rainbow symbolizes a covenant between God and creation that He would never destroy the world by a flood again."

Ireth looked at her quizzically. "That's interesting. Here, the rainbow is a prophetic sign that the Word is returning!"

"The Word left?" Ryann asked.

"The Word has been silent for over four hundred years. Following the reign of Aodan, each race and similar kind scattered, making separate colonies and scorning communication. It has not been until recently that someone came along to unite Aeliana in Myraddin again," Ireth noted skeptically.

"I would think that would be a good thing," Liddy said, trying to piece it together. "You don't seem so convinced."

"Narcissus is the current ruler. There are many who support him, and there are those who are not so sure."

"Is Narcissus human?" Terell asked.

For the first time a smile broke out across the elf's stoic face. "Ha! Narcissus, human? He would be insulted by that. No, Narcissus is a unicorn, as black as a moonless night, including his mane, tale, and horn."

"Will we meet him?" Liddy wondered aloud.

"Oh, I'm sure you will, young lady. Narcissus has his Peacekeepers everywhere." She sneered, "Peacekeepers are what he calls his guards. I would be surprised if he didn't know you were here long before you meet face to face."

Ireth hadn't moved for so long that Ryann was startled when she began her stroll around the small pond. Glancing down at his staff, the blinking fourth light caught his eye. A quick image popped into his head. He grinned.

Everyone jumped at the sudden appearance of the wolf. Teeth bared and frothing at the mouth, it raced across the surface of the pond in their direction. Ireth whirled around, drawing an arrow from her quiver in the process and launching it at the snarling beast. Liddy and Terell gasped as the arrow pierced the outer skin of the wolf until it was completely enveloped and then shot out the other side. Within seconds the watery beast stopped and collapsed in a small splash. All eyes turned toward Ryann.

"What? What? Oh, come on. It was a joke!" Ryann laughed awkwardly.

Ireth's face remained stoic, analyzing the mixed messages of the situation. "With great privilege comes great responsibility."

Ryann's face flushed pink as the elf continued her fluid movements in their direction. She stopped in front of Liddy. "May I see the book?"

Liddy extended the book out to its rightful owner with a look of respect. It was only when Ireth brought her hands up to receive the faded leather book that Liddy noticed she had a different color band on each of her fingers. The colors of the ring-like bands corresponded with the colors of the rainbow.

"Will we be able to hear the rest of the stories?" Liddy asked. "We've only had time to read a few ourselves."

"That may be possible, but you still have unfinished business here," she answered, pointing toward the mound rising out of the pond.

"I'll take care of that," Ryann announced, plunging into the water and quickly moving toward the box. Crystal clear water engulfed his legs to mid-thigh as he approached the brilliant colors flowing into the small island in front of him. The wooden cube, about the size of a mailbox, was sealed on each side. A wooden knob adorned the lid on top.

Reaching out for the box, Ryann's hand jerked back violently.

"Yoww!"

"What happened, dude?" Terell shouted.

"I don't know. Some sort of force repelled my hand. It didn't really hurt, but it took me by surprise."

Ryann eyed the box suspiciously, moving to the side slightly and reaching out his hand again.

"I wouldn't—" Ireth started to say.

"Yoww!" he yelped. "There it is again!" His arm snapped back another time.

Liddy stifled a laugh. "I'm sorry," Liddy said, turning her attention toward Ireth. "What were you about to say?"

"Only that the book of prophecy is very specific when it says a maiden with golden flowing hair will retrieve the treasure from the rainbow."

Terell broke the silence that followed. "Yo, Ryann? I might have bad eyesight, but I don't think you fit that description!"

"Ya think?" Ryann shot him a disgusted look as he turned to wade back to them.

Ireth nodded at Liddy, who stared back at her in disbelief. "Really? You think it's me? How many years ago was this book of prophecy written?"

"We have estimated it at 450 years. This is the first known rainbow since then, and you are the only one with golden hair in its presence. It comes to reason—"

"'Reason' is her middle name," Terell interrupted. "Come on! You go, girl!"

Shaking her head at Terell's sarcasm, Liddy turned her attention to the prize at the end of the rainbow and stepped into the same water Ryann had just exited. Focusing on the box as she approached the isle of dirt, she jumped at the shout from Ryann behind her.

"Look at the lights! They're moving!"

Glancing above her, Liddy watched in awe as the tiny sparkling white lights dotting the place where the rainbow entered the clearing began to swirl. Standing where Ryann had been only moments before, she tentatively reached out her hand, wincing at the thought of being shocked. When her hand passed the spot where Ryann's had been shoved backward, she relaxed and reached out with her other hand to retrieve the box. Cradling the wooden container, she looked up at the mesmerizing sight. The twinkling lights spiraled around the rainbow down into the box in her hands. It wasn't until every sparkle disappeared into the treasure that she pulled it away.

"Let's open it!" Ryann said excitedly as Liddy stepped out of the pond.

"Whoa, look!" Terell yelled, pointing toward the rainbow. "Up above!"

As if being absorbed through the hole in the canopy of trees, the rainbow began to sink into the island where it had illuminated the chest. Like a falling star, the streak of multiple colors erased itself. Their eyes followed the closure of the prophecy as the rainbow disappeared into the brown earth. Silence greeted them as they waited to see if anything else would happen. The gentle trickles from the rocky brook created a sense of peace and serenity.

"Hello? Anyone home? Come on. Wake up, people," Terell blurted out in a jovial, sing-song tone, clapping his hands for emphasis to bring some levity to the situation. "Liddy, how 'bout opening the box?"

Kneeling on the thick grass, she set the box down before her while the others gathered around. She looked up at Ireth. "Does the prophecy disclose what's in the box?"

"The prophecy says this about the rainbow:

Colors will appear across the sky,
Opening the way for the Word.
To bring the truth and stop the lie
The choice will be for shield or sword.
Three from afar will enter the fray;
True color will reveal friend or foe.
A moon will fall to bring a new day.
By a horn, Aeliana will know."

"Three from afar? Is that talking about us?" Liddy asked softly.

"It is becoming more and more apparent to me in the brief time I have known you that it is so," the elf confirmed.

Terell pretended to clear his throat. "Liddy, the box."

As much as she wanted to ignore Terell, Liddy turned away from Ireth to focus on the box. She grasped the wooden knob on top and lifted. Liddy gasped as the lid and box disappeared before her very eyes. Squeezing her fingers together, she realized she was no longer holding anything. Instead, a black leather pouch lay on the grass, pulled tightly together with a pewter-tipped drawstring.

"Whoa, how weird was that?" Terell asked.

"It appears the box was simply a temporary container for the real treasure," Ireth concluded.

Liddy picked up the leather pouch and loosened the twisted cords. She could feel the lumpy contents. Turning the bag upside down, she gave it a shake. Five smooth blue stones dropped into her palm.

"What do you think—?" She held them out.

Each of them picked a stone out of her hand to examine them more closely. Ryann turned his all around. "They don't seem to be anything out of the ordinary, but then again, neither did the disappearing box."

"I'm sure there's a purpose to them," Liddy said, "but for now it'll have to remain a mystery."

With a sheepish grin, Ryann stretched out his hand. "Well, it's obvious the stones were meant for you to find, Liddy, so it's appropriate that you should carry them with you in the satchel."

"In case anyone wants my vote," Terell said as he rolled his eyes, "I think Liddy should carry them as well."

Ireth provided Liddy with a makeshift belt for her to securely tie it on her hip.

"We should go," Ireth said, cautiously looking around the clearing at the shadows growing in the late afternoon sun. "We've been here a long time, and it is not certain whether Narcissus might have sent a group of Peacekeepers out to pursue the rainbow."

"Where to?" Ryann asked.

"Myraddin. Despite the dangers it may present, you need to see what it has become over the past four hundred years."

"Myraddin it is, then," Ryann concurred, looking to the nodding heads of Terell and Liddy.

"We head north and will sleep at the edge of the Southern Forest before following the Pedr River up to Myraddin in the morning." Ireth turned to lead them into a small parting in the trees the way she had come.

CHAPTER 12

The Peacekeepers

RYANN ROLLED LAZILY to his side, away from the light shining directly onto his face. Rubbing the sleep out of his partially opened eyes, he propped himself up on his elbow and glanced at his surroundings. Thick trees and the sound of rushing waters greeted him. The spongy moss ground covering he used as a bed was an additional reminder that the previous day's events were not a dream. Ireth sat off to his right on a large rock, reading in the early morning rays of sunshine. Travelling from the clearing to the edge of the forest had been fairly uneventful. Only once had they heard the screeching sounds of a griffin, forcing them to seek cover. Ireth explained how the griffins had sided with Narcissus and that they were responsible for patrolling the borders of Aeliana.

Movement by Liddy and Terell caught Ryann's attention, and he studied each of their faces as they awakened. Judging by their expressions, he knew they were going through the same realizations he had just moments earlier.

"Can you believe we're actually in Aeliana?" Ryann asked.

Terell and Liddy sat up, but it was Ireth who answered from behind him. "Oh, you are, and it is that reality which urges us to move on from here."

Ryann looked on as Liddy and Terell brushed themselves off and readied themselves to begin hiking. Liddy looked in Ireth's direction, and Ryann could see how she focused on the book she had surrendered to her the day before. Ireth soon noticed her blank stare as well and quickly engaged her in conversation.

"I remember being told stories by my mother about three children that came from a faraway place and fought the evil that came to destroy our land. She had heard the stories from her mother, which had been passed down through the generations. And now," she patted the book at her side, "I have the actual recordings myself. As I read through some of the accounts this morning, I was amazed at how accurately the stories had been passed down from over all these years."

Liddy's eyes brightened. "I'm glad you're having a chance to connect with the past."

"So am I," Ireth replied, smiling for only the second time that Ryann had observed. The friendly expression lasted only a moment, and then she was serious again. "Now, we must continue toward the castle. It is not good for us to be so far from Myraddin alone. The Pedr River is just ahead. If you listen closely, you can hear its rushing waters." She hesitated a minute to give them a chance to hear, then continued. "We will reach its banks and then head north until we reach Myraddin later in the day."

"I don't know about everyone else," Terell spoke up, "but my stomach's growling for some of my momma's scrambled eggs, grits, and a side of bacon."

"Oh, I'm sorry," Ireth said. "Here, I meant to give you this before we got started."

She handed out what looked like a piece of green beef jerky. Ryann put it up to his nose and sniffed.

"It's a special variety of dried vegetables and spices called cala-falas," Ireth announced proudly.

Ryann and Liddy took a bite. Terell stared at it as if unsure how to proceed. "Like I said, I could go for some of Momma's scrambled eggs, grits, and bacon!"

Ryann smiled, shaking his head. "Don't mind him, Ireth. He's like that with everyone."

Coming out from underneath the canopy of trees, they were welcomed by an open plain. Rolling, grassy hills scattered with rocks of varying shapes and sizes reminded Ryann of the Irish countryside he recalled seeing on a Discovery Channel episode. Being out in the open left them exposed to whomever might come their way, but Ireth had reviewed with them what to do in the event they were confronted. She would stay out in front and do the talking while everyone else gathered in tightly behind. Ryann had asked Ireth if she wanted him up front for his staff's power, but she dismissed the use of it, thinking it would bring more attention to them than was necessary.

As they walked along, Ireth sought details about Ryann's quest. "And you say that after delivering the sword to Aodan in Myraddin, Gabriel tasked you with finding a shield?"

"To be specific, he called it the shield of faith, but I have no idea where to start looking. In the first quest, I at least had a few clues," Ryann replied.

"Hmm, the story of your first journey has been passed from generation to generation here, but the part about the shield is new. I feel you should have every reason to believe it will be revealed to you at the appropriate time."

"Yeah, that's what I was afraid of," Ryann rolled his eyes. "Time and I aren't always the best of friends." He heard Liddy and Terell chuckle from behind him.

Ryann changed the subject. "What about these Peacekeepers? Who are they exactly?"

Ireth's alert eyes darted back and forth across the horizon in front of them while answering, "The Peacekeepers are a race of people known as Hugons. They are mostly human but part dragon. It's not known exactly how they came into being, but some of our oldest writings indicate that a race of small black dragons who rebelled against the Word intermarried with a remote village of humans in the farthest corners of Aeliana. This may be why the Hugons' skin is gray in color."

"Do they look like dragons?" Ryann asked.

"No, not exactly. There are some obvious resemblances, like their skin, which is gray and looks like rough leather. Their hands are larger than a human's, with fingernails that some might call claws. But one of the most apparent differences is their ears. They have slits in the side of their heads with a scaled flap that folds back over it."

Liddy shuddered. "I'm not so sure I'm looking forward to meeting them."

"Hopefully later rather than sooner," Ireth said. "They're all over Myraddin."

"Why the name 'Peacekeepers'?" Ryann continued his questioning.

"That was Narcissus's doing. Not long after he came into power, he brought in the Hugons for the citizens' protection, calling them Peacekeepers. Those who do not accept Narcissus as the rightful heir to the throne realize that the Peacekeepers are really his way to control the people, not protect them."

Screeeech!

They jumped at the shrill scream overhead and instinctively looked up in its direction. Having heard the sound the previous day, they knew it came from a griffin. Squinting to block out the morning sun, they could only make out the silhouette of the creature's body and flapping wings, which grew larger as it continued downward toward them. As rehearsed, Ryann, Liddy, and Terell moved in close behind Ireth as the griffin swooped down, landing twenty feet in front of them. The creature was much larger than it appeared in the sky. Eyes from the large, hawkish head carefully looked them over. Ireth maintained a confident stance as she addressed the bird-lion.

"I am Ireth Silimaurë of the elven clan. I am travelling in peace with friends of mine."

The griffin spoke. Its high-pitched voice surprised Ryann. While authoritative and loud, he had expected a deeper sound associated with a lion. "These friends of yours, they are not elves. Where are they from?"

"They're from a village just outside the borders of Aeliana," Ireth said. "I'm taking them to see our glorious capital city."

The griffin's eyes looked them over again. No one spoke in the ensuing awkward silence. Finally the griffin blinked and rendered its decision. "We will see if what you say is true. In the meantime, I will let Narcissus know of your whereabouts."

Its conclusion reached, the griffin stretched out its wings and in an instant was airborne, streaking across the sky in the direction of Myraddin.

"Whew," Terell breathed heavily. "I–I–I thought I was going to faint."

Ireth turned to face them. "So much for arriving in Myraddin unannounced, not that I thought it was really possible." She shrugged her shoulders. "I hear the sounds of rushing water just ahead. We'll stop at the river to rest and eat something, then walk along it to the city."

"Oh, boy." Terell grinned. "I hope we're having more calafalas. It's my new favorite."

The Pedr River was similar in size to the Elan River they had traveled on during their last trip to Aeliana. Ireth suggested they take a drink from the stream and then gather behind a few of the large rocks along the river's edge to block them from any unwanted visitors. Once seated as comfortably as possible on the hard ground, Ireth passed out more calafalas.

Ryann asked, "These Peacekeepers and Narcissus, when did they come into power?"

"It didn't occur overnight," Ireth answered. "Following Chancellor Aodan, there was a void of leadership. Oh, there were other chancellors who followed after him, but it was never the same."

"Why was that?"

"The chancellors that followed stopped leading through the Word. Slowly they came to believe that they were more important, embracing the power instead of the responsibility."

"That's terrible," Liddy said.

"It got worse. Much worse." Ireth shook her head as if vividly recalling. "As the leadership drifted away from the Word, so did the people. New ideas that were completely opposite of what the Word spoke at the annual feast were accepted as the new truth."

"New truth?" Liddy asked.

"Yes, the Enlighteners formed with their new ideas and ways of doing things. At first it appeared harmless. They were friendly and continued adding to their numbers daily. I remember attending one of their meetings. The leaders had a way of engaging your emotions by appealing to freedom from authority and elevating personal pleasure as the utmost of importance."

"What happened, then?" Liddy leaned forward, listening intently as Ireth continued.

"It dawned on me that everything they said was focused on the creature and not the Creator. They made up new words and phrases to explain things and moved away from the laws that the Word had given us."

"Surely, everyone didn't let this small group change the way of the Word," Ryann said.

"Oh, but they were clever. The Enlighteners were willing to take their time. They worked themselves into positions as instructors of the young and spread out into villages across the land, making friends and engaging in their doublespeak."

"Doublespeak?" Terell questioned.

"Yes, they would say things like, 'May the Word bless Aeliana,' in one sentence and then in another talk about how a creature fulfills his own destiny. But I believe the raids are what were responsible for the new regime that took over."

"The raids?" Ryann furrowed his brow. "What were they?"

"The raids brought fear to Aeliana. At first they were small disturbances along the border towns, a skirmish on one dwelling in the middle of the night. But then they grew fierce, with attacks conducted in broad daylight. The uproar from the people reached the ears of the chancellor, who by then was a very tired, old man. That's when Narcissus stepped in."

"So Narcissus was an Enlightener?" Liddy concluded.

"I believe he is more than that, but being an Enlightener made it that much easier for him to gain the trust of so many Aelianians who had abandoned the Word and were focused on themselves. As a young, powerful black unicorn, he was not only a charismatic leader, but he had a plan for taking care of the raids. Under pressure from the people, the weak chancellor was more than happy to appoint Narcissus second in command."

"Did the raids go away?" Ryann asked.

"Narcissus made it his first order of business to establish the

Peacekeepers. Ironically, they went out and did battle against the raiders and became heroes of the people. That made the citizens more than willing to give up some of their freedoms to ensure that they were kept safe."

"How long ago did that happen?" Ryan asked.

"It has been ten years now, nine since Narcissus took over."

"What ever happened to the chancellor?"

"That's a great question." Ireth rubbed the side of her face. "The story goes that he died unexpectedly in his sleep, and then Narcissus became the ruler of Aeliana."

"You mean the next chancellor, right?" Liddy asked.

"No, under the new ways Narcissus has decreed himself the first king of Aeliana."

"A creature as king in Aeliana?" Ryann blurted out. "I thought the Word was the only king."

"That's the way it was intended, but the people for the most part have given themselves over to Narcissus and the ways of the Enlighteners. It hasn't helped that the Word has been silent for almost three hundred years now."

"Three hundred years?" Liddy cried out. "What about the annual feast?"

Ireth cringed in a combination of sadness and distress. Getting to her feet, she motioned to them. "Come on. We need to get moving again. I'll tell you about it along the way."

CHAPTER 13

Enter the Unicorn

IDDY TWISTED TO the side, using one of the boulders to help lift herself up. Her toes tingled with the aftereffect of her legs being locked in one position so long. Stomping her feet to rid herself of the annoying prickling, she was interrupted by a soft clatter behind her. Turning, she noticed her pink cell phone lying on the rocks. Ireth bent over to pick it up.

"What's this?" she asked, carefully rotating the phone in every direction.

Liddy glanced over at Terell, who rolled his eyes.

"Um, well, it's a device that we call a 'cell phone' in our world, and we use it to communicate with each other."

Ireth handed the phone to Liddy, who flipped it open and continued her explanation.

"Everyone has one. You could be hundreds of miles away, and I could speak into my phone and you'd be able to hear me and speak back to me on yours."

"You live in an amazing place!" Ireth's eyes sparkled as she spoke. "I would like to come visit you there someday, but for now, you should put it away. Creatures here will think you're sorcerers."

"I guess it would be like taking technology back in time, where people wouldn't get it," Liddy agreed. "I've always thought it would be pretty cool, but I'll take your advice."

Continuing along the shore of the Pedr River, Ireth said, "I'd estimate from here that it's going to take us at least three hours to get to Myraddin."

The rushing waters provided the background music for this leg of their journey. Liddy stepped gingerly over the rocky soil, littered with patches of dry, yellowing grass. A gentle breeze reminded her of the cool forest shade they had left behind earlier in the day.

Ireth picked up the pace, motioning for them to hurry. "We need to make up for our extended lunch break."

Liddy sped up, working hard to keep up with her. For the next hour she never looked back. When Liddy thought she was going to have to call out for a break, Ireth seemed to sense her companion's weariness and slowed. It was then that she solemnly began speaking about the lost years of the Word.

"In my lifetime, I have never been to a feast with the Word, nor has anyone in my immediate family. I have only read about it in the annals. What was it like to be in the presence of the Word?"

Ryann and Liddy looked at one another. Ryann nodded for Liddy to answer.

"It was the most amazing feeling I have ever experienced. On one hand, I had a respectful fear, pressed down against the floor on my hands and knees with my eyes closed. At the same time, I felt more love and peace than ever before as the voice of the Word penetrated into my soul. On the outside I heard the words with my ears, but on the inside they came alive and seemed to flow through me. Even now as I think about it my skin tingles and I want the feelings to come back so I can experience them again."

Ireth had stopped, hanging on to every word Liddy spoke. "I'm jealous of you, Liddy," she acknowledged, "in a positive way. I hope that during my lifetime I may be able to experience the Word in the same manner you've described."

Liddy's eyes welled up with tears as she connected with the elf. Ireth turned away. "Come on. We need to keep moving. I'm sure we'll be met by some of the Peacekeepers within the hour."

Ireth could not have been more accurate in her assessment. A short time later when they came over the crest of a small hill, two dark figures appeared along the river in front of them. Ryann gripped his staff firmly while Ireth motioned them into a line behind her as they continued toward the oncoming creatures.

Even with Ireth's description of the Hugon race, Ryann was shocked as the two figures closed to within speaking distance. Their grayish skin looked like rhinoceros hide. Most of it was protected by additional black leather armor. Swords dangled from their sides, which Ryann thought was a little ironic based upon the length of their claw-like fingernails. Unlike the griffin's voice, which had surprised him, the Hugons sounded like what he had imagined—low and raspy.

"Stop and state your business!" the one with the red armband demanded.

Ireth returned their request with a firm reply. "I am Ireth Silimaurë of the Southern Forest elven clan, and I am escorting these travelers to Myraddin."

The dragon-like creatures stared with black, uncaring eyes at the three children as if to size them up as possible threats.

The leader gave a firm response. "Make sure that you don't create a disturbance in Myraddin and that they remain in your presence."

"I will keep watch over them at all times." Ireth nodded.

The Hugon responded in its guttural voice, "As we will over you."

The foursome continued on in their northerly direction, but it wasn't until they were out of earshot that Terell attempted to lighten the moment with his subtle sarcasm. "Ya know, the one on the left had an uncanny resemblance to an uncle of mine."

The castle in Myraddin rose high above all the surrounding dwellings. The small town they had visited previously had grown into a full-fledged city. No longer were single-story houses lined up in an orderly manner around the castle. Now buildings were built on top of buildings and in every open space, no matter how small. Stopping at the city gates, Ryann sought to absorb as many of the changes as possible prior to entering.

"It's so different from before," Liddy said.

"I suppose it had to change," Ryann agreed. "Nothing stays the same. It either continues growing toward its ultimate design or moving to ruin."

"What do you mean?" Terell asked.

"Well, it kind of reminds me of our own country," Ryann said. "You know, Washington, DC, has grown quite a bit over the two hundred plus years since the founding of the United States. I suppose that over a four hundred year period the capital of Aeliana would have changed significantly or been in ruins from an invading army."

"Good point," Liddy said. "But all the same, I wish that it would have stayed like I remembered it since we didn't get to grow along with it."

Terell laughed. "If we did, we'd be dead of old age!"

Ireth had her hands on her hips, listening to the banter back and forth. "Are you ready to proceed?"

Ryann had been staring at the castle towers since he'd last spoken and raised another question. "What happened to the flag?"

Liddy followed Ryann's gaze. "Yeah, the huge flag that used to fly over the castle—it used to be purple with a large gold *W*."

All of them stared at the new black flag, getting a glimpse of the red letters as a gust of wind unfurled it. The letters were now *A* and *M*.

"What does *AM* mean?" Ryann asked.

Ireth answered in a disgusted tone. "It's one of the subtle changes since Narcissus came to power. As part of the enlightenment, he took the *W* and added a few lines to form an *A* at the beginning and an *M* out of the end. It stands for 'Alpha Myraddin.'"

"As in alpha and omega, the beginning and the end?" Liddy asked.

"Sort of. Narcissus says it's the new beginning of Myraddin," Ireth answered, shaking her head. "Personally, I fear that it's the beginning of the end."

"What do you suggest we do now?" Ryann asked.

"The markets will close in another hour or so, and then Narcissus will speak from the steps of the castle." She looked them up and down. "It's obvious that you're foreigners from the clothes you're wearing. I suggest that we mingle with the crowds in the marketplace and find you something more local to wear so you can hear from Narcissus without drawing attention to yourselves."

Making their way to the markets, they only had to endure a few stares. Heavy cloth tarps bathed in a multitude of colors protected the merchants from the elements. The coverings also trapped the raucous banter of bartering between buyers and sellers inside the marketplace.

Glancing up and down the rows, the majority of the crowd appeared to be very human-like. The main differences were in stature, such as that of the dwarves, and some of the more subtle features, like the pointy ears of those of elven origin. Ireth had said that woodland creatures by nature did not desire to live in the city. However, they would come into town at the end of the day to hear Narcissus speak.

Even in the crowded markets, a bear, panther, and a pair of fauns were noticeable. The Hugons, with their darker, leathery skin, stood out from the rest of the townspeople. To Ryann, it was apparent that Ireth was avoiding them as she confidently led them to a safe location.

Fascinated by the tables of goods each merchant was selling, Ryann concluded the orderliness among the chaos was in keeping with one of the many street fairs they had back in Mount Dora. Each seller had a small area with a few tables. The selling booths lined up one next to the other. Jewelry, clothing, small weapons, and cooking spices appeared to be in the majority. Shuffling past each stall brought its own unique aroma—fragrant perfumes were followed by the smell of fish roasting over an open fire-pit with a hint of blackened spices, and then by a candle-maker kiosk, where aromas brought back memories of the Timeless Keepsakes shop back home.

Squeezing past the coarse hair of several brown bears, Ryann noticed one of the trader's stalls had its cloth sides and front down. As they approached, Ireth motioned for them to follow and quickly ducked through the loosely closed flap in front. Once all of them were safely inside, she tightened the opening. After a few minutes, their eyes adjusted to the dimly lit space.

Ireth put her finger up to her lips, "Keep quiet. This trading booth is run by those who are true followers of the Word. I saw one of them as we headed into the market and gave our signal for help. Someone should be entering soon."

No sooner had she finished her sentence than the back flap opened and another female elf slipped through. They heard Ireth's soft whispers, and she exited as quickly as she had come in.

Ireth explained, "Shamara is a kindred elf who has lived in the city for two decades now. She'll be back in a few minutes with clothes for you to wear. Then we'll make our way out the back and over to the castle entrance. Between the crowds and your new clothing, you should blend in well enough not to be noticed."

Ireth led them toward the marketplace exit, which was opposite of the direction they had come. Ryann and Terell were dressed in plain brown pants and shirts, with leather belts to tighten up the estimated sizes the mysterious elf had brought them. Surprisingly, the lace-up boots fit perfectly.

"Nice threads, Liddy," Terell whispered. Ryann looked at the simple, cream colored dress that hung loosely on her athletic frame. It wasn't much of a fashion statement, but the common garment for young ladies in Aeliana would allow her to blend in.

"Thanks," she responded sarcastically. "At least you got boots. I can already tell my feet are going to be filthy in these sandals." With each step she kicked up dust from the dirt floors of the bazaar as they traipsed past the final tables out into the late afternoon sun. Three dwarves off to their right were causing a commotion with their loud arguing. Ireth stopped within earshot to eavesdrop. Ryann noticed her pointed ears twitch as the dwarves carried on. He shuffled forward to listen in on their conversation.

"I'm telling you, it had the makings of a rebellion to me," the dark-bearded dwarf insisted.

The second one agreed. "You know how those red-haired dwarves can be. There's a reason why they call 'em fire dwarves!"

The first dwarf chuckled. "Yeah, cuz of their hot temper!"

"Where was he?"

"Out west toward the old canyon."

"And what exactly did this crazed dwarf say?" a skeptical third dwarf asked.

"I can't recall exactly, it was a type of proclamation, announcing a liberator that was coming to free Aeliana," the first dwarf answered, then stopped suddenly to look around.

Ireth motioned for Ryann and the others to continue following her, acting disinterested as she looked away. She whispered out of the side of her mouth, "Keep walking and don't turn around."

A reverberating gong rang loud enough to be heard for miles. Staying close to Ireth, they traveled toward the looming castle. Ryann noticed other Aelianians were headed in the same direction. A second gong rang.

Ireth stopped them in the middle of an open space in front of the castle. Many creatures who had been milling about were now maneuvering for the best vantage point for viewing. Others filled in behind them.

After the third gong, Liddy asked, "What does the ringing mean?"

"It's both an announcement and a summons. Following the sixth ringing of the gong, Narcissus will come out to address those gathered," Ireth replied.

"Why six?" Ryann asked.

Ireth's eyebrow raised as she looked at Ryann and replied, "Aelianians still remember that the Word considers seven the perfect number. Narcissus says that he rings six times because there is one coming after him who will sit on the throne and be much greater."

The sixth gong rang, immediately changing the restlessness and chattering of the crowd to a rigid silence. Ryann felt strangely out of place as those to his left and right gazed intently at the dark entrance to the castle. A resounding neigh blasted forth from within the fully shadowed passageway, reminding Ryann of a giant mouth stretching wide in a violent scream. The black flags with the new *AM* hung down from the walls on either side of the doorway. His eyes widened expectantly as he waited to see what would exit from the bowels of Castle Myraddin.

Emerging from the darkness, the ominous shadow took the form of an enormous unicorn. Black as a moonless night, with two bright stars for eyes, he strode confidently out into the open and stood before them. The great black horn extending from his head produced an aura of both regality and power. Shiny wet nostrils flared rhythmically with his steady breathing. Not a cough, whinny, nor growl escaped from the thousands of creatures gathered around. Heads around him began bowing in a great wave of reverence. It was then that the great black unicorn panned the crowd until it peered directly into Ryann's face. Ireth's sharp whisper grabbed his attention.

"Look down!"

Ryann quickly dropped his stare, bowing his head slightly to focus on the tail of a faun in front of him. He wondered if the unicorn was still looking in his direction. A low, booming voice brought his gaze upward again. He was relieved to notice those around him raised their heads as well.

"My fellow Aelianians, as you know, the new age of enlightenment we call Alpha Myraddin has brought peace to our land. Through this new way of believing, we know that the power of Aeliana itself is available to each one of us. By focusing within yourself, you can tap into this power to be a better creature and to attain the riches of your heart's desire."

Ryann carefully gazed around at the hundreds of creatures focusing on Narcissus. Hanging on his every word, their rising energy level was exhibiting itself through wide grins, stomping hooves, and nodding heads. Shouts of "Alphadin" erupted from several creatures nearby.

"I do not want to dwell on the closed-minded teachings of the past," Narcissus continued, "but, it was once thought that there was only one way to everlasting happiness in the hereafter. Omega Myraddin will be an eternal place of rest and happiness for *all* who believe. All will be able to be a part of this glorious place, for who am I to say that there is only one way? As each of you understands the openness of this new truth, you will feel more and more empowered to fulfill your destiny. Truth is different for each of us. Just as each of your desires is different from your fellow creatures, what's right for one might not be right for another. Embrace your desires. Seek your own way. For the road to paradise is wide and paved with many paths of gold!"

Cheers rang out in a deafening mixture of roars, shouts, and jungle sounds Ryann couldn't begin to distinguish. He panned the great gathering, the euphoria in sight and sound washing over him. Glancing back at the castle entrance, Ryann locked eyes with Narcissus, who seemed to be singling him out of the cheering throngs. He looked away and urgently tugged at Ireth's cloak. "Where do we go now?"

Ireth didn't hesitate. "Follow me. We have a dwarf to visit out west."

CHAPTER 14

Dragon Rider

K EEPING THE RIVER to their left, they traveled for an hour before Ryann stole one last glimpse back at Myraddin. He thought he could still see a lone tower rising up above the horizon. The image was so small he wondered if he would have mistaken it for mountain peak if he hadn't known any better. The Elan River flowed rapidly in the same easterly direction they had traveled on their previous adventure. While the town of Myraddin had proliferated into a vibrant city, along the river Ryann could not see any evidence that four hundred years had passed.

As they trudged along the riverbanks, visions of Drake's army, bows in hand, resurfaced in his memory. He recalled the horde coming out of the thick brush along the shores, his narrow escape, and that further down the river the scenery would open up in rocky, barren areas with patches of dried grass. Thin trees with broad willow canopies had sprung up along the banks of the river, providing welcomed shade as they walked single-file into the desert. Off in the distance to the south lay miles and miles of sand and rocky wasteland. If he had his directions correct, eventually past the desert there would be the Pedr River and beyond that the transition to the mountainous region.

Ireth stopped under one of the larger trees. The shady covering extended out over the river. "Let's get a drink and rest here for a few minutes."

Ryann dropped to the sandy bank and took off his boots. They fit perfectly when he first put them on, but the angry red spots where they were rubbing told a different story. The sounds of Terell slurping at the river water carried up the embankment as he turned his boots upside down and watched the sand pour out like an hourglass. He looked around for Liddy and saw her sitting downstream at the river's edge dangling her feet in the cool, rushing water. The scene reminded him of one of his family's vacations out west to Arizona and resting along the rocky sandbanks of a sparsely shaded Sedona stream.

He welcomed the few minutes to drink his fill of water and massage feeling back into his toes. Ireth waved them over, and they gathered in a circle along the top of the riverbank at the base of a sturdy oak tree. Ryann noted Terell had the prime seat with his back resting against the tree trunk, legs limply splayed out in front of him.

"We shouldn't be too far away now," Ireth began. "From what I gathered from my contacts in Myraddin, this dwarf they speak of is at the edge of the ancient canyon where you found the sword on your previous visit."

"You read that in the book as well?" Ryann asked.

Ireth nodded.

"I feel like a historical figure that's come back to life," Liddy said. "I mean, can you imagine having someone we've read about in history class coming to Mount Dora?"

Ryann turned to Ireth. "How many Aelianians have read about us?"

"Oh, very few, and then it is just those in my clan."

"That's good."

"But—" Ireth hesitated.

"But what?"

"There are always legends, rumors, and stories passed down from generation to generation. Historical accounts can be good and bad depending upon whose point of view it's coming from. That magnifies the importance of having the written word from firsthand witnesses. It conveys the truth about what happened and cannot change from storyteller to storyteller over time."

Nodding, Ryann shifted his attention toward Terell. His friend's eyes were wide open and his mouth formed a large oval.

"G–gu–guys!" He raised his shaking hand to point behind Ireth.

Knowing Terell only stuttered when he was very nervous or excited, Ryann turned in the direction he was pointing. An enormous white creature the height of the tree stood quietly watching them.

"Dra–dra–dragon!" Terell finally spat out.

Ryann glanced at the others. Liddy had a quizzical look on her face, and Ireth showed no fear.

"Sorcha?" Liddy asked meekly.

They stared at the imposing dragon silently gazing back at them with frosty blue eyes. Stunning white scales adorned her massive torso. Her wings stretched out thirty feet on both sides and, except for the frayed edges tinged a pinkish blue, were equally brilliant white. The dragon's streamlined head began with a small pointed beak at the tip of her snout and arched back over crests that staggered to its scaly neck. A few teeth protruded from her closed mouth, which curved slightly upward. Ryann wasn't sure if she was grinning or not.

"Greetings," the great white dragon replied. "Surely you can't be the same Earth children I met four hundred years ago?"

"Oh, but we are," Liddy eagerly responded. "We've come back only a year older, but time has passed much faster here. How is it that you're still alive? Uhh, no offense."

"None taken. It is the privilege and curse of being a dragon. When we first met, I was only a juvenile dragon of twenty-five years, and now I am an adult. So many friends have come and gone, the creator choosing to give them shorter lives. For some reason, He allows dragons to live a thousand years or more."

Liddy turned to Ireth. "And elves? I had read somewhere that you're immortal and live forever."

"If you mean our souls, all of us live forever, for the soul cannot die. Only our location changes," Ireth explained. "We either spend eternity with the Word in heaven or with Abaddon in the place prepared for him and his followers. If you mean our current life forms—like the Creator choosing to allow dragons to live in their temporary body for a thousand years—then yes, He gives elves one hundred years to live here, and then we cross over to our final destination without having to die in this one."

"So you can't be killed?" Ryann asked.

"It's certainly possible, but it requires extreme measures to do so."

Having regained his nerve, Terell joined the conversation. "Let me just say how much I appreciate this being a happy reunion and that we're not her lunch," he said, pointing to Sorcha. "But I don't recall meeting you on my last visit."

"Nor I you, dark one. A dragon's memory is quite keen. I do recall meeting the other two briefly. I believe it was at the nine-tieth feast of the Word."

Ireth's ear twitching caught Ryann's attention, and he watched her hesitate, glance across the river, then make eye contact with Sorcha and nod her head in that same direction.

Sorcha's mouth opened wide. Terell yelped as a cone of white frost erupted from her mouth with a loud, windy rush. Shooting across the river, the freezing blast expanded, blanketing an entire row of bushes in a thick mass of ice.

"Whoa, that was cool!" Terell shouted.

Ireth's eyebrow raised. "That is stating the obvious." Ireth started down to river's edge, motioning to the trio as she said, "Follow me."

At the edge of the stream she stopped and turned to the dragon. "Sorcha? If you please," she said, pointing toward the water.

Sorcha hopped into the middle of the river, the water rising up to wing level. She spread her wings wide, forming a bridge from one side to the other. Ireth started across and motioned for the others to follow. Ryann didn't hesitate after watching Ireth step across with ease but was surprised at the sturdiness of Sorcha's wings. He expected to sink down with each footstep, like stepping onto a trampoline. Instead it was more like walking across a flat wooden bridge with barely any noticeable give. Once they had crossed, Sorcha rose out of the waters, shaking like a dog to rid herself of the cool river water.

"What was that all about?" Liddy asked.

Ireth waved them forward, leading them around to the back side of the eight-foot block of ice. Frozen within was the body of a Hugon, mouth open in shocked surprise, his last moment encapsulated in the block.

Liddy gasped, "Is he—"

"Dead?" Sorcha finished the question. "No, not dead; just frozen in suspended animation for a few hours until the ice melts away. In this heat, it might be a little quicker."

"What was he doing?" Ryann asked.

"He's one of Narcissus's Peacekeeper spies," Ireth answered, displaying a rare grin. "This will slow down his report on our whereabouts."

Liddy looked from the frozen Hugon to Sorcha. "I take it you're not on good terms with Narcissus?"

Ryann noticed the same look he previously thought was a grin before Sorcha answered. "You could say that. Narcissus and the enlightened ones do not like the fact that I am a link to the past. They work hard to rewrite history in the minds of the young so it suits their purposes for the present and future. I am a bridge to the past that is a thorn in their side, especially since I lived it. They would prefer I not be around. But for now, since dragons are revered in the culture, it would not look good for them to kill me."

"For now?" Ryann asked.

"I am not naïve enough to believe that circumstances will not change. There is a time coming when Narcissus will turn even the Aelianians against dragons, unless—"

"Unless what?" Liddy looked intently into Sorcha's thoughtful light blue eyes.

The dragon's eyes sparkled with an obvious tinge of excitement. "Unless the chosen one comes first."

"The chosen one?" both Ryann and Liddy asked in unison.

"Yes, He is the one written about in one of the lost books. A gallant creature will be sent by the Word to rule Aeliana and restore her to greatness."

Ryann turned toward Ireth. "Have you read this in one of your books?"

"No, Sorcha is right in saying that the book is lost. I've only been privileged to hear the stories of a great king that will come to rule over Aeliana. There are many who have heard the stories passed down from their ancestors and believe that Narcissus is the one spoken about."

"He is not the one!" Sorcha spoke confidently.

"How can you be so sure?" Liddy asked.

"Because Narcissus came to power in a different way than the ancient books foretold. The books are no longer around to confirm this, and the Enlighteners have changed the stories over time; but the elves and dragons still remember."

Ireth added, "The book said, 'There is one who will call out in the desert and prepare the way for the king.' This is what intrigues me about the dwarf we are seeking. Rumors abound in Myraddin about all of the crazy things he is saying."

"Without the book, how can you be certain that what is passed down is accurate?" Liddy questioned again.

Ireth hesitated for a moment, her eyes squinting as she gazed into Liddy's eyes. "Faith, Liddy, faith that brings confidence in knowing what the Word has done for Aeliana in the past will be completed in the future. I am convinced that there are many who would doubt the Word is sending us a new king even if they had the book to read it for themselves."

Sorcha continued, "What Ireth is saying is true, and her faith shows she is a better creature than me. For like you, Liddy, I wanted proof for myself, so I have spent years in search of the lost book, which prophesies the coming of a king."

Ryann's attention was drawn to Sorcha, who now sat silent in reflective thought. The late afternoon sun danced across her glistening white scales. A soft scratching noise caused him to look down and focus on the dragon's feet. It was the first time he noticed the long, sharp talons protruding from her feet. They scraped across a small boulder.

"You've found it, haven't you?" Ryann blurted out to the surprise of the others.

They looked at him and then quickly back to Sorcha.

Sorcha stretched her neck out to the point that she was face to face with Ryann, only a few feet away. "You are very perceptive for one who is so young. Yes, I have found the book."

"Sorcha! This is great news," Ireth shouted, displaying the first real emotion any of them had seen since meeting her. "And where is it now?"

"Back in my lair in the Marrow Mountains, for safekeeping," she answered.

"I can't believe you kept this a secret. Did it reveal any clues about the One?" Ireth asked, eyes wide in anticipation.

"There are passages which give signs for what to look for around His coming."

"And?"

"For now I think it is best that I alone look through eyes jaded by this information. However, I would like to join you in travelling to see this dwarf you have been talking about. He may play a role in all of this."

"We would be honored to have you join us, Sorcha," Ireth spoke, then solemnly bowed her head.

Sorcha looked skyward and announced, "We have a few hours of sunlight left." Gazing back at the four of them, she nodded to Liddy. "Climb on my back. We'll fly ahead and scout out an area at the end of the river in preparation for nightfall."

Liddy felt her breathing increase. Certainly it was the ultimate fantasy of any dreamer to ride a dragon, and yet there was also the uncertainty of actually doing it. Any fear she harbored was quickly pushed aside as she scurried around behind one of the dragon's wings.

Sorcha sensed her hesitation. "Don't worry about hurting me. Just climb up however you can and hold on tight," she said, stooping low to provide better access.

Liddy needed no further encouragement and scrambled up Sorcha's scaly back using the dragon's muscular crevices for handholds and steps for her feet. Moving up into a flat space below Sorcha's neck, Liddy found a spot narrow enough to straddle and get a strong footing atop each of the dragon's wings. The lowest spine on Sorcha's neck was dull enough for her to grip like a saddle horn without cutting her bare hands.

"Ready!" she announced confidently. No sooner had she finished uttering the word than it changed into a high-pitched scream as Sorcha leapt into the air, snapping her tail downward and pushing off with her hind legs. Gripping the horn-like spine with all her might, Liddy squeezed her knees into the dragon's body as the laughter from Ryann and Terell quickly faded behind her.

"Are you okay back there?" Sorcha asked with a hint of sarcasm.

"You could have given me a little warning," Liddy yelled over the wind whipping her hair all about.

After several hundred feet of vertical ascent, Sorcha leveled out and began circling in a wide swath. Liddy looked down trying to make sense of the topography below them. Her hair now safely blowing behind her, she reveled in the powerful position of sitting atop a flying dragon. Sorcha leaned to her left, and they veered past another river to the north. *That must be the Bryn*, Liddy mused. She recalled three rivers split off the main river coming from Myraddin: the Bryn, Elan, and Pedr. The Bryn was the only one she hadn't seen. *Those green bumps dotting the land farther north must be the Joynnted Knolls.*

Having flown in airplanes before, Liddy had wondered what it would be like to ride on the wing outside the cozy confines of the plane's cabin. It felt different than she had expected, more like riding a rollercoaster that had left its tracks and soared into the sky. Her brief daydream was broken by Sorcha's long neck swinging around to give her a warning. "Hold on, young one!"

Without the warning she might have been thrown off by Sorcha's sharp left turn. Looking out over the western horizon, Liddy caught a quick glimpse of Castle Myraddin. She had hoped to have a closer look but thought Sorcha was probably using great care not to be spotted from the highly populated city.

To the south she saw the Pedr River, with jagged, snowcapped mountains rising just beyond as a backdrop. Sorcha again whirled her large head and provided some useful information. "The Marrow Mountains are where I've made my lair."

Liddy thought that made sense. A white, frost-breathing dragon would naturally live in an ice cave.

At the end of the snaking Pedr River, she could make out a vast blue area, which, if she had her bearings correct, was the same sea where the cave was located. She thought to herself, *It seems like weeks ago, but I know it has only been two days.*

Completing the big loop, they returned to the Elan River and headed east. Far below she could make out the shapes of three figures walking along the riverbank. Sorcha looked over her shoulder again with that now-familiar grin. "Let's have some fun!"

Liddy gripped the horn tighter and hunched down with her face almost touching Sorcha's shimmering white scales. Sorcha plummeted toward the ground, rapidly building up speed with her wings retracted close to her side. Within a few hundred feet of the rocky earth, her wings shot out fully extended, and the white dragon thrust her head up, pulling out of the dive.

Why her? Ryann thought. *You'd think the one tasked by Gabriel to find the shield would get to ride the dragon.*

Trying to rid himself of the negative thoughts creeping into his head, he decided to give Sorcha the benefit of the doubt and assume she was giving a fellow female a ride.

Captivated by the shadow in front of him growing larger and larger, Ryann didn't think much of it until Terell yelled, "Look out!"

Ryann looked skyward, expecting to see one of the griffins descending upon them. Instead he was greeted by the broad smile of Liddy, clinging to the back of Sorcha as the dragon pulled out of her steep dive to narrowly graze the tops of the trees. Instinctively, the three of them ducked their heads, catching the gust of wind and a cheering Liddy as she raced past them and down the length of the stream until they were out of sight.

CHAPTER 15

A Voice in the Wilderness

DARK FISSURE IN the earth expanded as Sorcha glided downward. Following her torrid pace along the winding river, she bolted back up to soaring heights again to best determine where to land. "How are you enjoying yourself back there?"

"It's the best!" Liddy shouted as the wind whipped through her hair, "I love flying across the endless blue sky."

"Hang on. We're headed down now!" Sorcha warned.

"Thanks for the warning."

Sorcha dove toward the canyon entrance in front of her. As she rapidly approached the ground, she flapped her wings in hearty earnest while stretching out her claws to brace for a swift landing. Liddy didn't say a word, but she squeezed hard with her legs to hold on.

Settling down next to the large rocks, Sorcha said, "These boulders will make a protective resting place for the night."

"I really don't want to have to get off," Liddy sighed.

"Don't worry," Sorcha said. "There will be other times."

Liddy slid off of the dragon's back. "I'll look around for some dead wood for a fire tonight."

Sorcha nodded in approval. "My senses tell me the dwarf will be in the canyon." Looking skyward, she continued, "The others should be here before the sun sets."

"What else should we do?" Liddy asked.

"After you gather some kindling, we can prepare our surroundings," Sorcha answered and winked. "They will be weary from taking the harder route."

Liddy smiled. *I think the two of us are going to become good friends.*

Ryann's eyes snapped open, aroused from a deep sleep. He lay still, listening for any sound that might alert him to something amiss. The arrival at the makeshift campsite the previous evening had been uneventful, with the exception of dinner. Fresh roasted fish, scooped out of the river by Sorcha and cooked by Ireth, proved to be a meal he would elevate above anything he had experienced back in Mount Dora. He suspected it was due, in part, to the long day's activities, which left him famished by the time they had arrived.

As he strained to hear anything out of the ordinary, Ryann lay motionless for several minutes. The brightening grayish hue announced the coming dawn. Hearing nothing, he turned his head to observe his peaceful surroundings. Sorcha's massive body formed a large semi-circle wrapping around the camp, with her spiked head at one end and her barbed tail on the other. Boulders closed in the opening formed by her u shape, providing the others with the ability to sleep safely in the center. Ryann noticed Ireth and Liddy had found a spot by Sorcha's front legs. Terell and he made their bed by the dragon's tail.

Glancing skyward, Ryann noticed the last few stars in the fading darkness dimmed with the coming day. A bright blue moon peeking over the sand dunes on the horizon captured his attention. The last time he had seen a moon like that was when the three blue moons had converged together for the Feast of the Word.

He continued staring at the moon as the pink twilight officially announced the dawn of a new day. Ryann prayed silently for God's hand in directing their steps in the coming hours. There was no doubt in his mind that his quest to find the shield was of God. The challenge, as before, would be in the process of discovering its whereabouts, and the blue moon was a positive sign that they were on the right path.

Sitting up to glance over at Ireth, Ryann saw her returning his gaze. He looked away, embarrassed that his subtle movements had awoken her. *With her elf hearing, she would probably be aware of danger much more quickly than I would,* he contemplated. As the pink sunrise blended into orangish-yellow, Liddy and Sorcha woke and stretched. Terell rolled over on his side, trying to ignore the waking movements of those around him. His efforts didn't go unnoticed by Sorcha, who with a slight twitch of her tail caught Terell in the head. He bolted upright.

"All right. All right. I'm gettin' up."

As soon as the laughter died down, Ryann pointed out the moon.

"What do you think it means?" He looked first to Ireth and then to Sorcha.

Ireth, who seemed to have an answer for everything, hesitated, deferring to the great white dragon.

"Indeed," Sorcha began, trying hard to contain her excitement, "it has been four hundred years since I last saw the blue moons. During those days, the three blue moons would come together into one, and the Word would speak to us. Ireth's clan recorded the annual messages in the great Book of Life. Your arrival back into Aeliana is not a coincidence. It appears as if the Word is going to show Himself again."

"If that's the case, Sorcha, shouldn't we see two more moons?" Ireth asked.

Twisting heads scanned the sky in an attempt to be the first to spot the other moons. "There's one!" Terell pointed out excitedly off in the opposite horizon from the first.

Searching the heavens for another five minutes proved fruitless. "There is a mystery here," Sorcha concluded. "Perhaps it will show itself shortly. Let's continue our journey and move down into the canyon."

Deep rumbles echoing off the canyon walls greeted them as they shuffled to a halt at the end of their descent. For Ryann, the scenery hadn't appeared to change over the four hundred years elapsing in Aeliana. Parts of the chasm's reddish-orange walls may have collapsed, but without trees to reveal the passage of time, the rocks and sand left scant evidence of change. Ireth admitted to never having been in this part of Aeliana, while Sorcha recalled flying over but never landing. They walked in silence toward the noise. Ryann extended his staff, readying himself for whatever they might find. He was fairly certain that Sorcha's lumbering mass wouldn't allow them to sneak up on anyone. The counter to that was her display of power over the Hugon the previous day.

Moving along the canyon floor, the echoing rumbles sharpened until it was recognizable as a shouting voice. The echoes intensified as they drew closer, becoming apparent they were not shouts of despair or a cry for help. As they rounded the last bend in the ravine, Ryann spied a red dwarf atop a flat boulder, yelling as he paced back and forth. His fiery-red hair splayed in disarray while spittle flew from his mouth.

A small gathering of creatures watched the spectacle with great interest. Ryann noticed a reddish-brown fox, two hill dwarves, a male elf, and a pair of muscular black bulls, all shifting uncomfortably in front of the crazed red dwarf.

As they approached, the bold dwarf proclaimed his final arguments as he flayed his arms for emphasis. His eyes were glazed over as if he were in the middle of an active dream.

"Prepare the way for the redeemer, make straight paths for him," he shouted. "Every valley shall be filled in, every mountain and hill made low. The crooked roads shall become straight, the rough ways smooth. And every creature will see the Word's deliverance!"

With his final words he collapsed in a heap, head hung down, looking like a giant red-haired mushroom. The creatures in front of him watched in bewildered silence. They looked to one another and back to the mute dwarf. When nothing new occurred, they walked away slowly, one by one. The male elf glanced their way, making eye contact with Ireth. Ryann observed the two. There didn't appear to be any noticeable communication, yet Ireth broke away from their group and made her way toward him.

"Okay, that was different," Terell said, sarcastically trying to lighten the moment.

"What does it mean?" Liddy asked Sorcha.

"I'm not exactly sure, young one, but somewhere in the recesses of my mind are cloudy memories concerning a prophecy of proclamation."

"Look," Ryann interrupted. "Here comes Ireth."

The elf returned, expressionless in her typical smooth gait, while her male counterpart hurried off to catch up to one of the others.

"Well?" Terell asked.

Ireth put a finger up to her mouth, motioning for them to be silent, then whispered, "My fellow kinsman has been listening to the red dwarf for weeks trying to understand his ranting. His message shifts between accusing the creatures of Aeliana from rebellion against the Word to appealing to them to recant of their evil behavior and return to the worship of the Word."

"Hmm, most interesting," Sorcha added. "The book did allude to a forbearer who would be the voice of one calling in the desert." Sorcha stopped, distracted by the sky. "Look above. The moons are drawing closer."

Looking up into the cloudless, pale blue sky, two full, radiant blue moons shone brightly against their tepid backdrop. Rising from the horizon where they had previously viewed them, the moons were on a collision course to intersect directly above them.

"Come," Sorcha continued. "Let's talk to this wild red dwarf and see what knowledge he has of things to come."

Sorcha led them the short distance to the balled-up dwarf. They formed a semi-circle around him and waited. Sorcha stretched her neck upward to her full height. Looking down on the hairy-topped dwarf, she boldly asked, "What is your name, red dwarf, and what is your business here?"

The mane of red hair rolled backward as the dwarf nonchalantly raised his head in response to Sorcha's questions.

Peering through his stringy hair, he replied, "Ah, yer breath is as foul as you look, ya pale monster!" rasped the disheveled dwarf.

Sorcha reeled back in surprise at the dwarf's curt words. Undeterred by the vast difference in each other's stature, the red dwarf jumped up to his full height of four feet and continued his monologue.

"There is one coming of whom I am not worthy to brush His coat. He is to be loved yet feared. The alpha and the omega. He will save Aeliana from itself!"

Ryann heard Liddy gasp then felt a tug on his shirt. "Ryann, look around his neck at the medallion he's wearing," she whispered. "It's the gift I gave to Essy the last time we were here!"

Ryann looked at the medallion resting on the dwarf's hairy chest. Stepping forward, he used his most authoritative voice, "Dwarf, we ask again, what is your name?"

The dwarf looked to the sky, ignoring him.

Ryann continued, "Where did you get that necklace?"

The accusatory question brought the dwarf out of his catatonic trance. His scrunched-up face turned toward Ryann as he eyed him up and down with his black, beady eyes. "My name is Eljon, and as for this medallion, I found it here in the canyon a few years ago. What's it to you?"

Liddy's face reddened as she stepped up next to Ryann. "It was a gift I gave to a noble leopard over four hundred years ago!" she shouted.

Eljon's gaze shifted from Ryann to Liddy, and in a dramatic transformation, his icy stare melted into a pool of compassion. "I can sense that what you say is true, my lady. A gift can never be taken. It can only be given and received. Despite my attachment to its unique properties, I will return it to its rightful owner."

Reaching behind his neck he untied the leather cord with the *E*-shaped medallion to hand it to her. Dropping it into her waiting hands, he looked up and froze. Ryann saw the dwarf's eyes widen in surprise as he looked over Liddy's head to something behind all of them. The others picked up on his shocked expression as well and turned with Ryann to see what captivated his attention.

CHAPTER 16

Blue Moons Descending

NOTHING COULD HAVE prepared them for the amazing sight now before them. A gleaming white unicorn, so white it made Sorcha appear dusty in comparison, stepped majestically in their direction. Rippling muscles moved in perfect harmony as the sure-footed creature strode confidently across the rocky ground. The glistening horn that adorned its head spiraled to a fine point, projecting an aura of authority.

Just as they were capturing the full beauty of the unicorn, Eljon's voice thundered from behind them, "Look, the atonement of the Word, who takes away the sickness of Aeliana!"

Fixated on the regal presence of the new creature entering their midst, the silence was only eclipsed by his clomping hooves against the orange desert stone. Terell broke the silence with urgent shouts. "Look! Up in the sky," he pointed.

All heads but Eljon's looked up to see the two full blue moons within moments of touching one another. Four hundred years earlier, three blue moons had come together annually into one for the Word to declare his annual proclamation. "Wh–wh–will the Word speak?" Terell asked.

"I don't know," Ryann whispered, "but we'll find out soon enough. They're coming together now."

He glanced back to the unicorn. Eljon had moved around and lay prostrate in front of the noble creature, his face literally kissing the earth. Ryann marveled in fascination as the unicorn spoke to the

dwarf and stomped the ground. Eljon tilted his head up, peering fully
into the unicorn's peaceful face while maintaining his prone posture.

Ryann barely heard the whispering words the unicorn spoke.
"Eljon, through the ages, you will be known as the first of the faith."

Overhead the two glowing moons merged together into one radi-
ating blue sphere. Ryann peered into the stream of light shining
down on them. As the intensity increased, he found himself slowly
bowing, then kneeling, and finally lying on the ground in much the
same way Eljon lay stretched out. He felt the same mixture of fear
and peace that he had felt in the castle at Myraddin the first time he
had heard the Word.

> *I am light. In me there is no darkness. If you claim me as*
> *your king yet walk in the darkness, then you deceive yourself*
> *and do not live by the truth. But if you walk in the light, as*
> *I am in the light, then you can claim me as your king.*

The weight of the Word's glorious expression lifted, and with
painstaking effort, Ryann struggled to rise. He noticed that even
Sorcha's muscular frame had been pressed flat to the sandy earth as
she labored to regain her footing.

The intensity of the blue glow lessened to the point that they
could look upward again without shielding their eyes. A collective
gasp rang out from each of them as one of the moons dropped out of
the sky and moved toward them. The closer the moon floated down
to them the smaller it became until it matched the size of a small
dragon hovering above the canyon walls.

"Wh–wha–what do we do?" Terell panted.

"Don't panic," Ryann cautioned. "The Word is good. Just stay
where you are and watch."

Whirling past with a trail of glowing blue, the moon headed toward the unicorn as the thundering voice of the Word called down from the heavens.

This is the one whom I cherish...follow him!

The strong voice roared as the blue moon washed over the unicorn, encapsulating him in a sphere of gaseous blue hues. In one instant the unicorn was completely covered and in the next the blueness began dissipating. In less than a minute, the moon had evaporated completely.

Liddy screamed as the white unicorn rose up on his hind legs, letting loose with a loud battle cry that echoed through the canyon. Knowing she was safe, Ryann scanned the area looking for any sign of the blue moon. Seeing none, he returned his gaze to the unicorn. He wasn't certain if his eyes were playing tricks on him or not—so much had happened in such a brief amount of time—but from his angle it appeared as if a blue aura were outlining the unicorn's horn. Above them the one remaining blue moon was retreating back into the heavens.

"What just happened here?" Ryann asked.

"You have been witness to the Word's shattering of time, space, and dimension," Eljon responded. "Nothing will be the same from this point forward."

"You speak in riddles, little one," Sorcha responded. "We are witnesses to this event, that much we cannot deny. However, we are not sure what we have seen."

"You will understand in the future, for as it was here, so shall it be with all of you. My purpose has been fulfilled. I must leave you now," Eljon responded flatly, ignoring Sorcha's comments.

"You can't just leave," Liddy said indignantly. "I mean, we need you here."

Eljon looked into her eyes for a brief moment as if considering the consequences of her request, then turned away. "I was born a messenger for such a time as this. I am honored that my message has been delivered in full and that I lived to see this day."

The weathered skin of the wild, red-haired dwarf glowed, and his red hair was now streaked with white highlights.

"The three of you—" He froze mid-sentence, staring catatonically straight ahead.

Ryann glanced over to the unicorn. No one moved for fear of upsetting the dwarf. Just when Ryann was about to say something, Eljon continued, "No, five of you, yes, five, will see the fulfillment of the assurance."

"The assurance?" several mouthed, but only Ryann was heard.

Eljon continued walking directly toward one of the sheer cliff walls.

"Come with us!" Liddy shouted to him.

Surely he's deranged, Ryann thought as the dwarf continued toward the rock wall rising several hundred feet straight up out of the ground. *There's nothing in front of him but rock.*

Their silence was broken by the eerie echoes of Eljon half-singing, half-shouting a Celtic-sounding folk song.

> O worship the King,
> All glorious above,
> And gratefully sing
> His power and His love:
> Our Shield and Defender,
> The Ancient of Days,
> Pavilioned in splendor,
> And girded with praise.

Mesmerized by the tune, Ryann's inkling to warn Eljon that he was going to walk directly into the canyon wall was suppressed. Instead, Ryann looked on with the others in awe as the dwarf never slowed and ended the last note of his song by disappearing into the rock face. Silence ensued as they waited to see if he would return.

Terell spoke first. "Okay, can you say 'freaky'?"

"Terell, this is serious," Liddy said. "Our best connection to what's going on around here is gone now."

"Maybe not," a strong yet kind voice said.

Their attention was immediately drawn back to the white unicorn, still relaxing on his haunches, observing them. There was nothing about him that would warrant their being afraid, yet none of them moved. Ryann looked into the crystal blue eyes sparkling back at him. Then the noble beast took the time to look at each of them. Instead of feeling awkward, Ryann felt like rushing over and throwing his arms around the unicorn with a hug reserved only for those closest to him. None of the others moved, so he willed himself to remain still.

Rising in one smooth motion to his feet, the unicorn said three words, "Come, follow me." Then he turned and walked slowly up the canyon the way they had entered.

The words reached their ears at the same time, yet the simple utterance had a different effect upon each of them.

Ryann's skin tingled with confidence, in a similar fashion to when he was around Gabriel. His fingers wrapped tightly around his staff, and he planted it firmly in the ground in front of him.

Liddy felt the warmth of friendship flowing through her. The image of hugging the leopard, Essy, the last time they were together popped into her head, yet now she felt as if she were the one receiving the hug. Opening her eyes, she realized she had closed them to fully embrace the sensation and looked down to see if arms were wrapped around her.

The three simple words crashed down upon Terell like a tidal wave, breaking open the locked latch on a chest of anger, for which he thought he had thrown away the key. The rage rose from his father deserting his mother and him at an early age. A whirlpool of emotions flooded through him. Pain, shame, and abandonment all swirled around. Then in an instant, the churning waters stopped, and Terell pictured a perfectly still lake with not one ripple on the glassy surface. The sting of desertion was replaced with a sense of belonging—*Come, follow me.*

The image of the white unicorn morphed in Ireth's mind into Aodan, the wise white-haired chancellor who had led Aeliana during its greatest years. A small tear formed in the corner of her right eye as she dwelled on the hopelessness that followed the void of leadership left by Aodan's passing, then trickled down her cheek as new hope blossomed within her.

Ice-cold flames surged through Sorcha's veins as the call to follow echoed inside. Her eyes flickered with the vision of a grassy battle-field as far as the eye could see. An army of Aelianians, all outfitted in various types of white armor, lined one side, with the white unicorn and Sorcha standing out front, leading the march. A great red dragon, a black unicorn, and a sea of gray Hugons and evil creatures awaited them on the far side. She imagined this would be her moment of glory!

Leading them through the familiar surroundings of the canyon, the unicorn didn't look back until they reached the exit. From behind they were able to observe his decisive gait and powerful leg muscles with each step he took. The flowing mane and tail hair was as pure a white as the rest of the unicorn's body. His head unexpectedly swiveled around momentarily, catching them off guard. Instead, they were greeted by inviting blue eyes. To Ryann they revealed a desire for belonging and friendship. Hesitating, they waited for him to speak. When no dialogue began, the unicorn swung his head back around and trotted up the embankment, flinging up sand and gravel as he headed out of the canyon.

No longer in sight, they scrambled up the winding pathway after him.

"Do you think he's left us?" Ryann asked.

Ireth didn't hesitate in her response. "No, everything about him seems very purposeful to me."

"Well, I think it's about time we had a talk," Terell said. "I mean, we're following him, and he hasn't even told us his name."

None of them spoke again, as they focused on maintaining their balance and conserving energy for the steep ascent. The energy expended to follow the unicorn out of the canyon further emphasized the grace and strength with which he had ascended. Ryann reached the summit first, followed quickly by Terell and Ireth. He turned back to ensure Liddy and Sorcha were behind them. Ryann grinned as he watched Liddy climbing up on Sorcha's back for the short flight up to meet them.

"So, Terell, are you ready to talk now?"

Ryann watched Terell's eyes bug out as he whirled around in response to the unexpected comment. Staring back at them in the late afternoon sun, the white unicorn introduced himself as Terell froze silently in place, his mouth hanging open.

"My name is Carwyn."

"What just happened back there?" Ryann asked.

Carwyn's blue eyes sparkled back at them with noticeable pleasure. "I received the blessing of the Word to begin fulfilling my purpose."

"Then," Ireth hesitated thoughtfully, "you are the one foretold in the history books of Aeliana who will liberate every creature?"

Carwyn responded in his smooth, comforting voice. "It is my desire that all creatures would put their loyalty in me, yet I know that not all will choose this path."

Rising well above them, Sorcha entered the discussion. "I was a youngling during the Aodan years and was witness to the changes that took place when darkness first entered Aeliana. It was my hope that I would live to see the day you entered our world. I have seen what evil does to those who embrace it, and I pledge what strength I have and my loyalty to you."

Carwyn's mouth curled upward in a smile before he spoke. "Sorcha, my big friend, you are set apart already for your unwavering acknowledgement and insight, which the Word has given you."

Sorcha bowed her towering, scaly white head low to the ground, closing her eyes briefly. As she rose back to her full height, she addressed Carwyn for the group. "Wherever you go, we will follow."

Carwyn looked into the white dragon's eyes then took a few more minutes to again gaze deeply into each of their eyes before responding. "I can see that your hearts are pure, but your motives are not united. Blessed are the pure in heart, for they will see the Word."

Turning away, Carwyn gallantly trotted in the direction of the Elan River. Ryann didn't hesitate to respond, "Come on, let's go. We can't afford to lose Carwyn like we did Eljon."

CHAPTER 17

The Chosen

PURSUING THE WHITE unicorn ended up being more of a challenge than Ryann anticipated. At the point they seemed close enough to speak, Carwyn would suddenly appear to be just out of earshot. They sprinted briefly, and while he didn't look as though he was moving at a faster gait, he again stayed just out of earshot. It was as if opposite poles of a magnet were keeping them apart.

At last they caught up to him, stopped at the river's edge in front of a small human-looking creature. Ryann led them right up to Carwyn. The unicorn looked up and made a simple introduction, "I would like you to meet Rowan," then a statement of fact. "She will be joining us."

Before they had a chance to speak, Carwyn turned upstream and ambled in the direction of Myraddin.

The slim girl, a head taller than Eljon had been, faced them and smiled meekly. Her auburn hair flowed gently around her pointed ears and seem to reach down to the middle of her back. She wore a simple dark green tunic, which was cinched at her waist with a frayed leather belt. Well-worn leather boots, laced in a criss-cross pattern, covered her legs from just below the knee down. Both her hands gripped a wooden spear, pressed into the ground at her feet.

"Awkward," Terell whispered behind Ryann.

Sorcha cut through the uncomfortable moment by acknowledging the young female and making a suggestion. "Welcome, Rowan. My name is Sorcha. I'm sure we will have time to get to know you when we stop for the evening, but for now I recommend we keep up with Carwyn."

Her green eyes grew wide as she looked up at Sorcha. Her slight smile disappeared as she spoke. "Great white dragon, I am humbled to join such a noble group and vow to strengthen you as best I can."

Glancing around at the onlookers, Ryann thought he detected a questioning scowl from Ireth. She caught him staring and relaxed to her normal unemotional state.

Sorcha assumed the position up front, leading them in pursuit of Carwyn, with Rowan scurrying to join her. Terell and Liddy followed a few feet behind while Ryann maneuvered to join Ireth at the back.

"Is Rowan an elf?" Ryann asked.

Ireth scowled, "Mmpf, don't insult me. Didn't you notice her diminutive stature and eyes set wider apart than normal?" She hesitated briefly, but Ryann remained silent.

"She's a halfling," she spat.

"And?" Ryann asked.

Her eyes narrowed as she lowered her voice and spoke through bitter lips. "They're an outcast race that's half elf and half dwarf. In the years of Aodan when the red dwarves rebelled against the Word and followed Lord Ekron, there were a group of elves from our clan who were enticed by his power and left the light to join darkness. They're shorter than elves due to their dwarf ancestry and retain the mark of their auburn hair as a symbol of their evil past."

"So you'd characterize an entire group because of what they look like?" Ryann asked.

Ireth raised an eyebrow as if bewildered by the question. "Of course."

"Carwyn seemed to trust her. Maybe we should get to know her as an individual before judging her," Ryann suggested.

"Perhaps you can," Ireth stated flatly, "but I won't trust her." Picking up the pace, she raced ahead to catch up with the others. Ryann stayed back, contemplating her words.

They had traveled for only a few minutes when a rhythmic cracking sound resonated over the rushing waters of the Elan River. Ryann was roused out of his deep thoughts over Ireth's bitter feelings toward Rowan. He looked down the river to see Carwyn standing still. The splintering resonance came to an abrupt halt at the same time. Ryann sprinted as fast as he could along the uneven riverbank, passing everyone until he came within a few feet of the unicorn. He slowed to walk for the last few yards. Breathing heavily, Ryann arrived in time to hear the only two words Carwyn uttered to a heavy-set dwarf in front of him.

"Follow me."

Carwyn turned to his followers. "We only have a few hours of daylight left. Up ahead, where the Elan and Pedr Rivers meet, there will be two more creatures to join us. After that, we will be close to our resting place for the night."

Seeing he blocked the dwarf from being seen by everyone, Carwyn stepped to the side and made an introduction.

"This is Garnock, one of the river dwellers. He will be joining us. Welcome him."

As with Rowan, they were left standing awkwardly in front of a new companion. Ryann thought it odd they were expected to make the dwarf feel welcome while Carwyn continued down along the riverbank. The dark-haired dwarf facing them was a stark contrast to the slightly-built halfling. Stringy black hair stuck to his sweaty face and compact, muscular body. His right hand gripped a battle-ax, its head resting on the burnt orange rock at his feet. Chopped wood from a fallen tree lay strewn about, evidence of the cracking sounds they had heard.

Ryann looked into the wrinkled face of the heavily bearded dwarf. Dark circles around his eyes gave them a recessed appearance, with two black pupils peering out from within. His blocky torso was covered in thick, fading black leather. A brown undershirt and pants extended out to his matching black leather gloves and boots. Ryann wasn't sure what Carwyn saw in the dwarf that was worth inviting him to join them, but he wanted to take the lead on introductions this time around.

"Welcome, Garnock. My name is Ryann, and my companions," he pointed to each of them as he spoke, "are Terell, Liddy, Ireth, Sorcha, and Rowan."

"Pleased to meet you," the dwarf grunted in a deep, gravelly voice.

"I'm sure we'll get to know one another better after we stop for the night," Ryann replied. "But for now, I suggest we keep moving."

Somewhat reluctantly, he motioned for the dwarf to join him.

Garnock didn't hesitate, effortlessly picking up his battle-ax and trudging over to join Ryann.

"Lead the way, lad," his voice rumbled from deep in his chest.

His long hair, full beard, and mustache hid most of his face, so it was hard to discern his emotions. Ryann forced a smile before following after Carwyn.

With Carwyn no longer in sight, Ryann was concerned that they had been abandoned. Scanning the natural riverbank pathway ahead of them, there was no sign of the brilliant white unicorn. A slight movement off to his left among some trees caught his attention. Carwyn's head was bent down, tearing at one of the few grass clumps sprouting in the shade of the willows. Ryann was about to call out when the unicorn looked his way and signaled for him to be quiet.

"Shh," he mouthed, before motioning down the river with a nod.

They followed his head motion and were immediately drawn to a flurry of activity at the bend in the river. Large brown shapes whirled in a tumultuous blur, flinging water in every direction as they splashed violently through the river. Ryann squinted and moved his head from side to side trying to determine what was causing all the commotion. Seemingly oblivious to their new audience, the two mountainous creatures ran out of energy and plopped down in the shallow edges of the river. Only then did Ryann recognize them as bulls. Brown and ivory colored horns proudly adorned the top of their wedge-shaped heads. Captivated by their heaving chests as they gaped for air, Ryann jerked back in shock as Carwyn let out a battle cry. A white blur passed in front of him, galloping in full stride toward the two bulls.

Weary from their strenuous antics, the two muscle-bound mammals didn't notice the galloping unicorn until he was almost upon them. Leaping through the air, Carwyn landed in a great splash between the bulls as they struggled to get to their feet and out of the way.

"Hey! What do you think you're doing?" one of the bulls shouted, his face drenched with water.

Carwyn's head reeled backward, all of his teeth exposed as a great laugh roared out from deep within.

Ryann watched the action unfold as if in slow motion. The two bulls looked at one another, scurried out of the water onto the river-bank and prepared to attack. Their eyes narrowed as they lined up their target. Lowering their heads, each of them dug at the sand with their right hooves. Their wet nostrils flared in and out several times, then they charged.

Knee-deep in the river, Carwyn continued laughing; his head tilted upward, giving them a glimpse of his vulnerable, smooth chest. Ryann looked back and forth between the two opponents and saw no possible escape for the unsuspecting unicorn. He gripped his staff firmly and waited until the last possible instance.

"Look out!" Ryann yelled, pushing down on button 4.

A thick wall of water flew up between Carwyn and the bulls, but not in time for the two charging creatures to stop. The others watched in shock as the bulls crashed through the wall, sending a shower of water in every direction. In the drizzling mist that remained, the bulls' heads jerked back and forth looking for their target, but none was to be found. Carwyn had disappeared.

"Are you looking for me?" they heard a familiar voice call out from the other side of the river.

They followed the voice to a smiling unicorn standing on the river-bank completely dry.

Heavy huffing brought Ryann's attention back to the two bulls. Their wet nostrils flared rhythmically in and out in the same cadence as their clenching jaw muscles.

"Friends," Carwyn jovially announced. "I apologize if my abrupt actions startled you. I've been looking for the sons of thunder, Taran and Mellt."

"Uhh, that's us. I'm Taran, and this is my brother Mellt."

Ryann noticed a light blue aura outlining Carwyn's horn as he spoke.

"Almost identical twins," the unicorn said, "except for the birthmarks on your foreheads."

Ryann looked closer at the white splotches on their brown hair as Carwyn explained. "Taran's mark resembles a cloud or thunder, and Mellt, your jagged line is the symbol for lightning."

"That's right," Mellt tentatively answered. "Have we met before?"

"No, but I've watched both of you grow up and have looked forward to this day. Today you have the choice to follow me."

Taran pondered the question, briefly looking from Carwyn to the rest of the followers on the other side of the river, and back again. Nodding toward Ryann and the rest of them he asked jokingly, "Do the rest of them come as part of a package deal?"

"Yes," Carwyn replied.

Mellt shook violently, his drenched hair standing on end as he attempted to dry off. "Well, I was dying of thirst travelling through the desert," he joked. "But after this refreshing bath, I don't think I'll ever be thirsty again."

"Everyone who drinks this water will be thirsty again," Carwyn replied seriously. "But whoever drinks the water I give them will never thirst. Indeed, the water I give them will become a spring of water inside welling up to eternal life."

"We're in!" the brothers answered in unison.

Carwyn smiled, addressing them in a loud, booming voice. "We'll stop for the night just ahead where the three rivers meet."

Keeping true to his previous actions, the unicorn turned and galloped off in the direction of their final destination without looking back.

Ryann welcomed the bulls as they followed after Carwyn. He heard Ireth mutter angrily under her breath as the rest of the group fell in behind them. "What a horde this is turning out to be."

"So, how long have you been travelling with this unicorn?" Mellt inquired.

The lightning-shaped birthmark distracted Ryann as he answered, "Hmm, we met him for the first time today."

"Really?" Taran cocked his head to the side. "Why'd you follow him?"

"There's something different about him," Ryann said. As they strolled along the river, he explained what had happened with the blue moons and the wild, red-haired dwarf.

"This is most interesting," Taran said. "My ancestors passed down stories about the blue moons and how someday they would return."

"I'm more curious about how he could have watched us grow up. I don't think he's that much older than us," Mellt said.

"Yeah, and what does he mean by never thirsting again?" Taran asked.

"In my world we have a Savior who came in an unexpected way," Ryann said. "He talked about living water and how you could drink it and never thirst again. In a way, Carwyn reminds me of Him. Like you, I'm hoping we get more answers tonight."

Ryann glanced over his shoulder. As he suspected, everyone had paired off. Liddy was continuing to walk alongside Sorcha, Terell was laughing at something he had said to Rowan, while Ireth and Garnock walked along with scowls on their faces. There were small groups within the group, and Ryann wondered if they would be able to overcome their differences and really get to know one another. Even

Carwyn, with his majestic stature and peaceful presence, seemed distant. He secretly hoped that somehow everything would work out when they got to their encampment for the night.

"Look! Is that a Pegasus?" Terell yelled.

Up ahead, the rushing waters of the Pedr and Elan Rivers flowed together. On the peninsula of land where they met, Carwyn was talking with a winged horse. From a distance, they appeared as brilliantly white twin horses. A closer view helped identify the distinguishing features of a horn atop Carwyn's head and the wings alongside the Pegasus. Neither turned to acknowledge the large party that traipsed up, partially enclosing them in a semi-circle.

"That's Adain," Ireth whispered to Ryann. "The Pegasi are very rare. In fact, he's the only one I've ever seen."

Looking on, it was apparent something was amiss as the winged horse knelt in front of Carwyn. One wing looked normal and was tucked smoothly along his side. The other wing was bent at an awkward angle. As if reading his thoughts, Ireth whispered to Ryann again, "This is dreadful. His left wing is broken. Dark powers must be at work."

"Why do you say that?"

"The wings of a Pegasus are almost indestructible. It would take an incredible evil to break them."

"Won't it just heal over time?"

"No, Ryann, it is well known in our world that a broken wing on a Pegasus is beyond healing. He will probably never fly again."

Ryann nodded, "That's the way it is with horses in our world. If they break a leg, they never run well again."

As Adain knelt, Carwyn spoke.

"Adain, do you pledge your allegiance to the Word?"

"I do."

"Do you have faith that the one who sent me can heal you?"

"I do."

A blue aura slowly intensified around Carwyn's horn. One by one he gazed into the eyes of each individual creature around him.

"So that all of you may believe," he announced to them, and then turned back to Adain and continued, "and because of your faith, you are healed!"

Carwyn nodded, touching the broken wing with his glowing blue horn. For a moment, nothing happened, then Adain's wing began glowing with the same blue luster. Each feather along his wing fluttered with life as the attaching bone snapped back into alignment.

Ryann cringed with the loud cracking noise, yet the Pegasus maintained his humble bow, showing no sign of pain.

"Spread your wings and fly," Carwyn said.

Adain rose up on all four legs, tentatively flapping both wings. Squinting his eyes tightly, he cautiously flapped them, rising thirty feet in the air. Looking down, a mighty "Yes!" erupted from deep inside as he bolted heavenward.

Ryann enjoyed the air show as the rejuvenated Pegasus tested his wings with a variety of maneuvers. Dropping out of the sky, he made a soft landing in front of Carwyn. Adain bowed and proclaimed, "My allegiance is to you and you alone."

"Come, follow me."

CHAPTER 18

Tree of Life

ARWYN AND ADAIN led the way as they traveled the short distance to the ford of the Pedr River. Ryann was encouraged as the mood slowly changed from one of subdued hesitation to excitement and hope as they trailed behind the unicorn and Pegasus. Coming to a stop at the V in the river, Carwyn waited for the rest of their party to gather and then announced, "We'll sleep here tonight."

As Carwyn gave each of them tasks—to find bedding, fetch water, or gather firewood—feelings of gratitude welled up inside of Ryann. Many times when asked by his parents to do chores of less magnitude, he resented it and became irritated. With Carwyn it was different, and he wondered why as he scoured the area of twigs and dead sticks. Carrying an armful of wood back to the camp area, he surmised that it was one of two things: either being on an adventure and part of a team, or possibly his actions conveyed that he had more respect for the unicorn. Feeling a tinge of guilt, he dropped his gatherings into a growing pile in the middle of their camp and distracted himself by looking for Terell.

Gentle flames swayed in a rhythmic dance above the burning pile of firewood they had gathered. The glow emanating from the fire reflected off of each watching face. Outside the ring, the darkness was held at bay. Ryann looked around the circle, noticing that in addition to Carwyn, Liddy, Terell, and himself, there were seven

Aelianians. His mind worked in numbers, and he wondered if there was significance to the number eleven.

"Friends," Carwyn began, "it has been a long day." Having finished dinner, they were reclining and basking in the glow of the fire, but Carwyn's clear and purposeful voice had them all shifting to a more attentive position.

"You are not here by chance. I saw each of you long ago, and you were chosen for a specific purpose. This evening marks the beginning of a lifetime journey, a quest for which there will be no turning back. While I have chosen you, you in turn must also choose to follow me. Today no tribulation, hostility, or persecution arose for following me, but in the future, all of these things will happen."

Ryann had the urge to look around and see the reaction of the others, but he didn't dare take his eyes away from Carwyn and the seriousness of the moment. Deep inside he was convinced that Gabriel's task to find the shield was somehow linked to Carwyn. At the first opportunity he could get him alone, Ryann would ask the question.

Carwyn paused, allowing his weighty words to permeate within each of his listeners. "When you come to a divided path, you must choose to go right or left. You cannot choose to go down each one simultaneously. So, I ask you again tonight, Will you follow me?"

An ember popped during the brief silence before Garnock grunted out his one-word reply, "Aye!"

Taran and Mellt chimed in with a hearty "aye," followed by a chorus of "yeahs" and more "ayes."

Carwyn bowed his head in a gracious nod. "Welcome. From this day forward, these three humans and these seven creatures of Aeliana will be known as the Chosen. With this privilege will come great responsibility."

"Ahem!" Garnock cleared his throat with a loud, guttural hack.

With all eyes focused on the gruff, hairy dwarf, he shifted uncomfortably. Recognizing his apparent gaffe, he was slow to continue. "Err, your sireship—"

A few stifled snickers escaped.

"—and other noble creatures," he nodded skeptically around the circle before returning to Carwyn, "uhh, what exactly will this great responsibility be?"

The flickering flames lapping outward to push back the darkness revealed ten solemn faces eagerly awaiting the answer from Carwyn. Blinking a few times as if to clear a distracting memory, the great white unicorn rose up slightly and addressed them.

"Happiness is fleeting. It is an outward emotion, which can lure you at innocent moments into a desire to pursue its temporary pleasures at all costs. Your ultimate well-being comes from inclusion in the kingdom of the Word. Joining those ranks is worth everything. This fire will slowly burn out tonight as we sleep, but I am confident the breath of life I impart to you will burn eternal. You will be a light to Aeliana and the yet-to-be-discovered realms of this world. A fire like this burns brightly and we gather around for its warmth and protection from the darkness. In the same way, you must let your light glow before every creature, so that they will see your good character and praise the Word. This is the great responsibility."

"Wise teacher?" Sorcha interrupted.

"Yes."

"Does every creature include the Hugons?"

"You mean the one whom you froze today?" Carwyn asked.

The white dragon lowered her head shamefully, then recovered. "Wait? You saw that?"

"Yes," Carwyn answered with a grin, then continued. "Sorcha, my beloved friend, all creatures of every race are children of the Word.

Many have lost their way and no longer acknowledge that He even exists. Admittedly, as we look at His creation, it is hard to believe that so many could be so blind, but that is His calling. He has chosen you to be His messengers. The Word does not seek to force His will on anyone."

"I was born with this breath of ice. Is there never a time to fight against evil?"

"Ah, Sorcha, do not misunderstand, nor the rest of you, there is a time for everything, and a season for every activity under the heavens. There is a time to be born and a time to die, a time to kill and a time to heal, a time to weep and time to laugh, a time to love and a time to hate, a time for war and a time for peace."

Ryann observed the discourse between the wise dragon and the unicorn with great interest. Leaning forward, he started to ask a question, but Sorcha interjected first.

"So, the Word says there is a time to kill and to hate?"

"Everything is judged by the intentions of the heart. The difficulty creatures have with this is that many things done out of seemingly pure motives may not be in keeping with the will of the Word."

"How can we know His will?"

Carwyn nodded in the direction of Ireth. "The elven clan has recorded the annual messages from the Word, have they not?"

Sorcha nodded.

"And now, He has sent me to be with you."

Again Ryann thought to ask a question, his hand involuntarily lifting off his lap as he was conditioned to do in a classroom setting when he wanted to be called upon by the teacher. Looking around at the others, he thought better of it and willed his hand to stop, lowering it again into his lap.

"What?" Liddy whispered, noticing the movement of his hand.

"I was going to ask him about the shield, but I'm not sure if it's something everyone else should know about."

Ryann turned his attention back to Carwyn, who was gazing back at him. He shifted uncomfortably as the unicorn announced, "We have a long day ahead of us tomorrow as we head toward the Tree of Life. It is time to rest."

Ryann thought it remarkable neither the Enlightened nor the Hugons stopped their large group on their way around Lake Penwyn to the Tree of Life. At times dark shadows appeared to loom larger than normal, but he never caught sight of anything recognizable. Reviewing the numerous stops they had made along the way, he tried to make sense of it all.

He had stopped for a beaver, whose two prominent front teeth were badly chipped. Rumors had traveled quickly about a Pegasus wing being healed, and the beaver sought Carwyn out to restore his teeth.

Remarkable, Ryann thought, grinning to himself and shaking his head as he recalled Carwyn's horn producing that wonderfully soft blue aura and gently touching the mouth of the wide-eyed beaver. One second the teeth were chipped, and in a blink of an eye they were perfectly new again!

Several more healings came to mind—a panther's hip out of place, a faun's food poisoning, an open wound on a gazelle, and even a hyena's laugh. *They all seem to have one thing in common—they believe He will heal them. No one is being turned away, no matter how small or insignificant they appear to be on the outside. He's treating them all the*

same. What will he do at the Tree of Life, and how does this all fit into
Gabriel tasking me to find the shield?

From a distance the most famous living memorial in Aeliana
emerged as a lone tree deceptively similar in size to those they were
currently passing. The illusion changed as the gap closed, and the
normal trees seemingly shrunk, appearing like bushes in comparison to this symbol of strength and common heritage.

"Man, I think this tree is even larger than when we last saw it,"
Terell said. "I mean, it was big back then, but now—"

"Yeah, I know what you mean," Liddy said. "It does appear larger,
but I'm more concerned about its health."

"What do you mean?" Ryann asked.

"Well, look at it," she replied.

Large, oval-shaped fruit hung from the drooping branches. Some
of them were a vibrant shade of pink, while others were black or a
mixture of black and ash gray.

"I think those are quants," Ryann said.

"Say what?" Terell answered with a scowl.

"The fruit on the tree," Liddy explained. "They're called quants.
Ryann and I ate one at the Feast of the Word. Quite tasty actually, but
they're supposed to be that pink color, not black. My guess is that the
tree is sick."

"Okay, Mother Nature, thanks for the analysis," Terell quipped.
"Let's see what Carwyn has to say about it."

The Chosen gathered around the base of the tree while Carwyn
addressed them with his back to it. "My friends, no good tree produces
bad fruit, nor does a bad tree produce good fruit. You wouldn't pick
oranges from thorn bushes or grapes from briers. A good creature
says good things out of the good stored up in his heart, and the evil

creature says evil things out of the evil stored up in his heart. That which the mouth speaks is simply overflowing from the heart."

The twin bulls snorted simultaneously, and Mellt spoke out, "Wise one, what about the Tree of Life you are standing in front of? It appears to have both good and bad fruit?"

"The Word planted this tree to represent the life that Aelianians could have in a relationship with Him," Carwyn replied. Then he asked, "Has it always had both the good, pink fruit and the bad, black fruit?"

Taran answered, "No, it's been passed along from generation to generation that the tree's fruit began changing when evil entered our world. Isn't that true?"

"That's correct," Carwyn replied. "This tree is symbolic of every individual creature in Aeliana, reflecting the condition of their heart. Watch out for deceptive leaders. They come to you in sheep's clothing, but inwardly they are ferocious wolves. By their fruit you will be able to recognize them. While this tree represents all the creatures of Aeliana, individually a good tree cannot bring forth bad fruit and a bad tree cannot bring forth good fruit. In the end, every tree that does not bear good fruit will be cut down and thrown into the fire."

One of Ireth's eyebrows rose slightly. "Does that mean that in the end, not everyone will become pink fruit, err, good?" Ryann noticed her quick glance toward Rowan.

As he spoke, Carwyn's gaze moved among his chosen. "Not everyone who says I am their prince will enter the kingdom of the Word, but only the ones who do the will of the King, who is ruling there. There will be many creatures who will claim to have taught others about me, fought demons, and performed magic in my name. I will tell them plainly, 'I never knew you. Away from me, you evildoers!'"

Finishing his monologue, a great silence settled over the group. Pondering his prophetic words, Ryan didn't dare to move and break the somber moment. A black quant fell from a branch high above, crashing through the limbs below and landing with a wet splat that oozed a black nectar onto the ground.

Liddy gasped.

The unicorn turned away from them. A blue aura swirled around his horn as he leaned forward and touched the point to one of the black quants hanging on the tree. Immediately it transformed to a perfectly ripe, pink quant.

Carwyn turned to face them again. "Yes, there was a time when all of the fruit was good, which is the way the Word designed it. Then, as you said, Taran, evil entered Aeliana, and many chose its wide path versus the straight and narrow path provided by the Word. Now all fruit is born black."

His strong neck turned, and his horn, which no longer glowed, pointed toward the pink fruit. "There is the opportunity for it to change, just as there is the opportunity for all creatures to be transformed."

Rowan's eyes darted back and forth between Ireth and Carwyn. Curling and uncurling her hands several times, she finally asked, "So, will we all have that opportunity?"

Carwyn smiled, "You have already chosen by answering the call to follow me. A creature that trusts in me is like a tree firmly planted by the water. It does not fear when heat comes. Its leaves are always green. It has no worries in a year of drought and never fails to bear fruit."

Ryann pondered what he was hearing. *So much of what he says sounds like what I've read in the Letter to the Romans in my Bible: "Sin came into the world through one man, Adam, and then death spread to everyone because all have sinned." Who exactly is this Carwyn?*

CHAPTER 19

Phantasm and Faith

R YANN OPENED HIS eyes to a heavy fog blanketing the grass field surrounding the Tree of Life. Liddy and Sorcha slept off to his right, while Terell and the bull brothers dozed on his left. The others were scattered around in ones and twos as dark lumps covered in the gray mist.

Where's Carwyn? Jumping to his feet, he walked away from the tree toward the distant roar of Glenys Falls. *Surely he didn't leave us.*

The haze grew thicker. Looking down, everything below his knees had disappeared in the dense fog. Hesitating, he cocked his head and listened again for the sounds from the crashing waterfall to give him some sense of direction before continuing.

"Ryann," a faint voice called to him from within the mist ahead.

"Carwyn?"

"Come, follow me."

"Carwyn, is that you?" Ryann asked.

"Follow me and I will give you the desires of your heart."

The voice came from up ahead. It was clearer now. Ryann felt like a blind man as he ran through the fog. Even with his eyes wide open, he could see only white. His feet hit something. *Is it a log?* he thought as he pitched awkwardly forward, landing in a heap. Struggling to his feet, he was surprised to see his legs clearly now. The fog was lifting.

Wispy streaks of white and gray replaced the thick cloud-like fog around him. Turning to see what he had tripped over, Ryann let out a gasp. *Garnock?* The river dwarf lay face down in the grass like a felled log.

"Ryann," the voice called from behind, "follow me."

He spun around, a warm glow spreading through his body at the approaching outline of a unicorn coming through the thick mist ahead of him.

"Carwyn! Thank goodness you're—"

Ryann's mouth dropped open at the sight of Narcissus strutting into the open. His eyes glowed red. "I am where the true power rests, Ryann," he said confidently. "It's me you want to follow."

Shock still overpowering his expectation of Carwyn, he barely got out one word. "Never!"

The large black beast swung his head to the left, then right, as if looking for something, and then returned his attention to Ryann. "Very well. We all make choices we must live with," he paused, a grin crawling up both sides of his mouth, "and die with!"

Dark figures approached on either side and behind Narcissus as the mist cleared. Hundreds of dragon-men clad in leather armor stood at attention with spears in hand.

A shiver ran down Ryann's spine. *Hugons!*

"He's made his choice," the dark unicorn announced to his small army. "Take him!"

Ryann's first thought was to blast them with his staff, but then he realized he wasn't carrying it. *I must have left it back at the tree.*

He turned. Garnock's body was gone! Narcissus's laughter coursed through Ryann's soul as he began sprinting back in the direction of the tree and safety. He had to warn the others!

The harder he ran, the slower he felt. The fog began moving in again. *Was it more to the left? Or right? It has to be just up ahead!*

He burst out of the fog into a clearing surrounding the Tree of Life and stopped in his tracks in disbelief. Narcissus was standing in front of the tree, his red eyes glowing.

It's not possible!

"You look surprised, mortal," the midnight-black unicorn sneered.

Ryann glanced up into the tree branches. Every quant was black except for one.

"The tree! What did you do to it?" Ryann shouted.

"Black is such a beautiful color," Narcissus said, ignoring his question. "Only one more to go, and my mission will be complete."

Turning his attention to the one ripe quant without a single blemish or discoloration, the unicorn thrust his horn through it. A sickening squishy, wet sound filled the air. For a moment, except for the hole gored through it, the quant remained a pinkish-orange. Then from the horn outward black decay crawled slowly over it until the entire quant was dark.

Ryann watched the event unfold in a trance of terror, his emotions boiling up into one vacuous scream. *Noooo!*

Ryann sat up straight, eyes darting left and right. He gasped for air. He could feel his damp hair matted to his forehead. He looked

down at the goose bumps dotting his arms. His clammy-looking
skin made him feel sick to his stomach. The gray light indicated it
was early morning. Lying back down, he took a moment to view his
surroundings. Everyone was still sleeping.

It was only a nightmare! His heart still racing, he took a deep
breath and exhaled slowly. *It all seemed so real. Narcissus, the army of
Hugons, the tree. Where was Carwyn?*

Carefully scanning around the camp, he accounted for everyone
else. Movement at the edge of his peripheral vision grabbed his attention. Turning in that direction, he saw Carwyn standing off to the
side of the Tree of Life. Ryann looked up into the tree, estimating
that half the fruit was black and half appeared normal. He shifted his
attention back to Carwyn, who swung his head away, indicating his
desire for Ryann to join him.

Silently, Ryann rose from his makeshift bed and stepped gingerly
through the campsite to avoid waking anyone. Carwyn had already
sauntered off ahead of him. Increasing his walk to a slow jog, he
caught up and blurted out, "I had a horrible nightmare!"

"That is not surprising."

"Really?" Ryann questioned. "Why not?"

"The Tree of Life has been imbued with a source of spiritual
energy by the Word. There is a great deal of mystery that surrounds
it. You have been sleeping nearby, and while it seems to be sending
you messages, evil is intent on stopping it."

Walking so close to the white unicorn for the first time washed
Ryann in waves of peacefulness. He didn't want the feeling to go
away. Carwyn maintained his pace as Ryann peered into the one blue
eye he could see.

"Is my dream going to come true?"

Carwyn continued a few more steps, then came to a stop at the edge of Lake Penwyn. The panoramic view of the cascading waters of Glenys Falls was a glorious sight to behold.

"Ryann, some dreams are symbolic, some are caused by inner turmoil or excitement, and others do indeed come true."

"Which one is this?"

Carwyn turned and looked directly into Ryann's eyes for the first time since they had left the camp. The blueness was so deep and comforting that Ryann felt as if his previous worries were no longer important.

"All three play a part in the dream you had."

"Wha—"

"Ryann," he interrupted, "never forget that faith overcomes."

Ryann started to respond, then thought better of it and again turned to look across the lake to the falls. Standing side by side, Ryann admired the view until he was reminded of Gabriel's task.

"What about the shield? Gabriel told me to seek the shield of faith."

"Ryann, everyone has his own journey through life. They must experience their own trials and struggles, successes and failures. I can't tell you where the shield is, but I can tell you what everyone needs for true success in their journey."

"What's that?" Ryann asked, still casting his view across the water.

"The Word will save you from the fowler's snare and from the deadly fangs. He will cover you with His feathers, and under His wings you will find refuge. His faithfulness will be your shield and rampart."

Ryann turned his attention back to Carwyn. "I...I'm not sure I understand."

Carwyn continued, "Let me put it this way, if you have faith in the

King, then no harm will befall you. He will command His angels to guard you in all your travels. They will lift you up in their hands so that you will not endure permanent injury. You will beat down the fanged flyers and the dark army. And you will trample the evil hoofed one and the red dragon."

"All this by seeking the shield, or faith in the Word?"

"The shield and faith are joined together. You cannot separate one from the other. Right now you might not be able to fully understand this, but in time you will. Now, before the others awaken, let's return. Today we enter Myraddin."

CHAPTER 20

Creatures and Cretans

I'M TELLING YOU I don't trust her," Ireth whispered to Ryann. Glancing over his shoulder, he smiled at Terell and the bulls, who engaged in their own conversation.

"Why not?" Ryann whispered back.

"Because," she hesitated, "she's a halfling."

"And—"

"And what?" she seemed surprised.

"And why can't we trust her?"

"Because she's a halfling," Ireth whispered more emphatically. "I told you this before. Everyone knows that you can't trust halflings."

"Okay, let me make sure I have this right. A halfling is a creature who is half elf and half dwarf."

She nodded.

"And they can't be trusted because they come from two different races, one of which is yours but the other's ancestry was part of a rebel dwarf tribe hundreds of years ago?"

"Yes!" She smiled. "Now you've got it."

Ryann continued walking silently alongside her, trying to relate her comments to people back home.

"What?" she asked, noticing his questioning demeanor.

"Well, I've been taught not to characterize an entire group of people, err, creatures, but to evaluate each individual based upon his or her actions."

"That's naïve," she said. "What about the Hugons? Every one of

177

them is raised to follow Narcissus and at an early age pledges their loyalty to him and him alone. Do you trust them?"

"Hmm, that's a good point. I hadn't thought about it that way. But I'm still not convinced you can assume all of them are bad."

"So, you'd wait until you have one of their claws gripping you around the neck before arriving at your conclusion?" Ireth asked. "It's a little late then."

"I suppose." He considered her reasoning. "I'm going to have to think about this more. Maybe I'll get to know Rowan a little better and then give you my final thoughts on the matter."

"Suit yourself, but I'm sure you'll come to the same conclusion."

"We have company," Liddy yelled back from the front of their procession.

Slowly they bunched together behind Carwyn and Adain as they stopped. A broad-shouldered stag with antlers jutting up in multiple points stood before them. Bowing his head so that the tip of his horns touched the ground, he paused respectfully, then rose again.

"Noble one, my youngest lies at home in terrible pain and on the verge of death."

Ryann had that feeling he got when a beggar came alongside his parents' car back home. He crossed and uncrossed his arms, not sure what to do with himself. Looking toward the others, each of them was avoiding eye contact with the stag, waiting to see what Carwyn would do next.

"What is your name?"

Moisture gathered in the sturdy buck's eyes. "Javell," he replied, fighting tears.

"Take me to your home, and I will heal him."

"Majesty, I do not deserve to have you come under my roof. But just say the word, and I know my son will be healed. I have authority over many creatures as an officer in the Aeliana Army. If I give one of my soldiers a command, they do it. I believe you can do the same."

Carwyn's ears perked up as he took a step back. Looking to the Chosen gathered around him, he spoke. "What you are witnessing now is the greatest faith I have seen anywhere in Aeliana." Carwyn turned back to the buck. Gazing directly into his face, he replied with authority, "Go! Your son will be healed, as you believed he would."

"Thank you, sire." The buck bowed his head again. A comforting smile spread across his face. Turning away, he bounded towards the woods and out of sight.

Carwyn turned his attention to the Chosen. He looked from creature to creature. Every face revealed varying degrees of amazement and admiration. Ryann watched him stop on Terell and wait.

"You have something to ask me, Terell?"

"Y–ye–yes," Terell stammered. "I be–believe y–you can heal me too."

Tears dripped down Terell's face as he looked into the unicorn's face.

Carwyn smiled and touched Terell's head with his horn. "Your faith has healed you."

Terell's eyes brightened. "Thank you!" he cried. "Thank you!"

Ryann and Liddy rushed over and hugged their friend. Terell leaned close to Ryann and whispered, "I saw the blue aura."

"It is always appropriate to celebrate great faith," Carwyn said, "but now I need you to gather around and sit. I want to talk to you before we enter Myraddin."

They settled down on the grass alongside the worn pathway. Again Carwyn took his time looking at each of them before speaking. Ryann sensed Carwyn was judging his heart through his eyes.

"How do you gain the inheritance of eternal life and enter the kingdom of the Word?"

Silence.

Turning his gaze toward Ireth, Carwyn asked, "What is written in the books your people keep? How do you read it?"

Ireth didn't hesitate. "All elves of my clan are required to begin reading the books as young elflings. It says to love the Word with all your heart and with all your soul and with all your strength and with all your mind and love your fellow creatures as yourself."

"You have answered correctly," Carwyn replied. "Do this, and you will live."

Ireth grinned knowingly.

Carwyn continued, "And Ireth, who are your fellow creatures?"

Confusion betrayed her normally composed face. She replied, "It would be those who live around you. Those you care about."

All eyes returned to Carwyn, awaiting the confirmation of her answer.

"Let me answer you in a story, Ireth. There was an elf who was travelling from his home to Myraddin by way of a seldom used path through the Marrow Mountains. While walking through a narrow passageway, he was attacked by thieves, who took all his possessions, beat him, and left him just off the pathway in the high grass, dying. A scholarly elf from another clan came along a little while later and saw him lying there bleeding. Looking about nervously for the ones who had committed this atrocity, he pulled out a small dagger to defend himself and hurried on his way.

"Soon after that an official of the forest dwarves passed through the same passageway and heard the elf groaning off in the brush. Aware that he was required to be at an important meeting of the forest council, he quickly looked away and convinced himself that he must have imagined hearing something.

"Lastly, a halfling passed by, and upon seeing the elf in his vulnerable condition, he took pity on him. Reaching into his leather pouch, the halfling pulled out one of his shirts, tore it into strips for bandages, and tended to the elf's wounds. With great effort he helped the elf get to the closest village, sought medical attention from the village doctor, and purchased a room for him at a lodge. The next morning, while the elf was resting, the halfling took out several silver coins and gave them to the innkeeper. 'Look after him,' he said, 'and when I return I will reimburse you for any extra expenses you may have.' Which of these three do you think was 'a fellow creature' to the elf who fell into the hands of robbers?"

Ireth did not hesitate. "The one who had mercy on him."

Carwyn smiled and nodded. "You should do likewise."

Ireth locked eyes with Ryann. Face flushing a light pink, her eyelids shut as she lowered her gaze.

"Now, let us rise and go. It's time to enter Myraddin," Carwyn said.

Heads turned at the eclectic band of sojourners making their way through the cobblestone streets. Unicorns, Pegasi, and dragons were rare sightings on their own in Aeliana, let alone one of each parading through the center of the capital city. Onlookers rushed door to door in an attempt to be the first to spread the news. Within minutes of entering Myraddin, the Chosen found themselves joined by city-dwellers curious about their intentions. Three Hugons joined the impromptu parade as a fourth raced toward the castle.

"This should be interesting," Terell said, guarded on either side by Taran and Mellt like a witness under protective custody by the Secret Service.

"Don't worry, we're ready for any trouble that might come our way," Taran replied, winking at his twin.

"Where do you think Carwyn's headed?" Ryann asked Sorcha.

"My instincts tell me the cathedral next to the castle. It would be in keeping with his love for the Word."

Ryann glanced back at the hundreds who were following them. Hugons intermingled with otherwise eager and joyous faces. "I hope he knows what he's doing."

"This will be a test of his leadership," Sorcha nodded, "but I have the feeling Carwyn is more than prepared for it."

Ryann looked up. Dark clouds drifted towards Myraddin from every direction. The cheering throngs were either ignoring the thunder or they were so caught up in emotion the darkening skies were blocked from recognition. Passing the castle, he noticed a red glow high up in one of the turret windows. A black form moved in front of the flickering light, and then it disappeared.

The cathedral was indeed their destination. They traversed the granite steps to the entrance platform. Carwyn directed them to split up, five on the left and five on the right. Liddy, Sorcha, Adain, Ireth, and Garnock were on one side; Ryann, Terell, Taran, Mellt, and Rowan were on the other. Turning to face the crowd, they were stunned to see the parade of one hundred or so following them had grown into a crowd of several thousand. The roar of the crowd crashed around the city square like turbulent rapids. Overcast skies blocked out the sun entirely as Carwyn stepped forward. The crowd hushed when he closed his eyes.

Ryann watched Carwyn's lips moving as the light blue aura glowed around his horn. "Do you see it?" he whispered to Terell.

"What?"

"His horn glowing."

"What?"

"His horn!" Ryann raised his voice. "It's glowing. Can't you see it?"

"No, it looks like it usually does."

Light poured down from above. The Chosen and the crowd looked into the sky in time to see the clouds being pushed back.

Ryann looked back at Carwyn, whose eyes were shut, lips moving. His back was to the sky. The dark clouds surrounded the city like an attacking army laying siege. Within the town, sunshine beamed down from an untainted blue sky.

"Fellow Aelianians!" Carwyn began.

The crowd looked on expectantly.

"There was a time when Aeliana was perfect. No sickness, no death, no suffering. Everything was alive. Flowers had smells you could taste. Biting into a piece of fruit would send tingles coursing through your body. Chancellors governed with integrity."

Murmuring rolled across the creatures nodding their heads in agreement.

"Then the dark day came. Evil made its way into your midst. Some of your ancestors embraced this evil, while others rejected it and continued in the way of the Word. Chancellor Aodan and the council braved the evil's fury and quelled the immediate threat, yet it only went into hiding. It never died."

"We have Narcissus!" a skeptical voice yelled from somewhere in the throng.

"He has replaced Aodan as our king!" another agreed.

Ryann listened as a second wave of muttering washed over the creatures below them. Picking out individual faces, some were smiling and others were angry.

A black-cloaked figure stepped out from the shadows of the cathedral door. Coming alongside Carwyn, this official raised his arms to the crowd. From behind Carwyn, Ryann could only see the dark, scraggly hair reaching down just past the creature's shoulders. The pale white skin of his hands extended out from the long sleeves of his baggy robe.

"Aelianians!

The crowd calmed.

"As bishop of Myraddin, I believe it is our duty to know more about our friends, who have obviously come here peacefully."

Sweeping his arm to one side as if to officially present them to the town, the bishop glared at each figure. Waving his other arm through the air toward Ryann's side, the bishop took his time to stare deeply into their faces.

Ryann looked into the face of the bishop and was taken aback. He had expected someone much older. Instead, a middle-aged man with dark circles under his eyes, like he hadn't slept for weeks, greeted him. A closely manicured beard and mustache covered the lower half of his face. Half his lip curled upward as he spoke.

"Now then, it's not every day we are graced by the presence of a unicorn, Pegasus, and dragon. Who are you?" he asked.

"If you mean the name given to me at birth, it is Carwyn."

"Well, Carwyn, I am Bishop Dolek. Let me continue your history lesson," he announced to the crowd. "After Aodan, there were many chancellors. At one point, rogue assailants began attacking the citizens. Possibly this was due to the evil you speak of. One creature stepped in to put an end to the chaos and restore order. His name is Narcissus."

Cheering erupted from the onlookers until the bishop raised his hands. "Look around you. Narcissus has rebuilt Myraddin into a strong fortress. Aeliana is great once again. And what say you?"

Cheers and clapping erupted from the crowd.

Carwyn waited patiently for the noise to die down. "Unless the Word builds the castle, its builders labor in vain. In frustration you wake up early and stay up late, toiling in your own efforts, but the Word grants rest to those He loves."

"And why wouldn't the Word love us?" Dolek replied. "We strictly enforce the laws and follow the rules He gave us!"

Carwyn looked into the eyes of the bishop as he spoke, "You honor the Word with your lips, but your heart is far from him. Your worship is in vain because your teachings are creature-made rules."

Turning his back to Dolek and facing the crowd, Carwyn continued, "Be wary of leaders who put their agenda before the Word, those who seek to control you with a system created to set you free. My friends, do not be afraid of those who can kill the body and after that can do no more. Fear him who, after the killing of the body, has power to throw you into the pit of fire. Whoever acknowledges me before others, I will acknowledge before the Word and His army of angels. Whoever disowns me, those creatures will be disowned before the Word and His angels."

"Outrageous!" Dolek seethed, his pale skin prickling into a pink rash. "Who are you to make such outlandish statements?"

Murmuring rumbled through the crowd.

"I am the way, the truth, and the life," Carwyn replied, "and no one comes to the Word, except through me."

"Ahh!" Dolek yelled, grabbing his robe in the center with both hands and pulling it apart.

Screams erupted from the masses. "Seize them!" the bishop ordered.

"Quick. Run to the left!" Liddy yelled.

"No, to the right!" Garnock bellowed.

Ryann looked for Carwyn. *His horn is glowing again!* he noticed.

Carwyn's mouth moved, and Ryann heard the familiar words "follow me" resonating inside his head. Even amidst the chaos, he assumed the Chosen had heard their leader as well.

Carwyn strode down into the crowd, horn aglow. The crowd parted around him. Chaos reigned all around them, yet an invisible hedge pressed outward against it. The Chosen filed behind him, two by two. As Carwyn pressed onward, head high and calm, the masses separated and eventually closed up again as they passed.

Ryann ventured a glance back to the cathedral steps and Bishop Dolek. His eyes flashed back at him, filled with rage. The bishop clenched his jaw so tight that snake-like veins flared out on both sides of his neck. Black clouds rolled in above him, and he vanished in the enveloping darkness.

Like waking from a horrible nightmare, one moment they were in the midst of a crisis and the next they were away yet still shaken from the experience. Shocked and silent, they followed at Carwyn's pace until they were amidst forest trees above Glenys Falls. Wandering into a small clearing, Carwyn stopped and simply said, "Sit and rest."

Ryann looked for the halfling. "Rowan, would you like to get a drink?"

She looked questioningly back at him, then shrugged her shoulders. "Sure."

Heading toward the distant sound of the fall's rushing waters, Ryann and Rowan walked along in increasingly awkward silence.

"That was quite amazing," Rowan finally said.

"Huh?"

"You know, back there in town."

"Oh, yeah."

A small tributary appeared in front of them, and they squatted down to scoop up some water.

"Ryann? What's wrong?"

"How does it feel to be a halfling?" he blurted out.

Her eyes narrowed. Ryann sighed and avoided her stare while repeatedly cupping the cool water into his hand.

"I resent it," she said, "but I've come to an understanding over the years."

"What do you mean?"

"When I was younger, being half-dwarf and half-elf, I was picked on by dwarves and elves. Sometimes it was only words, but other times it turned into a fight."

"Were you ever hurt?"

"Physically? Not really. But," she hesitated, "to be honest, the words hurt the most."

"We're taught a little rhyme growing up," Ryann said. "It goes, 'Sticks and stones may break my bones, but words will never hurt me.'"

"Hmm, whoever says that is in denial," she replied.

"What?"

"Scrapes, cuts, and broken bones will heal and go away. Words don't go away. They stick with you throughout your entire life. They can change the way you view yourself and how you interact with everyone around you."

"How so?" Ryann looked at her for the first time.

A burst of anger flashed in her eyes. "How would you feel if everyone around you made fun of you," her eyes glazed over into a watery pool as she continued, "or ignored you just because of how you looked?"

"Well—"

"Did I have any control over who my parents were?"

"No, I suppose not."

"No! Not at all!" she said angrily. A tear dropped from her eye before she could turn away.

"Rowan, I'm sorry. I really am."

"That's okay, Ryann. You just asked a question. You're normal, so you really can't understand."

He grimaced. "I can't help who my parents are either, Rowan. We're all on a journey, and while I might not be able to fully understand your plight, I can try."

He watched her back rise and fall heavily with each deep breath. "I'm okay."

Ryann placed his hand on her shoulder and patted it a few times. "How did you feel when Carwyn told the story about the injured elf and who our fellow creature is?"

She turned, took his hand between both of hers, and looked into his face. Ryann peered back into her sparkling eyes, still wet from tears, as she grinned.

"At first I was nervous because he was bringing attention to my being a halfling, and I didn't know what he was going to say. Then as he proclaimed the halfling to be the one who did right, I felt comforted. It was like drinking a warm drink on a cold day as the feeling spread through my body. It's hard to explain, but for the first time I felt loved by someone other than my parents."

"Carwyn seems to have that comforting effect on whoever's around him."

"I don't know about that. Bishop Dolek didn't seem very pleased with him." She smiled.

"Ha! You're right about that," Ryann laughed, then blushed when he realized they were still holding hands. Releasing his grip, he pulled his hand back.

"We should probably get back to the others," she said with an awkward grin.

"I suppose you're right."

"Ryann?"

"Yes."

"Thanks for taking the time to walk with me and for getting to know me."

"I'm glad I overcame my nervousness." He grinned.

"Where'd the two of you run off to?" Liddy asked.

"I wanted to get to know Rowan better," Ryann said. "I don't think Ireth understands what it's like not to be accepted. I hope Carwyn's story made an impression on her."

"She went off into the woods with Garnock, who's a full-blooded dwarf, so I'm not so sure."

"What did you think about today?" Ryann asked.

"The town? Pretty wild, huh? I thought we were gonna get attacked."

"Did you see Carwyn's horn glowing?"

"No, when was it doing that?"

"When the black clouds were held back so the sun could shine down and then again when the crowds parted for us to get away. You didn't see that?"

"Sorry, no I didn't. We were all looking at him. I wonder why you were the only one who could see it glow."

"Shh, he's coming out to speak," Ryann whispered.

Again, the Chosen gathered in a circle around their leader, anxiously awaiting what the one who called them had to say. Ryann expected an explanation for the day's events, but instead Carwyn asked them a question.

"Who do the crowds say that I am?"

"I heard someone say you were Aodan reincarnated," Mellt said.

Sorcha spoke up. "I heard someone say that you were a sorcerer using magic to make yourself appear as a unicorn."

"I overheard a Hugon say you were a cursed ghost, banished from the afterlife," Garnock growled.

Carwyn listened, respectfully nodding his head at each one. "And you," he replied, "who do you say that I am?"

Silence.

Ryann's eyes grew large as the blue aura returned around Carwyn's horn. Looking around the circle, he noticed the others' eyes were downcast, avoiding their leader.

"You are the ancient of days...the deliverer of Aeliana!" Ryann blurted out.

Carwyn smiled.

"You are blessed, Ryann Watters, because this was not revealed to you by any creature, but by the Word from above. If anyone seeks to join me, he must deny himself and show complete dedication daily and follow me. For whoever wants to save his life will lose it, but whoever loses his life for me will save it. What good is it for a creature to gain the riches of the world, and yet lose his very soul?"

"Ireth, can I speak with you for a minute?" Ryann asked.

The stoic elf responded in her usual calm voice, "Of course, Ryann, how can I be of assistance?"

"Well, I'm not so much looking for help," he said, sliding his feet back and forth over the ground. "I'm wondering if you had a chance to think about what we talked about before."

"Which is?"

"You know, what Carwyn was talking about. Who your fellow creature is."

"Ryann, that was a good story, but not very realistic."

"Huh?" he looked at her incredulously. "What do you mean?"

"Let me put it to you this way. There are so many different types of creatures in Aeliana with diverse backgrounds, traditions, and beliefs. It would be nice if they all could get along together. But such ideas are pure fantasy."

"How can you say that?" Ryann's voice rose. Ireth glanced off to her left and right, hinting at whom he might be including in their discourse.

"How can you say that," he asked again more softly, "especially when he's here to save Aeliana?"

"Save Aeliana? Is that why you think he's here?"

Ryann felt his face flush with embarrassment as she challenged him.

Ireth patted him on the shoulder. "Ryann, you must remember that we elves are the keepers of the books of the Word. We have studied them from generation to generation and passed this knowledge along. While I believe Narcissus is evil, I also know whoever removes this darkness will do so on the battlefield, not through words."

Ryann shook his head. "I can't believe you think this way. What about the miraculous healings we have witnessed or the power he displayed today over the skies and crowd?"

"Where you come from these may be out of the ordinary, Ryann, but here in Aeliana there are many unexplainable powers. Do you have winged horses, dragons, and elves like me in your world?"

"No."

"Then I would not be so quick to draw conclusions. Carwyn is a noble creature who I believe means well, but the Son of the Word will come with an army of angels, setting up his kingdom again here in Aeliana, as it was in the beginning."

Ryann remained silent and unmoving.

"I do hope that we can remain friends, but if you will excuse me, I am going to make my bed for the night."

Standing in place a while longer, Ryann watched Ireth walk to her resting place. Questions seeped into his mind. *What if she's right? Who is Carwyn, really? What is my part in all of this?*

Deep in thought, he returned to his makeshift bed, walking past Liddy without acknowledging her presence.

Ryann?

"Yes."

Ryann?

"Yes!"

Rolling black and gray mist swirled around him. Turning in every direction, it was all the same. Darkness. Nothingness. "Who's there?"

Hooves galloping in the distance came toward him. He turned to face the sound. Closer and closer it came until a white horn pierced the black veil. *Carwyn!*

"Ryann, I am the way, the truth, and the life. No one comes to the Word but by me."

"Is it true?"

"Don't forget the ring you were given."

Ryann glanced down at his hand. His ring glowed white. Turning back to Carwyn, there was only darkness.

Jerking awake into a sitting position, he tried to focus. A dream; it was only a dream. Looking down at his ring, it was clear. A light caught his attention off to the side. *My staff—the fifth button is lit up!*

Turning in the direction of Carwyn's bed, he searched the ground for the sleeping unicorn. He was gone!

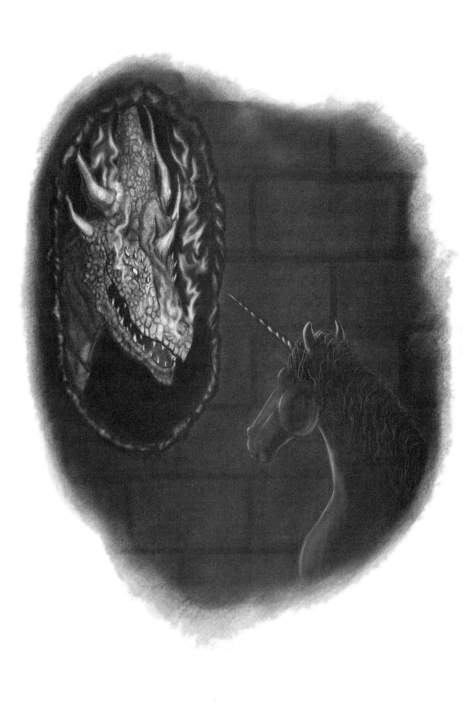

CHAPTER 21

The Dark Lament

THE BLACK UNICORN stared out the window of the west tower, grinding his teeth as the white unicorn led the procession through the streets. He knew his name, Carwyn. He knew his place of birth, Cloverdale. He'd been born to Gensoff and Marryna, two unicorns who met accidental deaths while making their annual trek to Myraddin for the feast. Only it wasn't an accident. A smile crept across his face, relieving the tension in his jaw. He knew everything about this creature that some called the anointed one.

He watched Carwyn lead his small group of followers past the castle. *Who does he think he is, parading through my streets as if he has power or authority over my subjects? I can cut him down with a single command!* Spittle dripped from his mouth onto the floor as he shook his mane. He clenched his jaw harder than before. *There needs to be a plan. Moving too fast will confuse the simple peasants who mindlessly chant their allegiance to me. They don't even realize who they've elevated to the most powerful position in Aeliana. Fools!*

Six large, red candles flickered awkwardly in the drafty, isolated room. Their flames produced eerie shadows dancing along the carved stone walls. *From this vantage point they shouldn't be able to see me.* Peering through the upper window he focused on each of the creatures as they passed. *His followers hardly know who it is they are following. My Hugons and griffins have reported their every move.* "The Chosen." *Ha!* The smile returned.

The white Pegasus and dragon followed close behind the unicorn.

Ahh! I hate white. A Pegasus will garner the town's attention, and Sorcha—won't that meddling fool of a dragon ever go away? She's been a thorn in the side of the Enlighteners for a hundred years!

He paced to one end of the isolated room and back. The sound of his heavy hooves clacking on stone echoed around the room. He paused in front of the candles. Red wax pooled around the diminishing flames as they sank deeper into the hollowed candles. *Blood. Red like blood.* His wet nostrils flared and he felt his breathing hasten.

Dropping his head, he held his horn over the burning flames. At first it was warm, and then it burned. Clenching his jaw, he let the hatred boil over inside. *Pain...blood...red...black.*

Picturing the white unicorn tied to an altar in front of him, he began thrashing down over and over again with his horn, stabbing at the whiteness. *Again, again!*

Hot red globs of wax splattered in every direction. *This feels so good.* One last candle remained upright, the flame sputtering to stay lit. His grin was the largest yet. *So good I can hardly stand it!*

His frantic flailing subsided. Slowly, very slowly, he lowered his horn into the hot pool of red wax. Bubbling redness covered his horn. The wax burned and made him feel alive. *Yes, burn, burn!*

He raised his head and kicked the last upright candle across the room. It splattered against the far wall with a sickening sound, like an over-ripened piece of fruit. Staring across the room, he looked into the full-length mirror. Delivered to the castle when he was a yearling by black dwarves, the ancient mirror had befriended him. The reflective glass was framed in a mysterious wood with an origin no one could trace. It had taught him many things when he was younger but had been dormant ever since.

He looked at the reflection, baring his teeth. Their whiteness disgusted him. *I wish they were fangs, like the bats in the caves under the castle.* His horn was a mixture of swirled red and black. Splotches of red wax covered his mane and torso. *Mmm, it looks like blood. My old teacher would like this.*

Flames burst to life in the cold, woodless fireplace to his right. *Huh?*

"Narcissus!"

That voice. Is it coming from the fire? Within myself? Or both? Would anyone else hear it if they were here in the room? He shuddered. *I like this.*

"Yes, my lord."

"I have work for you."

Yes, it's my old teacher. I could never erase that voice from my memory. How long has it been?

He stared into the fire. The flames shifted, taking shape, morphing into the image of Carwyn and his followers.

"I am not pleased with what is happening in Myraddin today," the voice bellowed. The imagery shifted so he could see the white unicorn addressing the creatures gathered in front of the cathedral.

Hold your tongue, Narcissus, he cautioned himself. *If he wants you to speak he will ask.*

"As you should know, they call themselves the Chosen." One of the ten images burst into flaming fragments and disappeared. "I can sense weakness within them. Some of them are unsure about the one they follow."

A second image exploded, then a third and fourth.

"There is one who can be exploited. I can feel it!"

Five, six, seven, eight. Soon only two were left. He stared at the two images remaining in the fireplace, conscious of his eyes widening and teeth clenching in anticipation.

One of the remaining figures erupted in a ball of flames and into a residue of ash. The last creature grew larger, filling the fireplace.

"This is the one you must focus your efforts on."

Staring intently at the flaming figure, he burned the image into his mind. *I'm going to enjoy this.*

The last shape erupted in a fiery, gaseous ball, leaving behind the cold, lifeless fireplace. A small ash heap was the only proof of the supernatural experience.

"You must lure this one over to our side. I sense vulnerability for the promise of power."

The voice. Where is it coming from?

"Turn around, Narcissus. It's time you met your father, face-to-face."

Father?

Whirling around, he looked into the mirror and took a slight step back.

A red dragon?

Molten-yellow orbs returned his stare. *My father?* Outside of his eyes, jagged spikes dotted the dragon's skull. Flames licked up from his nostrils to the frilled horns on his head.

"You look surprised, Narcissus."

"But how?"

"That is for another time. You are the incarnation of my deepest desires. Rebellion personified in the image of the Word's son. I will give you the power, and you will help me defeat him."

"Yes, father. I am ready."

"Then go!"

Narcissus was left peering at a dim reflection of himself. Overcast light filtering through the half-drawn curtains created an atmosphere of doom.

The fools don't even realize that one of them has been chosen as the betrayer. The wicked smirk returned. *My father is king of this world, and as the prince of darkness I will sit on the throne of darkness and rule it. I will be their worst nightmare.*

CHAPTER 22

Déjà vu

WAKE UP! WAKE up!"
A mixture of groans and "What is it?" greeted him.

"Carwyn! He's gone!" Ryann shouted louder.

More shuffles and groans.

"Everyone spread out and look around the camp," Sorcha directed.

"Maybe he's just gone down to the river," Terell suggested through a yawn, making him barely understandable.

Mellt kicked Taran in the ribs, rousing him out of a deep sleep.

"What? Who? Where? Am I still dreaming?"

Terell laughed. "Nice one, Mellt."

"Anyone see him?" Ryann yelled out again over his friend's antics.

Thirty minutes later, they gathered together in the camp clearing. He could read their faces. Carwyn was gone.

"What do we do now?" Terell asked.

"We can wait," Ryann answered. "I'm sure he'll show up soon."

Ireth muttered something under her breath that sounded like, "Figures."

"What is it, Ireth?" Ryann called her on it. "Do you know something we don't?"

Her eyes narrowed. "I'm sorry if I seem a bit cynical, but I just find it remarkable that our leader chooses to run off in the middle of the night."

"That's quite an accusation without knowing all the facts," Liddy said.

"Liddy's right," Sorcha said. "There's probably a perfectly logical reason why he's not here right now."

"Well, I don't like it," Garnock huffed. "A real leader doesn't desert his troops."

"Troops?" Adain asked. "I didn't realize we were going into battle."

"Mmpf! Well, that's why I'm here—to overthrow Narcissus and his ugly cronies!" Garnock said gruffly.

The dam broke in a flood of indistinguishable voices arguing back and forth over the location of Carwyn and the purpose of the Chosen. Separating themselves as the jousting comments persisted, they faced off as two groups: Ireth, Garnock, the bull brothers, and Terell on one side; and Sorcha, Adain, Rowan, Liddy, and Ryann on the other.

"Quiet!" Ryann yelled.

The shouting drowned him out.

Gripping his staff firmly, he thrust it up into the air in frustration, while simultaneously squeezing the fifth lit button.

"I said quiet!"

A two-foot flame roared out of his staff, hurling a ball of fire skyward.

The whoosh of the flame drew everyone's attention, silencing the argument.

Terell spoke first. "Wicked cool!"

Ryann released the button as the fireball dissipated high above their heads.

"Now, let's discuss this in an orderly manner."

"Sounds good to me," Terell said, "but first tell us when you got the power to shoot a fireball. I haven't seen that come out of your staff before."

Recounting his dreams was his first concern. The power of the staff could wait. It wasn't like Ryann to have nightmares, and he wanted everyone to know about them so he could listen to their responses. There was no way he would have expressed something as personal as a dream back home, but in Aeliana he had a sense that this type of thing wasn't out of the ordinary. When he finished the first dream about Narcissus and the Tree of Life, he barely hesitated before beginning the second dream. It was more pleasant talking about Carwyn, how his ring had turned white, and then the fifth button on his staff lighting up.

"What does it mean?" Ryann asked.

The Chosen from Aeliana turned toward Sorcha.

Ryann overheard Liddy whisper to Rowan, "Why's everyone looking to her?"

"Dragons have a sixth sense known as blindsense. It allows them to see things that are invisible and understand the unreal—dreams, nightmares, visions, that sort of thing."

"That's right. I remember reading about it in *All About Dragons*."

"I can tell you one thing," Garnock huffed, "I don't like the idea of me lying facedown on the ground like a rottin' log!"

A snicker from Terell drew a stern glare from Liddy.

She turned back to Sorcha, whose eyes were now clamped shut.

"How long will it take?" she whispered back to Rowan.

"Who knows? Blindsense is something that's talked about but rarely witnessed."

Sorcha opened her eyes. Her long neck swiveled around, gazing intently at each of them as if looking for something.

"What is it, Sorcha?" Adain asked.

The white dragon spoke solemnly. "I can discern three things from what you've told me. One of us will sacrifice himself to save the others, one of us will save himself to sacrifice the others, and one of us will deny he is a part of us."

"Who?" Ryann blurted out. "When?"

"I'm sorry. I'm at a loss," Sorcha replied. "Normally my blindsense is much clearer, but—"

"But what?"

"Darkness. A murky cloud of darkness and evil is distorting everything."

Heads turned, looking at each other as if they could determine which three of them fit Sorcha's descriptions from some external sign. Liddy verbalized what everyone was thinking. "So, what you're saying is that we have a hero, a betrayer, and a denier among us?"

"That is correct."

"Mmm, that's three out of ten, but I suppose you can't be included."

"That is not knowable. What I do know is that our hero, betrayer, and denier will be responding to evil. When confronted by evil, I know how I want to respond. But until that moment comes, can one ever be totally sure?"

"I can tell you right now," said Terell, pointing to Taran and Mellt, "me and my boys here aren't going to be betraying or denying anyone."

The bulls grinned.

Liddy shot him a dirty look.

Everyone began chiming in at once about his or her loyalty to the Chosen. Ryann quickly cut them off.

"That's enough," Ryann said. "Sorcha, are the things you spoke of certain? Meaning, there's nothing we can do to change the future?"

"The future is both knowable and unknowable," Sorcha responded.

"That's true," Ireth said, adding, "the Word has given us a glimpse of things to come in the books but not all of the details."

"What are some of these glimpses?" Ryann asked.

"The most important one is that in the end, good will triumph over evil and the Word will reign over all," Ireth said.

Sorcha nodded. "We must band together for strength and encouragement in numbers."

Ireth squinted skeptically, "So back to our initial dilemma. Where's Carwyn? Perhaps he is the betrayer and is turning us in to the Hugons as we speak for being disloyal followers of Narcissus."

"Bite your tongue, elf!" Adain snapped. "Carwyn healed me, and I have pledged my loyalty to him. He is not capable of such a thing."

Ireth slumped back at the bristling feathers of the Pegasus. "Perhaps," she muttered.

"Look!" Liddy motioned back to Sorcha.

With her eyes shut, the white dragon was stiff as an ice sculpture.

"Now what?" Garnock asked.

Sorcha's blue eyes sprung open. "Glenys Falls. Something is going to happen. We need to go there."

"Eh? The Falls?" Garnock questioned, his cold demeanor melting. "Sure, why not? At least we have a plan of action now."

"Adain, you fly on ahead and report back. I'd like to know exactly what we're getting into before we get there," Sorcha said.

"Gladly," the Pegasus responded, immediately springing into the air, his great wings extending. With a few short bursts, he was above the tree lines.

Heading toward the sound of rushing waters, Sorcha led the way at a slow, lumbering pace. Ryann quickly glanced over his shoulder and stepped in line next to Rowan. Ireth looked about, impatiently waiting for everyone to fall in line so that she could follow at the end.

Ryann hoped eventually they would all get along. For a time, the Chosen had been energetic and united in following their leader. Now, in a brief period, fissures of dissent and anger opened up, breaking them apart.

One of us will sacrifice himself to save the others, one of us will save himself to sacrifice the others, and one of us will deny he is a part of us. He reviewed Sorcha's words again and again, each of the faces in front and behind him flashing before him.

Who would sacrifice himself to save the others? Sorcha? Yeah, she probably would. Adain? He certainly seems loyal enough. Would he? Ryann wasn't sure how he'd react when the time came.

Who would betray everyone? Ireth came to mind immediately, although he couldn't imagine her going through with it. *Garnock? He appeared gruff enough, but a betrayer?* An image of Terell popped in his head. He had betrayed him back in Mount Dora when Drake threatened to beat him up. He didn't want to believe it could happen, but what if someone or something intimidated Terell again?

Who would deny they even know us, or more likely, that they were a member of the Chosen? He glanced at Rowan out of the corner of his eye. *She certainly is skittish. Not exactly well thought of by the full bloods, Ireth and Garnock.* Ryann pushed the thoughts away. He would get back to it later. For now, he was curious about what lay ahead at Glenys Falls.

Winding along the well-worn path, a familiar clearing would appear and then disappear just as quickly. Ryann had the nagging feeling he had walked this way before. The roar of the falls grew louder and the trail steeper as his mind searched for the moment in time that fit this place. *Raz!* His mind screamed, eyes widening. *This was the same path I followed Raz on to the top of Glenys Falls the first time I came to Aeliana!* He could picture it now. He had tried to keep up with the scampering raccoon racing up the pathway, eager to show him the majestic views from the top of the falls. He smiled at the thought of seeing his first and best friend in the land.

It seems like it was just a few months ago.

Reality and déjà vu collided as his mind wrestled with the fact that he had indeed been here earlier this year, but in Aeliana time hundreds of years had passed. *There was no way Raz could be alive. Raccoons don't live that long, do they? Even in Aeliana?*

A loud bray cracked his daydream, drawing his focus to Adain's arrival. Ryann watched in amazement as Adain effortlessly descended through the blue sky toward them, the great wings of the Pegasus extended fully. It was only as the flying horse tilted forward to land that he noticed the dark ball of hair curled on his back. A small creature clutched at Adain's mane to keep from falling.

Nah, it can't be, Ryan thought. *But it does look like a raccoon! Raz?*

"Adain, my friend, what have you brought us?" Sorcha asked with a grin.

The smallish raccoon sought safety behind Adain's mane, peering through the coarse hair at the huge dragon.

"He says his name is—"

"Raz! My name is Raz, and I can speak for myself," the high-pitched voice answered.

Adain grinned as the self-assured raccoon rose up on his hind legs. "He hasn't stopped talking since I mentioned Ryann, Liddy, and Terell back atop the waterfall. You might as well hear him out."

"Ahem." The raccoon confidently cleared his throat. "I am Raz the Fifth, a proud descendant of my fourth-times-great-grandfather." Focusing primarily on the dropped jaws of the humans, he continued. "The story has been passed down from generation to generation about his adventures in fighting the original evil as it entered Aeliana. He was the first creature in Aeliana to encounter Ryann Watters and was charged by Chancellor Aodan to accompany Ryann into the desert in search of the King's sword."

"Y–you're a descendant of Raz?" Ryann stammered. "I'm Ryann!"

The raccoon's masked eyes widened. Jumping off Adain, he landed softly on his back feet and in one smooth move lowered his head in a deep bow. "It is an honor to meet someone so revered as you." Rising up slightly, he continued, "But how? The story has been passed down that time moves more slowly in your world. But it's been four hundred years. Is that possible?"

"It's true. I'm not sure how, but it is. Time travels much more quickly here. So much has changed since we were here last."

Raz looked to either side of Ryann and grinned. "Then you must be Liddy and Terell."

"We are," Liddy answered. "Do you recall any stories with a leopard by the name of Essy? Well, actually, her real name was Esselyt."

Raz scratched his head. Ryann grinned at the mannerisms, which were so similar to the original Raz.

"Of course, she was in the original stories. I seem to recall that one of my ancestors tried to track her family down, and at some point no cubs were born."

"I hate to interrupt," Sorcha said, "but I sense that we are to continue to the Falls. You are welcome to join us, Raz, and continue your conversation while we walk."

"Thank you." He looked from the dragon to Ryann and back. "I believe I will."

The Chosen continued their ascent to the peak of Glenys Falls. Ryann, Liddy, Terell, and their new friend drifted to the back of the line, eager to get to know one another. With Raz's relentless bantering, it became hard to distinguish the old Raz from his heir.

Having listened to the raccoon's story and then catching him up on what had occurred since arriving, Ryann decided to ask the young creature's advice.

"Now that you're up to speed, what do you think I should do to find the shield?"

Raz continued strolling alongside them in silence for a few moments, then replied, "I'm not so sure you should do anything."

"What do you mean not do anything? I have to do something. Gabriel gave me the first task to find the sword, and I did, and now he's told me to search for the shield of faith!"

"There is a difference between doing and searching, Ryann. Searching requires not only looking on the outside but also looking on the inside."

Ryann's eyes widened. *That sounds so familiar*, he mused.

Liddy interrupted, "Ryann, your ring!"

The line jerked to a halt as her exclamation caused everyone's heads to turn and stare at Ryann's hand. Light blue sparkles radiated from the bubble-topped ring.

"Aww, man!" Terell demanded. "Now what?"

"Blue is for nearby water, and in the past gold was for the portal back and forth," Liddy stated. "But light blue?"

"The falls!" Ryann shouted. "We need to get to the falls. Come on!"

Racing passed the questioning looks from Liddy, Terell, and Raz, Ryann darted around Sorcha and up the path. Overgrown bushes on both sides began narrowing the trail, and soon the dirt path was covered with moss and other foliage. Swatting a few low branches away from his face, Ryann yelled over his shoulder, "Raz! Does anyone travel this way anymore?"

He jumped at the reply coming from almost underneath him. Raz was right on his heels, ahead of Liddy and Terell. "I haven't seen anyone come through here in years. At least, no one from Myraddin.

Lower-travelling creatures like myself don't see a need to keep a wide pathway cleared."

Despite his urgency, Ryann laughed to himself. *That is the same type of comment the first Raz would have made.*

With the sounds of cracking branches and bushes being trampled, he pictured Sorcha's scaly body forcing a wide swath for the rest of the Chosen. Ducking under a large branch, Ryann stumbled forward into the late morning sun. Shielding his eyes, he could see the path ending at the edge of the plateau. Off to his right, the greenish-blue waters rushed over the peak, creating the illusion of being level with the horizon.

"Hold it up! Hold it up!" Raz shouted from Ryann's feet, back at the others. "Or someone's going to get hurt!"

Crack!

Without looking, Ryann knew it was the sound of the last limb he had ducked under being snapped like a twig by Sorcha clearing the way.

"Whoa!" the bulls breathed together as they came alongside Terell.

Light blue sparkles glowed fiercely from Ryann's ring. Turning around to face the Chosen, he announced, "Gabriel said the ring might lead the way, and it led us to Aeliana again. When it did, it was glowing blue like this!" Ryann held the ring up for all to see.

"How exactly did you get here?" Adain asked.

"Through a swirl of blue-and-white mist," Ryann answered. "We walked up a ladder through it."

Heads turned from side to side and up and down looking for the blue swirl. Sorcha's eyes narrowed, and she took a few steps forward, leaping into flight. The focus changed from their surroundings to the flight path of the white dragon as she rose above them, making a wide swing around the falls.

"Here it is!" Sorcha bellowed. "Step forward to the edge of the cliff!"

Sorcha's expansive wings flapped in a rhythmic pattern, holding her in a hovering position a short leap away from the precipice.

Moving forward over the barren rock jutting away from the woods, they lined the edge.

"Look down," Sorcha said.

Twenty feet below, a swirling blue-and-white mist created a sweeping circular pattern that reminded Ryann of the hurricane pictures they would show on television back home during the storm season. One hundred feet below that was Lake Penwyn.

"How do we get through it?" Terell asked, craning cautiously to look over the edge from several feet farther back than the rest.

Liddy scratched her head as she focused on the cascading waters from the falls crashing far below into the lake. "Maybe it's rising up," she suggested.

"I think we're supposed to jump," Ryann said.

"What? Are you insane?" Terell asked.

Ryann smiled at his friend as he looked from the ring on his hand to the swirling aura. He nodded, "Yep. I think it's a test of faith. I mean, we are trying to find the shield of *faith*, aren't we?"

"You got that right," Mellt said.

Taran added, "Yeah, your faith had better be strong, cuz if you're wrong—splat!"

Terell scrunched his face up at the bulls. "Thanks, guys. You've been helpful."

"You're welcome." They grinned at each other.

"Are you serious, Ryann?" Liddy asked.

"I am."

Liddy bit her lip, looking down at the swirling fog and then beyond into the dark waters below.

"Can I make a suggestion?"

"Sure."

"Let's suppose Terell and I go along with your idea to jump off this perfectly safe cliff. Can we have Sorcha and Adain fly below the mist to catch us? You know, just in case?"

"Sorcha! What do you think?" Ryann asked.

Still hovering, his blue eyes flashed in response. "Your faith is strong, and I sense that it's true. Liddy's pragmatic behavior is understandable. Adain and I will fly below to help expand their faith."

"We should go now," Ryann said. "It probably won't stay open much longer."

"You might want to change back into your old clothes," Ireth interrupted. "I've got them here in my satchel."

"Good idea," Terell said. "If we come back in broad daylight, we'd get some crazy looks dressed this way."

Ireth handed the bag to Ryann, who handed out their clothes. He and Terell sprinted into the woods off to the left, while Liddy veered off to the right. The boys were finished first and stood at the edge of the cliff when Liddy ran up and positioned herself between them.

"Ready?" she grinned.

"Ready!" Ryann and Terell shouted.

She grabbed Terell's hand, then reached over and grasped Ryann's staff, since his hand was unavailable.

Adain took to the air, joining Sorcha in flight down below the whirling haze. As they disappeared, Ryann looked from side to side and addressed the remaining Chosen.

"My new friends, I'm confident that we'll see each other again soon. Find Carwyn and let him know what we've done."

Nods of agreement acknowledged his request.

Ryann's eyes lit up as he pulled the staff away from Liddy. "Let me try something."

Peering down into the swirling mist, Ryann tossed his staff through the air into it.

"Are you outta your mind?" Terell asked.

"You see anything come through?" Ryann shouted down to Sorcha and Adain.

"Nothing yet!" Adain yelled back.

Ryann grinned and took Liddy's hand. "Okay! On the count of three. One. Two. Threeeeeee!"

Pulling one another forward, the trio ran a few steps and then jumped off the cliff into the empty space in front of them. Liddy's scream pierced the air as they plummeted together toward the mist. They entered the kaleidoscope of frantic energy swirling around them in a mixture of sparkling blue lights while high-pitched screams escaped from within.

CHAPTER 23

Mount Dora Mayhem

SPLASH!

Water rushed into Ryann's screaming mouth as white bubbles exploded around him. Instinctively he released his friends' hands and clawed at the surrounding water to propel himself to the surface. Ryann gasped for a breath of air as his head popped out of the murky water. He looked around wide-eyed for signs of Liddy and Terell. A full moon glowed in the dark sky, reflecting brightly off the surface of the black water. Liddy's head surfaced first, followed quickly by Terell.

"Oh, my gosh!" Liddy cried. "Are you guys okay?"

Terell spat water out of his mouth and gasped several times before answering. "I'd be a lot better off if I were a fish and could breathe water!"

"He sounds fine to me," Ryann laughed.

Treading water in place, they looked around to see where they had landed.

"Looks like we're back!" Ryann said. The familiar sight of Mount Dora's most famous landmark, the lighthouse on Grantham Point, stood in front of them like a sentinel, proudly illuminating the port of Mount Dora.

"What time is it?" Terell asked.

"If it's anything like our last trips, it's probably about the same time as when we left," Ryann said.

"Remember," Liddy added, "we were at my house, looking through my dad's telescope."

"Oh man, your dad thinks we went inside for a drink," Terell said. "How are we gonna explain this?"

"Come on, let's get out of the water," Ryann said, swimming toward the shore. "We'll think of something,"

Gathering around the base of the small, thirty-five-foot lighthouse, their clothes dripping on the brick pavers, they broke out in laughter at the sight of one another.

"Ha! Nice 'do, Liddy!" Terell joked.

"Yeah, and if you had hair, you'd look the same," she jabbed back with a grin.

"Anyone missing anything?" Ryann asked. "I'm assuming my staff made its way back to my closet again."

"All I can say is, I'm glad my glasses stayed on," Terell said. "My mom would'a killed me if I'd lost 'em again."

Liddy checked her back pocket. "Darn! My cell phone's wet." She grimaced. "I hope it still works!" Setting it down on the short brick wall that circled the lighthouse, she felt around her neck. Liddy smiled and pulled the E-shaped medallion out from under her shirt. "I've still got my memory of Essy!"

"Good!" Ryann looked at both his friends. "Now we need to figure out how we're going to explain this to our parents."

"Oh no!" Liddy exclaimed, patting her hips. "They're gone!"

Terell looked in her direction. "What's gone?"

"The stones!" Liddy cried, still patting her hips while looking frantically between the water and the ground around her feet. "They were in the leather satchel tied around my waist, and now they're gone!"

Ryann took a step toward her. "Are you sure?"

"Do you see them attached anywhere, genius?" she snapped. "First I break the horn, and now this?"

"Hey, hey," Ryann tried to speak calmly. "Maybe they'll show up. Ya never know. Kinda like my staff."

"You think?" A glimmer of hope rose in her voice.

"Yeah, maybe," Ryann reassured. "Now what about our parents?"

"My mom's gonna freak," Terell said. "I never wanted to worry her about Aeliana, so I've never told her about it."

"My parents don't know either," Liddy said, "and even if we came back at the same time we left, by the time we get back to my house from here, my mom and dad will be looking for us."

"Not to mention the fact that we're soakin' wet," Terell added.

"We've got to tell them the truth," Ryann said. "Maybe we can get them all together at one time."

Terell rolled his eyes. "That sounds like fun."

Liddy squatted down to fix her sneakers.

"Better late than never. Now we'd better get going," Ryann said.

"Just a sec," Liddy said. "My shoe almost fell off when we landed in the lake, and I need to get it back on right and retie it." As Liddy worked to tie her wet shoelaces, a perfectly oval hole at the base of the lighthouse caught her eye.

"That's odd. I don't remember this being here," she muttered to herself, running her fingers across it.

"Come on!" Ryann urged, heading off the lighthouse peninsula. "We have a two-mile walk back to Liddy's."

"Coming." Liddy hopped up, grabbed her cell phone, and punched *one* as she trotted to catch up to the two sets of water-logged tennis shoes squishing ahead of her.

"Yeah, Dad, we're okay. Can you come pick us up in the parking lot by the lighthouse?"

Ryann and Terell whirled around, puzzled looks on their faces.

"Boys!" Liddy shook her head. "You didn't think I was going to walk two miles in the dark, did you? With soaking wet sneakers rubbing my feet raw?"

Liddy's father hopped out of the car and headed up the walk to their house. Ryann glanced at his watch—9:35. His parents were supposed to pick up Terell and him at 10:00.

"That was weird," Liddy said as they got out of the car. "My dad hardly said anything. He wasn't even mad."

"He's a cool dude," Terell said.

"Yeah, my dad would have been lecturing us the entire drive," Ryann added.

Liddy stopped them at the front door. "My dad may be cool, but I'm sure he wouldn't want us traipsing through the house in our wet shoes and socks."

"Good idea," Ryann said, pulling his first shoe off and wringing his sock out on the porch.

"Come on, let's get inside," Liddy said. "We can get something to drink while we wait for your dad, Ryann."

"Yeah, I still need something dry to wipe my glasses off with," Terell said as they walked through the front door. "The lake water really—"

"Hello, Mr. Watters!" Liddy yelled over Terell's comments. "Mrs. Watters. Mrs. Peterson. Uhh, so nice to see all of you."

Their parents sat on the large sofa in the family room. Liddy's mom sat in one of the oversized armchairs next to them. A plastic painter's sheet lay spread out across the carpet. Three plastic chairs from the patio were strategically positioned on top of the sheet facing the couch.

"Hey, Mom and Dad," Ryann said with mock enthusiasm. "What are you doing here so early?"

"Mrs. Thomas gave us and Terell's mother a call while Mr. Thomas went to pick you up. Now, why don't you sit down and tell us what's going on?"

The tone in his father's voice indicated he wasn't making a request. With their wet clothes and hair, Ryann knew there wasn't a way to make up a story. The three of them hadn't been alone long enough to concoct one if they had wanted to. Between his father's Naval Academy training rubbing off on him and Ryann's weekly Sunday school lessons, he knew it would be best to be completely honest.

Mr. Thomas sat down opposite his wife in the matching oversized armchair. Ryann plopped down in the plastic chair between Liddy and Terell. Each of them shifted uncomfortably in their wet jeans and clingy shirts. Terell's eyes darted to his mother, whose arms were folded and lips tightly pursed.

"Ryann," Mr. Watters said firmly, "go ahead and tell us exactly what happened. Oh! In case you're wondering, I've already briefed

Liddy's parents and Terell's mother on the reality of Aeliana. I was surprised to learn that they knew nothing about it."

Ryann could see both his friends squirming on either side of him. At least he wouldn't have to go over that later. He had discussed his last adventure in Aeliana with his parents in great detail.

"...and then we landed in Lake Dora," Ryann concluded.

He had summarized everything as accurately as possible, while trying to minimize as much of the danger as possible. The concerned look on Terell's mom's face had him worried that if they were to try and return she might object. Several times, Liddy's parents and Mrs. Peterson had started to interrupt, but Mr. Watters had intervened and encouraged them to wait until Ryann was finished.

Mr. Thomas was the first to speak. "You can't honestly expect me to believe all this, can you?" he asked, looking back and forth between the kids and Ryann's parents, as if expecting them to jump up at any moment and yell, "Surprise!"

"I knew you'd say that," Liddy said, shaking her head in obvious disappointment.

Ryann recalled vividly her doubts when he had first confided in her about Aeliana.

"Come on, Liddy," her father answered. "It's all pretty far-fetched, you know. I mean, *dragons*. Really?"

"I knew you'd respond that way. That's why I took this!" Liddy answered with a mischievous grin while holding up her cell phone.

"What's that?" Mr. Thomas asked.

"That would be a picture of Sorcha, the dragon I've ridden, and off to the side is Garnock. He's a river dwarf."

"How?" Ryann asked.

"Just because there isn't cell service in Aeliana," she interrupted, "doesn't mean the battery and camera don't work."

"Honey, I–I don't know what to say," her father stammered, staring at her phone.

"That's okay, Dad. The 'show me' tendency runs in the family." She smiled sheepishly.

Amazement gripped each viewer in the form of contorted facial expressions and breathy *whoa*s and *ahh*s as Liddy's phone was passed around. Mrs. Peterson was the last to view it but the first to make a comment.

"It doesn't sound or look very safe," she concluded.

Ryann cringed.

"Actually," Mr. Watters interjected, "I feel pretty good about it after having been visited by Gabriel myself."

"Yeah, Mom, you wouldn't believe Aeliana," Terell said. "All of the creatures there can talk. It's the most amazing place I've ever been. I know that doesn't mean much since we hardly ever travel, but I never dreamed I could be part of an adventure like this!"

"Well, I don't know."

"Mom, I was exposed to more violence when we lived in downtown Atlanta."

"Terell?" Her voice rose.

"Yes, ma'am?" he answered politely.

She started to say something else and instead stared at him with a puzzled expression.

"Terell, what happened to your stutter?"

Terell grinned, then jabbed Ryann in the ribs with his elbow. "Ryann left out that small detail in his story because he was so busy talking about himself," he laughed. "Carwyn healed me!"

"Say what?"

"The white unicorn, Carwyn, he touched me with his horn and healed me from my stuttering. It's not that big a deal."

"I'd say it is, honey." Her eyes began to water as she tried to continue, "You've had that stutter since you first started talking."

"I mean, he healed other creatures of a lot worse things. I think the worst was an antelope—"

"It was a stag," Liddy interrupted.

"Whatever…A stag that asked Carwyn to heal his dying son, and the son wasn't even with him. He was still back at their home in bed."

"I'd love to meet this Carwyn and thank him personally." Mrs. Peterson smiled as a tear ran down her cheek. "He sounds so much like Jesus."

"You know, you bring up a good point," Mr. Watters said. "Everything you kids have told us definitely points to a supernatural being of some sort. I'm going to have to think about this a little more."

"Even so, it still sounds dangerous to me," Mrs. Thomas said.

"Mom, please, I've never come back hurt," Liddy groaned.

"Well, riding a dragon doesn't sound very safe to me!" She hesitated. "I can honestly say that's something I thought I'd never say."

"Are you going back?" Mr. Watters asked.

"I'm sure I will," Ryann answered. "Gabriel tasked me with finding the shield of faith, and I haven't found it yet."

"Ahem." Terell feigned a cough. "You mean *we,* don't you?"

"Yeah, man, sorry. We!" Ryann said pointing to Terell and Liddy. "Uh, us."

"Oh my!" Mrs. Peterson exclaimed. "It's almost midnight." She looked up from her watch. "We're gonna have a mighty struggle getting up for church tomorrow." She gathered her purse and stood up.

"Thanks for coming over on such short notice," Mr. Thomas said. "I hope we can continue this discussion and come up with a solution for how to handle it from this point forward."

Liddy scowled at her father.

Following the cordial good-byes, Ryann sat in silence on the short drive home. Questions swirled around in his head, but the two most important kept resurfacing. How long would it be until they returned to Aeliana, and how much time would have transpired there while they were gone?

CHAPTER 24

Ɗ. Ҡ,

YANN POUNDED HIS pillow for the fifth time trying to make the perfect resting-place for his head. Ten minutes later he was still wide awake. Shadows loomed ominously across the far wall of his room from the glow of the streetlight seeping through his window. One form took the shape of a black unicorn.

Flipping his desk lamp on, the shadows scurried into hiding. Ryann opened his Bible to the concordance in the back and looked up *darkness*. There were many verses listed, but his eyes were drawn to the psalms.

Psalms and Proverbs have so much encouragement and wisdom. Maybe I can find something to calm me down.

He opened to Psalm 18, his finger scanning down the page to verse 28.

> You, O Lord, keep my lamp burning; my God turns my darkness into light.

There it was, darkness. *God keeps my light burning, and it causes the darkness to vanish, replacing it with light.*

> With your help I can advance against the enemy; with my God I can scale a wall. As for God, his way is perfect; the word of the Lord is flawless. He is a shield for all who take refuge in him.

A shield?
He read the line again, meditating on each word.

> He is a shield for all who take refuge in him.

Maybe "he" is the shield of faith?
Out of the corner of his eye, the red glow of his digital alarm peered back at him—2:14 a.m.

Reaching up to turn off the lamp, he thought about what he had just read and left the light on. He hopped into bed, glancing back over to the far wall. Light had replaced the shadowy unicorn. Smiling, he closed his eyes. This time sleep came quickly.

Within minutes his mind drifted away from the reality surrounding him to the other reality awaiting him. The world of Aeliana beckoned throughout the night. He was there alone, on top of Glenys Falls. A voice echoed behind him. "Who do you say that I am?"

He turned in time to see the white backside of a horse galloping into the forest.

"Carwyn?"

Running after him, he entered the shadows until the light behind him faded away.

The voice came again from behind him. "Who do you say that I am?"

Heavy breathing tickled his neck. He whirled around.

"Car—?" Ryann stopped mid-word as he stared into two red eyes. The black unicorn grinned.

Mrs. Goodwill glanced up from her Bible as the blond teen sauntered into her Sunday school class. Ignoring the distraction, she continued reading aloud to the class.

Ryann plopped heavily into the empty seat between Terell and Liddy. Both teens' eyebrows rose in response to the unusual circumstance. Ryann Watters was never late. He looked at Terell, then Liddy. His eyes felt puffy as he strained to open them wider. Smiling weakly, he shrugged his shoulders and opened his Bible.

"You okay?" Terell asked.

"Yeah, I didn't sleep well last night."

"Boys! No talking, please," Mrs. Goodwill said.

"Yes, ma'am," Ryann automatically responded.

Sunday school and church service were a blur of disjointed messages as Ryann fought to stay awake. Subtle jabs in the ribs by his father continually interrupted his feeble attempts for sleep. As the organist began playing "Amazing Grace" for the offering, Ryann glanced at his watch. It was 11:45 a.m. *Only fifteen more minutes*, he thought.

"Dad, I need to get a drink," Ryann whispered.

Mr. Watters scooted back in the pew, giving him enough room to get by. "Maybe it will help you stay awake," he whispered, giving Ryann a stern look.

The short walk out into the sanctuary foyer rejuvenated his senses. Looking up from the water fountain, Ryann noticed a familiar figure passing briskly by the glass entry doors.

D. K.?

Ryann looked at his watch again. It was 11:50.

Walking swiftly across the carpeted foyer, Ryann exited in time to see the dark-clothed figure dart around the corner.

"Don?"

Ryann jogged after him. *Noah was Gabriel in disguise. I know he's taken the form of this drifter, or if he can't shape-shift, then it's another angel.*

Rounding the corner of the building, Ryann smiled. *Man, he moves quickly for an old guy.*

Don lay fully extended on the same park bench where they had first met.

Sneaking up next to him, Ryann cleared his throat. "Ahem, you can't possibly be asleep already!"

The corpse-like body twitched, then a grin appeared on the drifter's face. "Eh, Ryann?" He opened both eyes. "Nothing gets by you, does it?"

His eyes are dark, but there was that familiar wink, just like Gabriel. I'll play along with his little game and assume he knows all about Aeliana.

"Aeliana was so different from last time," Ryann said.

"Really, how so?" D. K. asked, rising to a sitting position.

Ha! I tricked him.

Briefly recounting what had occurred, he ended with a question. "I'm concerned about the black unicorn, Narcissus, taking over. What do you think I should do when I get back?"

"I can see where you'd be concerned, Ryann, but I wouldn't worry about it too much."

"Why's that?"

"How much do you know about unicorns?"

"Not much," he admitted. "I mean this is the first time I've met one."

"Without going into a lot of detail," D. K. replied, "unicorns are unique creatures who live very long lives and are very peaceful by nature."

"I can see that in Carwyn," Ryann said, "but Narcissus has a very evil air about him, and many creatures don't trust him."

"A lot? Really? Like whom?" D. K. asked.

"Well, everyone in the Chosen."

"So how many is that?"

"Let's see, if you subtract out Terell, Liddy, and me, that would make seven, eight if you count Carwyn," Ryann answered.

"And what about the rest of the creatures of Aeliana?"

"They seem to follow him."

"So it appears as if only a small minority don't care for Narcissus."

The noise behind him signaled that the front doors to the church had opened with the end of the service.

"My belief," D. K. continued, "is that ultimately they will reconcile their differences."

"Seriously? That's hard to believe." The noise behind him grew louder as the congregation exited the building. "I've got to get going now. Will you be hanging around here in case I have other questions?"

"I'm planning to be in Mount Dora for another few weeks. Then I'll be moving on."

"Thanks, D. K. You've been a lot of help. It's okay that I call you D. K., right?"

"Yep, I definitely prefer that over Don or Mr. Korrel. See ya."

Ryann turned to leave, making his way back to the corner of the building before remembering he had forgotten to ask about the shield. Looking back to the bench, it was empty.

"Hey, homeboy, whatcha been doin'?" Terell asked with Liddy right behind him.

"You'll never believe what D. K. said." Ryann quickly caught them up on the conversation as they walked back to the foyer to meet up with his parents.

"I don't think there's any way the two of them would ever get along," Liddy scoffed.

"Why not?" Terell asked, putting his arm around Ryann. "I mean my main man here is white, and I'm black. And we get along just fine. Right?"

"Trying to be serious here, Terell." Liddy shook her head.

Terell's face beamed with a big, toothy smile. "Hey, maybe we can ask Carwyn about it when we get back."

"Yeah, if we get back. And if my parents let me go," Liddy replied sarcastically.

"What?" the boys said together.

"They didn't say you couldn't go back, did they?" Ryann asked.

"Not exactly, my dad said he thinks it's too dangerous, but he and my mom are going to talk about it." She did quotes with her fingers as she said the word *talk*.

Ryann tried to encourage her. "At least they haven't said no yet."

"Liddy! It's time to go!" Mrs. Thomas called from across the church patio entrance.

Liddy rolled her eyes. "See ya."

"I'd better get going too," Ryann said. "See you tomorrow at school, Terell."

"Cool. Don't forget to text if something comes up."

Ryann plopped down in the mushy leather chair as he looked up at the crossed sword and scabbard on the wall of his dad's study. A dark-framed oil painting of the Navy sailing team titled *The Chase* hung underneath. Being exposed to the military through his father had always given him the desire to be a leader.

I wonder if I have what it takes. The sword was one thing, but the shield is proving to be more of a challenge. Now, so many others are involved.

"So, what's on your mind, son?" his father asked, drawing him away from his thoughts.

"Huh?" Ryann tried to sit up.

"You said you wanted to talk, remember? I'm all ears."

Ryann shook his head. "Okay, um, where does evil come from?"

"Whoa. You don't give your dad any easy ones, do you? How about who's going to win the army-navy game this year?"

Ryann grinned. "Like I don't know how you'd answer that one."

His father got serious again. "So what's driving your question?"

"I'm just a little confused. The white unicorn, Carwyn, seems good to me, and Narcissus, the black unicorn, seems evil; but then Gabriel said they would end up getting along in the end."

"Gabriel talked to you?"

"Yeah, well, not exactly. Remember how he appeared as Noah Johnson before?"

His father nodded.

"I think he's back, pretending to be another drifter. Only this time his name is Don Korrel, or D. K., as I call him. He hangs out by the church."

"Interesting. Well, I know that when you were younger we read you the story of Adam and Even and how they were the first ones to sin, and I'm sure you've heard it at church—"

"Yes, sir. I mean before that."

"Okay, as Christians we believe that evil began with the rebellion of the angel Lucifer against God. Lucifer's pride caused him to claim he was on the same level as God."

"Wow! That's pretty outrageous." Ryann shook his head in disbelief.

"Not as much as you think, son. People do the same thing today. They just aren't as blatant about it."

"How so?"

"A lot of people say they believe in a God or a higher power, but they don't like how the Bible describes God. They don't want to follow His instructions for them in their daily living and how He's designed them to have a relationship with Him."

Ryann scratched his head. "So what do they do?"

"They create their own god."

"Huh?"

"They don't make an actual idol to worship," his father continued. "Instead they pick a few verses from the Bible that appeal to them, add in characteristics they like in a friend, and then blend that together with what fits into their schedule and makes them feel good."

"Really?"

"Sure. Most people don't worship the God who is; they worship the god they want."

"How can they find out if they're on the wrong track?"

"I bet you already know the answer to that one." His father leaned forward in his chair. "What's our guide for daily living?"

"The Bible?"

"That's right. God's given us the Bible to show us how we can have a relationship with Him. It gives the account of Lucifer and other rebellious angels being thrown out of heaven."

Ryann interrupted, "Like Lord Ekron?"

"Yep. We refer to them as demons now, and Lucifer as Satan."

"And that's where Adam and Eve come in, right?"

"You've got it, bud. They were created perfect and enjoyed a direct relationship with God. Then they were tempted by Satan in the form of a serpent."

"We studied that in Sunday school. They rebelled against God by eating the apple off the tree He told them not to eat from."

Mr. Watters grinned. "Almost. We don't know if the fruit was an apple or not. A lot of people just assume that. But they did disobey God. Do you know what the sin was?"

"Hmm. Satan told them to eat the fruit because it would open their eyes to right and wrong and—"

"And?" His father's brow furrowed in anticipation.

"That they would be like God!" Ryann's face lit up.

"You got it!" His father smiled. "And that's been the problem ever since. The decision everyone wrestles with is whether to be your own god by creating one that allows you to do whatever you want or to follow the one true God."

"Wow! That makes so much sense now, Dad."

"Good, I'm glad I could help. Keep reading your Bible. It'll provide you with a lot more truth and insight."

Ryann jumped up and headed to the door. "Thanks, again."

"Oh, not to change the subject," his father added as he started through the door, "but how do you plan to get back to Aeliana?"

Ryann looked back over his shoulder. "No clue, Dad. It's not something we've ever had control over. It just happens. See ya."

Mr. Watters was left alone in his thoughts. He reached up with one hand and rubbed his jaw.

Something Ryann said doesn't fit. Carwyn, Narcissus, Gabriel, Lord Ekron, Noah Johnson, and now D. K. I hope it comes to me before it's too late.

CHAPTER 25

Day of Reckoning

THE GLOW OF the full moon filtered through the window blinds, casting an eerie array of silent shadows around his room. Sleep continued to elude Ryann. He rolled to his side for a third time. Trying to block out everything else, he pictured Carwyn and the peace he felt around the unicorn. His breathing slowed and grew deeper. Moments later the realities of this world drifted away.

Everything was black.

Ryann looked down. He was barefoot, standing on flat blackness. His white pants matched his white shirt. *Odd*, he thought.

Something moved. He wasn't alone. Looking up, he saw Carwyn off to his right and Narcissus off to his left, walking toward one another.

He looked from one to the other for some sort of expression. *Are they brothers or enemies?*

Twenty feet. Ten feet. They were face to face, moist nostrils flaring, breathing on one another. Red eyes glared into blue, but neither blinked.

"Carwyn?" Ryann called out. His voice sounded strange to him. Both unicorns ignored him. Carwyn lowered his head and closed his eyes.

What's he doing?

The white unicorn held his head down for a moment, then raised it higher than before and looked skyward.

Narcissus lowered his head as if imitating Carwyn.

Maybe it's a customary greeting of some sort or respectful gesture? Ryann looked on. Narcissus kept his eyes open, watching every movement of the white unicorn. The black unicorn hesitated at the bottom of his bow, a sneering grin spread across his face.

What? Ryann focused on the shiny, pointed horn just before Narcissus thrust it upward into Carwyn's chest.

Everything came to a standstill. Ryann stared in disbelief at the black horn, half buried in the smooth white hair of Carwyn's chest. A small red circle appeared around the black horn and slowly began spreading outward, staining the unblemished hair.

"Noooo!" Ryann screamed.

His eyes snapped open. Sitting upright, darkness pressed in on him. A cool draft blew across his neck. Reaching behind him, he rubbed the matted hair on the back of his head, the moisture clinging to his hand. Breathing deeply in and out, Ryann tried to slow his racing heart. Slipping out of bed, he stepped over to the window and spread the blinds. Dark gray clouds blanketed the nighttime sky, hiding the full moon. The glowing red digits on his alarm clock read 4:37.

Two hours until I need to get up for school. It's just a nightmare. That's all it was.

Ryann bounced slightly as he sat down on his bed. Twisting around, he swung his feet up and leaned back against his headboard, staring straight ahead into the darkness.

"I'm telling you, guys, it was so real I felt like I was there," Ryann concluded.

Terell and Liddy listened attentively as they pulled various lunch items from their brown bags. The din of indistinguishable chatter filled the cafeteria as the trio hunched close together, forming a small circle of isolation.

Terell took a bite of his sandwich. "Do you think it means anything?" he asked between chews.

"I'm not sure," Ryann replied. "It scares me, though, because I've been having more and more nightmares lately."

Liddy finished neatly laying out her lunch items. "Why don't you ask Gabriel about it?"

"Huh?"

"You know, D. K."

"Hey, that's a good idea, Liddy. I can't believe I didn't think of it."

"Yeah, I'm smart like that." She flashed her bright smile.

"Thanks, Liddy. I'm on it," Ryann answered. "Right after school."

"Geez, Ryann," Terell rolled his eyes, "don't encourage her."

The last tick of the school clock concluded with a long, drawn-out bell signaling the end of school for the day and the beginning of a few short hours of freedom before it began all over again.

"See ya!" Ryann yelled, sprinting out of their last-period class.

Arriving first at the bike compound, he unlocked his ten-speed and peddled in the direction of First Presbyterian Church. *He's got to be there.*

Coasting down Alexander Street and around the front of the church, he came to a stop by the primary school playground. Like a statue, Don was in the same place he had spoken to him last. Ryann grinned. The drifter lay sprawled out across the park bench in a perpetual state of sleep. In keeping with the tranquil atmosphere, Ryann quietly got off his bike and walked it toward the vagrant's abode. *Maybe I can sneak up on him.*

As he got to within twenty feet of the bench, Ryann saw D. K.'s eyes open, as if an invisible force field warned him of someone entering his space. A peculiar sideways grin greeted Ryann until the drifter sat up. The grin grew into a normal smile.

"Ryann, my boy, it's so good to see you again."

Still breathing hard, Ryann dropped his bike to the ground instead of using the kickstand.

"D. K., I need your help."

The darkly dressed man's smile disappeared, replaced by a furrowed brow. "Sure, Ryann, what seems to be the problem?"

Ryann looked into the dark eyes gazing back at him. *Should I call him Gabriel? Nah. Not just yet.*

"I keep having disturbing dreams. Well, actually, they're more like nightmares."

"Tell me about it," D. K. encouraged in a silky smooth voice.

"Remember when I told you my concerns about the white and black unicorns, and you told me not to worry? That they were brothers who would resolve their conflict?"

"Yes," D. K. replied, drawing out his response eagerly.

"I had a nightmare last night, and the black unicorn stabbed the white unicorn in the chest with his horn."

"Did it kill him?" D. K. scooted forward to the edge of the park bench.

"Uhh, I think so," Ryann stammered. "He was bleeding badly. I woke up disoriented and yelling. At least I think I was. I screamed in my dream."

"Hmm." The drifter's eyes squinted as his pursed lips snaked into a slithery grin.

"What? What is it?" Ryann looked up and down at the man dressed in black with the strange grin.

"It's time you knew." D. K.'s grin grew into a broad smile as his eyes continued to narrow.

"Know what?"

"You're seeing the future."

"But, but I thought you said—" Ryann didn't have a chance to finish as the drifter waved him off.

"You thought, did you?" D. K.'s voice changed. The smooth, fatherly tone was gone, replaced by a much deeper one.

Ryann stared back, perplexed. He wanted to ask a question but his throat felt as though every ounce of moisture had been wrung from it. His mouth opened, and a wispy breath escaped.

"Mmwaa, ha-haaaaa!" An eruption of echoing laughter filled the void around him, as if a dozen drifters were laughing. Ryann looked frantically around him, but no. It was only one. D. K.

"You foolish, foolish boy. I tried to make it so easy for you. But alas, how naïve is the side of light."

"What?" Ryann rasped. "You aren't Gabriel?"

"Gabriel? Hmm." He looked around as if pondering the idea. "So, that's who you thought I was? Oh, you are going to be so disappointed. No, I'm not your little guardian angel, Gabriel. Not by a long shot!"

Ryann's stomach spasmed. He thought he might throw up. Too unnerved to reply, he watched D. K. squat down in front of him. Running his finger through the soft dirt, the drifter spelled out his full name upside down so that Ryann could read it.

Staring at the drifter's name as he stood up, the evolving, deep voice continued as he waved his hand over the letters he had just written.

"No, you might have thought you had a nightmare last night."

He hesitated as Ryann watched in amazement. The dirt-scrawled letters began moving and rearranging themselves from:

D O N K O R R E L

to

L O R D E K R O N

"No, Ryann. I am your worst nightmare!" he spat as he stood up.

Backing away, Ryann tripped over his bike, landing with a hard thud on the ground but never taking his eyes off the man whose evil was increasingly being revealed. "No, no, it can't be."

"Oh, but it is!" the old man cackled, whipping his long black trench coat up over his head. In one swooping motion, the old man transformed before Ryann's eyes. Curved black wings replaced the swirling coat. Black coloring, like spilled paint, coursed through the dark angel's hair, changing it from gray to jet black. His wrinkled disguise stretched tightly over a youthful, rugged face, returning him to the form Ryann had confronted in the desert of Aeliana. Ekron grew to a full seven feet in his dark angel form, looming over Ryann as he scrambled to regain his footing.

"It's not true!" Ryann now stood, defiantly confronting Ekron. "Carwyn is good, and good always defeats evil."

"Fool!" the demon shouted. "The world is moving faster in Aeliana. Since you returned it has been over a year there." He hesitated, watching Ryann's reaction. Lowering his voice, he spoke very deliberately, "And let's just say things are not going so well for the Chosen."

Ryann felt rage welling up within him. Clenching his fists tightly, he felt like charging the taunting demon, but he knew running away was his only real option. Ekron's demeanor grew more menacing as Ryann's loathing for this enemy boiled over.

"Yes, that's it. Feel the hate. It's powerful, isn't it?" Ekron hissed.

The demon's words brought Ryann out of his trance. What was it Gabriel had once told him? *For you were once darkness, but now you are a light. Have nothing to do with the deeds of darkness, but rather expose them in the light.*

He looked into Ekron's seemingly perfect face with restored confidence. The thin scar etched from the side of his forehead around to his chin revealed a weakness. He didn't know how or why, but he felt he should bring it up anyway.

"Where did you get that scar on your face?"

A flash of confusion illuminated the demon for one brief moment. Ryann felt the confirmation of a weakness and pounced.

"You didn't get it in a little swordplay with Gabriel, did you?"

"Silence!" Ekron roared. "I am returning to Aeliana through the portal you and your friends opened for me. I don't want to miss the tragic ending of Carwyn and his chosen ones. You, on the other hand, can count yourself lucky for not being there!"

"It was just a dream!" Ryann shouted. With a little less confidence, he added, "Carwyn will be fine."

Ekron's vivid black form began fading, but his voice rang stronger than ever. "Your precious white unicorn will be dead in less than two days your time, and there's nothing you can do about it. Ha, hahaa, haaaa!"

Shock over the demon's statement and the way he faded away riveted Ryann in place. *No! It can't be true. It can't happen this way. I've got to tell the others.*

Grabbing his bike, he jumped on. *Should I ride to Terell's? Call Liddy?*

He pulled out his phone to call Terell. Holding on to the handlebars with one hand, he quickly relayed what had happened as he pedaled home.

"No way, dude! D. K. is Lord Ekron, not Gabriel?" Terell asked.

"Yeah, I couldn't believe it either."

"What are we gonna do?"

"I don't know. Pray that we find a way back to Aeliana to warn Carwyn. I'll call Liddy."

Ryann clicked off and speed-dialed Liddy. Her response was the same, but with greater emotion.

"Oh, my gosh! D. K. is Lord Ekron?"

"What do you think we should do?"

"You know I'm all about logic and facts, Ryann, but logic can only take us so far. This is a supernatural battle between good and evil, angels and demons. We need to pray."

"You're right. I'm almost home now," Ryann said. "Start praying. I need to talk to my dad."

Ryann sat at the kitchen table, tapping his spoon over and over again against the wooden surface. His mom moved around the kitchen, preparing dinner with the unconscious confidence of someone who had rehearsed it a thousand times.

"You know, Ryann, tapping your spoon isn't going to make your father get home any faster," she said while opening the oven to check on the baked potatoes.

"Huh?" He noticed what he was doing for the first time and set the spoon down. "Oh, uh, sorry, Mom."

He had phoned his dad as soon as he got home, and following a brief silence his father had suggested discussing it at the dinner table with the whole family instead of alone in his study. Ryann wasn't so sure about including his brother and sister, but his father's final words before hanging up were growing on him: "Even though God chose you for this journey, Ryann, it still affects the rest of our family and becomes part of our journey as well."

The front door slammed, followed immediately by his father's familiar, "I'm home!"

"Henry! Alison! Time for dinner!" Ryann shouted.

Mrs. Watters smiled and shook her head.

Moments later they sat around the dinner table in their unofficially assigned seats. Ryann had heard Liddy say that a behavioral study had been done showing the human nature for groups, whether in schools, work settings, or home, is to subconsciously accept seating arrangements as permanent after only sitting in them one time.

Mr. Watters's prayer was followed immediately by the familiar sounds of utensils dinging dishes as food was passed clockwise around the table. After everyone had served themselves, Mr. Watters cleared his throat.

"All of you are aware of Ryann's task to find the shield of faith. Today, Ryann alerted me to the fact the drifter behind the church he thought was Gabriel was actually a demon."

At the mention of a demon, Henry Jr. stopped spreading butter on his bread, while Alison's fork halted midway to her mouth.

"The demon said the black unicorn currently ruling Aeliana is going to kill Carwyn, and he even went to far to say it would occur within two days, our time."

Both siblings turned to look at Ryann, who avoided their stares, poking at his food and moving it around his plate but not taking a bite.

"Ryann, I know you've told us that Carwyn is good and all, but don't you think the people in Aeliana realize that too and would help protect him?" his older brother asked.

Ryann stabbed his potato. "It's not that simple. The people of Aeliana are being manipulated by Narcissus and his army of Hugons."

"There isn't anyone that will help him?" Alison asked.

"There's the Chosen, but three of the ten of us are here, and even with ten loyal followers, they wouldn't have a chance," Ryann answered.

Mrs. Watters gently entered the conversation, "Followers. Chosen ones. An evil leader. It all sounds so biblical, like Jesus and the disciples being pursued by the corrupt Sanhedrin of His day."

Ryann stopped fidgeting with his food and looked up, a smile spreading across his face.

"What? What is it, son?" his father asked.

"Dad, now that we know there's another world out there we didn't know about before, do you think they would be in need of a Savior as well?"

Mr. Watters stopped mid-chew, cocked his head to the side and furrowed his brow. No one spoke as he continued chewing, deep in thought. It was rare not to have an immediate response from their father, even if his mouth was full. He swallowed and pointed his fork at Ryann.

"That's a very good question, son. I normally don't like to engage in hypothetical questions about whether there's life on other planets and how God might treat them, but this is different. We know Aeliana's real."

"And, your point is?" Ryann tried not to sound sarcastic.

"The Bible is pretty clear about the importance of not adding or taking away words from it. Therefore, I have to rely on what it says about God's character versus life on other worlds, since it was written about and for people on Earth."

Henry Jr. leaned forward with his elbows on the table. "So what you're saying is that even though there aren't any Scripture verses that talk about other worlds or other races of intelligent beings, we still might be able to figure out what God would do by what's written about Him in the Bible?"

"Cool, like science fiction!" Alison joined in.

Both brothers looked at their ten-year-old sister and rolled their eyes.

"Well, sort of," Mr. Watters continued. "The question of whether or not there are aliens on other planets has been discussed for centuries. No Bible passage proves that God has or hasn't, or will or won't create other races of intelligent beings. We know that God is the Creator and has a very creative spirit based upon the variety of creatures and nature we see around us. He created angels, who we know are different beings than we are, and now we know that there is life in Aeliana. Let's see if we can work backward from this new knowledge."

Everyone nodded in agreement at the almost game-like scenario with their father.

"Ryann, let's start with you. When you first traveled to Aeliana, what was it like?"

Ryann's eyes glazed over, reflecting on that first experience. "It was totally amazing. The colors were so bright, sounds were crisper—it was like everything was alive, and I could taste it!"

"Possibly like what Adam and Eve experienced in the Garden of Eden?"

"Yeah, maybe."

"And how did it change after Drake and the fallen angel, Ekron, showed up?"

"The same places were still there, but it was different. Plants and animals were growing old and dying." His voice softened as he continued, "There were still beautiful sites to see, but the excitement and freshness were gone."

"That's probably how Adam and Eve felt." He turned his attention to Alison. "Why did everything change in the Garden of Eden?"

Alison looked nervously back and forth between her mother and father. "Because they disobeyed God?"

"That's right, honey, and because of that disobedience, the relationship between the Creator and the created changed. Death entered the world both physically and spiritually. Henry?"

"Yes, sir!" Henry Jr. jumped at the sudden focus on him, banging his knees against the table. Alison giggled nervously.

"Sorry. Didn't mean to startle you." Mr. Watters smiled. "What did they need to make things right?"

"The same thing we need. A Savior who would come and restore the right relationship by taking on our wrongs and conquering death."

Mr. Watters winked at him. "Exactly! Now let's see if we can draw a conclusion." His eyes settled on his young daughter. "Alison, what does John 3:16 say?"

Alison proudly sat up in her chair and recited the first verse they had learned in Sunday school. "For God so loved the world, that He gave His one and only Son, that whoever believes in Him shall not perish but have eternal life."

Ryann looked confused. "So how does that apply to Aeliana?"

"Well, Ryann, we can't say exactly, but from knowing what we know about God's love and His creation, and that He continues to be in control of everything in the universe, there are a few conclusions I would draw. The first is that Aeliana is a separate world from Earth, so the sin of Adam and Eve here didn't affect them there. God sending His Son was for everyone in this world. Second, now that the people of Aeliana have sinned themselves, they're in need of a Savior, and it appears He may be coming in the form of Carwyn."

"Really?" Ryann asked.

"It's possible, from the miracles you've described and his teachings. Aren't the inhabitants of Aeliana mostly animals and non-human creatures?"

"Yes, sir."

"Then wouldn't it make sense that He would come in the form of someone they would relate to?"

"Well, yes, but how can we know for sure?"

"Observation is one thing, but the best way would be for you to ask him yourself."

The phone rang before Ryann could respond.

Liddy stepped from the kitchen into the family room. Long, rolling shadows flowed from the west side of the room across the antique furniture to the hardwood floor. Sunset would be over in a few minutes, she told herself, and the room would be blanketed in darkness. Once a week her parents went on a "date night," leaving her home alone to fend for dinner herself and do her homework. She didn't want to admit it creeped her out a little bit to be in the house alone at night, because she did actually enjoy the independence.

As she felt for the light switch, a small white glow reflected off the hardwood floor about six feet away. Hesitating, she looked around to see what might be its source of energy. The spot grew to the size of a small ball, as if it were coming from a flashlight. Her chest felt warm. Instinctively, Liddy brought her hand up to her shirt.

"Ouch!" she cried.

Jerking her hand away, she lost sight of the spot. Flicking on the light, she looked down at her shirt. The pewter-looking *E* pendant she had retrieved from Eljon dangled from around her neck. Tentatively, she reached up and touched it. The warmth emanating from it surprised her. It wasn't hot, but she understood how it had startled her in the dark. Pondering her options, Liddy reached over and turned the light off again.

The light reappeared in the same place in front of her. She cupped her hand and placed it over the necklace charm. The spot disappeared. Removing her hand, the spot reappeared, but only momentarily before moving a few feet farther away.

"What?" she gasped.

Even as she heard herself breathing heavily in the silent

surroundings, the spot returned to its original position for a brief moment and then moved away again.

It's like it wants me to follow it.

Liddy took a few steps toward the spot. When she came to within a few feet, it slid all the way across the family room and stopped at the bottom of the stairs.

"No way!" she muttered.

Scurrying over to the stairs, she tried to step on it with her foot. As her foot came down, the white blotch raced to the top of the staircase. She stood at the bottom pondering where it was going and watched in amazement as the spot slid back down. It stopped halfway. *Now what?*

The spot jumped up one step.

It's treating this like a game. Almost taunting me to catch it.

Forgetting her anxiousness about the dark surroundings, she felt her competitive juices flowing and bounded up the stairs after the spot. Taking two steps at a time, she reached the top and ran down the hall a few steps behind the light. Then it was gone.

Liddy stopped at the end of the hall. Rapid panting was the only sound she heard as she rested in almost total darkness. She hadn't turned on a light, yet she could see her shadow where the spot should have been. *How could that be?*

Raising her head slowly, a smile crept across her face. *The ceiling.* Her second realization was more telling. *The doorway to the attic!*

Liddy knew where the light spot was taking her as she pulled the small rope that would bring the retractable ladder down. Confidently feeling her way up the steps, a passing thought told her she should go get a flashlight, yet something in her heart knew she wouldn't need one. Halfway up the steps, she looked up into what should have been a dark hole. Instead, the entrance to the attic lit up like someone had already turned on the lone light bulb attached to the ceiling beam. Passing through the attic doorway, she glanced in the direction of the light. The spot had grown, completely bathing the familiar wooden chest in its glow.

Why had it led her to the old trunk? Her short breaths mixed with the creaking floor as she tiptoed over to the chest. She flipped the latch up on the trunk and listened to the creak as she raised the old lid. Instantly the room was swallowed in darkness, but for one small glow inside the chest. At the bottom of the chest was a small leather pouch, the same one she had used to store the treasure stones. *Could it be?*

Ryann jumped up first to answer the phone. "Hello?"

He listened attentively, then answered, "No way!" as he walked back toward his seat.

"You're kidding, right?" he asked as he sat down.

Covering the phone with his hand, he whispered, "It's Liddy," then spoke in the receiver. "Uh-huh. I think you might be right."

The family focused on Ryann while the higher pitched voice of Liddy coming from the receiver chatted non-stop.

"Just a sec." Ryann covered the phone again. "Liddy found her bag of stones in the attic and thinks she knows what to do with them."

"And?" Mr. Watters asked, making a circular motion with his hand to coax the answer out of his son.

Ryann returned to his conversation with Liddy. "Yeah, uh-huh, okay, I'll ask."

"She wants to know if we can come over and drive her to the lighthouse."

Mr. Watters looked at his watch. "Now?"

"Dad, we just got done talking about how important it is to get back to Aeliana. If there's a chance this might work, we've gotta give it a shot!"

"Henry, I'm concerned," Mrs. Watters voiced. "It sounds more dangerous now with one unicorn trying to kill another, Hugon armies, dragons. Do you think it's safe?"

Mr. Watters weighed both their comments before speaking. "Honey, the safe way isn't always the right way—"

Ryann grinned too soon.

"—but, you have a point." Turning to Ryann, he asked, "Is there anything to keep me from coming with you?"

"Henry Watters!" his wife exclaimed.

Alison giggled at her mom's sudden outburst.

"I think it's important that the kids try and get back to Aeliana if they can. They'll be under God's protection. He's the one who's given them the task. It would be disobedient not to try. But just to add a level of protection, and," he winked at his wife, "to quell a mother's anxiousness, I'll go to Aeliana."

"We'll be there in a few. Just give me a chance to call Terell."

CHAPTER 26

"Magic" Stones

MOONLESS NIGHT DARKENED the evening sky, elevating the lighthouse's pulsing glow to a haughtier sense of purpose. The gentle lapping of waves, pushed along by a slight westerly breeze, created a reflective disturbance within the reach of the beacon's glow.

Pulling the car to a stop in the asphalt lot next to the boat ramps still left them with a short stroll onto the peninsula and their final destination. Ryann slammed his door shut and walked steadily with Terell and Liddy toward the lighthouse. The *beep-beep* of his father locking the car doors with his remote pierced the silence.

Ryann looked up as his father approached, chuckling to himself.

The spot of his flashlight and the two others chased each other around the base of the city's landmark. It was a good thing he had insisted taking a few extra minutes to find more flashlights before rushing out of their house.

"See!" Liddy exclaimed. "I told you it was here."

"Okay." Terell's response dripped with sarcasm. "Congratulations, you found a hole."

"You can be so annoying sometimes, Terell," Liddy responded.

"Why don't you tell Terell and my dad what you told me on the phone," Ryann said. "That should clear things up."

"Mr. Watters, can you hold my flashlight?"

"Sure, Liddy."

"Thanks. Okay, here's the short version. Somehow the medallion on my necklace produced a light on my living room floor, and when I tried to touch it, the light moved away and eventually led me up the stairs to our attic."

"Really? What did your parents say?" Mr. Watters asked.

"Uhh, they didn't say anything. They weren't home."

"Liddy! They don't know you're here?"

"Sure they do. I left them a note."

Mr. Watters pointed his finger at her. "You need to call them right now. Sheesh. All I need is to have them come home and find you gone."

"Ooh, busted," Terell whispered to a grinning Ryann.

"Really, Mr. Watters, it's okay. This is my parents' date night, and they wouldn't want to be interrupted."

"Liddy, my better judgment says I should drive you home right now."

She pleaded, "Pleeease, Mr. Watters."

He raised an eyebrow at Terell. "Don't think I didn't hear your comment."

"Ooh, busted!" Ryann laughed.

Mr. Watters turned his attention back to Liddy. "Let me think about it, Liddy, while you relay the rest of your story. I'm assuming that's not all there is."

"No, sir. The light led me to an old chest, and when I opened it, I was shocked to see this pouch." She held it up for all of them to see. "It's the same one I used in Aeliana to hold the five blue stones we found at the end of the rainbow."

"Tell 'em what your theory is," Ryann prodded.

"When I poured the stones out into my hand, I started wondering what use there could be for them. I can't imagine a treasure like that at the end of a rainbow could be anything but magical."

"Supernatural," Ryann corrected her.

"Yeah, well, as I studied their color and then shape, I remembered the hole here at the lighthouse when we came back last night and that the stones were the exact same size."

"Mmm, pretty clever, Liddy," Mr. Watters said. "I assume you mean to put one of the rocks into the hole?"

"Yes, sir."

"And what do you think will happen?"

"Well, my hope would be that it will open a pathway into Aeliana."

"I see," Mr. Watters nodded. "So is that your guess or wish?"

"I get your point, Mr. Watters. I'm sure from my normally scientific ways my hypothesis is a little biased, but I'd hardly call what we're doing a controlled experiment. Like Ryann says, this stuff is supernatural and goes way beyond science."

"Very interesting. I like the logic behind it, especially based upon previous experience," Mr. Watters congratulated her. "Like I told

Ryann back at the house, Mrs. Watters and I would feel much better if I accompanied you on this trip—if, indeed, your hunch is correct."

"Fine by me," Liddy answered.

"Me too," Terell chimed in.

"Great, it's settled. But first I'm going to give your folks a call, Liddy," Mr. Watters said.

"Ya know, Mr. Watters, I think it will be okay. Based upon the time-space continuum between here and Aeliana, we should arrive back a few minutes from now."

Terell shook his head. "Really, Liddy, do you sit around thinkin' this stuff up? It sounds like we're in some sort of sci-fi movie."

"Ya think, Terell?" She pulled one of the shiny blue stones out of her leather satchel and held it up to emphasize her point. "I'll just take this *normal* rock and put it in this *normal* hole and see if something *normal* happens."

"I got it, I got it. You win," he conceded.

"Nice try, Liddy," Mr. Watters said. "Here, dial your parents' number in my phone or you don't go."

She conceded, typing each number in his phone and handing it back. "Here you go."

Mr. Watters walked a distance away from them, pacing back and forth for a few minutes. When he returned, he gave a nod to Liddy.

"Your parents have given their okay, mainly because I'm going."

"Thanks, Mr. Watters. I appreciate it." She smiled.

Liddy tied the black pouch with the four other stones to the belt loop on her jeans. Pinching the stone between her thumb and forefinger she held it just above the same-shaped hole. All three flashlights focused on the stone's ultimate destination.

"Ready?"

"Ready," the three onlookers voiced in unison.

"Here goes," she announced, gently releasing the stone. It settled in place an inch or so below the surface. Nothing happened as they watched in silence.

"Turn off your lights," Liddy whispered. "I think it's starting to glow."

A faint glimmer appeared in the hole, making the stone look like the last of a campfire's burning embers, only this ember's luminescence was pale blue. The silent observers' faces reflected the pulsing stone's light as more energy began emanating from within. Excited smiles spread across their faces as they looked on in confident expectation.

As a brilliant white flash blasted forth from the hole, four cries erupted into the darkness. Caught off guard and blinded by the unexpected intensity of the light, Ryann stumbled backward, landing on the pavement.

"Keep your eyes shut for a few minutes," Mr. Watters instructed. "It will help your pupils adjust quicker to the darkness."

Terell propped himself up to a sitting position. "Yo, dude, that was intense."

Ryann rubbed his eyes. "What happened?"

"Shh, listen!" Liddy whispered.

Eyes still closed, Ryann listened for whatever Liddy seemed to be hearing.

Terell tilted his head to the side. "What are we listening for?"

"Don't you hear it? Listen to the water," Liddy said.

Focusing on the sounds of the lake, Ryann heard it now. The gentle lapping waters had grown to a surf-like crashing of rolling waves onto the shore.

"Everyone open your eyes," Mr. Watters said. "You should be able to see fine now."

"The stone's gone!" Ryann shouted, focusing his flashlight on the hole.

"Yeah, but check that out!" Terell pointed behind them toward the lake.

A fiery blue-and-white circle blazed in the air just off shore. Ten feet wide, the outer edges crackled white in a clockwise swirling motion, while the aura darkened in various shades of blue toward the center. Liddy's hair fluttered around her shoulders as the breeze picked up.

"What now?" Mr. Watters directed his question to Liddy.

Ryann answered, "In Aeliana, we jumped through a circle like this to get back. I say we take a running leap through the center."

Mr. Watters's eyebrows rose.

"He's right," Liddy said. "Judging by the height and distance from the lighthouse platform, the worst thing that could happen is that we end up in the lake."

"Okay," Mr. Watters concurred. "Who wants to be first?"

They looked at one another. "I'll go first," Ryann said. "If it doesn't work, then I'll be the only one to get wet."

"That's very thoughtful of you, son. If it works, I'll make sure the rest of you get through, and I'll go last."

Ryann backed away from the seawall to give himself a running start. "I'm going to jump through feet-first. There's no telling what's going to greet me on the other side."

Sprinting forward, Ryann quickly covered the fifteen or so paces before he reached the edge. Pushing off with all his might, he jumped through the air with a loud battle cry.

"Aaahhhhhhh!"

Ryann's scream was cut off abruptly as his head disappeared through the swirling aura. Mr. Watters watched in amazement, waiting to see if there would be a splash on the other side. When none occurred, he spoke up.

"That settles that." He nodded to Terell. "You're up."

Terell didn't hesitate. Without stuttering, he uttered his final words. "See y'all on the other side!" Racing forward, he followed Ryann's lead and jumped through the air feet-first.

"Your turn, Liddy."

She hesitated, her eyes growing bigger.

"It's okay, Liddy, you can—"

Liddy cut him off. "It's not that, Mr. Watters. The circle is shrinking. Look!"

Mr. Watters glanced over his shoulder. The circle was, indeed, shrinking. He grabbed Liddy's hand and pulled. "Come on. We're going through together!"

Hand-in-hand he raced with her toward the edge of the cement pier. When they reached the edge, he shouted, "Jump!"

Headfirst, the two of them plunged through the diminishing circle, a tangle of flailing arms and legs. Liddy screamed. Only one of them heard the splash.

CHAPTER 27

Galloping Ghosts

O KAY, THAT WAS freaky," Terell said to Ryann as they waited for Liddy and Mr. Watters to come through. "Where are we?"

"I'm not exactly sure," Ryann answered. "But I think it's the same cave we entered from Liddy's attic."

"Really?" Terell looked around. Dark, rocky walls, the rock floor, and an opening with blue sky and sunlight peering back greeted him.

"Yep, definitely a cave," Terell concluded as Liddy tumbled in headfirst.

"Ugh!" she groaned, landing next to Terell.

"Nice!" Terell chuckled. "The judges give that landing an eight out of ten."

"You okay?" Ryann asked.

"I'm fine," she snapped, shooting Terell a dirty look as she brushed herself off.

"Okay, move out of the way. My dad should be coming through next."

"Oh no!" Liddy exclaimed.

"What?"

"The circle started getting smaller when it was my turn, so your dad and I grabbed hands and dove through together."

"Well, where is he?"

"I don't know. One second we were in the air, and the next his hand pulled away from mine. He must not have made it."

"As much as I'd like him to be here," Ryann said, "there must be a reason for the portal not letting him through."

"Look on the bright side, Liddy," Terell said. "At least Mr. Watters is still there to talk to your parents." Turning to Ryann, he asked, "What's our next move?"

"First we need to find Carwyn and warn him about Ekron's message and the plot against his life."

"Where do you think we'll find him?"

Ryann turned to Liddy. "Any ideas?"

Liddy stared past him, wide-eyed and silent.

"What is it?" he asked.

Raising her arm in response, she pointed toward the cave entrance, still not answering. Ryann turned to see what captivated her attention.

"Whoa," Terell answered for both of them.

Off in the distance, a white horse appeared to be galloping through the air.

"Is it Adain?" Terell asked.

Liddy snapped out of her trance. "I don't think so. It's not a Pegasus. I don't see any wings."

They rushed out of the cave entrance as far as they could go before reaching the edge of the cliff. Bright rays from the afternoon sun temporarily blinded them. Their eyes adjusting, Ryann called out, "It's Carwyn! He's galloping through the air!"

"Unicorns can't fly," Liddy cut him off. "It must be a ghost or mirage."

Ryann ignored her, cupped his hands around his mouth, and called out, "Carwyn! If it's you, tell me to come to you in the air!"

The white unicorn hovered fifty feet away. "Come!"

Liddy and Terell watched in disbelief as Ryann stared straight ahead at Carwyn and stepped off the edge. His friends expected him to plummet to his death. Instead, Ryann's foot came down on an invisible surface, allowing him to take a second step, then a third as he moved farther and farther away from them. Halfway to Carwyn, he glanced down. Hundreds of feet below, boulders littered the sandy beach as the sounds of the crashing waves resonated upwards.

Liddy and Terell watched in horror as the invisible platform Ryann seemed to be walking on collapsed like a trap door.

Flailing as he lost his balance and gravity took over, Ryann cried out, "Carwyn, save me!"

In a white blur, Carwyn accelerated downward under Ryann. Landing awkwardly on the unicorn's back, Ryann grappled to hang on and stop his descent.

"You of little faith," Carwyn said. "Why did you doubt?"

Ryann had no answer. His face reflected his disappointment.

Terell couldn't contain his excitement as Carwyn landed on the precipice alongside them. "That was amazing! Ryann confided to me that he thought you were the Word's son, and I wasn't sure. But that just confirmed it."

Carwyn grinned at Terell and then turned his attention to Liddy.

"What just happened is clearly a miracle," she said. "There isn't a scientific explanation for how that could have occurred. Obviously you have no attributes of flight and—"

"For crying out loud, Liddy!" Terell cut in, "Can't you just say, 'That was amazing,' or, 'Cool'?"

Liddy cocked her head, eyebrow raised, with her hands on her hips.

"All righty, then. We'll just leave it at that," Terell said.

Ryann slid off Carwyn's back, holding on for a few moments while he whispered in the unicorn's ear. Terell started forward, but was stopped by Liddy holding out her arm. Carwyn's eyes grew larger and a smile large enough to bare his teeth spread across his face. Turning back to face his friends, Ryann no longer wore a face of despair. Instead he held a fist up toward Terell, and they rapped knuckles.

"Dude, that was awesome."

"Yeah, I shouldn't have looked down though."

Carwyn's consoling voice spoke up from behind, "I'm proud of you, Ryann. Terell is right to admire your faith in stepping out. Next time your faith will protect you from greater harm than falling from this cliff. Come here, all of you."

Carwyn took a few steps toward the ledge and looked down at the beach far below them. "Do you see that sand?"

"Yes," three voices acknowledged.

"If you had faith the size of one grain of sand, you would be able to say to this mountainside, 'Jump,' and it would cast itself into the sea."

"Right," Terell nodded his head while dragging out his reply.

"Terell!" Liddy chided.

Carwyn cleared his throat. "Terell, did you just see your best friend walking on air?"

"Uhh, yes."

"He quite literally took a step of faith. That faith was in me, that I would not allow him to fall. I give you the ability to exercise your faith, but it is up to you to do so. In your world, so many claim to have faith and yet don't ever do anything to prove it's real. No one in Aeliana has confirmed their faith like Ryann. But they will."

Ryann savored each word Carwyn spoke, forgetting his original urgency until the unicorn finished. "Carwyn! The demon Ekron revealed himself to me back in Mount Dora and said that you were going to be killed by Narcissus!"

"You are right to be concerned, Ryann," he confirmed, nodding. "There is evil in the land. And yet, evil must be overcome or good will not last."

"Should we gather the Chosen, and anyone else who will join us, to fight?" Ryann asked.

Carwyn stared into Ryann's eyes, at first saying nothing.

Carwyn's vibrant blue eyes seemed so deep with emotion. *Like the ocean,* Ryann thought. *Alive with unlimited energy, real concern, love, power, and sadness all mixed into one longing gaze.*

"Let me comfort the three of you. When the Word's only offspring comes in His glory, and all the angels with Him, then He will sit on His glorious throne. The world will be gathered before Him. And He will separate them from one another, as the kindhearted prince separates the loyal subjects of the kingdom from foreigners only living in the land. He will put the loyal subjects on His right and the foreigners on His left. Then He will say to those on His right, 'Come, you who are blessed of the King, inherit the kingdom prepared for you from the foundation of the world. For I was hungry, and you gave Me something to eat. I was thirsty, and you gave me something to drink.'"

Ryann, Liddy, and Terell treasured each word as Carwyn unfolded the story to them.

"Then the loyal subjects will ask the prince, 'Lord, when did we do all of this that you are talking about?' The prince will answer and say to them, 'To the extent that you did any of these things to your fellow creatures, even the least of them, you did it to Me.'

"Then to those on His left He will say, 'Depart from Me, accursed ones, into the eternal fire which has been prepared for the devil and his angels for you did none of these things for Me.'

"Then the foreigners will ask the prince the same question, 'Lord, when did we see you in need like this?' Then he will answer them. 'To the extent that you did not do it to one of the least of these, you did not do it to me.' These foreigners will go away into eternal punishment, but the loyal subjects will enter into eternal life."

"Whoa," Terell muttered. "This is supposed to comfort us?"

"It should," Carwyn smiled. "Because the three of you are loyal subjects in the King's service."

"That's right," Ryann said. "We've found the King's sword and are now seeking to recover the shield of faith."

"Then you're okay with Ekron's threats against you?" Liddy asked. "You aren't just going to ignore that, are you?"

"I'll be okay, Liddy. Don't be afraid of those who kill the body but cannot kill the soul. You should be afraid of the one who can destroy both soul and body in the abyss."

"The King?"

"Yes, He has the power to do so. In this He is to be feared, but at the same time His love for His people knows no bounds. Once you are part of His kingdom, you can never be snatched away."

Liddy managed a weak smile. "That's comforting to know."

"It is. And it is another aspect of faith."

Emboldened by the words of Carwyn, which seemed to penetrate through his chest and grip his heart, Ryann spoke up, "We will follow you wherever you lead and against whatever evil we have to face."

The white unicorn's face shifted to an expression of solemnity. "That is a worthy statement, young Ryann. For whoever finds his life will lose it, but whoever loses his life for my sake will find it."

"I'm ready for that," Ryann answered. "Where do we find the Chosen?"

"You'll find them in the Western Forest. It's getting late. You should go to them, but first, go back into the cave and retrieve your staff."

"Huh? But I was jus—" Ryann stopped mid-sentence as Carwyn nuzzled into him, gently pushing him toward the cave.

"Hey!" Ryann chuckled in mock surprise. "All right. I'm goin'. I'm goin'. Come on, guys."

Liddy and Terell followed him back to the entrance of the cave. Just inside, his staff rested against one of the rock walls. Picking it up, he turned around to thank Carwyn. "Ya know—"

Carwyn was gone.

CHAPTER 28

Fighting for Friendship

S O THE THREE of them think they can just traipse through our world without opposition, do they?" Narcissus mused. Peering into the ancient wood-framed mirror, the black unicorn gazed in a growing obsession with their every move. Three adolescent humans scrambled up a sparsely covered knoll, hiking with direction and purpose away from the rocky beaches of the Morganwyn Sea. Blood-red eyes narrowed as Narcissus ground his teeth together. The dark supernatural powers of the mirror were a benefit and a curse. The focus of his hatred could be revealed in the smoky glass, but at a cost. Excruciating pain, like a flame searing exposed flesh, coursed through his bones. He learned to revel in the pain, welcoming the intense rage it brought, but even he was cognizant that prolonged use would severely drain his strength. He recalled the overuse of the mirror during a rebellion early in his dynasty. The strain had left him in a coma for three days.

"Where do you think they're headed?" Narcissus asked the dark angel, who had been waiting patiently in the shadows.

"My liege, it would appear they are headed toward the Western Forest."

"Around the north side of the Marrow Mountains, or south?"

"South. The path is easier and farther away from detection."

Droplets of sweat appeared on the muscled neck of the unicorn. He stomped his hooves several times. The echoing claps careened around the stone room as he continued, "What forces do we have in that area?"

"There is a small patrol of Hugons, my lord. Would you like me to contact them?"

A deviant smile snaked across the unicorn's face. Dragging one hoof across the stone floor, he created an abhorrent screech.

Ekron winced.

Narcissus envisioned the future, his red eyes glowing in the reflection of the blank mirror. "Yes," Narcissus hissed. "Send a griffin at once. They cannot be allowed to reach the protection of the Western Forest!"

"As you say, so it shall be done." Ekron bowed and stormed out of the room.

Ryann came to the conclusion that the plains below the Marrow Mountains would be the most direct route to the Western Forest, but it came with a downside. Rolling grass hills were easier to traverse, but they also provided no cover for hiding. It made for a lively discussion in regard to the benefits of trees—shade and stealth versus speed, exposure to the elements, and vulnerability. In the end they agreed expedience was most vital.

"If a griffin comes screeching through the sky, I'm gonna freak,"

Terell blurted out between short huffs as he strained to keep up with Ryann's pace.

"At least we can see anything coming our way. Remember, I'll keep a look out ahead; Liddy, you watch the sky; and Terell, look over your shoulder occasionally to make sure that nothing sneaks up on us."

"Oh, thanks!" Terell replied. "That's supposed to comfort me?"

Ryann ignored the sarcasm. "We've been walking for over an hour now. We should see the tree line of the forest's edge any minute now."

"Mmm, if this is walking, I'm glad we're not running."

"Ya know, Terell," Liddy said, "you really should lay off the video games and get a little more exercise."

"Thanks for the diagnosis, doc," he huffed between words. "I'll try to keep that in mind."

The soaring heights of the Marrow Mountains provided a dramatic view off to their right. Snow-covered caps adorned the top of each. Ryann recalled Sorcha mentioning her lair was carved into the ice of these mountains and wondered which one it was. He had purposefully kept a buffer zone between them and the rocky foothills near the mountain range. Too many crags and crevices for enemies to hide in and ambush them.

"Up ahead," Ryann announced. "I can see trees. It must be the Western Forest."

"Thank goodness," Terell gasped. "What a waste. We're in the midst of a walk-a-thon, and I don't even have any sponsors."

Ryann and Liddy looked at each other and grinned.

The smiles were short-lived.

"Hugons!" Terell screamed.

"Where?" Ryann scanned the emptiness between them and the forest.

Terell pointed to the left. "Over there. That way."

The Hugons' lumbering movements were now clearly visible as Ryann followed Terell's finger. While their features weren't distinctive at this distance, the shadowy outline of their unique dragon shape and walk were. Ryann roughly estimated where they might intercept one another.

"Come on! If we run, I think we can beat them to the forest."

A few minutes into an all-out sprint, Liddy was slightly ahead, followed closely by Ryann, with Terell falling farther behind.

"Come on, Terell!" Ryann looked back at his friend, trying to encourage him.

"I'm not gonna make it!"

Ryann slowed down to a brisk walk. "Sure you will. It's just a little farther." Looking between the Hugons and back to Terell, Ryann began to have doubts himself, and made a calculated decision.

"Liddy! Hold up. Wait for Terell."

"Huh?" She stopped as he hustled up to her.

"Wait here for Terell, and then the two of you continue on to the forest. I'm gonna try and catch the Hugons off-guard by heading right toward them and giving them a little taste of this." He patted his staff.

"Are you nuts?"

"Nah, I just think we need to buy a little time, and I'd rather play offense than defense."

"All right. It's your life, but be careful."

"Will do," Ryann replied as Terell staggered up, huffing and puffing.

"Thirty seconds, Terell. Then we've gotta get to the forest."

Ryann raced in the direction of the dragon-men charging directly toward him about a football field length away. Closing the gap, he quickly tried to put together a game plan. At fifty yards, he stopped, held the staff out in front of him and pushed button 5. Fire swirled around the staff in a hypnotic blaze then blasted in a straight, crackling line towards the Hugons.

Frantic curses filled the air as the flame grew into an orangish-yellow ball of fire. Slamming into the dry earth where a Hugon had leapt from just moments before, an explosion of sand and flames shook the ground around the reptilian warriors.

Ryann looked over his shoulder; Liddy and Terell were still a few minutes away from the forest. Ryann turned back around to survey the damage he had inflicted on the Hugons. The dry grass at the center point of the fireball was aflame. With a mixture of caution and uncertainty, the Hugons rose to a crouching position and began spreading out.

Good idea, Ryan observed. *That way I can't focus on all of them. I'll have to be careful. They're smarter than they look.*

"Mmm, let's see what they do with this," Ryann muttered to himself. In four successive clicks, Ryann pointed the staff to the left of the group, two times in the middle and once on the right. Short bursts of flame spewed forth from the staff, causing the Hugons to jump for cover. Intentionally aiming low, the balls of fire struck the dry grass in front of the patrol, setting it on fire. *That should slow them down*, Ryann thought, racing to catch up with his friends.

Ryann was glad they weren't able to sneak up on the Chosen. He had cautioned Liddy and Terell to tread softly across the forest ground in an attempt to see how alert their comrades were. Halfway into an overgrown hollow, Ireth and Garnock had jumped out in front of them, spears menacingly pointed in their direction.

"Hey! It's us!" Liddy shouted.

Ryann had his staff up ready to protect them. A few blinks later, Ireth and Garnock lowered their spears, smiles spreading across their faces.

"We thought we'd never see you again," Ireth admitted.

"What?" Terell said. "We've only been gone a few days."

Ireth and Garnock turned to each other with surprise.

"It's been almost three years here," Garnock replied. "Follow us. We have lots of catching up to do."

CHAPTER 29

The Waterfall of Grace

IRETH AND GARNOCK led Ryann, Terell, and Liddy deeper into the thickest part of the forest, where they joined the rest of the Chosen. Darkness poured into the hidden bowels of the woods, cutting short the happy reunion. Rowan started a fire and invited them to find a seat atop the flat rocks and newly chopped logs she'd arranged. By the light of the flickering flame, Ryann surveyed his circle of friends. Liddy sat on one of the rocks, leaning back against Sorcha's side. Terell positioned himself between Taran and Mellt, his head swiveling back and forth as they each vied for his attention. As expected, Ireth and Garnock sat next to one another. Ryann chose a place between Rowan and Adain.

The crackling fire provided both warmth and comfort amidst the din of whispered conversations. Sorcha broke up the tranquility of the moment by clearing her throat. "I sense that Carwyn will be with us soon. Before he shows up, I feel we should discuss what has occurred over the past two years our time, since you've been gone."

Sullen faces reinforced Ryann's presumption that not all had gone well. As Sorcha gave an account, he had the feeling the intention was not only for the newcomer's benefit but was also meant as an encouraging review of what they had overcome in the past twenty-four months.

"When you left us, we were in our infancy as a group. Since that time we have been travelling around Aeliana and meeting citizens on the road, in small towns, and on their farms. Carwyn has spoken in a

271

way that only a prophet, soothsayer, or king would. And while that is all well and good, it is also our dilemma."

"How's that?" Ryann asked.

"We're having an impact on the creatures of Aeliana, but we don't know what will happen next," Sorcha replied.

"More than that," Garnock grunted, "when does it end?"

"We come from so many different backgrounds," Sorcha continued, "that each of our species has formed their own story of the future king who will restore Aeliana." She nodded in the direction of Garnock. "The dwarves tell of a great battle in which an anointed warrior from the Word will overthrow the reigning kingdom. Rowan's clan has passed down tales of a liberator who meekly comes out of the wilderness to free people from their inner hatred, more as personal encouragement versus physical combat."

Liddy scratched her head. "Isn't there one true account that you can all agree upon?"

"Yeah, and what about Carwyn himself?" Ryann added. "Have you asked him?"

Amongst the nervous shifting and downcast eyes, Ireth stood up and addressed them. "We have the books of the elven clan. They are both historic and prophetic. While we can agree on the history, the prophecy has proven to be more difficult. Based upon our bias from our various upbringings, it seems to reinforce what we want it to."

"How can that be?" Liddy asked.

"Well, in some places of the books, there are accounts of great personal sacrifice and humility by an unassuming prince. Yet in others, there are descriptions of great battles, culminating in a final engagement to end all evil."

A thought popped into Ryann's head as Ireth sat down. "Have you considered," he hesitated as the attention now focused on him. "Have you considered," he repeated, "that possibly the accounts are not referring to one coming of a king, but two?"

Several eyebrows rose in consideration of the question. Sorcha closed her eyes while simultaneously encouraging Ryann with one word, "Continue."

Ryann looked at Ireth as he began. "I will not presume to know the words of your books, but I can say from experience that in our world we had a prince known by many names, including the Prince of Peace. He came the first time not as a warrior bent on destroying those in power, but to save the people from their sins. He, too, has been misunderstood over the ages by every culture."

"And the second coming?" Sorcha asked, her eyes still closed.

"That has not occurred yet. We're still waiting, but it is supposed to be as a conquering warrior."

Adain fluffed the feathers on his wings. "Doesn't that create confusion?"

"It does," Ryann answered. "There are some who believe this Savior hasn't come yet. But it's been two thousand years since the first coming, and they're still waiting. You'd think they might wonder if they have missed it. Still others are anticipating the second coming, and there are indications it could be soon. However, there are many who have gone their own way, creating their own gods or forsaking any higher power whatsoever."

A loud braying snapped them out of their quiet discussion.

"Carwyn!" Liddy shouted, jumping up and running over to the white figure exiting the darkened perimeter. The Chosen rose as Liddy escorted Carwyn over to them with one hand resting on the unicorn's smooth, white back.

"I'm glad to see you made it here in one piece," he said, nodding to Ryann and Terell. "So, have you been discussing why I'm here and what my purpose is?"

They avoided eye contact in silence. "You would do yourself good by listening to young Ryann. Though he does not have gray hairs of wisdom from years of experience, I included him in the Chosen for the insight he has been given in his world."

Adain's eyes narrowed. "So, you are coming twice?"

"Let me answer you this way. I am here with you now. At some point I will have to leave you for a short time, and then I will come again; but it will be different than the first time."

"When will this happen?" Ireth questioned him. "What will be the sign of your coming?"

Carwyn replied, "Watch out that no one deceives you. For many will come in my name, claiming, 'I am the anointed one,' and will deceive the masses. Kingdom will rise up against kingdom. At that time many will turn away from the Word and will betray each other. Many false prophets will appear, claiming to be me and performing great signs and miracles to mislead the masses, but those who stand firm to the end will be saved."

"What will be a sign for the Chosen to look for?" Sorcha asked.

Carwyn continued, "Immediately following the distress of those days, 'the sun will be darkened, and the moon will not give its light; the stars will fall from the sky, and the heavenly bodies will be shaken.' At that time the sign of the one true Prince of the Word will appear in the sky, and all the kingdoms in Aeliana will mourn. They will see the Prince coming on the clouds of the sky, with power and great glory. Legions of angels will be with Him, and a loud trumpet will sound as they gather the Chosen from the four winds."

"What about now?" grunted Garnock. "In case you haven't noticed, there are those who would like to put us to death today. Ahem, Narcissus for one!"

"Garnock, my anxious warrior. Trust me when I say that the Word's curse is on the castle of the wicked, but He blesses the home of the righteous."

"Mmpf, well, I'd like to be part of inflictin' that curse. If ya' know what I mean."

Carwyn swung his head, taking time to peer into each of their eyes. Ryann felt as if Carwyn were looking into his heart, and Carwyn confirmed it. "The eyes are a window into someone's soul. Do not entertain the thought that by doing evil, good may result. This is the twisted logic of those who shun the Word."

"There is great wisdom in what you say," Sorcha acknowledged. "But teacher, how can we best resist this evil?"

"Many say, 'Love your neighbor and hate your enemy,'" Carwyn said, looking in the direction of Garnock, who smiled back at him. "But I say, love your enemies and pray for those who seek to do you harm. In the meantime it has been the custom in Aeliana to annually travel to Myraddin for the Feast of the Word. I have not come to break tradition, but to fulfill it. Therefore, we will travel to Myraddin tomorrow."

Gasps and indiscernible comments erupted at the unicorn's announcement. Ryann knew they had been in hiding from Narcissus and the Hugons. They had discussed venturing into small towns with a watchful eye for potential trouble, so he knew it didn't seem plausible they would just stroll through the gates of Myraddin in broad daylight.

Carwyn spoke through the initial shocked responses. "This must be done to fulfill the prophecies in the books. I am here to provide a new path for you to the Word. The old one is blocked and impossible to travel on. Instead of waiting for the feast each year to hear the bishop's prayer and the voice of the Word, each of you should pray on your own."

Looking back at Garnock, he added, "If you forgive those who do wrong to you, the Word will also forgive you. But if you do not forgive other creatures of their wrongs against you, then the Word will not forgive you of your wrongs."

Garnock's neck burned red at the admonishment by Carwyn. The others looked on in silence to see if the hot-tempered dwarf would argue the point and were pleasantly surprised to observe the softening of his tense facial features.

"Good, it's time to rest," Carwyn continued with his calm demeanor. "Tomorrow will be a significant day in Aeliana folklore for generations.

Ryann brushed his hand across his face, wiping at what felt like wet dew. Roused from a deep sleep, heavy breathing wisped through his hair. Alertly opening his eyes, a dark snout flared inches from his face.

"Wha—?"

"Shh," the calm voice breathed.

Blinking several times, Ryann looked passed the wet nostrils and focused on the protruding horn of the white unicorn.

"Carwyn? What's going on?"

"Follow me," were his only words as he turned and silently strolled away.

Ryann snapped to his feet, disturbing the bed of pine needles he'd slept on, and hustled after Carwyn. The unicorn exited the familiar camp surroundings, still dimly lit by the smoldering fire, just as Ryann caught up to him.

Resting one hand on the hindquarter of Carwyn's sturdy frame, he gripped his staff firmly with the other as they entered the darkness. Crunching leaves underfoot spoke in the tiniest of voices as they sauntered along the otherwise predawn silence. Completely blind in the surrounding night, Ryann kept a trustworthy hand on his leader. It wasn't long until nature's transitioning filter from night into early morning brought some welcomed visibility. Ryann's first sight was the narrow path they were moving along. He gasped as he looked off the path to his left. A shear cliff dropped hundreds of feet to a rocky stream below. He cocked his head, listening for the familiar sounds of rushing water. Expecting it to rise from below, he was surprised to hear the sound of plummeting waters coming from just up ahead of them. The canopy of limbs arching overhead as well as thick under-brush to their right made him feel as if he were walking through a tunnel.

"Whoa!" Ryann cried as he bumped into Carwyn. "Sorry; I didn't see you stop."

"Listen for the waterfall," Carwyn said, not acknowledging the sudden jolt he'd received.

Ryann closed his eyes and focused. He could hear it now, and pictured the cascading waters as the tumultuous resonance played in his ears. Carwyn began moving again. Ryann kept his eyes closed, moving forward another twenty feet until the unicorn stopped again.

"Open your eyes."

Standing together on a precipice, a magnificent valley unfolded in front of them. The early dawn still had not introduced the sun, yet there was enough light to reveal the lush green lowland, split in half by the dark rushing waters of a spirited river. Tracing the river back toward them led him to its vibrant energy source. Three distinct waterfalls poured over the rocky cliffs nearby. The one in the middle was almost twice as high as the other two, and as the three crashed into the pool below the resulting overflow created a rapid tide of water exiting the canyon.

"Follow me," Carwyn said for the second time that morning.

His sight unimpaired, Ryann no longer needed the unicorn for direction, but he kept his hand on him just the same. The small path wound around the side of the hill and led them to a natural rock formation that formed a bridge over one of the smaller waterfalls. Carwyn stopped to allow Ryann a few moments to revel in the beauty up close. Moving forward again, the clopping sound of hooves striking rock could be heard over the waters rushing past.

Ryann walked across the stone bridge and stopped halfway across. A hidden alcove appeared behind the curved downpour of water from the middle waterfall. He hesitated and looked out over the valley again as Carwyn stepped onto the rock ledge behind the water. A sliver of yellow peered over the easternmost hill, awakening the valley for another day. Pulling himself away from the mesmerizing display developing in front of him, he joined Carwyn behind the falls.

Surveying the spot they stood on, Ryann noticed that it wasn't so much a cave as it was a hidden spot cut into the mountainside. Instead of dark cavern walls like he had expected, they were white and smooth. The first thought that popped into his head was limestone. He was sure Liddy would know, but that's how he'd describe it to his friends. It also occurred to him that the cavern was large enough for the Chosen to hide behind if the need arose.

"Whoa, this is cool," Ryann said, his voice bouncing oddly around the enclosed area, which was bordered on three sides by stone and one side by a sheet of thick, clear water.

"Wait!" Carwyn said. "Watch what happens in three, two, one—now!" On the pronouncement of *now*, the sun's rays lit up the cascading water in front of him. Like a stained glass window, the yellow light illuminated their secret room in a diffused array of dazzling glory. Ryann marveled in the glow encompassing the space.

"Ryann, do you know what *grace* means?"

"Uhh, to be kind?"

"Partly, but it's much more than that. The Word defines it as 'unmerited favor.'"

"Meaning?" Ryann continued looking at the falling water.

"That He extends His love to the faithful, even though it is not deserved. It is a free gift He chooses to give, and yet it comes with a great cost."

Ryann turned away from the waterfall and looked at Carwyn. His eyes held a hint of sadness. He thought about what the unicorn had just told him but was still confused.

"How can the gift be free and also have a cost?"

"I sense you are only thinking about how much you will pay for the gift, like it is something you purchase at the store. You have to approach grace from a different angle." Carwyn looked thoughtfully at Ryann and continued, "There is a great cost to the Word in giving the gift. As a recipient of the gift of grace, there may be a cost in the way you live your life."

"I think I get it. What you're saying is I can't do anything on my own to buy or earn grace?"

"That's right. You're saved by faith alone, and yet the paradox is that what you do has to confirm that faith. The person whose faith comes while on their deathbed may have but a few breaths of life to exhibit faith."

"Saved? Saved from what?"

"That's one of life's most important questions," Carwyn answered, "and sadly, many creatures go their entire lives without finding out. Remember when you fell face-first to the floor of Myraddin at the Feast of the Word?"

"Yes," Ryann nodded, recalling the event. "It was when I heard His voice."

"You were getting a glimpse of His glory and were unable to stand up to it. In fact, you couldn't even look at it. He allowed you a brief impression through the sound of His voice."

Ryann thought back to that intense feeling of both love and fear; fear at the power exuded throughout the great hall of the castle and yet love in the form of overwhelming security and comfort from such a powerful being.

Carwyn continued, "The Word is light and in Him there is no darkness. Not even the glimpse of a shadow. All creatures outside of the Word and His Son have darkness in their lives and need the light to be saved from the ultimate darkness."

"The ultimate darkness?"

"Everyone will give an account for their actions at their death or the end of days. You will be part of the light or part of the darkness. There is no in-between. It is only by His grace that this is even possible."

Ryann considered Carwyn's words carefully before posing his next question. "Does grace happen one time, or does it happen over and over again?"

Carwyn smiled. "Let me put it this way; you showed great faith when you stepped off the cliff to come to me. Your faith is the act of receiving, depending, trusting, and resting in the Word's grace. Your job is to stay constantly under the waterfall of the Word's grace. You can only receive what He gives, so stay under the waterfall."

Ryann followed Carwyn's gaze and looked into the waterfall. Its full brilliance was on display with the rays of the morning sunshine.

"Step into it, Ryann," Carwyn urged. "Step into the waterfall."

Ryann didn't hesitate. With several long strides, he moved from beneath the limestone roof into the cool, clear water flowing down. The initial shock of actually moving under frigid running water lasted only a few moments. It was replaced by pure energy, seeping from his head down to his toes. Ryann had never felt so full of raw emotion before, so full of life! He turned around and peered toward Carwyn through the water pouring over him. The unicorn's horn glowed blue. Raising his arms up on both sides, Ryann closed his eyes. Looking toward the heavens, he basked in the waterfall of grace.

CHAPTER 30

Falling Short

RYANN WAS SURE if they took a vote, no one but Carwyn would choose to go to Myraddin. The previous evening, they had relayed stories of the past two years. The Chosen had traveled throughout all the known lands of Aeliana. Some citizens had welcomed them, while others viewed them as crazy hooligans, ignoring anything they had to say. It was apparent to Ryann that Garnock, Ireth, and the bulls struggled with Carwyn's teachings of tolerance, while Sorcha, Adain, and Rowan admired that about him. Sorcha was adamant no one in Aeliana could teach the way Carwyn did. The sage dragon, who had lived so much longer than any of them, was unable to counter the unicorn's discernment and new way of looking at things. These new ideas he brought up, seemingly out of nowhere, were what caused ongoing debate among them. They did seem to be united around the miraculous wonders Carwyn performed.

Ryann stumbled on the narrow path as they descended from one of the foothills in the shadows of the Marrow Mountains to the grassy plain below. With Liddy in front of him and Terell behind, they peppered him with questions concerning his meeting with Carwyn prior to breaking camp.

"Why do you think you were completely dry when you returned, despite being in a waterfall?" Liddy asked.

"For the third time, I don't know." Ryann rolled his eyes. "One minute I found it hard to keep my balance because of the amount of water pouring over me, and the next I was walking alongside Carwyn completely dry."

"I'd be trippin' out if that happened to me," Terell said.

Ryann held his nose and blew gently to clear his ears as they descended to the rich green grass of the valley plains. "I'm ready to walk on flat ground."

"Yeah, it's easier to talk walking side by side," Liddy said.

Walking next to one other, they navigated a short rise, which took them between two massive boulders spread about ten feet apart. The sound of galloping hooves approaching took them by surprise.

Ryann pointed in front of them as they passed through the boulders. "Look."

Two fauns raced back and forth across the plain, so focused on what they were doing that they hadn't noticed the large party moving up on them. A few steps later, the surprise was gone. The two stopped to study the intruders.

Terell provided his own commentary. "Look! They're shootin' arrows."

"Sheesh," Liddy chided him. "We call that archery, genius!"

The half-human, half-goat creatures closed the short distance between them in a frenzied gallop. Eager smiles adorned their faces as they came to an abrupt stop in front of Carwyn and Adain. The rest of the Chosen bunched into a small crowd as they caught up to their leader. Turning away from their new acquaintances, Carwyn announced, "I would like everyone to meet Jasper and Jett, two young brothers who appear to be engaging in a little competition today."

A mixture of hellos and "nice to meet you's" were followed by Jett responding to Carwyn's statement with a broad grin. "It's actually not much of a competition, but we'll call it that for the sake of argument."

"I like him," Terell whispered to Liddy and Ryann.

"You would," Liddy snipped back.

Both of the fauns had bows slung over their shoulders and across their backs. In the distance, a bold target painted on a large hay-stuffed sack sat like a little island in a sea of green. "Would you mind a small audience?" Carwyn asked.

"Ha! We don't mind. Do we, Jasper?"

"No, I suppose you wouldn't." Jasper mimicked his brother's enthusiastic voice. "Jett's the archery champ in these parts, so a little exhibition should suit his ego just fine."

The Chosen gathered in a semi-circle behind Jasper as Jett raced out to position the target in front of them. Jasper pointed toward his brother, who was arranging the burlap sack, and explained the rules. "The red outer circle is worth one point; the inner white circle counts for three points; and if you hit the black spot in the middle, you get five points."

"Sprit," Ireth said.

"That's right," Jasper spoke to her. "The game is called *sprit*, and whoever scores the most points with three arrows wins. Have you played before?"

"A time or two," Ireth answered with no hint of emotion.

"Yeh, don't let her fool ya," Garnock said. "Elves are raised with a bow in their hand."

Jett galloped up with a broad grin on his face. "Ready to go, brother?"

"Looks like you have some competition today," Jasper replied.

Jett looked his brother up and down. "What?" he sneered. "Did you get a quick lesson from someone while I was settin' up the target?"

"My brother, your humility is only surpassed by your quick wit."

He nodded in Ireth's direction. "I'm sorry ma'am, I didn't get your name."

"Ireth, but I didn't say I wanted to—"

Shouts from the Chosen implored her to challenge the brash young faun.

"Please do." Jett bowed low with a broad grin across his face. "I promise to take it easy on you."

A pale, determined look replaced Ireth's blushing face. Her lips pursed together, she breathed deeply, then exhaled and acknowledged her competition. "I appreciate the gesture, Jett. It's very thoughtful of you." Smiling, she stepped forward, her hand outstretched. Instead of shaking it, Jett grasped her hand lightly in his and pulled it up to his lips. With a light kiss, he whispered, "The pleasure is all mine."

Jerking her hand away as if she had touched a hot flame, Ireth's face burned red again. Several snickers erupted behind her.

"Game on!" She pulled the bow from around her shoulders as she stepped forward. Without waiting for the faun, she retrieved an arrow from her quiver, effortlessly drawing it into her bowstring and pulling it. She let it fly. In rapid succession, Ireth went through the motion two more times before the first arrow had even landed. A hush blanketed the onlookers as the arrows struck the target with a *thud...thud...thud*. All three arrows struck the center black dot.

Jett's mouth hung open as Jasper gently chided him, "Good luck, brother." Wild cheers rang out from the Chosen. Jasper galloped out to the target, retrieved the three arrows and headed back.

Without hesitation, Jett reached back, grabbed an arrow from his quiver, pulled back on the bowstring, lined up the target, and let it fly. *Thud.* Black!

Looking over his shoulder, he winked at Ireth. Drawing his second arrow back, he hesitated briefly, then let it fly. *Thud.* Black!

As Jett pulled the third arrow from his quiver, Ireth gracefully strolled to his side, leaned over, and whispered in his ear. She returned to her place in the same elegant manner. Jett slid the arrow into the bowstring and pulled it back. Holding it in place, he stared across the plain to the target. Ryann watched him nod at the target and release the string. *Twang! Thud!* Gasps rose around him, and Ryann looked out to the target. The arrow stuck out of the white band in the target. Cheers erupted from the Chosen as they gathered around their victor to offer personal accolades.

"Congratulations, Ireth. That was amazing," Liddy said as she shook the elf's hand.

"I'm sorry I had to embarrass him that way."

"Where did you learn to shoot like that?" Terell asked.

"Garnock was correct in saying that our people are raised with a bow in our hands. I also happen to be the champion of my clan," she smiled.

Ryann noticed Carwyn speaking into Jasper's ear and then watched as the faun dashed away.

Returning his attention to Ireth, Ryann said, "I'm curious to know what you said to Jett before his last shot."

"Hmm, that's a secret." Her smile widened until she noticed Carwyn staring at her.

Ryann watched the interaction, and Ireth's face blush. He wondered why the unicorn didn't congratulate her but instead addressed them all.

"The contest we just witnessed is an example of life. Everyone has a target, or goals, that they shoot for each day. For many, their achievement comes through money or fame, while others focus on their talents in music or art. Some creatures will utilize the amazing minds the Word gave them for the good of others by pursuing scientific answers for sickness and pain. Ask yourself, what is your target in life?" He paused to allow each of them to consider their individual answer.

"However noble or unselfish your answer may be, even if it is to feed and clothe the neglected and downtrodden, there is one target you must hit before your life ends."

Carwyn stopped.

In the silence that followed, Garnock gruffly asked the question they all wanted an answer to: "Which target is that?"

Carwyn turned back to the open plain. "That one."

The target Jett and Ireth had fired upon was gone. Jasper galloped toward them from beyond where it was previously.

"There it is!" Adain shouted.

"Where?" Liddy asked.

"There, I see it too," Sorcha said. "It's that small shape on the other side of Jasper."

They waited for the faun to gallop back. His chest heaved up and down as he came to a halt, gasping for air.

Carwyn continued, "The target on the horizon represents the Word in all His glory and perfection. You must hit it to pass from this life to the next and the new Aeliana, a place which will be like the original Aeliana before the darkness came."

Terell squinted to make out the distant target. "What if we don't hit the target?"

"Then you will enter the place prepared for the angels who first rebelled against the Word. It is a place of both darkness and fire, of both separation from the Word and isolation from everyone condemned to go there." Carwyn's serious tone cast a heavy burden over all of them as he emphasized each significant point of what awaited those who failed to hit the target. "So, who will be first?"

One by one, each of them stepped up and let an arrow fly. Jett and Ireth went last, taking their time to strain and pull the bowstring back until Ryann thought it would snap. Their faces grimaced under the tension as they aimed the bow for the optimal trajectory to ensure the furthest flight. *Twang. Twang.* Both arrows flew well beyond the less experienced participants but well short of the target. They both tried several more times with the same result.

"It's impossible," Ireth uttered in disgust. "Even my best attempt was far short of the target."

"Good, good," Carwyn said, nodding in agreement.

"Good? How can you say 'good'?"

"You have acknowledged that it is impossible for you to hit the target. Most creatures go through life believing if they only try harder, they can hit it. They believe if they are good enough, they will go to the new Aeliana. The Word is perfect goodness, and only those who are without imperfection can join Him in His new kingdom. The first realization you need to come to is you can't try hard enough or be good enough."

Ireth's eyebrows scrunched together in concern. "That doesn't offer much hope, does it?"

"It is the only way to realize that the hope does not come from within yourself, but from the Word and the one He has sent to redeem His creatures."

"Who is the one?" Ireth asked.

Carwyn looked deep into her eyes, then raised his head and gazed at the weary assembly gathered around him. No one spoke as his eyes briefly formed shallow pools of water and dried again, but not before a small tear escaped and ran down the side of his face.

"A time is coming soon when I will have to go away for awhile."

"Surely we can follow you," Rowan said, half as a statement and half as a question.

"No, you will not be able to follow me on the path I am taking. But I will not be gone long, and when I return, we will celebrate the greatest victory of all time."

A buzz spread through the Chosen as they speculated on the possibilities that lay before them.

"I can't wait for the big battle and wielding my ax through the ranks of the filthy Hugons," Garnock gruffly mumbled.

"It will be glorious to fly over Castle Myraddin once again without fear of Narcissus and his agents of change shooting arrows into my underside," Adain nodded repeatedly in anticipation.

Liddy joined in, "While I don't live here permanently, I'm hopeful for future visits that go back to the way things used to be."

Ryann glanced at Sorcha, whose eyes were clamped shut. He maneuvered himself closer as the chattering continued around him. "What does your sense tell you?" Ryann whispered to the white dragon.

Sorcha's eyelids rose halfway and one eye lazily rolled in Ryann's direction. "It is very confusing. I sense a conflict of emotions. There is darkness, pain, and sorrow, yet at the same time rejoicing and excitement."

"What should we do now?" Ryann asked.

"I suggest we all follow Carwyn," Sorcha answered in a much louder voice, bringing the other conversations to a close.

Ryann turned back to the unicorn. He was gone.

"There he is!" Terell pointed down the trail following alongside the grassy plain in the direction of Myraddin.

"Come on, let's go," Ryann said, heading off after him.

The Chosen paired off and fell in line behind Ryann, with the exception of Ireth. She stood her ground until the others had all moved on. "You're welcome to come with us," she said to the fauns.

"Hmm, I don't know," Jasper hesitated.

"Come on, brother," Jett encouraged. "Where's your sense of adventure? It will certainly be more exciting than hanging around here."

Jasper looked from Ireth to Jett. "All right, all right, I'm in, but I don't want any trouble in Myraddin, if that's where we're headed."

CHAPTER 31

Righteous Anger

HE JAGGED SPIRES and walls of Castle Myraddin etched a distinctive shape against the backdrop of the rising sun and its soft yellow hues. Ryann thought through the previous day's events. Catching up to the white unicorn hadn't been difficult, but no one dared to initiate conversation. The mood had remained somber as Carwyn led them in a dinner prayer around a hastily constructed cooking fire, then their leader had reminded them they would be entering Myraddin on the traditional date for the annual Feast of the Word. Carwyn's final words before they lay down for the night still resonated in his mind:

"The Word began the annual feasts to communicate to His creatures, yet they strayed. Through his love, He will restore the fellowship of the feasts. No longer will the feasts be held in a formal manner. The wall of separation will be broken through his emissary, the Prince of Peace."

Ryann's eyes darted into the heavily shadowed forests on either side of the road as they made the final push into the capital city. He gripped his staff firmly, anticipating a confrontation with the Hugon guards at any moment. None came. It was as if the pathway into Myraddin had purposefully been cleared just for them. Surely a trap of some sort awaited them, he thought, yet Carwyn continued on, undaunted by the possibility.

The din of shouts and clamoring instruments reached their ears long before they reached the city gates. Some of the instrumental sounds were familiar to Ryann, others sounded like variations of trumpets and flutes. A hollow blowing noise kept a steady beat and reminded him of the didgeridoo wind instrument he had learned about when he wrote an essay on Australian aboriginal tribes.

Scrumptious smells wafted passed them next as the frantic bustle of creatures scurrying in and out of the city gates came into view. Ryann had experienced an annual feast once before and recalled the tart smell of roasted apples and sweetness from a bubbling vat of molasses. He thought he caught a whiff of something that smelled like bacon sizzling in the frying pan back home, but he didn't recall seeing meat at his first feast. *If there were meat, what animal would it come from?*

Carwyn continued through the stone-carved arches of the west gate of Myraddin with confidence. Adain drew his wings in close to his sides and followed, his head moving back and forth searching the crowd.

"Ryann, something's not right," Sorcha muttered. "There are always Hugon sentries at the gates of Myraddin."

Scanning the bevy of activity as he passed through the curved archway, he noticed a few heads turn to stare at the unusual collection of creatures strolling into town. Ryann was certain they would have garnered more attention if not for the commotion in the streets. He breathed a sigh of relief and tried to relax.

The assault on his senses as they moved into the celebration rushed over him like opening a door on a blustery winter morning. Urgent shouts of items for sale to passing customers mixed with intense whiffs of spices and herbs roasting on open fires. Brightly colored tents and tablecloths provided a kaleidoscope of coverings along the streets. Tables pressed together as far as he could see were adorned in assorted jewelry, precious stones, cookware, metal tools, fruit, vegetables, and freshly cooked food. A black banner stretched across the street, rippling in the pleasant breeze. The red lettering announced the day's festivities:

Annual Feast of Alpha Myraddin

The Chosen shuffled through the crowded street as townspeople, animals, and other creatures parted in front of them. Carwyn continued to lead, followed closely by Adain. Their white coats provided a stark contrast to the drab brown, forest green, and black clothing worn by most of the citizens. Ryann compared this event to a Saturday morning flea market at Renninger's in Mount Dora. He chuckled to himself at the idea of people back home mixing with elves, dwarves, panthers, stags, warthogs, bears, and a host of other creatures.

As Ryann moved farther into the crowds, his overwhelmed senses adjusted to the true antics of the bazaar and a different picture began to emerge. Shouts turned ugly as patrons haggled with sellers over prices, laughter morphed to cursing, and orderly shopping turned into shoving and arguing. His mind flashed to tragic stories he had read about after-Thanksgiving Day sales, in which customers trampled one another just to get a deeply discounted item. Peering over the blur of activity, the outline of a Hugon appeared in the shadows of an alleyway alongside a darkened shop. Scanning over the heads to the periphery of the bantering crowds, Ryann honed in on dozens of the dragon-men lurking in the shadows of the surrounding storefronts and side streets.

The farther they waded into Myraddin, the more raucous the behavior became. The heart of the activity seemed to reside at the entryway to the ancient cathedral. Pointy spires from the dingy building cast jagged shadows over the crowd. Ryann stopped as Carwyn came to an abrupt halt at the bottom of the stone steps. Whirling around, the white unicorn gazed intently at the frantic behavior raging all around him. Carwyn's brow furrowed together in a way Ryann had never seen. Jaw-muscles clenching in rhythm with his flaring nostrils, Carwyn stomped the stone street and scraped his hoof across the uneven stones.

Rising up on his two hind legs, his two front legs pawing at the air, Carwyn let loose with a hideous neigh drowning out every other noise. Heads turned immediately at the unusual commotion. Dropping back down to all fours, he galloped in and out of the crammed tables and tents. Caught completely off guard, the sellers jumped out of the way as Carwyn uprooted tents and knocked over tables. Coins, jewelry, and other metal items clattered onto the rocky ground. Kicking at a cart of fruit and vegetables, Carwyn's hooves crashed through the wooden sides, sending the food flying in every direction. Chaos ensued as shoppers dove for fallen items, stealing anything on the ground in the wake of the unicorn's rampage.

Jett turned to his brother. "Come on, Jasper, let's get out of here before Hugon guards start arresting folks and throwin' them in the dungeon."

"Stop!" Ireth cried out as they raced passed her. Neither turned as they dodged curious onlookers and sprinted toward the city gates.

Carwyn completed three loops around the cathedral square, kicking over more tables and knocking down any booths in his path. Coming to a stop, he rose up again and let out a final, resounding neigh. An eerie silence bathed the stunned crowd as his legs came down with a sharp click. Carwyn drew a deep breath before chastising the people in the sternest tone Ryann had ever heard him use.

"Myraddin used to be the jewel of Aeliana, the place where the Word would speak. Now you have changed it into a bazaar of greed and gorging. You have deserted the truth for a lie. Cursed are those who lead you down the path of destruction!"

The subdued crowd looked on in silence. Ryann took a moment to glance at the throngs of motionless creatures. A subtle movement from the darkened periphery drew his attention. Hugons left the shadows and moved through the motionless creatures, anchored in place, awaiting the next words from Carwyn.

Ryann turned toward Liddy and Terell. "How many do you think there are?"

Liddy frantically scanned the gray-skinned creatures moving in from all directions. "At least a hundred. What do we do?"

Clenching and unclenching his staff, Ryann thought through the repercussions of each button's power. *It's too crowded for me to use my staff,* he reasoned. Looking to the other members of the Chosen, all of them stood transfixed by the scene unfolding before them and unsure of what to do next.

Carwyn looked heavenward as the Hugons lumbered toward him

in a robotic manner. Stunned city dwellers appeared to be mere nuisances to avoid as the seething dragon-men formed a wide, three-deep circle around the unicorn.

Ryann's skin crawled with goose bumps as a sudden chill washed over him. His focus on the city guards surrounding Carwyn widened as he watched a line of darkness advance across the crowds like a midday eclipse pushing the sunlight away.

"Look!" Terell said, pointing up.

A blue sphere hovered above the city, slowly blocking the view of the sun. The rays saturated the town in a pale blue light. Hugons baring their jagged teeth growled, holding their ground as if waiting for their next command. Ryann peered across the crowds for a sign of Narcissus. A hooded figure cloaked in black lurked near the cathedral doors. He couldn't make out the face hidden within the hood, but Ryann was certain it was Bishop Dridak.

A roar erupted from the Hugons. Carwyn looked up in the sky at the blue moon. Bright rays streamed down, bathing him in shimmering light. He ignored a lone dragon-man rushing forward toward him. One after another, the Hugons lunged toward the encapsulated unicorn with clubs and spears, only to be rebuffed and have their weapons bounce off the blue illumination. Ryann lowered his staff, watching open-mouthed as Carwyn ignored the intense attacks raging around him. The unicorn's mouth moved, as if praying, while he focused on the brightly colored moon above him. The pale blue light intensified, drenching everyone gathered in the city square.

"Hail Carwyn!" a voice called out from among the masses.

"The true king of Aeliana!" another voice shouted.

Other cries joined in affirming the unicorn but were eventually drowned out by the growing cheers of the crowd.

"Can you believe it?" Liddy grinned excitedly.

"It's amazing!" Terell agreed.

Ryann smiled with his friends. Looking around at the Chosen, all of them grinned with pride at their leader effortlessly thwarting the enemy.

He noticed one of them was missing. "Hey, where's Garnock?"

"He's a dwarf," Terell cracked. "I'm sure he's hiding around here somewhere."

Plodding along as they entered the city gates, the tantalizing smells of grilled vegetables and spices lured Garnock into dreamy recollections of life in the forest before the Chosen. His stomach growled at the thought of sitting down to a meal of sautéed yellow peppers, sweet onions, and wild mushrooms. Shouts pulled him out of his cuisine-driven illusion. Already last in line, he'd drifted farther away amidst the frantic atmosphere.

Shuffling his feet to pick up the pace, a voice nearby caught him off guard.

"Garnock!"

The middle-aged dwarf turned and looked up into the handsome face of a black-cloaked human whose sole imperfection appeared to be a thin scar running from his right ear down to his chin.

"How do you know my name?" Garnock asked.

"Ah, Garnock the river dwarf is well known throughout Aeliana," the man replied.

"And your name is?" Garnock asked, scrutinizing him up and down.

"I'm sorry, how rude of me. My name is Ekron."

"I need to catch upta' the others, so if you'd like to walk beside me and chat that'd be fine, otherwise..." His voice trailed off as he regained his step.

Ekron walked easily alongside the shorter-legged dwarf, the sea of creatures in front of them opening a path as they made their way toward the middle of town. "Have you heard of Narcissus?"

"You mean the black unicorn? Yeah, what about 'em?"

"He'd like a few words with you, if you have a moment."

Garnock stopped. "Ya wouldn't be messin' with me now, would ya?" He placed both hands on his hips.

"I assure you I'm not. But don't take my word for it. He's right over there."

Garnock gazed in the direction the man pointed. In a darkened alleyway just to the back of the crowd, the silhouette of a unicorn was barely discernable. Looking in the direction of his comrades, he noticed they had stopped in the town square. *It don't appear as if they're goin' anywhere for the time bein'. Maybe I can get me some insights into this self-proclaimed prince.*

"All right, then. I might have a few minutes. Lead the way."

Garnock followed the man into the busy ruckus of vendors, customers, and wandering observers. Immediately, a clear path emerged in a direct line to the alleyway as an invisible wall temporarily blocked any traffic that might cross in front of them. Ekron ignored the surprised creatures bouncing off the transparent obstacle. Some were knocked awkwardly off their feet. A few others held their noses in anguish after colliding face-first with the unseen barrier.

"Ha! That's quite the little gimmick ya' got there." Garnock laughed as two unsuspecting children chasing each other through the crowds smacked into the wall with such force they were jarred off their feet, landing on their backs with a thud.

Garnock looked over his shoulder and noticed the crowd filling in behind them. *The invisible wall must be disappearing as we pass.*

Ekron stood off to the side of the alleyway and ushered Garnock into the shadows.

"Good morning, dwarf," a smooth, deep voice said.

"The name's Garnock," he replied, cautiously eyeing the black unicorn.

"Yes, of course it is. The famous river dwarf who bravely defended Aeliana during the ogre invasion at Lydorf Pass, correct?"

"That's quite right." Garnock puffed out his chest. "There should have been a monument for that, just so creatures wouldn't be forget'n."

"I find that interesting..." the unicorn's voice trailed off.

"What's that?"

"Well," Narcissus pondered aloud, "that a brave warrior such as yourself has joined up with the white unicorn."

"And what's that supposed to mean?" Garnock gruffly asked.

Narcissus squinted as he peered into the dwarf's eyes. "You do know that they call Carwyn the Prince of Peace, don't you?"

"Is that so?" Garnock nodded. "Well, I got it by good authority that he's gonna rule over all of Aeliana."

"Really? Well, it seems like that might be hard to do without a fight," Narcissus said. "And he doesn't appear to be the fighting type to me."

"O', he'll fight, all right," Garnock replied. "He just needs the right moment."

A grin slowly spread across the unicorn's face. Lowering his voice, he laid out a proposition. "What if I were to provide you with that right moment?"

Garnock cocked his head. "Git on with it. I'm listening."

"What if I could provoke your leader to action so that Garnock the river dwarf could once again lead a mighty battle and go down in Aeliana's history as one of its greatest warriors?"

Garnock shifted uncomfortably for the first time. Stealing a glance back to the festivities, he caught a glimpse of Carwyn frozen in place, staring into the sky. *If things are gonna happen, they sure aren't gonna happen standing around.*

Covenant Keepers

'M GLAD TO see that you made it out of the city unscathed, Garnock," Ireth said as they gathered under the shade of the Tree of Life.

"Aye! My shorter frame ain't the best for keepin' up in that kind of fracas."

Rowan wiped her forehead as she trudged out of the thick brush surrounding the great tree's clearing.

Carwyn looked around at the Chosen who were around the tree, then called over to the halfling. "Rowan, have you seen our newest friends, Jett and Jasper?"

"They weren't behind me," she replied.

Ireth spoke up, "I saw them gallop out of town. They were afraid of the consequences of being with us."

The crushing blow for the attacking Hugons had been a brilliant blast of light. All those harboring animosity toward Carwyn had been struck with temporary blindness. Convicted of their wayward actions, the townspeople tore down the festival banners, cheering as they escorted the Chosen out of town.

"Very well, Ireth, thank you," Carwyn replied. "Now, everyone please gather around!"

A few moments later, each of them settled into a comfortable position on the grass in front of their leader, eager for the explanation he had for what happened in Myraddin. The sun drooped on its afternoon downward trek, reducing the intense midday heat. Leaves bristled high above them in the Tree of Life.

Carwyn basked in the setting sun as he spoke. "Many things that happened to you today may seem strange. My hope is that through a tale I'd like to tell you, you might understand." He hesitated. "There was a farmer who went out to plant his seeds. As he was scattering the seed, some fell along the path, and the birds came and ate all the seeds. Some fell on rocky places, where there wasn't much soil. Sprouts sprang up quickly because the soil was shallow. But when the sun came up, the new plants were scorched, and they withered because they had few roots. Other seed fell among thorns. The weeds grew up and choked the plants. Still other seed fell on good soil, where it produced a crop many times what was sown."

Finishing his story, every eye looked on, pleading for more, but nothing else came. As the silence became uncomfortable, Adain finally spoke. "I don't understand how this story relates to what we saw today."

Carwyn grinned in a kindhearted way. "Ah, Adain, you ask what is on the hearts of your comrades. All of you have been given the secret knowledge of the kingdom. These mysteries are open to all creatures, but not all will seek to uncover them."

Ireth cleared her throat in the ensuing silence. "He speaks the truth," she said. "The books say:

'You will be ever hearing but never understanding;
you will be ever seeing but never perceiving.
For the people's hearts have become calloused;
they hardly hear with their ears,
and they have closed their eyes.
Otherwise they might see with their eyes,
hear with their ears,
understand with their hearts,
and turn to the One who will heal them.'"

When she was finished, Sorcha bowed humbly and spoke. "We are grateful for you allowing us to discern your words, my prince, but in the case of this insightful story about the farmer, can you explain the seeds?"

"Sorcha, do not dismay at your current lack of understanding. It will grow as your desire for truth grows. Many noble prophets and gallant creatures have longed to see what you now see and to hear what you now hear."

Carwyn nodded to all of them and began, "This is the interpretation of the sower. When anyone hears a message about the kingdom and does not understand it, the evil one comes and snatches away what was sown in his heart. This is the seed sown along the path. Most of Aeliana is like this. The one who received the seed that fell on the rocky places is the creature who hears the Word and excitedly receives it. When no root grows to take hold, that creature's belief lasts only a short time. When trouble or persecution comes because of the Word, he quickly falls away. Your faun friends, Jett and Jasper, who scattered at the first signs of trouble in Myraddin, are examples of this." Carwyn looked at Ireth as an unpleasant reminder that she had enticed the young faun into joining them. He continued his interpretation to the group. "The one who received the seed that fell among the thorns is the creature who hears the Word, but the worries of this life and the deceitfulness of wealth choke it, so that no fruit grows. Lastly, the one who received the seed that fell on good soil is the creature who hears the Word and understands it. He then produces a magnificent crop, yielding many times what was sown."

Carwyn rose on all four legs, admonishing everyone to remain seated as they moved to stand and join him. Reaching behind the tree with his head, he returned with a wooden basket. Holding the handle in his mouth, he approached Adain on his immediate left and offered him the contents of the basket.

Ryann looked on in fascination. Perfectly oval-shaped quants ripened in marbled pink hues were stacked on top of one another. He hadn't seen the unicorn picking them off the Tree of Life, but it was apparent he had the choicest of the bunch.

Adain attempted to stop him. "Wise one, you do not need to serve me. Let me take the basket and serve the others."

"No, Adain, unless I serve you, then you can have no part with me."

"Then, my prince, serve me two quants instead of one."

"One quant will satisfy your hunger, as well as the rest of you—save one." He looked from face to face until his eyes settled on Garnock. "You should go now and do what you have to do."

The stout dwarf's eyes widened at his words. He started to speak, hesitated just a moment as if something stopped him, and stood instead. As he rose his entire demeanor changed. Shock was replaced with grim resolve. Garnock's dark, bushy eyebrows narrowed, his jaw fixed tightly as a small snarl twisted the left side of his mouth.

Tearing his gaze away from Carwyn, he nodded his head in acknowledgement, turned, and walked in the direction of Myraddin.

Ryann leaned over and whispered to Liddy, "That's just how I
pictured Judas when he went to betray Jesus. Should we try to stop
him?"

"No," Liddy whispered back, her eyes still on Carwyn. "I don't
think it's our place to interfere. Terell, what do you think?"

"Are you serious?" Terell asked. "After what we just saw in
Myraddin I think Carwyn's plenty capable of handling himself."

Carwyn continued around the circle until each had been given a
piece of the hallowed fruit. "Eat," he said. "This fruit is a covenant
between me and you. It is given as a taste of what is to come. The
black quants on the tree are the hearts of the creatures of Aeliana.
I have come to put an end to death and to provide a pathway to the
Word."

Ryann bit through the thin-skinned exterior of the light pink fruit.
An explosion of sweet tingles raced through his mouth as he closed
his lips around the first bite. Squeezing his eyes shut, he basked in the
most enjoyable taste he could ever have imaged, a soft moan escaping
from deep within. "Mmm," he groaned. Looking at Liddy and Terell,
they grinned widely as their chewing became more vigorous. Juicy
spittle escaped Ryann's mouth, landing on his chin. Breaking to wipe
it off with his sleeve, he exclaimed, "This is unbelievable!"

"I've never"—*smack*—"tasted"—*smack*—"anything quite like it,"
Liddy said, causing both Ryann and Terell to laugh at the display of
such unbecoming behavior coming from their refined friend.

"It beats the juiciest mango I've ever tasted back home by a long
shot," Terell said, ending his last swallow with a wet burp.

"That's disgusting, Terell," Liddy responded, lifting her nose at
him as she took a delicate bite of her quant.

They turned their attention back to Carwyn as he began speaking. "Do you understand what I have done for you? You call me 'wise one' and 'prince,' and rightly so, for that is what I am. As your teacher, now that I have served you, you too should humbly be willing to serve others."

"We will commit to serve others," Adain pledged for the group.

"The Word watches over everything and sees how you interact with everyone. Your loyalty will be rewarded. Whoever proclaims allegiance to me before creatures in Aeliana, I will also proclaim them before the Word in heaven. But whoever disowns me before their fellow creatures, I will disown them before the Word."

"Our loyalty is to the rightful prince," Adain again responded. "We are at your service and will faithfully follow you."

"Dark times are ahead, Adain," Carwyn replied. "You are the one I would like to take over leadership of the Chosen while I am away."

"Where are you going? We'll follow you anywhere."

"Where I'm going you can't follow. But don't worry; I'll only be gone a short while. In the meantime I need to have a private talk with my human friends. Ryann, Liddy, and Terell, follow me. The rest of you stay alert."

Carwyn turned and walked toward the line of trees on the west side of the clearing. Ryann, Liddy, and Terell looked at one another blankly, then hopped to their feet and ran after him. Crashing through the underbrush into the forest shadows, they crunched to a stop atop a bed of dried leaves.

Before Carwyn uttered a word, Ryann preempted him with a question. "I'm still puzzled about finding the shield of faith. Where should I be looking?"

"Don't fret over finding the shield, Ryann. I'm confident that at the right time the shield will find you."

"It's hard to have faith about something when you've never seen it before, yet you're told to seek it out."

"There is more truth to that statement than you know," Carwyn smiled. "Now, the reason I brought the three of you aside is that, while you've been called to Aeliana for a purpose and are part of the Chosen here, I have been with you before you ever came to Aeliana."

"Huh?" Terell said, suspiciously raising an eyebrow. "I know I've never seen you in Mount Dora before!"

"Terell, don't be disrespectful," Liddy chided.

"Oh, he's correct, Liddy, at least in one sense. Would it make sense for a talking unicorn to show up on Earth?"

"No," she answered.

"Ryann has had this feeling for some time now. The Word sends me in the way that is most appropriate for His creatures who are in need of a redeemer. My mission has been, is, and always will be to restore relationship to the Word."

"Who did he send you as in Mount Dora?" Liddy asked.

"Deep inside, you know. It will be revealed soon enough, but a time is rapidly approaching when the Chosen will be scattered." He lowered his gaze. "You will leave me all alone."

"I'd never leave you," Terell said.

"Yes, Terell, you will, and the roaring of a bear will be a sign. You will deny you even know me. But I will not be alone, for the Word is with me. I am telling the three of you these things so that in me you may have peace. In this world and on Earth, you will have trouble. But take heart! I've overcome both worlds."

"But how will you overcome—" Shouting and screams from the clearing drowned out Terell's words.

"Come on!" Ryann shouted. "We have to get back and see what's happening!"

CHAPTER 33

Evil Unleashed

RYANN RACED BACK the way they had come with Liddy and Terell close behind him. Springing past the last trappings of the forest's protection, they landed in the midst of a raging battle. Ryann's head swiveled trying to assess the calamity.

Hugons were pouring into the clearing from the eastern woods, clubs swinging. Snarling growls lashed out from behind their jagged teeth. Three were encapsulated in ice from the freezing breath of Sorcha. As Ryann watched, the white dragon's tail swept behind her, sending several others flying through the air. Taran and Mellt stood back to back, surrounded by a dozen Hugons. Their adversaries stood out of harm's way, carefully eyeing the bulls' pointed horns.

Adain's back hooves kicked out with blinding speed, catching one of the gray-skinned Hugons in the chest. Hurtling backward, two other dragon-men were taken down.

Off to his right, Ireth plucked arrows from her quiver in the same rhythmic motion she had shown in the bow competition. Fifty feet in front of her, arrows stuck out of the arms, legs, and torsos of a horde of twenty to thirty dragon-men. Ryann could see she was going to run out of arrows soon. Rowan stood just behind Ireth, nervously gripping her wooden staff.

"Come on." Ryann motioned to Liddy and Terell. "Follow me." Racing toward the greatest need, Ryann raised his metal staff and aimed toward the closing gap between Ireth and the advancing

Hugons. He pushed button 2, unleashing a stream of fire. The fiery trail barely missed Rowan, sizzling into the grassy earth just in front of the gray-skinned monsters. As the turf erupted into a wall of flames, anguished cries rang out from the surprised Hugons. They fell backward, clamoring away to a safe distance.

"That should hold them!" Ryann shouted, advancing until he was alongside Ireth.

"Thanks, Ryann. I was almost out of arrows."

"What?" Terell boasted. "You've got three left. You had those uglies right where you wanted 'em."

"I'm really glad you three showed up," Rowan confessed. "I didn't relish having to take them on with my regular, wood staff."

Over the shouting of the battlefield, a commanding voice bellowed from behind them.

"Enough!"

Heads turned to the sound of Carwyn, his head held high as he continued his slow stroll up to the Tree of Life. "It is time to stop fighting."

Sorcha hesitated just before releasing another breath of frost. Ryann released the pressure on the button, and his wall of flames dissipated into a smoky mist. The Hugons cautiously advanced, waiting for the unicorn's next words.

"All who rely on violence will die violently. Don't you know that I can call upon the Word, and He will at once send legions of angels to my defense? This isn't the way the Prince of Peace will redeem his people."

"Yes! You should listen to him!" a mocking voice shouted from behind the Hugons.

"Ekron!" Ryann seethed.

A sly, curling smile spread across the dark angel's face. With a swoosh, his black, feathered wings fanned out behind him as he continued in his leering tone, "They don't intimidate me. I recall leading those legions before I chose to leave."

"Your mind has become clouded since your fall from grace," Carwyn stated. "You did not choose to leave. You were banished from heaven."

Ekron glared at the white unicorn. "Better to reign in the fires of hell than to serve in heaven."

"That's the same deceitful lie you tried to perpetuate on Earth, Ekron. And having failed there, I see you've moved on to new territories. The result will be the same."

"I think not," the dark angel raged. "Have you met my little friend here?"

Garnock stepped out from behind Ekron's expansive wings. "I think he wants to have a word with you."

The weary-looking dwarf stepped forward, avoiding Carwyn's eyes as he walked toward him.

Sorcha took a deep breath, glaring at their betrayer.

"Don't freeze him, Sorcha," Carwyn cautioned. "I'll talk with Garnock."

The Chosen, Ekron, and the Hugon guards looked on as the river dwarf approached the white unicorn and conversed for several minutes. Garnock bowed, stepping backward as Carwyn held his head high and announced, "I am innocent of any charges of conspiracy against the throne of Aeliana that may be levied against me. And as such, I will go quietly with them to Myraddin."

Ekron smiled. "Seize him!"

The Hugons hesitated, looking from the white dragon to Ryann and his staff.

"Now!"

Ryann looked around nervously and raised his staff.

"This is not the time," Carwyn said as he bowed his head, allowing the Hugons to throw a rope around his neck and cinch it tight. The dragon-men's eyes gleamed in delight as they attached iron shackles to each of the unicorn's legs. Working the chains across to connect each leg, they linked them together to prevent any sudden movements. Ryann seethed inside as one of the Hugons brought out a leather muzzle and secured it around Carwyn's face.

Torn between the order from Carwyn not to fight and the rage building within him to battle such an obvious injustice, Ryann was paralyzed. He clenched his fists over and over again, breathing rapidly as the gray figures led his leader into the tree line from which they'd come.

"Ryann, we can't just stand here!" Liddy broke the silence. "We have to do something!"

Ryann asked their appointed leader, Adain, "What do you think we should do?"

"I suggest you leave quickly!" a deep voice sounded from behind them.

Jumping at the surprising voice, they turned around.

Black, shiny nostrils poked out from behind the thick trunk of the Tree of Life, followed by the imposing horn and face of the black unicorn.

"Narcissus!" Adain glared at the intruder.

"Yes," he answered, drawing out his response with a sarcastic snarl.

"You shouldn't have come alone," Sorcha answered, her blue eyes glaring in disgust.

Narcissus strolled out into full view under the shade of the historic tree. "I'll have you know that the six of you and the three trespassers into our land are the only ones who stand in opposition to me. Being the open-minded leader of the Enlightened, I'd like to give you an opportunity to join me. Your dwarf friend chose wisely and is being rewarded with a sizeable sum of gold and his choice of living quarters in Myraddin."

Adain looked at the resolve in the faces of his comrades. "We would rather die than join you!"

"Tsk, tsk. So be it," Narcissus shook his head. "Oh, and in regard to your scaly white friend's assumption, I didn't come alone. Look around you."

Ryann glanced around the circular clearing, awestruck at the number of Hugons stepping out of the shadows of the surrounding trees. His jaw dropped.

"There are too many," Adain whispered. "When I give the signal, Ryann, you jump on my back; Terell and Liddy, get on Sorcha. Rowan, you and Ireth hop on our bull brethren and scatter. We'll regroup back here when it's safe."

Three Hugons carrying round, black iron shields with red dragons emblazoned on the front and torches in the other hand walked across the clearing to join Narcissus. "This is your final opportunity to join the new order," the black unicorn gloated. "The old way is being put to death today."

As he nodded to the Hugons, they moved closer to the Tree of Life, torches in hand.

Ryann watched the look of horror wash over Adain's face. "Noooo!" the Pegasus cried out. "You can't do this. It's an abomination to the Word!"

"Oh, believe me when I say I can and I will," Narcissus spat. "The Word is dead!"

Lifting their torches overhead, the emotionless Hugons lit the bottom limbs on fire. "Kill them!" Narcissus ordered.

"Now!" Adain countered.

Ryann held down button 3 and made a sweeping circular motion, firing at the ground of the approaching Hugons. White mist sprayed out of his staff, coating the grass with a layer of ice. Terell and Liddy climbed up Sorcha's tail onto her back as Taran and Mellt knelt down so Ireth and Rowan could hop on their backs. Hugons slipped and fell on the frosted grass. Ryann continued spraying the icy substance, buying them precious seconds. Finally releasing his grip, he climbed awkwardly on Adain's bare back and held on to his mane.

"Fools, don't let them escape!" Narcissus shouted.

"Taran and Mellt, head west!" Ryann shouted. "I'll cover you." Pointing his staff toward the Hugons to the west, who were trying to regain their footing on the icy ground, Ryann pushed button 5 rapidly three times. Three small balls of fire shot out of his staff, one after the other, rocketing into the ground along a thirty-foot section of the line of approaching Hugons. Dirt and flames erupted like small volcanoes as the dragon-men dove for cover. Smoke billowed from the scorched grass, adding to the chaos, while Taran and Mellt galloped toward the gaping hole in the Hugon ranks.

Sorcha bolted almost vertically with Liddy clinging to her neck. Terell yelled, straining to hold on to Liddy's waist. Adain followed, though not nearly as fast, flapping his wings mightily to lift Ryann's added weight. Rising above the ground provided a sense of comfort and fear. Their immediate threat was gone. However, Ryann's mind replaced it with the image of himself plunging to his death if he fell off the Pegasus in flight.

"I'll fly low toward the bulls," Sorcha shouted, "and see if I can freeze any Hugons that get in their way!"

Ryann glanced back toward Narcissus. Instead of looking up to them, Narcissus was facing the burning tree. Ryann watched in wonder as the black unicorn's horn cast a red aura over the Tree of Life.

"Look!" Liddy shouted. "The black fruit on the tree is moving."

Ryann's focus moved from the red aura to the flames licking their way through the tree limbs, and finally to the rotten, black quants. Indeed, they were shaking like bird eggs at the point of hatching. Instead of beaks pecking their way through a shell, the fruit swelled and exploded. Dozens of pieces went flying in every direction. Wings sprouted from the center mass with two red dots in the center. One after another, hundreds of explosions took place across the massive burning tree.

"Bats!" Liddy screamed.

Shrieks filled the air as the flying beasts opened their mouths, sucking in their first breaths of life and crying out for something to sink their fangs into. Like a newly hatched duckling imprinting on the first moving object it sees, the black bats flew skyward and honed in on their prey.

"Let's get out of here!" Ryann cried out to Adain.

The bloodthirsty bats filled the air like billowing smoke from the dying Tree of Life. Seeking their first life's blood, the oversized bats swarmed into a crazed feeding frenzy, forming a giant black cloud. Blocking out the sun setting behind them, they gave chase to their much-larger prey, instinctively relying on one unified mission for the multitude.

"Use your staff to scare them away," Adain said. "I'll keep us steady." Ryann took a firmer hold of Adain's mane. Looking back, he saw a stray bat out in front and pressed button 5. The end of his staff erupted in a swirl of orangish-yellow flames, sending a ball of fire hurtling towards the hideous red-eyed creature.

"Bull's-eye!" Ryann shouted gleefully as his fireball hit the bat, bursting its target into pieces of seared flesh that disintegrated along with the explosive fire.

Bolstered by his success, Ryann squeezed the button three times in succession, sending a trio of fireballs into the evil black swarm. More bats exploded like the first, leaving gaps in the dark veil of wings, which filled in quickly.

"There are too many!" Ryann yelled. "We'll have to try and out-fly them, Adain."

Flashing into his field of vision like a white comet, Ryann watched Sorcha fly past them in the direction of the shrieking bats. He turned his head in time to see her blow a white cone of air into the flapping mass of evil. Expanding as it blasted into the great wall of screeching fangs and red eyes, hundreds of black bats were immediately washed over in a glaze of white frost. Wings froze in midair. The momentum of the bats carried them forward another few feet before they plummeted toward the ground like giant hailstones.

Sorcha whirled around. Terell held on to Liddy with one hand and pumped his other fist in the air. "That's what I'm talking about!" he screamed.

"They're still coming!" Ryann pointed back.

Flying side by side, Sorcha laid out a plan to Adain. "I'll slow down and confuse them with a fog of ice-rain. You head toward your hollow in the Joynnted Knolls, and we'll loop around and head toward my lair in the Marrow Mountains."

Ryann leaned into the wind as Adain raced forward at full speed.

CHAPTER 34

Jailed!

ORCHA SLOWED TO put distance between them while blowing bursts of wet breath in every direction. Like chaff firing off the side of a plane to confuse incoming missiles, the bats' sonar began picking up multiple images. With Adain and Ryann sufficiently beyond danger, Sorcha gave a warning to Liddy and Terell. "Dragons are capable of flying over one thousand of your miles per hour. So hold on tight; we're going to lose them. *Now!*"

Liddy and Terell flattened themselves against Sorcha's white scales. Her wings whipped up and down in a blurred fervor. Wild screeches rang out as the confused bats scattered in hundreds of different directions. In moments, the shrieking sounds had passed and were replaced with the quickly dropping temperature of the headwind rushing over them. Sorcha's voice carried on the wind, "Another minute at this speed and we'll be there."

Adain extended his wings, galloping through the air in a gentle glide to match the speed of the approaching grass-covered lowland. If Ryann had been blind, he wouldn't have noticed a difference between flying and the smooth gallop Adain effortlessly transitioned into.

"The hollow I call home is just up ahead in those trees," Adain pointed out. "We'll stay there tonight and make plans for what to do tomorrow."

Liddy shivered within the confines of the icy cave. Despite being out of the sub-zero gusts among the peaks of the snowcapped Marrow Mountains, she was still wearing her sleeveless pink top. While appropriate for the year-round climate of Florida, it provided little protection for Sorcha's glacial home, which was chiseled into the side of the mountain. Sorcha described with great pride the numerous tunnels and chambers she had carved into the ice. Her greatest accomplishment was completing a back entrance escape route. Burrowed down under the mountain, the tunnel ran out a short distance and rose up into a spring-fed lake.

"D–d–do you think we can start a fire?" Liddy asked, crossing her arms in front of her and rubbing her shoulders.

"I don't know why you'd want to disturb this perfectly good ambiance with a fire," Sorcha answered, then smiled at Liddy's raised brow.

"Here," Sorcha said. "This is the lost book I spoke of. It's actually called *The Prophecies of Aeliana*. See what you think while I go out to fetch the two of you some firewood."

The white dragon swooped out of her cave, illuminated by the smallest amount of light reflecting off of ice crystals, stalactites, and stalagmites. Huddling next to one another for warmth, Liddy and Terell opened the book and began reading to take their minds off the bitter cold.

Four Hugons donning heavily padded black armor tugged on chains fastened to a thick iron collar around Carwyn's neck. The unicorn looked up briefly and noticed a red dragon logo sewn onto the chest of the senior guard. Leading him along the dark passageway, they passed through two carved wooden doors into a large hall with massive gray pillars. Two of the pillars had heavy metal rings attached to them. Sneering as they attached the chains to the metal rings, one of them mocked the unicorn, while another spat on him.

"You're going to enjoy your time in here," the spitter laughed.

The Hugons stood off to the side in pairs at attention. The clunks of echoing boots marching into the dank room broke the silence. The sound continued methodically across the stone floor until it stopped in front of the chained prisoner. Carwyn's head drooped low, staring at the worn stone inches from his nose. The new voice cackled in front of him.

"It's so nice to have the mighty self-proclaimed prince with us!"

Carwyn ignored the taunt.

"Look at me," the voice rasped.

With great effort, he raised his head and stared into his captor's black eyes. Hands on his hips, Ekron leered back smugly.

"How does it feel to be on the other side?" the dark angel asked.

"Whether I am in heaven, on Earth, or here in Aeliana, my feelings do not change my loyalty to the Word," Carwyn responded.

"Spoken like the naïve, submissive son that you are. Only when you leave the boundaries of your Father's kingdom will you experience true freedom."

"You were a brilliant star in charge of a legion of angels, Ekron. As you well know, the Word is the one true ruler. He was at the beginning, and He knows the end. You will not be so arrogant when that time comes."

"Silence!" Ekron shouted. "We are in the process of changing the ending, and it begins right now. Guards! Give this pathetic creature forty lashes and then lock him in the dungeon."

Two pairs of yellow eyes peered from the dark recesses of the musty cell. Ears perked in advance of the echoes bringing another forlorn soul down the seldom-used passageway. One flickering torch anchored to the cave wall just outside the cell bars provided just enough light to see the cell door and scattered, mildewed hay.

Labored clacking mixed with the shuffles and grunts of Hugons bounced off the stone walls, increasing to a crescendo just outside the wooden door. Two Hugons entered first, chains in hand. The eyes watched as the chains pulled their prisoner through next. A unicorn with its eyes closed staggered in with the violent tugs from the guards.

"Both of ya better stay back!" one of the guards ordered as he fumbled through a dozen skeleton keys to open the interior iron-barred door.

Two more Hugons entered to unlock the prisoner's shackles, while the first two opened the creaking cell door.

"Get in there!" the Hugon handling the keys snapped, kicking the unicorn in the hindquarters. The flame provided a ghastly view of the beaten animal as it stumbled through the cell door. Dark red streaks crisscrossed over the once brilliant white backside of the abused creature. Limping forward a few more feet, the unicorn collapsed in an awkward heap on a pile of straw in the middle of the cage.

The pairs of yellow eyes emerged, one on each side of the downed unicorn. Mangy, gray wolves with oily, matted hair slinked into the flickering light, exposing their open sores and missing tufts of hair.

Sniffing at the bloodied, horse-like body, the smaller of the two wolves spoke.

"He smells just like Carwyn, the unicorn I saw over two years ago. It was rumored he claimed to be the rightful prince sent by the Word."

"Are you sure it's him?" the larger wolf asked skeptically.

"Of course I'm sure. This nose never forgets a smell," he chuckled.

"Mmpf, if it's him, then he took a wrong turn on the way to the throne room," the big wolf growled.

The unicorn whispered, startling the two wolves, "A cloud of darkness has descended upon Aeliana." He raised his head, taking a moment to look into the eyes of his cellmates.

The smaller wolf's eyes lit up. "Are you Carwyn, sent by the Word to save us?"

"I am."

"Ha! If you're really the prince, then save us!" the large wolf snapped.

"Hush! Don't you fear the Word?" his cellmate admonished. "You're under the same sentence as me. We're being punished justly for the evil deeds we've done. But this creature has done nothing wrong."

"The only thing I did wrong was get caught," the larger wolf answered bitterly, turning back into the darkness.

"Prince?" The remaining wolf looked into Carwyn's face. "Remember me when you establish your kingdom."

"You're right about your past when you say your wickedness is great. However, in one moment of faith, you have left that all behind." Carwyn laid his weary head down on the rough straw. "Be at peace." He closed his eyes and whispered, "I will speak to the King on your behalf."

CHAPTER 35

ꓱanishment

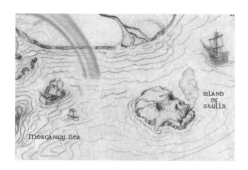

EFORE SHE OPENED her eyes, Liddy knew the fire was out. Her eyeballs felt like round ice cubes inside the thin lids meant to protect them. Sorcha had returned with leaves for bedding, wood, and a torch from a family of hill dwarves who lived at the foot of her mountain. Liddy had warmed by the small fire and quietly dozed off to sleep. It was cold and dark now. *It must be early morning,* she thought.

Scooping a handful of leaves together, she tossed them onto a few of the embers that still glowed with life. A thin trail of smoke rose from the leaf pile, building into a small cloud before a tiny flash ignited it. She reached over Terell and grabbed the last three logs, one at a time, and placed them gently in the fire pit.

"Wake up, sleepyhead," she said, shaking Terell's shoulder.

Sorcha emitted a low growl as her mouth stretched open in a huge morning yawn.

326

"Phew! Now I know where they get the term *dragon breath*," Terell said, frantically waving his hand in front of his face.

Blowing gently while fanning the new flames, Liddy asked, "Sorcha, I read something interesting last night in the scrolls and wanted to know if you knew what it meant."

"I've read them countless times over the years, yet that doesn't necessarily mean I understand it all. What perked your curiosity?"

"From an outsider's perspective, so much of the prophecy fits the life of Carwyn that I wanted to get your thoughts."

"I have carefully scrutinized the prophecies in the annals of Aeliana and have lived a thousand years waiting for the one who would fulfill them," Sorcha noted solemnly. "You have been here only a short time, but I believe you can trust your instincts."

"Well, if that's the case, the puzzling part is here," she said, pointing to a specific line in the book. "It says, 'The Word's Son will be delivered into the hands of the evil ones, be sacrificed, and then on the third day, overcome Azriel.'"

"I am familiar with that phrase," Sorcha acknowledged.

"Carwyn's been captured by the evil ones." Liddy paused. "If He's the Son, then the prophecy says what happens next. Who is Azriel?"

"Azriel?" Sorcha peered into her eyes. "He's the angel of death."

Wind whipped through Ryann's wavy blond hair, causing him to smile and reflect, *I could get used to flying through the skies of Aeliana, if only circumstances were better.* As he continued flying atop Adain, he played back the past few hours in his mind.

When he awoke, the Pegasus had left to procure a few items from his neighbors. Ryann found a few edible items to serve as breakfast and then looked around Adain's hollow. It reminded him of a spacious stable built into the side of a hill. Deep piles of hay on one side were used for sleeping, and he presumed the troughs on the side were for eating from and entertaining guests. He had laughed at the absence of a table, but it made sense when he thought about it. Unicorns didn't sit at tables to dine or cut food with a fork and knife. He was curious to know who had helped Adain construct the wood-planked ceiling and walls, which gave the space the overall effect of a log cabin.

Adain returned with what he explained to Ryann was a tai'ir, the traditional, coarse, loose-fitting garment of a monk. It had an over-sized hood to hide Ryann's face from view and draped down to just above the ground. The hope was that by wearing it, he wouldn't rouse suspicion from anyone in Myraddin. Adain had also found a "bark sleeve." It consisted of the bark of a fallen tree branch, eaten out by bugs that had no appetite for the exterior. The sleeve was the length of his staff, and Ryann slid it over the smooth metal finish to complete his disguise.

Ryann snapped out of his deep thoughts as Adain swooped down to a lower altitude. "There's a wooded area just north of the city. I'll drop you off there, and you can complete the remainder of the journey by foot."

"I wish you could come with me."

"As do I, but unfortunately my wings and white coat would be hard to conceal. Even if I could be made to look like a horse, I'd draw attention to you. It's better this way."

"Where will you wait for me?"

"Don't worry about that. I'll fly around the city out of view and see if I can locate the others. If anything goes wrong, meet up at the Tree of Life. Hopefully it didn't burn to the ground."

Raucous shouts, grunts, howls, and roars echoed around the center square as the town creatures scurried and jostled for the best view. Ryann stopped at the edge of an alleyway, peering through the small opening in his hood. As Adain had explained, Narcissus's first in command, Lord Ekron, presided over all judicial punishment throughout the year. Annually they held the traditional guilt offering, in which one criminal would be sentenced for banishment to the Island of Skulls. This creature, according to the Enlighteners, was guilty of the most despicable crimes in Aeliana and was given over to the Word as appeasement for everyone's transgressions.

Ryann was intrigued by the Island of Skulls and had asked the Pegasus what he knew about it. Adain answered that it was the ultimate form of punishment, arousing fear in the most courageous creatures. He had flown near the remote island once, but never close enough to see anything living. The most intriguing aspects were that from above it resembled the shape of a skull. Two dormant volcanoes were positioned at the approximate location of eye sockets, while a live volcano was located at the site of the skull's mouth. The remainder of the dead island was covered in gray rock, ash, and driftwood. Adain's last comment was that the names of those exiled to the island were carved into a wooden plaque in the alleyway alongside the cathedral. As far as he knew, none of them had ever returned.

Baaawaaaaaaa!

The first of the six trumpet calls announcing the judgment blared across town. Those gathered grew more anxious as they tried to push their way to the front.

Ryann kept his hood pulled down, making it harder to see where he was going, but it was a small sacrifice to hide his identity. By the time the fifth horn sounded, he had circled around the edge of the crowd and positioned himself behind a short stone wall of steps leading into a closed store. *I hope Liddy and Terell made it. I'm sure Sorcha had to drop them off on the outskirts of town as well.*

Baaawaaaaaaa! The sixth blast sounded.

The heavy wooden doors of the castle swung open, bringing a dramatic hush over the eager onlookers. Ryann focused on the dark opening, anxious to see who would exit first. Striding out confidently in his black garb, Ekron took his place on the right side of the dais, nodding to the crowd before beginning his remarks.

"Citizens of Aeliana and fellow Enlighteners, we solemnly gather here today for the annual guilt offering to the Word. Every year, from the time I became ruler of Aeliana, we have found two creatures who have violated the laws and brought them before you to determine who will be set free and who will be sent as our sacrifice to the Island of Skulls. Today will be no exception. I bring before you Xanth, an albino troll from the uncharted lands."

Boos erupted from the crowd.

With a wave of his hand, like a circus ringmaster introducing the next act, Ekron ushered forth two Hugon guards pulling chains. Next out of the cave-like castle entrance strode a seven-foot monster with a noticeable limp. The crowd gasped as the pale, wart-covered troll shuffled out. His pink nose protruded out like a banana, dangling down over his mouth to make his broken, half-toothed smile more noticeable. Wild, moss-green hair lay atop his head like an abandoned bird's nest. His clothing consisted of an animal hide hanging from his bloated waist to just above his knobby knees.

"Xanth's crime is the devouring of two six-month old fauns—alive!"

The troll grinned at his dubious introduction as the crowd booed.

A few rocks, thrown by enraged town creatures, bounced off his leathery skin.

As the crowd's outrage subsided, Ekron motioned to the Hugons, and the guards tugged the troll over to the other side of the platform. Two more Hugons emerged from the darkness pulling chains attached to a white unicorn.

Ryann struggled to contain a scream. *Carwyn!*

A low murmur rolled in waves across the crowd as the unicorn willingly stepped out, followed by two more guards with their chains attached to shackles on his legs. A purple blanket with a gold *W* embroidered on it covered his backside up to his midsection.

What could they possibly accuse him of? Ryann's chest felt heavy, like a giant weight was pressing down on him. *The disparity between the two of them couldn't be greater.*

Lord Ekron began, "The second heinous creature of the day is Carwyn, the Prince of Peace, as he calls himself. Not only does he claim to be the rightful heir to the throne of Aeliana, but he seeks to overthrow our king as well."

Rage boiled within Ryann. *That's a lie!*

Lord Ekron walked over to Carwyn, slapping his hand down violently on the blanket. Carwyn winced.

"Do you deny it?"

Carwyn remained silent.

"Haven't you organized a group of rebels called the Chosen?" Ekron yelled.

"He has!" someone in the crowd called out. "I've seen them together."

"And," the dark angel drawled out, "didn't you come into town to demolish the festivities surrounding the annual celebration of the Word?"

"He did!" a dwarf up front cried.

"I saw him kicking over tables, destroying booths, and fighting the king's guards," another creature voiced.

Ryann felt the frustration tearing at his insides. *That's because they were making a mockery of the celebration!*

"That is just the beginning of the horrific acts this rogue unicorn has committed. Do you want to know the worst of it?" Ekron asked.

"Yes!" the crowd roared.

"Are you sure you want to hear the worst of it?" he asked again, raising the crowd's emotions to a feverish pitch.

"Yes!"

"He has committed the unpardonable sin! He has burned down the Tree of Life!"

"No. It's not true!" Ryann yelled out this time, but the violent chants of the enraged crowd drowned him out.

"Banish! Banish! Banish!"

Tears welled up in Liddy's eyes. "It's not right; he's lying," she cried out to Terell.

The pandemonium of the distracted crowd ignored them as Terell replied, "I know, Liddy, but there's nothing we can do about it. We just need to be patient and see what happens. Maybe we'll have an opportunity to help." He looked around. "Do you see Ryann anywhere?"

Liddy scanned the crowd. "No, but I'm sure he's here somewhere," she said, trying to pull herself together. "Maybe he'll use his staff to intervene somehow."

The noise from the crowd returned to a dull rumble as Ekron raised his hands and extended his wings.

"I ask you, creatures of Myraddin, citizens of Aeliana, who should I release today? The troll, Xanth, or the prince-imposter, Carwyn?"

"Release Xanth! Release Xanth!" the mob chanted over and over again in unison.

Terell focused on the individual faces of the crowd. Enraged faces turned red to the point that ropy veins popped out on necks. Numerous Hugons positioned themselves throughout the masses, encouraging the emotional cries.

"This isn't going to turn out pretty," Terell yelled into Liddy's ear, as he tried shoving back against the mob pushing into them.

"What should I do with Carwyn?" Lord Ekron yelled.

"Banish him! Banish him! Banish him!"

A coarse-haired black bear shoved his way between Terell and Liddy, separating the two. Screaming town creatures filled in the gap between them, pushing them further apart. "Terell, help!" Liddy cried.

The dark angel's hands came down, and as if by signal, new flags were unfurled around the walls of the city. The purple-and-gold flags, which had evolved from a *W* to *AM* for *Alpha Myraddin*, were removed and replaced with black flags emblazoned with a fire-breathing red dragon.

"Today is the dawning of a new age in Aeliana. King Narcissus and the Enlighteners present our progressive symbol of empowerment!"

With the crowds gawking at the new flags, the jostling stopped temporarily and Terell was able to glance back to the platform. A Hugon behind Carwyn replaced the old blanket on his back with the new black-and-red dragon emblem. Terell gasped at the fresh, red streaks across the unicorn's back as the change was made. Looking at Carwyn's face, he came in direct contact with his shining blue eyes. For a brief moment, his soul felt refreshed.

"I release to you, Xanth the troll!" Lord Ekron declared.

The mob cheered at the announcement. The Hugons chanted, "Banish Carwyn!" and the mindless mob joined in.

"Lead him away to the ships!" Ekron screamed.

The ships? Where are the ships? Ryann wondered.

Enraged throughout the mock trial, it was all Ryann could do to keep from pulling out his staff and pushing every button at once. His chest still pounded from the vision he had of the condemning crowd ablaze in flames or white with frost.

He took a few deep breaths and tried to think. *Ships? They have to be down by the channel that leads to the Pedr River. The Pedr flows out to the Morganwyn Sea, doesn't it?*

A Hugon hesitated and looked his way. Ryann turned and melded into the dispersing crowd that was cheering and heading in the direction of the river. Ryann pulled his hood down tight and flowed with the tide of delirious creatures.

"Hey, aren't you one of the Chosen?" a young elf girl asked.

"Huh?" Terell replied, looking around to see if she was talking to him. "No, not me."

"Yeah, she's right," the older female holding the girl's hand agreed. "I saw you with the others the last time you came to Myraddin."

"No, you must be mistaken," Terell answered. Turning to walk away, he bumped into a stocky dwarf.

"Hey, watch where you're—wait a second, you're that human who was with Carwyn!"

"I'm telling you," Terell countered, "I don't even know the white unicorn!"

"Get outta my way!" roared a bristling black bear who had brushed by him earlier.

"Run, Terell!" Liddy cried out, speeding toward him as a Hugon guard pointed in her direction and called for more guards.

They ran west, back the way they had come and toward the Tree of Life. The thinning crowds following after Carwyn and the procession of guards provided space for them to sprint toward the city gate.

"Do you think it's smart going back to the tree?" Liddy asked, looking over her shoulder.

"That's not my plan," Terell replied. "First we need to put some distance between us and the guards."

Running out the city gate, they headed for the trees.

"I see six of those monsters following us!" Liddy cried.

"Come on, this way," Terell said, running up a pathway to his right.

Liddy followed Terell into the trees. "The path is easier around the lake," she yelled to him.

"That's right, but the top of the falls is our way of escape!"

Liddy stole one last look as they entered the forest. The Hugons still followed.

Ryann stayed to the shadows, skirting along the row houses and shops as he made his way down the sloped alley. The riotous crowds provided a distraction, but his hood limited his vision and caused him to stumble on the uneven street stones. He caught a glimpse of Carwyn's horn and mane as he stopped at the corner and tried to get his bearings. Brooms and sticks crashed down on the unicorn's head and back, but Ryann never heard Carwyn cry out. He tried to ignore the curses and insults.

Lord help me, Ryann prayed to himself. *I need to find a way to help him.*

Passing through the south city gate, Ryann recalled the last time he had come this way. Griffin, the red fox who was a member of the high council, and the rest of them had boarded a small boat in search of the King's sword. Their travels had taken them to the tri-river area where the Bryn, Elan, and Pedr rivers split off to the northeast, east, and southeast.

The Pedr River was the one near where we came out of the cave, Ryann thought. *How long ago was that trip?*

At the bottom of cobblestone road, he stopped. The crowd continued across a grass lawn dotted with mature oaks and white wildflowers. Loosening the grip on his cloak, the hood opened up, allowing him a more panoramic view of the river shores. "Whoa," he muttered. "This doesn't look anything like the last time I was here."

CHAPTER 36

Island of Skulls

RYANN RECALLED A few small boats tied to wooden pylons on his previous quest. Since then the river had been dredged and widened to accommodate six wooden sailing vessels. They reminded him of pirate ships as the crews busily ran provisions up and down the gangways. *I'd call this more of a wharf than a boat dock.*

"Hey, you!"

Ryann's heart skipped a beat, hoping the voice wasn't speaking to him.

"Where've you been, Relyk? I haven't seen you in ages."

Whew! Ryann ducked behind an unhitched wagon piled high with bales of hay. *That was close. Maybe I can lay low here for a few minutes.*

Plopping down around one of the large wooden-spoked wheels, he lowered his head and pretended to be asleep.

"You running from the law too?" a tiny voice asked.

He jerked, smacking his head against the wheel.

"Oh, sorry to startle ya. I suppose ya are if ya be jumpin' like that."

Ryann raised his head slightly and peered with one eye out of the dark confines of his hood. He saw no one.

"Up here, lad."

Ryann raised his head higher. A two-foot-long rat returned his stare from between two bales of hay. He looked old and bedraggled, with wet, matted fur sticking out in every direction. A black patch covered one eye and a few of his pinkish-gray claws were missing.

"Name's Rutland."

Ryann nodded his hooded head up and down. The chants on the other side of the cart began again. "Skull Island! Skull Island! Skull Island!"

"Poor soul," the rat said. "I've seen many a creature shipped out, but ne'er seen one of 'em come back."

"What are you wanted for?" Ryann asked, talking low to disguise his voice.

"Eh? Ya do talk, huh? Well, they be wantin' all river rats outta the wharf. Can ya believe they think we're dirty? What's the world comin' to?"

Ryann heard the clip-clopping of hooves on wood, then more commotion from the crowd, and finally a few orders yelled clearly over the murmuring throngs.

"Okay, the spectacle's over now. You can go home. The ship will be departing in an hour, and then the rebellion will officially be over!"

"Tsk, tsk, tsk. What a waste," the rat said, shaking his head sadly. "Another promising rebellion stopped in its tracks."

"Uhh, excuse me, Rutland, but I have to see what boat they put the unicorn on."

Getting to his knees, Ryann scooted over to the side of the wagon and peered around the hay. The six boats were still moored in front of him, pointed out toward the river. Carwyn was nowhere to be seen.

Terell and Liddy raced up the mountainous path they had traveled along just a few days earlier. In Aeliana time, it had been three years.

Wild grass and fallen branches covered much of the trail, a clear sign it had not been not well traveled.

"Just a little farther," Terell said.

"What makes you so sure the portal out of here will be in the same place again?" Liddy asked.

Terell stopped as they reached the top, breathing heavily as sweat dripped lazily down his forehead. He smiled at her. "Faith!"

"Terell, this is no laughing matter. You'd better be right. Come on." She pulled on his hand, leading them toward the edge of the cliff.

Stopping a few feet from the precipice, Terell put his hands over his eyes. "Well?" he asked, peeking through the fingers on one of his hands.

Liddy shuffled forward a few more inches and peered over the edge. "It's there!" she squealed. Jumping back to Terell, she grabbed his hand, "Let's go!"

"Wait a second, Liddy. I've been dying to do this ever since we first saw those Hugons."

"What? Come on, they'll be here any—" Shouts interrupted her.

Crashing off the overgrown trail onto the hilltop, the Hugons raised their hands to block the sun's glare.

Terell turned and backed up until his heels were hanging off the edge of the cliff.

"What are you doing?" Liddy whispered, as she prepared to jump.

"Watch this," Terell smiled. "Hey, ya big uglies. Over here!"

The Hugons raised their clubs, grunted, and charged toward them.

"See ya!" Terell saluted. A big smile spread across his face as he fell backward.

Liddy jumped off feet-first, screaming, "You're crazy!" as they plunged through the swirling blue light.

Which one? Which one? Ryann's eyes darted between the ships for some sort of movement or clue as to which boat Carwyn was on. *I've got to get on board while no one's looking.*

Every ship in the tiny fleet looked ready to set sail. Crewman checked mooring lines, and supplies were piled up around each boat. A few creatures walked along the pier, but Ryann was afraid to approach any of them. *Which one would Ekron use?*

Carved across the stern of each vessel was the ship's name, painted with red lettering across a black background. Ryann mumbled the names aloud to himself—*"Aeron, Palunder, Gwril, Serapis, Jackyl,* and *Cynan.* Mmm, there's something familiar about this, but what?"

Ryann read the names over and over again in his mind. "That's it!" he said excitedly. "Carwyn said that with the Word there are no coincidences." Making his way down the pier with an air of authority, Ryann strode towards the *Serapis.*

It's the only one named after one of the six ships that John Paul Jones commanded, he reasoned. *There are six ships here. It has to be this one!*

Ryann walked up the gangplank and made a quick turn toward the stern. Muffled voices shouted from inside the main cabin as he passed amidships, moving aft. Cargo of all shapes and sizes stacked on the main deck looked suitable for hiding. Ryann was standing there considering his options when the cabin door creaked open.

"Where is his majesty?"

Ryann listened from between a stack of crates on one side and rope-bound blankets on the other.

"He will arrive when he chooses," answered a voice Ryann recognized. *Ekron!*

More voices and movement followed, jumbling together in an indiscernible tangle of yelled orders, doors banging, and chains dragged across the deck.

The clomping of hooves on wood caught his attention. Wedged between the cargo, Ryann pressed back against the blankets and scooted toward the opening at the end. He peered out and caught a glimpse of what he thought would be Carwyn. Instead, the clomping hooves coming up the gangplank were black and belonged to Narcissus.

"All hands, ahh...ten...shun!

A whistle blew six short blasts. Two Hugons grabbed the gangplank and pulled it aboard, scraping it across the bulwark.

"Cast off!" the voice ordered. "Set the jib and foresail."

Movement coming his way caught his eye. Ryann pushed himself back, then sunk down to the deck, making himself as small as possible. The ship was obviously underway as the gentle rocking up and down brought a methodical trance to his sleepy eyes. Initially, he fought the urge to sleep, then his mind convinced him otherwise. *It'll be a while before they reach Morganwyn Sea. If I stay low like this, no one will be able to see me. I'll just close my eyes for a minute.*

"Set the mainsail!"

Ryann's eyes shot open. A salty breeze whisked over him with each dramatic up-and-down movement of the ship. His ears perked up at the voices speaking nearby.

"Are we out of sight of land now?"

"We are, my lord."

"Then bring the captive on deck and shackle him to the mainmast."

"I'll get the king."

What now? Ryann sat up, carefully sliding his staff out of the bark encasement. He clenched his jaw. *I know this much, I'm not going down without a fight.*

The melodic blowing of a whistle by the ship's boatswain was followed immediately by the gruff order, "All hands on deck!"

Feet pounded across the wood deck heading toward the bow, allowing Ryann the opportunity to escape from his hiding place. On the other side of the cargo area he found a ladder and climbed up to the top of the vessel's wardroom. Peeking through the slated railing he had an unobstructed view of the open deck around the mainmast. The ship's crew gathered in a semi-circle around the mast. He noted they were primarily Hugons with a few burly dwarves pushing their way up front.

Ryann thought through the options he might have with his staff. He contemplated burning the sails, or maybe freezing some of the crew or blasting a fireball.

He looked down at his staff. Button 4 was blinking. *Now there's an idea!*

"Make a path! Make a path for your king!" Ekron ordered as the fifty seamen parted for him to pass. Two guards followed, pulling the chains attached to Carwyn. The blanket that had covered him earlier in the day was gone now and the red streaks cut into his hindquarters were painfully visible. Turning him around to face the crew, the guards forced Carwyn to a sitting position. They pulled back roughly on the chains fastened to his neck, wrapped them around the mainmast, and locked them in place. With his head forced back, Carwyn's neck, chest, and stomach were exposed and vulnerable. Chains around each of his forelegs were pulled down and fastened to the base to keep him from kicking. A low, guttural sound spread through the sailors' ranks but was quickly silenced by the short motion of Ekron's hand across his neck.

"Now, all bow for his majesty, King Narcissus."

Heads bent down reverently as the black unicorn swaggered through the same path they had led Carwyn. Brushed to perfection, his smooth, black coat gleamed in the afternoon sun. "At ease," Narcissus said as he turned to face his crew.

"The purpose of our voyage today is to extinguish the rebellion of this dissident and his rogue followers. He has the audacity to claim kingship over me and my kingdom. For those of you who have never been to the Island of Skulls, there is a reason that no one ever comes back alive." Narcissus sneered as he let his words settle on his eager listeners, then calmly uttered, "Gordak, it is time."

Ryann's eyes widened at the sight of the enormous gray creature exiting the shadows of the wardroom. He resembled a Hugon but was a foot taller than the tallest guard Ryann had ever seen. His thick, muscular frame made for heavy, labored movement as the bulky creature moved through the crew to stand alongside Carwyn. Reaching up with one massive, clawed hand, he gripped the unicorn's throat and squeezed. With the other hand, he grabbed Carwyn's horn. Veins on the giant Hugon's neck bulged. Grimacing, he emitted a low growl through his clenched teeth as he strained.

Crack!

Ryann gasped. Most of the sailors jumped at the unfamiliar sound. Carwyn moaned in pain as the triumphant Hugon held the broken horn high above his head.

Shocked at what he had just witnessed, Ryann froze in place. He looked up as cool air gusted through his hair and around his face. Within moments, the sky had shifted from blue and cloudless to ominous, dark clouds moving swiftly toward them from the horizon.

A wicked smile crept across the black unicorn's face. "A unicorn's horn can never grow back. In fact," he lectured, "a unicorn's lifeblood is in his horn, and he will die within hours after it breaks."

Lightning crackled across the backdrop of a foreboding storm gathering in the distance. The sudden change in weather sent murmurs through the crew.

He's going to die? Ryann clenched his staff as the ship unexpectedly rose on a large wave. Crashing back into the sea, an eruption of water splashed over the bow.

"Hold your places, knaves!" Ekron ordered as the Hugons closest to the side gripped the ship's railing to steady themselves.

Narcissus looked skyward. The ship's sails billowed violently in the stormy winds, while above them the heavens swirled in blackness.

Turning back to his captive, the eyes of Narcissus glowed red. "There's no reason to delay the inevitable!" he cried out. Lowering his head, he thrust his head up viciously into Carwyn's exposed white chest. The sharp horn pierced through the white hair like a spear through soft flesh. Carwyn's mouth opened wide, his eyes white saucers of astonishment. A high-pitched whine escaped and was lost in the violent skies.

"Noooo!" Ryann wailed, standing up.

Boom!

White heat seared down to the deck of the ship as lightning cracked the sky. Sailors screamed and scrambled away from the mainmast. Ryann blinked several times, trying to clear the image of the white light that had temporarily blinded him. He saw Carwyn's chains broken and lying on the deck. The unicorn's body slumped over in a heap, blood running out from under him across the wooden planks.

Narcissus appeared surprised at both Ryann's boldness and at the broken chains, releasing Carwyn. It didn't last long.

"Gordak!" Narcissus ordered. "Throw this cursed unicorn over-board and the storm will pass!" He turned to the sailors. "The rest of you, kill that boy!"

The giant Hugon lumbered forward to Carwyn's lifeless body, gripped his legs like a small pony, and raised him up over his head. Blood dripped from the open wound in the unicorn's chest and splat-tered on the gray skull of the dragon-man.

Ryann's sorrow morphed to rage. He glared with hatred at the black unicorn. Pushing the blinking button on his staff, he pointed it toward the sea and conjured up the most gruesome monster he could imagine. Hugons scaled the wooden ladders leading up to his perch as water frothed and bubbled violently in the tumultuous waves. With a massive *swoosh*, a geyser of seawater erupted higher than the tallest mast. The distracted Hugons looked over in terror as the body of water transformed itself into a grotesque sea creature. The bubbling monstrosity looked down on the ship and opened its frothy mouth.

Crying out, some sailors scrambled for cover behind the cargo and others escaped into the hold of the ship. Ekron spread his wings and took flight up into the dark skies. A flash of fire caught Ryann's eyes as Gordak stepped to the ship's railing, grunting under the strain of Carwyn held above his head. Ryann looked over at the flames and was shocked to see they were covering the body of Narcissus. The fire wasn't burning the unicorn but appeared to be a part of him. The horn atop his head was gone.

"He's a Nightmare!" a sailor yelled.

His disguise gone, Narcissus glared at Ryann with his red eyes as smoke billowed out his nostrils. "I am the ruler of this world, Ryann, and there's nothing you can do to stop me. Your King is dead!"

Gordak tossed Carwyn overboard, his bloodstained body splashing into the tossing waves. Fire spewed from the Nightmare's mouth, churning directly toward Ryann. Diving off his platform, he pictured his hideous sea monster crushing the wooden vessel. A ball of fire exploded behind him, searing his back with a blast of heat. A moment later he plunged into the dark waters.

Frantically looking about, Ryann caught sight of Carwyn's billowing mane sinking deeper. He let go of his staff and clawed at the water, kicking furiously to propel himself toward the unicorn. He went down, further and further. Ryann's head pounded, knowing that lack of oxygen would soon become his enemy.

I see his broken horn and head. Almost there. His lungs burned. *His eyes are open. He's looking at me.* Carwyn's mouth opened. No sound carried through the water, but Ryann clearly heard him speak. "It is finished."

Darkness enveloped them. *Where is he?*

A glowing white light appeared in the darkness. Ryann's chest felt like it was going to burst. *Swim for the light. Swim for the light.* A few more kicks, and he burst through a veil of white. Opening his mouth, he gasped for air.

Chapter 37

End of a Nightmare

RYANN SUCKED A big gulp of air. The light blinded him, and he was forced to close his eyes. Wiping the water from his face, his chest heaving up and down, he stood, trying to orient himself.

I'm standing up?

Shielding his eyes, he looked up into blue skies. A midday sun stared back at him.

I was swimming down to the light. Now it's daytime?

He turned around and stared in disbelief. Across the small inlet, the Mount Dora lighthouse stood guard over its peninsula.

What? Where's Carwyn? How did I get here?

He had too many questions. Ryann slogged his way through the lake muck. Grabbing a fistful of wild grass on the shoreline, he pulled himself out of the water by the gazebo in Evans Park.

I wonder if Terell and Liddy made it back. I've gotta get home and tell Dad what happened!

Ryann sprinted as best he could in wet jeans and waterlogged sneakers. At the top of the street, he cut across the wild grass and railroad tracks to Alexander Street. Slowing to catch his breath, he ignored the stares of the lunch crowd eating at the outside cafés. He jogged past the church, half expecting Ekron to be standing there laughing at him to complete his living nightmare. As he broached the crest of the hill near his neighborhood, Ryann felt a tinge of adrenaline and dashed the rest of the way home.

"Mom! Dad!" he called out as he burst through the side door.

"In here!" his mother called out.

Following his mother's voice through the kitchen, he darted into the next room and stopped in his tracks. His mother and father sat on the main couch, while Liddy and Terell sat in a smaller sofa next to them. Between them on the coffee table were two cans of soda and two glasses of iced tea. Mrs. Watters's mouth opened in shock as she stared at her son's feet.

Ryann glanced down at his wet, mud-covered shoes standing on the family room carpet. "Uh, sorry, Mom! Let me go change." Backpedaling into the kitchen, he called out, "I'll be right back!"

"Grab a soda on your way back!" Mr. Watters yelled after him.

"...and just before I dove for the water, Narcissus changed. One second he looked like his normal, evil black unicorn self, and the next his horn was gone and he looked like he was on fire." Ryann shook his head. "It was like he was burning without being burned, as if the fire were part of him. I heard one of the crew call him a Nightmare."

Mr. Watters scooted forward on the coach. "If I'm not mistaken, from my limited knowledge of mythological creatures, a Nightmare is one of the most treacherous demons, who serves an even greater master."

"Great," Terell said, "that's what we need. More evil."

"Shh." Liddy jabbed him with her elbow. "Let Ryann finish. What happened next?"

"I dove off the ship just in time to avoid a fireball he shot out of his mouth. Before I landed in the sea, I directed the water serpent to destroy the ship."

Ryann hesitated as he relived the moment in his mind. "I saw Carwyn's legs as he sunk, and I swam down after him. I got close enough to make eye contact, and even though we couldn't talk, I heard him say, 'It is finished.' It was just like the first time we entered Aeliana when we could hear each other in our heads as we traveled through the water."

"Yeah!" Liddy inched forward on the couch. "I remember that."

"Shh." Terell mocked her. "Let homeboy finish up. What happened next, Ryann?"

"Well, then it went completely dark. I felt like my lungs were going to burst and that I was probably going to die!"

"Oh, my," Mrs. Watters said under her breath. Mr. Watters put his hand on her knee.

"But a light appeared, and at first I wondered if maybe I had died and I should head for the light, you know, like those people that say they've died and come back. I kicked my feet and swam like crazy toward it. When I burst out of the water, I found myself in Lake Dora with the noonday sun shining down on me. Weird, huh?"

"Where did Carwyn go?" Mr. Watters asked.

"I don't know, but I'm pretty sure it's not here."

Liddy breathed a deep sigh. "Well, what now?"

"I thought about that while I was running back here," Ryann quickly replied. "Remember what Carwyn said: 'Where I am going you cannot follow, but I will only be gone a short time.' I think he was talking about right now. Narcissus killed him, but he's going to come back."

Mr. Watters looked intently at his son. "You mean like Jesus did dying on the cross, being buried, and then rising from the dead three days later?"

"Yeah, Dad. I know we speculated about it over dinner with the family, but I'm convinced that Carwyn isn't like Jesus. He *is* Jesus."

Silence blanketed the room as the idea fully sank in.

Liddy spoke first. "Logically, it makes a lot of sense."

"You may be right, son," his father said.

Ryann looked at his mother. She rocked back and forth on the edge of the couch, rubbing her hands together. "What?"

"Just curious, Mom, what do you think?"

"Hmm, well, my first thought is, I don't think we need to bring this up to the pastor or we might get run out of the church."

Everyone laughed.

"My second thought is—" She got up from her seat, shuffled over to Ryann, and gave him a big hug.

"Aww," Liddy sighed.

Terell reached over with a smile on his face and slapped his friend on the back. "It takes a big man to be hugged by his mom in front of his friends."

"That still brings us back to my earlier question," Liddy said. "What do we do now?"

"Do you still have the stones?" Ryann asked. "They got us back to Aeliana last time. I think we should use one of the other four to go back again and see what happened."

"Yep, they're right here." She patted the small leather pouch attached to her belt loop.

"Okay, I'll go make sure my staff made it back to my closet, and then we'll head back over to the lighthouse."

"Whoa, whoa, whoa," Mrs. Watters's voice cracked. "Isn't it getting just a little too dangerous in Aeliana now? I mean, weren't you just attacked by those dragon men, then almost blown up by a fireball? And last but not least, you could have drowned!"

"Mom, I've got a guardian angel, for crying out loud. I don't think Gabriel's going to let anything happen to me."

"He's got a point there, honey," Mr. Watters said. "Remember, Gabriel did contact us before the quest started with the sword. I think he's in good hands."

She sighed. "You're right, but I just wish you could go along."

"Believe me, it's killing me to miss out on the adventure of a lifetime, but the portal wouldn't let me through. I think this is their journey," Mr. Watters said.

"All right. Let's do it!" Terell said.

Mr. Watters grinned. "I love the enthusiasm, Terell. I spoke with your mother, and she's very pleased with how much you've matured through this whole ordeal."

Terell's eyes grew wide as his jaw dropped open.

Liddy and Ryann chuckled. For the first time, their friend was speechless.

Mr. Watters looked at his watch. "Based upon what you guys have told me. I figure fifteen minutes here equates to one day in Aeliana. If we go with that logic, then you had better get going. It's been a little over thirty minutes since Ryann got back, so by the time you get to the lighthouse, three days will have passed in Aeliana. But let's pray first."

Ryann's, Terell's, and Liddy's parents gathered around a few of the picnic tables under the moss-covered trees near the lighthouse. Mrs. Thomas spread out a red-and-white checkered tablecloth on one of the tables just in time for Mrs. Peterson to set her picnic basket down. As she pulled tinfoil-wrapped plates out of the basket, Terell noticed and commented to Ryann and Liddy. "Look, my mom's made all my favorites—cornbread, stove-fried chicken, sweet potato casserole, and peach cobbler. I can't believe I'm leavin' that behind."

"The way my dad sees it," Ryann said, "is that they can wait right there, and we'll be back in around five minutes our time, and the food won't even be cold yet. That is, if all goes well."

"Thanks for adding on that last part, bro."

"My parents have finally stopped being so skeptical about the whole thing," Liddy said. "I'm glad we decided not to try and keep this a secret. It's more fun knowing we have their approval without having to feel guilty about it."

Ryann gripped his staff. "Okay, Liddy, put in one of your stones."

"We'll be back in a few minutes!" Terell yelled to their parents.

Ryann waved good-bye, then grabbed his friends' hands and ran toward the swirling blue portal a few feet off shore.

CHAPTER 38

Clash of Angels

RYANN EXPECTED TO end up back in the cave they had entered twice before. Everything around him looked the same except for a white glow, which confused him. *It must be nighttime or we'd see the light coming through the cave entrance. Is that a star? It seems too close.*

"Everyone okay?" Ryann asked.

"I'm fine," Liddy answered from the darkness.

"Me too," Terell said. "But what's that glow?"

"I was wondering the same thing," Ryann said. "It's too close to be a star."

The ball of light floated down like a feather blowing in the wind. As it entered the cave, it hovered in the air between them. Their faces radiated with anxious expressions that quickly relaxed into knowing smiles as the glowing ball took the shape of a figure they instantly recognized.

"Gabriel!" they shouted in unison.

The angel allowed himself to grin, which was a first as far as Ryann could recall.

"Greetings, friends! Welcome back to Aeliana."

"It's great to be back," Ryann said. "What's happened since we've been gone? Have you seen Carwyn?"

"While it is dark outside now and indeed is the middle of the night, the blackness has covered Aeliana for almost three days now. Panic has set in among the citizens, and many have come to realize that they were wrong to voice opposition to Carwyn."

Liddy spoke up. "Is he here?"

"Carwyn is in the midst of a battle that is coming to a close, but we have yet to begin our own."

Ryan piped up again. "What do you mean 'our own'?"

"It is time to retrieve the King's sword, which is still locked up in the armory from your last quest. Come, let's move outside." Gabriel exited the cave onto the precipice overlooking the Morganwyn Sea. The sound of waves crashing ashore could be heard in the vast darkness below. Above them, thousands of white stars dotted the black sky, providing the only means for navigating the moonless night.

Gabriel opened his mouth and shattered the air with a piercing whistle. For a moment there was only the distant sound of crashing waves, then wind whipped rapidly in front of them like a hovering helicopter. Liddy recognized it right away.

"Sorcha!" she cried as the dim starlight revealed the dragon.

"Hey! Don't forget me," Adain said, gliding gently onto the rocky overlook.

Gabriel interrupted their brief reunion with somber instructions. "We will fly to the castle in Myraddin. I suspect there will be heavy resistance. If that is the case, leave Ekron to me."

"Hop aboard," Sorcha said. "Let's fly!"

Moments later they soared through the starry skies with the snowcapped peaks of the Marrow Mountains off to their left. Ryann glanced over to Sorcha from atop Adain and laughed. Liddy's hair whipped back and forth across Terell's face. His friend struggled to hold on with one hand while swatting at the nuisance with the other.

"There it is," Adain called over his shoulder. "Just up ahead."

Gabriel led the way, his white wings stretched out, gliding down toward the highest spire. The sentry looked over a second too late, and the angel's boots slammed into his chest, sending him backward into the stone wall.

Adain and Sorcha touched down on the now-crowded tower. Sorcha froze the unconscious guard with a breath of icy air, then closed her eyes.

Gabriel briefed Ryann, "You and I will head down the tower to the armory." To the others he said, "Lay low here and wait."

"Aww, man, I was hopin' for some action," Terell quipped.

The angel turned toward Terell with a stern face but said nothing.

"Nice," Liddy commented, shaking her head as Ryann followed Gabriel through the door.

"Wait," Sorcha said, opening her eyes. Ryann and Gabriel turned around to listen. "My dragon sense tells me that there is much darkness before us."

"There's a lot of evil around us," Liddy said. "Can you be more specific?"

"I can only see darkness and a death. Someone is going to die, but I can't see who it is."

"The Word is with us," Gabriel spoke plainly. "Stay hidden." He disappeared into the tower with Ryann shadowing just behind him.

Wall torches lit the darkened passageway from the bottom of the tower to the armory. Spaced evenly along their route, the flickering light cast an orange pall over small sections of their pathway followed by dark shadows, before repeating the sequence again. The angel moved with precision and confidence. Ryann was glad to have a guide the caliber of Gabriel. Following close behind, he held his staff at the ready. With his attention focused on potential enemies, Ryann bumped into the angel when he stopped suddenly.

They stood before a ceiling-high iron gate. On the other side of the bars lay an array of weaponry. Giving it a cursory glance, Ryann saw an assortment of spears, shields, swords, daggers, and full-body armor. Gabriel grabbed the gate and pulled. It was locked.

Ryann winced at the sound of rattling metal echoing through the cavernous space. He wondered how far the sound would travel. Gabriel widened his stance and grabbed two of the iron bars. The hinges cried out with a high-pitched whine as he pulled up and back.

Snap! The hinges broke free, and he carefully lifted the gate and set it off to the side.

"I'll find the sword," Gabriel said. "You look for the shield of faith."

"Okay," Ryann answered. "Hey, wait a minute. What's it look like?"

Gabriel started on the left side of the room. "You'll know it when you see it."

Ryann started on the right, quickly bypassing the weapons, his eyes focused solely on shields. There were hundreds of black shields with red dragons. Halfway around the room, the shields began to vary by metals and shapes. A shimmering gold shield stood out from all the rest. Next to it was a half-oxidized, bronze shield. He moved further around the room and discovered several highly polished wood shields, both round and rectangular. A glow appeared out of the corner of his eye. He looked down at the orange glimmer coming from his ring, the same color it had turned when he found the King's sword.

Ryann stepped around the wood shields and saw a lone shield leaning up against the wall. *This has got to be it!* The shield looked to